The Duke of Cleybourne let out a low curse. "You don't look like any governess I have ever seen."

Jessica's hands flew instinctively to her hair. Her thick, curly red hair had a mind of its own, and no matter how much she tried to subdue it into the sort of tight bun that was suitable for a governess, it often managed to work its way out. Now, she realized, after the long ride in the carriage a good bit of it had come loose and straggled around her face, flame-red and curling wildly. Embarrassed, she pulled off her bonnet and tried to smooth back her hair, searching for a hairpin to secure it, and the result was that even more of it tumbled down around her shoulders.

Cleybourne's eyes went involuntarily to the bright fall of hair, glinting warmly in the light of the lamp, and something tightened in his abdomen. She had hair that made a man want to sink his hands into it, not the sort of thought he usually had about a governess—indeed, not the sort of thought that Richard allowed himself about any woman.

* * *

"Readers who enjoy historical regencies by Christina Dodd and Amanda Quick will find this book utterly irresistible."
—*Booklist* on *So Wild a Heart*

CANDACE CAMP

The Hidden Heart

HQN™

ISBN 0-373-77161-4

THE HIDDEN HEART

www.HQNBooks.com

Printed in U.S.A.

The Hidden Heart

Prologue

The Duke of Cleybourne was going home to die.

He had decided it the night before, as he was standing in his study, gazing up at the portrait of Caroline that Devin had painted for him as a wedding present. Richard had looked at the picture, and at the smaller, less satisfactory one of their daughter, and he had thought about the fact that it was December, and the anniversary of their deaths would be coming up soon.

Their carriage had overturned and skidded over the slick, icy road and grass into the pond, breaking through the skin of ice on top of the water. It had been only a few days before Christmas when it happened.

He could still smell the heavy scent of fir boughs that decorated the house for the holiday. It had hung in his nostrils all through his illness and convalescence, like the cloying odor of death, long after the boughs had been taken down and burned.

It had been four years since it happened. Most people, he knew, thought he should have gotten over the tragedy by now. One mourned for a reasonable period of time, then gathered oneself together and went on. But he had not been able to. Frankly, he had not had the desire to.

He had left his country estate, taking up residence in the ducal town house in London, and he had not returned to Castle Cleybourne in all that time.

But last night, as he looked at the portrait, he thought of how tired he was of plowing through one day after another, and it had come to him, almost like a golden ray of hope, that he did not have to continue this way. There was no need to walk through the days allotted him until God in his mercy saw fit to take him. The Cleybournes were a long-lived group, often lingering until well into their eighties and even nineties. And Richard had little faith in God's mercy.

He did have faith in his own pistols and steady hand. He would be the bringer of his own surcease, and the dark angel of retribution, as well.

So he rang for his butler and told him to pack for the trip. They would be returning to the castle, he said, and felt faintly guilty when the old man beamed at him. The servants, who worried about him, were pleased, thinking he'd thrown off his mantle of sorrow at last, and they packed both cheerfully and quickly.

And it was true, he told himself. He would end his sorrow. In the most fitting way and place: where his wife and child had died, and he had not saved them.

1

Lady Leona Vesey was beautiful when she cried. She was doing so now…copiously. Great tears pooled in her eyes and rolled down her cheeks as she took the gnarled hand of the old man lying in the bed. "Oh, Uncle, please don't die," she said in a piteous voice, her lips trembling slightly.

Jessica Maitland, who stood on the other side of General Streathern's bed, next to the General's great-niece Gabriela, regarded Lady Vesey with cool contempt. Her performance, she thought, was worthy of the best who trod the stage. Jessica had to admit that Leona looked lovely when she cried, a talent that Jessica suspected she had spent some years perfecting. Tears, she had heard, worked enormously well with men. Jessica herself hated tears, and when she could not keep them at bay, she gave in to them in the quiet and solitude of her own room.

Of course, Jessica, a supremely fair woman, had to admit that Lady Leona Vesey was beautiful when she was not crying, as well. She had been one of the reigning beauties of London for some years now—

though she was considered far too scandalous to be admitted into the best houses—and if she was reaching the last few years of that reign, the golden glow of candlelight in the darkened room hid whatever ravages time and dissipation had worked upon her.

Lady Vesey was all rounded, succulent flesh, soft shoulders and bosom rising from the scooped neckline of her dress, more suitable for evening wear than for visiting the sickroom of an aging relative. Her skin was smooth and honey toned, complementing the gold of the ringlets piled atop her head and the tawny color of her large, rounded eyes. She reminded Jessica of a sleek, pampered cat—although she was apt to change into something more resembling a lioness when she was angered, as yesterday, when Leona had slapped a clumsy maid who had spilled a bit of tea upon Leona's dress.

Jessica had itched to slap Leona herself at that moment, but, being only the governess of the General's ward, she had kept her lips clamped firmly together. Though in normal times Jessica kept the General's household running efficiently, Leona was not only above her in rank but, being the wife of General Streathern's great-nephew, also had a claim of kinship. From the moment she and Lord Vesey had swept into the house, Leona had taken over, treating Jessica as if she were a servant.

"Oh, Uncle," Leona said now, dabbing at her tears with a lacy handkerchief. "Please speak to me. It lays me low to see you this way."

Jessica felt Gabriela stiffen beside her, and she knew what the girl was thinking—that the General was no real relation to Lady Vesey, being the great-uncle of her husband, and that Lady Vesey's spirits were anything but lowered at seeing the General lying in his bed at death's door.

In the six years that Jessica had been at the General's house, the Veseys had visited but rarely, and usually those visits had been accompanied by a request for money. She had little doubt that it was money that had brought them flying to the old man's bedside now. Less than a week earlier, General Streathern had received a letter telling him of the death of an old and dear friend. He had jumped to his feet with a loud cry. Then his hand had flown to his head, and he had crumpled onto the carpet. Servants had carried him to his bed, where he had lain ever since, inert and seemingly insensible to everything and everyone around him. *Apoplexy,* the doctor had termed it, with a sad shake of his head, and held out little hope of recovery, given the General's advanced years. The Veseys, Jessica was sure, had dashed to his bedside because they hoped to be named in the General's will.

Jessica had tried her best to put aside her antipathy to Lord and Lady Vesey. They were, after all, Gabriela's only living relatives besides the General, and, as such, she knew with a cold queasiness, in all likelihood Lord Vesey would become Gabriela's guardian if the General did indeed die, which seemed more likely with each passing day.

She told herself that some of her dislike of Lady Vesey stemmed from that woman's voluptuous beauty. Jessica had grown up stick-thin, with a wild mop of carrot-colored hair, her eyes and mouth too big in her starkly thin face. As an adolescent, she had towered over all the other girls—and most of the boys, as well—gangly and awkward and feeling hopelessly unfeminine next to the soft, small, rounded females all about her. And even though her figure had eventually ripened into womanhood and her face had filled out and softened, and her hair had deepened into a rich, vibrant red, so that she had become a statuesque and striking-looking woman, Jessica still felt twinges of envy and awkwardness around women like Leona Vesey, who used their lush femininity as a form of weapon.

Also, she admitted that she had prejudged the woman because of letters from Viola Lamprey, the lone friend who had stuck by Jessica through all the scandal concerning Jessica's father. Viola had married rather late but startlingly well, becoming Lady Eskew three years ago and living at the height of London society. She and Viola had continued to correspond all through the years after the scandal, and Viola loved to keep Jessica amused with her witty, entertaining tales of the scandals and excesses of the Ton.

Lord and Lady Vesey were often the topic of gossip. He, it was said, was much too fond of very young females, and she had been carrying on a very well-known "secret" affair with Devin Aincourt for over a decade. A few months ago Viola's letters had been full of the stories circulating through London concerning Aincourt's sudden marriage to an American heiress and the subsequent termination—by Aincourt, not Lady Vesey—of the long-standing affair. The ladies of London were gleeful. Leona Vesey had few friends among them, having often made it a point to demonstrate how easily she could take away any of their husbands or suitors.

Jessica knew she should not have judged Lady Vesey on the basis of gossip. After all, she had certainly been at the center of a great deal of unfair gossip herself ten years earlier. When the Veseys had arrived here, she had made an effort to look at Lady Vesey afresh, untainted by preconceptions and prejudices. But it was soon clear to her that gossip had, if anything, not painted the lady black enough. Leona Vesey was selfish, vain and mean-tempered. She was contemptuous of all those of lower station than she, and she was pleasant only to those whom she thought could help her, usually men. The Veseys had been here for only three days, and already Jessica could barely stand to be in the same room with either of them.

She felt Gabriela tense beside her, and she suspected that the girl was about to unleash her anger on Leona, so Jessica quickly linked her arm with Gabriela's, casting her a warning look. She was worried for Gabriela's future. If the General should die and she was given to Lord and Lady Vesey as their ward, her life would be hard enough without her already having earned the enmity of Lady Vesey.

"Oh, please, Uncle," Leona said, her voice breaking as she bent over the still form of the old man, waxen in the dim light. "Please say some parting word to me."

Suddenly the old man's eyes flew open. Leona let out a small shriek and jumped back. The General stared at her with piercing hawk eyes.

"What the devil are *you* doing here?" he asked, his voice scratchy and fainter than his usual bark, but his annoyance clear.

"Why, Uncle," Leona said, recovering some composure, though her voice was still a trifle breathless. "Vesey and I came because we heard you were ill. We wanted to be with you."

The old man glared at her for a long moment. "Afraid you might lose your share of my estate is more like it. Ha! Well, I have news for you. I ain't dying. And even if I was, I wouldn't be leaving anything to you and that roué of a husband of yours."

"Uncle…" Lord Vesey, standing behind and to the side of his wife, tried an indulgent laugh. "You will give everyone the wrong idea. Others are not aware of your little fondness for jokes…."

"I wasn't talking to you," the General pointed out sharply, sounding stronger with each passing moment. "Damme! Nobody invited you here. You're a damned nuisance."

"Oh, Gramps!" Gabriela burst out, unable to restrain herself any longer. "You're all right! We thought you were dying."

The General turned his head and saw Gabriela standing on the other side of the bed, Jessica behind her, and he smiled.

"Now, would I do a thing like that?" he asked, extending his hand to the girl.

Tears spilled out of Gabriela's eyes, and she

leaned forward to take her great-uncle's hand. "I am so glad you are all right. We were horribly scared."

"I'm sure you were, Gaby." The old man squeezed her hand with only a remnant of his former strength. "But no need. I'm still breathing."

He looked toward the foot of the bed, where his doctor and the village vicar stood, staring at him in astonishment. "No thanks to you, I'm sure," General Streathern went on, talking to the doctor. "Go away. You look like a couple of damned crows standing there. I'm not dying."

"General, you must not excite yourself," the doctor said in a calming voice. "You have been unconscious for almost a week now."

"No, I haven't. Woke up last night. Just went back to sleep."

"It must have been the sound of Lady Vesey's voice that got through to you," the vicar said, with an admiring smile in that woman's direction.

"Humph!" the General responded. "Well, you were a fool when you were young, Babcock, so no use expecting you to be any better when you're old. Hearing that baggage's voice is more likely to send me over than bring me back."

"What!" Leona exclaimed, setting her hands on her hips indignantly. "Well, I like that. We left London and drove all the way up to this godforsaken place just because we heard you were ill. And this is the thanks we get?"

"I didn't ask you to come here," the General said reasonably. "Nobody did. You came because you hoped there was money in it for you. It's the only reason the two of you ever set foot in this house, and I told you last time not to return. You're damned nervy, that's all I can say, to come strutting back in here. You are a conniving bit o' muslin, Leona, and I thank God you're not my blood relative. I wish I could say the same about that piece of trash you're married to.'' He broke off his harangue long enough to shoot Lord Vesey a malevolent glare. ''Now get out, both of you. I don't want to see your faces again.''

''Perhaps we had best go back to our rooms,'' Lord Vesey suggested to his wife, looking a shade paler than he had a few moments before.

''Your rooms? You're staying here?'' The General's face reddened alarmingly.

''Why, yes, of course,'' Leona replied. ''Where else would we stay?''

''I told you you were not welcome in this house,'' the General snapped, struggling weakly to sit up.

''Please, General, calm yourself,'' the doctor said, hurrying around the bed to put his hands on the old man's shoulders and push him back down flat on the bed. ''You will bring on another apopolexy if you don't watch out.''

''The devil take it!'' General Streathern glared at the doctor, but he didn't have the strength to defy him. ''I want them out of my house, do you understand?''

''But, General,'' the vicar protested. ''Lord Vesey is your nephew. And Lady Vesey—''

He broke off abruptly as the General fixed him with a glare.

"This is my house," General Streathern said coldly, "and I am in charge of who does and does not stay here. Don't tell me who I can have in my house, Babcock."

"No, of course not, General," the vicar said, forcing a smile. "I did not mean to be presumptuous. It is just—they traveled so far, and where are they to stay?"

"Let 'em stay with you, if you like them so much."

Reverend Babcock chuckled indulgently, a sound that seemed to irritate the irascible old man even more.

"There's an inn in Lapham," he said, naming the local village. "Let them stay there if they're so bloody-minded they have to remain. But I refuse to let them torture me with their whinings and cryings and making my servants unhappy. Nothing worse than having the maids weeping all over the place because *he's* backing them into corners and taking liberties or *she's* screeching at them like a harpy and slapping them. If a man cannot have peace when he's been at death's door for a week, then I don't know what the world's coming to."

"Of course you can have peace," the doctor told him soothingly, sending an expressive look in the direction of Lord and Lady Vesey. "My lord..."

"Yes, yes, of course." Lord Vesey gave a smile that looked more like the death rictus of a corpse. "Anything to make the General feel better. Lady Vesey and I will take our leave right away."

He took his wife's hand, and they started from the

room. The General turned his head toward Jessica. "Jessica. Make sure they leave."

"Of course, General," Jessica told him with a smile. "I shall be happy to." She faced the others remaining in the room. "Gabriela, Vicar, why don't we let the General talk to the doctor now?"

The clergyman was obviously eager to leave the sickroom—whether because he feared the General or was hoping to find Lady Vesey, Jessica wasn't sure. Gabriela fairly skipped down the hall, keeping up a constant stream of chatter directed at Jessica.

"Oh, Miss Jessie, isn't it wonderful? I was so sure that Gramps was going to die! I should have known that he was tougher than some old apoplexy."

Jessica smiled at the young girl. At fourteen, Gabriela was already promising to turn into a beauty. Though her figure was still as slender and flat as a boy's, there was a litheness to her walk that promised a future grace, and her skin was fresh and creamy, her face lively and well put together, with large, dancing gray eyes and a tip-tilted nose.

Jessica was glad to see her charge so happy, but deep inside she could not keep from having a few doubts herself. The General might have awakened and seemed his old self. He might regain his full strength. But Jessica had noticed, even if Gabriela had not, that the left side of the old man's face had not moved much when he talked, and his left hand had not curled around Gabriela's in response to her taking it in hers. He had been unconscious for some time, and if nothing else, he was bound to be far weaker than normal. He was an old man, and the old were always susceptible to fevers and coughs, especially when they were weakened by illness.

She worried about the General, not only because she was fond of the him, but also because his sudden illness had brought home to her how vulnerable Gabriela was. Underage, orphaned, she might very well be left to the mercies of such people as the Veseys. Jessica had taken care of Gabriela, been her companion, teacher and confidante since the girl was eight, and she loved her as if she were her own sister. But in the eyes of the world, hers was only a paid position, and if the General died, whoever became Gabriela's guardian could terminate Jessica's employment, and she would have no recourse. She had worried over the matter ever since the General fell ill.

Gabriela went upstairs with the promise that she would work on the studies she had neglected during her great-uncle's illness, and Jessica turned into the kitchen to find the butler, Pierson, and inform him of the General's miraculous recovery and his subsequent banishment of the Veseys. Nothing, she knew, could make the servants happier than those two events.

As she expected, the butler beamed when she told him what had taken place in the General's bedchamber upstairs and assured her that he would assign two maids, not one, to packing up the Veseys' baggage and would personally escort them to their carriage.

Jessica returned to the nursery upstairs, where her and Gabriela's bedrooms lay, separated by the schoolroom. As she passed the Veseys' room, she heard the sound of something breaking, followed by Leona's high-pitched, angry voice and Lord Vesey's lower-pitched but no less furious one. Jessica smiled to herself and continued on her way.

The doctor left, and not long after that, Lord and Lady Vesey also quit the house. Humphrey, the General's valet, stayed by the old man's side throughout the rest of the day and that night, relieved—after great resistance—for a few hours at a stretch when Jessica or the butler or the housekeeper took over his role of nursemaid.

The General slept much of that time, waking up now and then to complain of feeling hungry and devouring first a bowl of consommé, then gruel and, finally, demanding soup with some substance to it. With each irascible command or gripe, the spirits of the household lightened. The General was becoming more and more normal.

Jessica visited the old man with her charge every morning and evening, and she could see visible improvement in him each time. She was very happy, not only for Gabriela's sake, but because she was fond of the General. When the scandal broke and her father was cashiered out of the army, most of their acquaintances and friends, even the man she had thought loved her, had turned away from her, but General Streathern had not. He had come to pay his condolences after her father's death, a courtesy few other of his military friends had seen fit to exercise.

Her father's death had left Jessica penniless. She had refused to seek the help of her father's family, who had scorned him after the scandal. For a time she had stayed with her dead mother's brother, but it had been an untenable situation. He had five daughters of his own, all coming up to marriageable age and making their debuts. The last thing they needed was another young female about the place, and Jessica, whose father had raised her to be strong-minded and independent, was accustomed to running a household, not living meekly in one. She and her aunt did not get along, and she had soon seen that she could not live with them, either. There had followed a series of positions as governess or companion, but she was generally considered too young or too attractive or too tainted by scandal to be hired, and when she was, she often found herself leaving because of the unwelcome advances of a male of the house.

It had struck Jessica as grimly ironic that she, who had struggled through her younger years as a gawky, clumsy ugly duckling of a girl, had now somehow become the unwelcome object of male lust. She knew that the development of her late-blooming figure had had something to do with it, but she had difficulty recognizing that her despised riot of flame-colored hair was a lure to men, or that her features, once too large for her face, had matured into striking beauty. So, rather cynically, she laid the bulk of the blame for her attraction for men on the fact that they were drawn to her because she was no longer under her father's protection. They wanted her, in short, she decided, because they thought she was an easy target now, a woman who was at their mercy because she had to work for a living.

Dismayed and embittered, she had stopped applying for positions as a governess and had managed to scrape out a living taking in fancy sewing. She had a good eye and hand for needlework, and when she swallowed her pride and went humbly asking for work, a number of women of wealth and position had paid for beautiful embroidery. Still it was a difficult and minimal living, and there were times when she despaired. Winters were the worst, for it cost more to live, as she had to heat her small room. She tried to save on coal, but she could not do the fine threadwork with fingers that were freezing. One winter, about six years earlier, the amount of sewing that she had been given had fallen off, and then she fell ill and had to turn away work for a week. She found herself suddenly on the brink of disaster, and she was forced to consider going back to live with her uncle or even asking her father's stiff-necked family for help.

It was then that the General had appeared on her doorstep, a gruff, unlikely angel of mercy, and had offered her a position as companion and governess to his great-niece, Gabriela, whose parents had died a month earlier, leaving the General her guardian. The General had immediately thought of Jessica, with whom he had retained contact throughout the years. In fact, she had long suspected that he was behind some of the bonuses and gifts that she had received from her customers over the years. Jessica had seized on the offer of a position with joyful relief, and she had never regretted her decision.

Her time here had been happy. She soon grew to

love her charge, and as she stayed, she took on more and more of the running of the household. The servants relied on her for advice and orders, quick to realize her competence, and the General was happy to turn such "women's things" over to her. She enjoyed her life here, and it seemed almost as if General Streathern and Gabriela were her family. She did not think she could have been more concerned for the old man or happier that he was coming out of his illness if he had been her own grandfather.

After another day of convalescence, the General informed his valet that he did not need a "damned nursemaid sitting up and staring at me all night," and ordered him to go to bed and end his nightly watch. The following morning he sent Humphrey to Jessica with the request that she come to his room. She left Gabriela with a paper to write and went to see the General, wondering what he wanted. Knowing the General, it could be anything from an accounting of the household budget to a game of chess to alleviate his boredom.

In this instance it was neither. General Streathern was sitting up in his bed, looking much stronger than he had the day before. He smiled when he saw Jessica, and she noted that the expression still did not reach the left side of his face. His left arm, too, was held across his lap and did not move much as he talked. But his color was much better and his gaze was alert, and when he spoke he sounded much like his old self.

"Well, girl, had you given me up for dead, too?" he barked.

"I was very worried," Jessica admitted.

"Doubter."

"You had been unconscious for a week, General," Jessica pointed out. She had grown up speaking her mind, for it was the way her father had trained her, and she had been greatly relieved to find that the General was the same sort of man.

The old man chuckled. "I can always count on you to tell me the truth, Jess." He patted his bed. "Come, sit down where I can see you without having to break my neck."

Jessica went forward and sat down on the edge of his bed, facing him. "I am very glad to see that I was mistaken."

"I am, too, my girl." General Streathern let out a sigh. "I have to tell you, I gave myself a scare. I wouldn't let on to that old sawbones, of course, but I know I had a close brush with death. I can feel it." He patted his left arm. "Haven't got full movement here, you know." He shook his head. "It's a frightening thing, your brain attacking you."

"I imagine it is. But you are better now. And perhaps your arm will grow stronger."

"I hope so. It's damned irritating. Not as irritating as waking up and finding that scoundrel Vesey in my room, though. Don't know how my sister could have produced a grandchild like that. Nothing wrong with her daughter—course, the Vesey line has always had bad blood. I told Gertie that no good would come of it, but it was out of her hands. Her son-in-law always did have batting for brains."

"I am sorry they were here."

"Not your fault. But I told Pierson not to let them back in. Now that he has my orders, he'll keep them out. And if he does go all weak, you remind him of what I said."

"I will."

"Gave me a turn, seeing Vesey." The General fell silent for a moment, looking down at his hands. He was not one to speak of personal feelings, a military man to the bone. "It made me think. I could die. I am seventy-two years old. I've had more than my time on earth. I guess I always thought I could some-how fight it off. But it was sheer luck this time. When I read that letter, saw that Millicent had died…"

"I am sure it was a shock to learn of your friend's death."

"It was indeed." Sadness fell over the old man's features. "I loved her, you see."

"Of course."

"No. I mean, really loved her. Loved her for al-most fifty years."

Jessica, startled, looked keenly at the General. There was a softness in his eyes that she had rarely seen there.

"She was married to another man. Not a bad fel-low. I knew him. I met her at a party Lady Abernethy gave. I was thirty-four at the time. I hadn't married. I had been too busy with my career for things like that. After I saw Millicent, I knew I never would. Terrible thing to live with, knowing that you would be ecstatic if a good man died. Course, he did, many years later. But by that time, we had gotten old.

Grown into the way of being friends, settled in our own lives and neither of us too eager to give that up. It was enough for us the last few years just to see each other now and then, and to maintain our correspondence. I would have done anything for her, though.''

He sat lost in reverie. Jessica remained silent, too, trying to absorb this new picture of the crusty old military man as a devoted swain, loving a woman he could not have.

"Ah, well." The General seemed to shake off his thoughts. "That's not what I called you here about. Not directly, anyway. The thing is, when I read those lines, there was a terrific pain in my head, and then the next thing I knew I was waking up here with that silly cow Leona blubbering all over me. Now I realize how presumptuous I was all these years, thinking I could fight off death, as if it were an enemy soldier. I couldn't do a thing. I was just lucky to come back. Next time, I might not be so fortunate."

Jessica did not know what to say. The General was right, and it was hard to say something optimistic in response.

"Seventy-two. Some would say it's about time I figured out I wasn't invincible." The General let out a little chuckle. "Thing is, what about Gaby? Oh, I've provided for her in my will, no worry about that. And her father left her a nice trust. She will have plenty of money. But she needs more than that. She needs someone who loves her."

"I will stay with her, General. I promise. You know how much I care for her."

The General smiled at her, and it touched Jessica's heart with sorrow to see how one side of his mouth did not curl up with the other. "I knew I could count on you. But I wanted to make sure you understood what to do if anything should happen to me. I have provided for a guardian in my will. It's the same man that her father named as successor should anything happen to me. I don't know him well, but he was a friend of her father's and reputed to be an honorable sort. He will look after her money and her welfare. I just wrote him a letter. There…"

He gestured toward the small table beside his bed, on which lay a letter, closed by a blob of red wax bearing the General's seal. "Take it. I want you to escort Gaby to his home if anything further should happen to me. Give him this letter, as well as the will. In it, I've asked him to keep you on. I told him that Gaby relies on you and trusts you."

"I will. Don't worry. But let us hope that there will be no need for it. You will recover and live long past Gaby's marriage, I'm sure."

"I hope so. But I haven't said all I want to say. Once Gaby is with her new guardian, I won't worry. He is a powerful, influential man—the Duke of Cleybourne. Vesey would be able to do nothing to him. But until then…I fear Vesey."

"Lord Vesey? But surely, if you name someone else her guardian, that will put a stop to any danger from him."

"I would count on nothing when it comes to that man." General Streathern's lip curled. "He is vile, and his wife is no better. I would not trust him not to seize Gaby if he has the opportunity. I left the man nothing, and he would love to get his hands on Gaby's money. And that witch of a wife of his is able to twist honest men around her finger. I don't trust the pair of them.'' He frowned, then went on slowly. ''I would not otherwise sully your ears with such a tale, but you must know the full extent of his wickedness. The man is a lecher, and I have heard that he has a…a preference for young girls. Girls of Gaby's age.''

Jessica sucked in her breath sharply. ''General! Do you mean—you think he would—''

''I do not know how low the man would sink, but I would not be surprised at the depth of his depravity, either. Let us just say that it would be safer if she were never under his control, even for a day.'' He looked at her sharply from beneath his thick white eyebrows. ''Your father was one of the best soldiers I ever commanded.''

''Thank you, General.'' Jessica felt emotion swell unexpectedly in her throat.

''I am counting on you to have his same spirit.''

''I hope and pray that I do,'' Jessica replied, adding firmly, ''You can rely on me to keep her away from Lord Vesey.''

''Good.'' He relaxed, easing back against the pillows. ''Thank you, Jessica. If I should die, either now or later, he will come like a vulture. Get her away from here as soon as the will is read. Be packed and ready to go. You understand me, don't you?''

''Yes, I will waste no time. I swear it to you. She

and I will leave immediately after the will is read, even if it means leaving the luggage for later.''

He nodded. ''You're a sharp, sensible girl. I know I can trust in you. Take her to the Duke of Cleybourne. His estate is in Yorkshire, near the town of Hedby, no more than a hard two days' ride by carriage.''

''I will.'' Jessica reached over and took the old man's hand. ''But, please God, that time will not come for many years, and Gaby will be a married woman by then.''

''God willing.''

It was late at night and the house was dark, everyone tucked up in their beds, when a side door opened quietly and a dark figure slipped inside. The man stood for a moment, still and watching, then moved with equal silence down the hallway and up the servants' stairs to the second floor. Once again he waited, poised at the top of the stairs for the slightest sound before he went on to the door he sought. He opened it and peeked inside. There was no sign of the General's valet or a nurse keeping watch over the old man.

He slid through the door and closed it softly after him, then glided across the floor until he stood beside the bed. He stood for a moment, gazing down at the old man. The General looked so frail that for a moment he wondered if this was really necessary. The man had just, after all, almost died. There was always the possibility that he would not regain his health, and then General Streathern would be of no danger to him.

As he watched, the old man's eyes opened, as if he had sensed the watcher's presence. His eyes narrowed. "You!" he rasped. "What the devil are you doing here? Didn't I tell you—"

"Yes, yes, I know," the younger man said lightly. "I am never to taint you with my presence. But, I thought it best to talk to you. You see things have changed."

"Yes, they have." The General pulled himself up into a sitting position against his pillows. His uninvited guest noted that it was something of a struggle for him.

"I wanted to make sure that you were not thinking of doing anything foolish."

"You mean revealing what really happened? What makes you think I wouldn't?" the General shot back, rather injudiciously. "I have no reason to keep silent anymore."

"There is the slight problem of your not having brought the matter up years ago, when it mattered. It would not reflect well on you. Your name would be ruined."

"Perhaps that is as it should be," the old man remarked heavily.

"Easy for you to say, when you are facing the grave, anyway. I, on the other hand, have many years to live, and I have no desire to do so under the taint of scandal."

"It would be worse than that."

"Indeed? I think not. Only your word against

mine, and you are an old fool who has just suffered an apoplexy. Everyone would assume that your brain simply was not working properly any longer.''

''Oh, they would believe me,'' General Streathern said, contempt and hatred lighting his eyes. ''I have proof, you see.''

The other man's eyes were as cold as the General's were heated. He surveyed the old man for a moment, then said, ''Well, I am sorry to hear that.''

Swiftly he picked up a pillow from the bed and put it over the old man's face. The General struggled, but he was weak from his illness, and it was not long before his struggles ceased. The visitor waited another long moment after that, then lifted the pillow and set it back with the others. He pulled the old man back down in the bed so that he was no longer sitting up but would look as if he had died peacefully in his sleep.

He cast a quick glance around the room, and it was only then that it struck him: if the General truly had proof against him, he could still be in danger. His jaw clenched, and he glanced at the still man in the bed, anger surging up in him. The old fool had made him so angry, he had acted in haste. He should have made him reveal where and what the proof was before he killed him.

He went over to the chest across the room and began to search through it, realizing even as he did so how difficult it would be to find what he needed. To begin with, there was the possibility that there was no actual proof, that the General might have been merely bluffing, hoping to scare him. And if the old goat had been telling the truth, he still had no idea even what the proof consisted of. *Was it an object? A piece of paper?* Whatever it was, he was certain that the General would have secreted it away somewhere. A safe was the most likely choice, so he searched the room but found none, knowing even as he did so that the safe was just as likely to be downstairs in the old man's study or smoking room, or even where they locked up the precious silver. Finding it would be a daunting task in the best of circumstances. At night, with a houseful of people around who might wake up and discover him, it was almost impossible.

Even as he thought it, he heard the sound of the doorknob turning. He darted into the shadowy spot between the wardrobe and the corner of the room and waited, holding his breath. He heard the shuffle of an old man's feet across the room and saw the flickering low light of a candle. Fortunately the light did not come close to where he hid. He, however, could see the features of a man close to the General's age, dressed in nightclothes and dressing gown. The General's valet, he thought.

The servant stopped at the foot of the bed and stood for a moment. Then he began to frown and edged around the bed to stand beside the old man. He sucked in his breath and let out a low wail. "Oh, no, oh, my lord, no!"

He moaned again, then turned and left the room at a pace close to a run.

The intruder did not hang far behind. He raced to the door after the servant and saw him shuffling down the hallway, moaning and crying out, "He's gone! The General's dead!"

He did not pause, but slipped along the hall in the opposite direction, running lightly down the main stairs and out of the house.

2

The carriage rolled to a stop, and Jessica pushed back the curtain to peer out into the dark, a question on her lips. As soon as she saw what lay before them, the question died unanswered. The coachman had stopped, no doubt, just as she would have, because of the looming dark bulk that lay ahead of them. It was a massive structure of dark gray stone, obviously built centuries before in a time of frequent strife, and added onto throughout the years until it was a sprawling hulk of sheer stone walls, battlements and Norman towers. Lights burned on either side of its open gateway, doing little to alleviate the darkness. It was gloomy and foreboding, dominating the countryside from its seat on a slight rise. *Castle Cleybourne.*

Jessica had little trouble believing that it was the country seat of an old and powerful family. Nor was it difficult to imagine the place being besieged, war engines hammering away at its massive walls, soldiers on the battlements shooting down arrows on the troops below. What was harder was to picture it as a welcoming place to bring an adolescent girl who had just lost her last loving relative. She could not hold back a sigh.

Perhaps it had been a mistake, after all, to act this precipitously upon the General's orders. It had shaken her so when the old man's valet had run through the halls, wailing out the news of his death, that she had immediately set about readying Gabriela and herself for the journey to Gabriela's new guardian. General Streathern's death, following as it did hard on the heels of his seemingly prophetic words to her, jolted and frightened her, lending an eerie importance to what he had said. Had he foreseen that his death would come that swiftly? And had he foreseen other things, as well—things that had made him urge her to take Gabriela safe out of Lord Vesey's hands?

She had sat up with Gabriela the rest of the night, holding the girl while she cried out her grief until Gaby fell, finally, into a restless slumber. Jessica had remained by the girl's side, dozing by fits and starts in the padded rocker beside the bed, thinking about the General and letting her own tears flow for the man who had been so kind to her, standing by her when the rest of the polite world had scorned her. She had not cried like this for anyone since her father's death ten years ago.

The next morning, she had told Pierson, the butler, about the General's last instructions to her, and he had immediately set two of the maids to packing up her and Gabriela's clothes and other necessities for the journey. He would not have ignored the General's orders in any case, nor would any of the other servants, but Jessica could see in his eyes that he agreed with the General about the wisdom of removing Gabriela from Lord Vesey's vicinity.

Jessica had gone about her business, seeing to the funeral arrangements and notifying all who needed to be notified of the old man's death, including Lord Vesey at the inn in the village—even though it was like a stab wound to her chest to think of that loathsome man's probable pleasure at the news. She had penned letters to the General's friends, telling them of his demise, and another to the Duke of Cleybourne explaining the situation, while the servants went about the necessary arrangements to the house—draping crepe above doors and turning mirrors to the wall, muffling the door-knockers. Every spare moment, Jessica had spent with Gabriela, trying to ease the pain of this new death and separation.

The girl was white and hollow eyed but calm, not giving way to tears again until the last moments of the funeral. Jessica's heart was heavy for her. Gabriela had had to suffer more sorrow than a fourteen-year-old should bear—losing both her parents when she was eight, and now losing the man who had been a grandfather to her, her only real remaining relative, for one could scarcely count Lord Vesey. Now all she had left were Jessica and the stranger who would be her guardian.

Despite the girl's sorrow, Jessica knew that she had to explain to her why they must leave as soon as possible. She did not, of course, explain Lord Vesey's depravity to her, deeming it unsuitable for a young girl's ears, as well as exceedingly frightening for her. However, as it turned out, she did not need to justify leaving. As soon as Gabriela learned that they were going away in order to avoid Lord Vesey, she was eager to leave.

"I hate him," she told Jessica vehemently. "I know it's wrong. He is old and deserves respect…but he gives me the shivers. The way he looks at me…it's as if a snake had crossed my path."

"I understand. It is an apt analogy," Jessica agreed. "He is a wicked man. Your great-uncle thought so, too. You must never be alone with him. If he comes into a room, you leave."

"I will."

At the funeral, Leona wept in her lovely way. Jessica wondered why the woman bothered, since the General was dead. Did she hope to influence the attorney who would read the will? Or was she simply unable to pass up an opportunity to focus everyone's eyes on herself?

Jessica herself struggled not to cry, sitting beside Gabriela and holding her hand. She knew that she needed to be strong, for Gabriela's sake, but she could not help remembering the many kindnesses that General Streathern had shown her, until finally she could not hold back the tears any longer, and she, too, had cried, silent tears rolling down her cheeks.

Afterward, in the formal drawing room of the General's house, his attorney, Mr. Cumpston, read the General's last will and testament to them. It came as no surprise to Jessica that the old man left his house and his entire fortune to Gabriela and nothing to the Veseys. It was what he had told her the other night. It did come as a shock, however, when she learned that General Streathern had left Jessica his favorite inlaid wood box, containing several of his mementos, as well as a sum of money. She stared at the attorney, amazed, oblivious to the venomous looks the Veseys shot at her. It was not a large sum, she knew, compared to Gabriela's fortune. Leona, she felt sure, would consider it mere pin money. But it was enough, if invested wisely, to provide Jessica with a livelihood for the rest of her life. She would not have to scrimp and save, and she would never again be at the mercy of others. It was freedom from the painful, frequently humiliating existence into which her father's scandal had plunged her, and it made her heart swell with gratitude and affection for the General.

Lord and Lady Vesey, as she had expected, had protested the contents of the will long and vigorously.

"I am his nephew!" Lord Vesey had cried. "There has to be a mistake. He would not have left money to his butler and valet and…and *her*—" he pointed contemptuously at Jessica "—and left nothing to a relative!"

"It's because of you!" Leona added, her eyes shooting into Jessica like daggers. "I think we all know why he left you money, don't we? The sort of services you performed for the old—"

"Lady Vesey!" Mr. Cumpston exclaimed, shocked. "How can you say such a thing about the General? Or Miss Maitland?"

"Quite easily," Leona retorted scornfully. "I am not a country innocent like you."

"I was friend to General Streathern for many years," Mr. Cumpston replied. "I knew him well, and I know that there was no taint of scandal attached to him or Miss Maitland. He explained all his wishes to me."

"He was influenced by her!" Leona cried, her lovely face contorted into something far less fetching. "Her and that chit!" She waved her hand toward Gabriela. "They worked on him. Convinced him to exclude us."

"That's right," Lord Vesey agreed. "Undue influence, that's what it was. He was an old man, and feeble. He probably didn't know what he was doing. I shall take this to court."

"Very well, Lord Vesey," the attorney said with a sigh. "Certainly you may do so. But I think you would simply be throwing away money on such a suit. The General was in full possession of his faculties until he was felled by apoplexy that day, and there are a large number of respected people in this community who will testify to that. The witnesses to the will were Sir Roland Winfrey and the Honorable Mr. Ashton Cranfield, who were visiting the General at the time. They, too, can testify as to the General's ability to know what he was doing, and I think you will find few who would dispute the word of either of those gentlemen."

Lord Vesey sneered but fell silent. Jessica had no very great opinion of his intelligence, but she suspected that even Lord Vesey would realize he had little hope with two such respected men as witnesses against him. He and Leona left the house soon afterward, and Jessica sincerely hoped that was the last she and Gabriela would ever have to see of them.

Mindful of her promise to the General, she and Gabriela had also left that afternoon, after packing up the last of their things, putting the lovely wooden box the General had given her into one of her trunks, then bidding the servants of the household a tearful farewell and promising to send them word from the home of Gabriela's new guardian and trustee.

They had traveled throughout the night, stopping only to change the horses at post houses along the way. She and Gabriela slept as best they could in the rumbling carriage, woken often by jolts and jars. Though the carriage was well-appointed and as comfortable as such conveyances could be, it was a hard drive, and it was a relief whenever they stopped at an inn to change horses and could get out a bit and stretch their legs, free from the constant motion of the coach.

Now, having arrived at the duke's stronghold the next evening, Jessica was swept by a new dismay. The castle did not look like a welcoming place.

"Are we there?" Gaby asked, pushing aside the curtain beside her and looking out. She sucked in a breath as she saw the looming structure. "Oh, my…it looks like something out of a book—you know, the romances Gramps disapproved of my reading. Doesn't it look as if it holds ghosts and villains?"

"And at least one mad monk," Jessica added

dryly, pleased when the younger girl let out a little chuckle. "Well, shall we venture forward?"

"Oh, yes. It looks most interesting."

Jessica smiled at the girl. Gabriela was handling everything so well it was amazing. Jessica felt sure that many another young lady would have fallen into a fit of the vapors by now, given the events of the past few days.

She ordered the driver to proceed and settled back in her seat. She hoped that the Duke of Cleybourne would not be too offended by their arrival after dark. It was not the best time to impose on someone, but she hoped that he would understand the exigencies of the situation. It was too bad, she thought, that Gabriela's father and then the General had chosen someone so lofty in lineage and rank to be the girl's guardian. She was afraid that he would be so high in the instep that it would be difficult to talk to him. Jessica had been raised in good circles: her father's brother was a baron, and her mother's father was a baronet. But that was a far cry from a duke, the very highest title one could have below royalty. Some dukes were even royal themselves. She feared that he might dismiss her, thinking Gabriela's schooling and training in the polite arts was not good enough for the ward of a duke. She kept such thoughts to herself, however, not wanting to upset Gabriela.

The carriage rolled up to the gates, stopped for a moment, then rolled on into the courtyard beyond. The entrance had once been the outer wall of the castle, Jessica supposed, with huge gates that were closed at night, but in these modern times, the gates no longer stood, only the entrance. Inside the wall lay a small courtyard paved with stones. The coachman pulled up to the front steps of the house, then climbed down to help Gabriela and Jessica out.

The house was imposing, the timeworn stone steps leading up to a large and beautifully carved wooden door. Concealing her nerves, Jessica went up the steps, Gabriela on her heels, and knocked firmly on the front door. It was opened almost immediately by a surprised-looking footman.

"Yes?"

"I am sorry to intrude so late at night. I am Jessica Maitland, and this is Gabriela Carstairs. We are here to see the Duke of Cleybourne."

The young man continued to stare at them blankly. "The duke?" he asked finally.

"Yes." Jessica wonderd if the man was not quite right in the head. "The duke. Miss Carstairs is the grandniece of General Streathern. Her father was a friend of the duke's."

"Oh. I see." The footman frowned some more but stepped back, permitting them inside. "If you will, ah, just sit down, I will tell His Grace that you are here."

It was not, Jessica noted, the pleasantest of greetings. Her unease grew. *What if the letter had been delayed and the duke had not gotten it yet?* They had traveled very quickly, and it was possible they could have outstripped the mail.

The footman was gone for some time, and when he did return, it was with another, older man, who came forward to Jessica.

"I am very sorry, Miss…Maitland, is it? My name is Baxter. I am the butler here. I'm afraid that this is not a good time to see His Grace. It is, after all, nine o'clock, rather late for visiting."

"I sent him a letter," Jessica said. "Did he not receive it? I explained the circumstances of our arrival."

"I, ah, I'm not sure. I, there has been mail, of course, but I do not know whether he has read it. His Grace did not seem to expect you."

"I am very sorry if he has not received the letter. But if he has it and has not read it, it would be a good idea for him to do so now. It will explain everything. I am sure it must appear odd to him, but I really must meet with him. Pray go back and tell him that it is imperative that we speak. Miss Carstairs and I have traveled quite a distance. She is the duke's ward."

The old man eyed Gabriela somewhat skeptically. "Ward?"

"Yes." Jessica instilled her voice with all the iron she could muster.

The butler bowed and left, but a few minutes later, he returned, looking apologetic. "I am sorry, ma'am, but His Grace is adamant. He is, um, not one who engages in much social intercourse. He suggested that you contact his estate manager, Mr. Williams, tomorrow."

"His estate manager!" Anger flared up in Jessica. She was tired, thirsty and hungry, as well as grimy from the dust of the road. She wanted nothing so much as a chance to wash off, then tumble into bed for a long sleep. It was galling that the obnoxiously proud duke did not even have the courtesy to meet her. During the years since her father's death, she had grown used to slights and snubs, to the small, painful pinpricks of humiliation that the rich and powerful all too frequently gave out. But they never failed to raise her ire, and this one was far worse, because it was a snub and insult to Gabriela, as well.

She glanced over at her charge and saw that Gaby's pretty young face was pale and apprehensive. She would no doubt worry now that her guardian had no liking for her, that he might refuse to be her guardian or, even worse, be a harsh one. The sight of Gabriela's small hands twisting together in her lap touched flame to the fuel of Jessica's anger.

"I am so very sorry that it is inconvenient for your master to come downstairs and meet an orphan who has been placed in his care," Jessica snapped. "But I am afraid that he has no choice in the matter. *He* is Gabriela's guardian, not his estate manager, and I intend to talk to *him*. We have traveled for a day and a half to see him, and I have no intention of going back to the village at this hour to get a room at the inn."

The butler shifted nervously under Jessica's flashing eyes. "I am most awfully sorry, miss...."

"Oh, stop saying that! Just tell me where he is, and I will give him the message myself."

The old man's eyes widened in horror. "Miss! No, you cannot—"

But his words fell on empty space, for Jessica

walked past him, saying to Gabriela, "Wait here for me, Gaby. I'll be back in a trice."

The butler hurried after her, his hands fluttering nervously. "But, miss, you cannot…His Grace is not receiving. It is very late."

"I am quite aware of the hour. And I frankly do not care whether His Grace is receiving or not. I intend to talk to the man, and I am not leaving this house until I do," Jessica said as she strode into the huge central room beyond the stairs. "Your only choice is whether you will tell me where he is or let me yell for him," she informed him over her shoulder.

"Yell?" The man looked as if he might faint from the horror of the idea. "Miss Maitland, please…"

"Hello?" Jessica called loudly, cupping her hands around her mouth. "I am looking for the Duke of Cleybourne!"

The butler gasped behind her. "No! Miss, you must not, it isn't seemly."

"And is it seemly for a man to ignore his duties to a dead friend, to tell a fourteen-year-old girl who has just lost everyone dear to her that she should go back to an inn to spend the night and then talk to his estate manager? I may be unseemly, but I am not wicked."

She walked toward the main corridor leading off from the Great Hall, shouting again, "Cleybourne!"

Down the corridor a door was flung open, and a man stepped into the corridor. He was tall, with an unruly mop of thick black hair and eyes of nearly as dark a color. His cheekbones were wide and sharp, his jaw firm and his cheeks hollowed. He was dressed in breeches and a shirt, his jacket and cravat discarded, and his shirt unbuttoned at the top. He glowered down the hallway at Jessica.

"What the devil is going on out here? Who is making that racket?"

"I am," Jessica replied, walking purposefully toward him.

"And who the devil are you?"

"Jessica Maitland. The one whose message you just flung back in her face."

"I am sorry, Your Grace." The butler hurried toward him, puffing.

"Never mind, Baxter. I shall take care of this myself." The man swayed a little, putting a hand up to the doorjamb to steady himself.

"You're bosky!" Jessica exclaimed.

"I am not," he disputed. "Anyway, the amount of my inebriation is scarcely any business of yours, Miss Maitland. I am still not at home to every hopeful debutante who passes through with her harpy of a mother and hopes to put up at my home. Ever since that fool Vindefors married the chit who put up at his house after an accident, every grasping mama in the Ton has tried to emulate her."

"I have no idea what you are talking about," Jessica said impatiently. "But it has nothing to do with me or my purpose here, as you would know if you had listened to what your butler said."

The man's brows soared upward. Jessica was sure he was unused to hearing anything he said or did disputed, given his rank. "I beg your pardon," he said icily.

"As well you should," Jessica retorted, purposely taking his words in the wrong way. "Miss Carstairs and I have had a long and difficult journey, and it is entirely too much to be told to take ourselves off to an inn at this hour of the night."

"Some might say that it is entirely too much to expect a stranger to take one in at this hour of the night." The duke crossed his arms, glaring back at her. "And who in the bloody hell is Miss Carstairs?"

"She is the daughter of a man who thought you were his friend," Jessica replied. "So good a friend that he named you her guardian."

His arms fell to his sides, and Cleybourne stared at her. "Roddy? Roddy Carstairs? Are you saying that Roddy Carstairs' daughter is here?"

"That is precisely what I am saying. Did you not get my letter? Or have you simply not troubled yourself to read it?"

He blinked at her for a moment, then said, "The devil!"

He turned around and strode back into the room from which he had emerged. Jessica followed him. It was a study, masculinely decorated in browns and tans, with leather chairs and a massive desk and dark wood paneling on the walls. A fire burned low in the fireplace, the only light in the room besides the oil lamp on the desk. A decanter and glass stood on the desk, mute testimony to what the duke had been doing in the dimly lit room. On the corner of the desk was a small pile of letters.

Cleybourne pawed through them and pulled one out. Jessica's copperplate writing adorned the front, and it remained sealed. He broke the seal now and opened it, bringing the sheet of paper closer to the lamp to read it.

"I will tell you what it says. I am Miss Carstairs' governess, Jessica Maitland, and her great-uncle, General Streathern, passed away a few days ago, leaving her entirely orphaned and still underage. As you were named in her father's will as her guardian if her uncle could not serve, he thought that you were the proper man to become her guardian upon his death."

The duke let out a low curse and dropped Jessica's letter back onto the table. He looked at her again, still frowning.

"You don't look like any governess I have ever seen."

Jessica's hand flew instinctively to her hair. Her thick, curly red hair had a mind of its own, and no matter how much she tried to subdue it into the sort of tight bun that was suitable for a governess, it often managed to work its way out. Now, she realized, after the long ride in the carriage, a good bit of it had come loose from the bun and straggled around her face, flame-red and curling wildly. Her hat, as well, had been knocked askew. No doubt she looked a fright. Embarrassed, she pulled off her bonnet and tried to smooth back her hair, searching for a hairpin to secure it, and the result was that even more of it tumbled down around her shoulders.

Cleybourne's eyes went involuntarily to the bright

fall of hair, glinting warmly in the light of the lamp, and something tightened in his abdomen. She had hair that made a man want to sink his hands into it, not the sort of thought he usually had about a governess—indeed, not the sort of thought Richard normally had about any woman.

Since Caroline's death, he had locked himself away from the world, eschewing especially the company of women. The musical sound of their laughter, the golden touch of candlelight on bare feminine shoulders, the whiff of perfume—all were reminders of what he had lost, and he found himself filled with anger whenever he looked at them. The only woman he regularly saw besides the maids and housekeeper was his wife's sister, Rachel. She was, perhaps, the most painful of all women to see, as she looked more like Caroline than anyone, tall and black haired, with eyes as green as grass, but he was too fond of her to cut her off, and she, out of all the world, was the only one who truly shared in his grief.

But never, in the four years since Caroline had died, had he looked at a woman and felt a stab of pure lust. Oh, there had been times when he had felt a man's natural needs, but that had been simply a matter of instinct and the amount of time that had passed since he had known the pleasure of a woman's body. It had not flamed up in him because of the look of a particular woman's hair or the curve of her shoulder or the sound of her voice.

It seemed absurd that he should feel it now, with this harridan of a governess. God knows, she was beautiful—vivid and unusual, with startlingly blue eyes and pale, creamy skin and that wild fall of hair—and her tall, statuesque figure could not be completely toned down by the plain dark dress she wore. But she was also loud, strident and completely without manners. He did not know if he had ever met a less feminine-acting woman.

He did not want her in the house—neither her nor the young girl whose guardian she claimed he was. He had come here to end his days in this place where his life had stopped four years ago, even though his heart had continued vulgarly to beat. How could he do it with this virago and some silly girl in the house with him?

"How do I know that any of this is real?" he asked her abruptly. "What proof do you have of it?"

Jessica had tried unsuccessfully to wind her hair back into a knot, but finally she had simply let it go. She bridled at his words. "I would hate to be as suspicious as you," she said bitingly. "First you assume we are some sort of rapacious husband-hunters, and now you doubt whether a poor orphaned girl is actually your ward."

"One learns to be suspicious through hard experience," Cleybourne said flatly. "Well? If your story is true, there must be some proof."

"Of course there is proof." Jessica had stuck the folded will and the General's letter into her pocket when she emerged from the carriage, and now she reached in and pullled them out, handing them over to the duke. "Here is the General's will, as well as a letter that he wrote to you, explaining the circumstances. I do not have a copy of his death certificate with me, however, if you doubt whether he has actually died.''

Cleybourne's mouth tightened, and he snatched the papers from her. His eyes ran down the will until they reached the clause naming him guardian of General Streathern's great-niece, Gabriela Carstairs, the daughter of Roderick and Mary Carstairs. He sighed, folding the will back up. *Poor Roddy.* He remembered well when his friend and his wife had died, both felled by a vicious fever that had swept through the south of England that year. Their young daughter had survived only because the doctor had insisted that she and her nurse be quarantined in her nursery, never visiting her parents.

He opened the letter and read it, squinting to make out the scratchings of an ill old man. At one point, he exclaimed, ''Vesey is her only living relative! Good God!''

''Precisely.'' Jessica was relieved at his reaction to Vesey's name. From the way the man had been acting, she had been afraid that he might decide to hand Gabriela over to Lord Vesey rather than trouble with her himself. ''The General was afraid that Lord Vesey might try to wrest the guardianship away from you—I'm not sure how, exactly. That is why he insisted that we leave immediately after the reading of the will and drive straight here. It has been a long and exhausting journey. Gabriela is very tired.''

''Yes, of course.'' His eyes flickered to her, and he noticed for the first time the pale blue half circles of weariness and worry beneath her eyes. ''You, too, I should imagine.'' He sighed and laid the documents on his desk. "Well, there is nothing for it but for you to stay here, of course." He paused, then added stiffly, "My apologies for your reception when you arrived. I had no idea who you were. I—everyone will tell you that I am not a sociable man."

Jessica felt like retorting that this was scarcely news to her, but she held her tongue. The man might be a snob and a boor, but she did not want to offend him so much that he took Gabriela out of her care. She swallowed her pride and said, "Thank you, Your Grace. We are in your debt."

"I will direct Baxter to set you up for the night."

"Thank you." Jessica started for the door, then paused and swung back to him. "I—I suppose that you would like to meet your ward. Shall I bring her here?"

"No!" His answer was swift and adamant, and his face, which had relaxed its lines somewhat, was suddenly as set as stone. He apparently realized the rudeness of his response, for he added, "That is, I think it would be better not at this time. I am sure that Miss Carstairs is quite done in by her journey. Meeting me would only be an unnecessary burden to her."

Jessica met his eyes unflinchingly for a long moment. "Very well," she said quietly. "Until tomorrow, then."

"Yes."

She turned and went out the door, passing Baxter, who was worriedly hanging about in the hall. She heard the duke call to his butler as she marched back to the entryway, seething as she went. One would think the man could have had the courtesy at least to meet his new ward! Simple politeness would have compelled most people to greet her, even if they had not expected or wanted to have such a burden placed upon them.

She saw Gabriela waiting for her, sitting alone on a marble bench near the front door. The footman stood a few feet away from her, almost as if he were standing guard. Gabriela was swinging her feet, scuffing them against the marble in a way that under normal circumstances Jessica would have reprimanded her for. But as it was, all she could think was how thin and young and lost Gabriela looked, and her chest tightened with sympathy.

"Gabriela."

The girl whirled around, rising to her feet apprehensively. Jessica smiled at her.

"It is straightened out now," she told her with all the cheerfulness and confidence she could muster. "The duke had not read my letter yet, so he did not understand why we were here. It was, you know, so hastily done...."

"Yes, of course. But now it is all right?" Gabriela's face brightened. "He wants us to remain?"

"Of course." Jessica omitted the man's reluctant agreement that they must stay. No matter how much she might dislike him, she did not want to influence his ward's feeling for him. "He remembered your father with affection and sorrow. I think he was merely caught by surprise, not expecting anything to have happened to the General."

"Am I to meet him now?" Gabriela shook out her skirts a little and began to brush at a spot.

"No, I think it is best that we wait for that. He was quite considerate and pointed out that you must be very tired and not up to meeting anyone yet. Tomorrow will be much better."

"Oh." Gabriela's face fell. "Well, yes, I suppose it would be better to meet him when I am looking more the thing." She paused, then went on curiously, "What manner of man is he? What does he look like? Is he tall, short, kind—"

"In looks he is quite handsome," Jessica admitted, pushing back her other, less positive, thoughts of him. "He is tall and dark." She thought of him, the brown throat that showed where his shirt was unbuttoned, the breadth of his chest and shoulders beneath that shirt, owing nothing to a padded jacket as some men did, the piercing dark eyes, the sharp outcropping of cheekbones. "He is, well, the sort of man to command attention."

"Then he looks as a duke should look?"

"Oh, yes."

"Good. I was so afraid he would be short and pudgy. You know, the kind whose fingers are like white sausages with rings on them."

Jessica had to laugh. "That is most unlike the Duke of Cleybourne."

"I'm glad. Is he nice, though? I mean, he's not high in the instep, is he?"

"He did not seem to stand on ceremony," Jessica told her carefully. She did not want to describe the man's cold reception or his reluctant acceptance of

Gabriela, but neither did she did want to paint too rosy a picture of him or Gabriela would be severely disappointed when she met him. "As to what sort of man he is, I think we must wait and get to know him better. It is difficult to determine on such a brief meeting, after all."

"Yes. Of course." Gabriela nodded. "I will be able to tell much better when I meet him tomorrow."

"Yes." Surely, Jessica thought, the duke would be in a better mood tomorrow. He would think about the General's letter and his old friend Carstairs, and by tomorrow morning he would have accepted the situation—perhaps even be pleased at the idea of raising Carstairs' daughter. He would not be so rude as not to invite Gabriela to his study for an introductory chat.

They did not have to wait much longer before the butler came to them. Jessica was pleased to see that the old man bowed with not only politeness but a certain eagerness, as well, as though he was pleased to welcome the girl to the household.

"Miss Carstairs. My name is Baxter. I am His Grace's butler. I am so pleased to meet you. I remember your father quite well. He was a good man."

Gabriela's face lit up with a smile. "Thank you."

"The maids have made up your rooms now, in the nursery. I am sorry we were so ill prepared for your visit. But hopefully you will find everything to your satisfaction."

"I am sure it will be," Gabriela replied with another dazzling smile, and the old man's face softened even more.

He led them up the stairs to the nursery, tucked away, as nurseries often were, far from the other bedrooms, in the rear of the house on the third floor. It was a large, cheerful suite of rooms, with a sizable central schoolroom and playroom, and three smaller bedrooms opening off it.

Gabriela's bedroom was very pretty, if a trifle young for her, with a yellow embroidered coverlet and a lace canopy over the bed, and wallpaper of cheerful yellow roses climbing a trellis. There was a rocker beside the bed, as well as a white chest and a small white table and chairs.

Jessica's room, beside Gabriela's, was much starker, with only a small oak chest for her clothes and a narrow oak bed, but Jessica did not expect anything more. Governess's rooms, in general, were neither large nor particularly accommodating. At least this one boasted a small fireplace, which had not been the case in every house where Jessica had stayed.

She was overwhelmed with weariness as soon as her eyes fell upon the bed, and it was all she could do to take the time to wash her face and change into her bedclothes. At last, with a grateful sigh, she stretched out between the sheets and closed her eyes.

Tomorrow would be better, she told herself again, and she fell asleep, thinking about the troublesome duke.

3

Lady Leona Vesey crossed her arms and looked over at her husband as if he were a rat that had just run into the room. They were sitting in the single private dining chamber in the Grey Horse Inn in the early afternoon, waiting for their luncheon to be brought. Leona had had more than enough of the uncertain service and unsophisticated amenities of a village inn. As if those things were not irritation enough, Lord Vesey had just told her that they were going back to the General's manor house.

"Have you gone mad?" she asked in a scathing voice, her tone implying that she had already answered her own question. "Why in the world would we want to go back to the General's house—I'm sorry, I should say, to that misbegotten brat's house? I, for one, have no liking for having the door slammed in my face."

Her husband scowled back at her. He had spent the evening after the reading of the General's will comforting himself with a large bottle of port, and, as a consequence, this afternoon his tongue felt coated with fur and his head seemed to have acquired an army of tiny gnomes hammering away.

Lord Vesey did not like his wife at the best of times. Right now he was entertaining cheerful visions of putting his hands around her throat and squeezing until her eyes bulged. "The door won't be slammed in our face."

"Your brain is obviously soaked in port. Don't you remember? The General kicked us out."

"Yes, you bollixed that one up, all right," Lord Vesey agreed.

"*I?*" Leona exclaimed, her eyes widening. "*I* bollixed it up? You were the man's great-nephew. It was you who made him despise you."

"Ah, but you were supposed to be able to wrap an old man around your finger. Remember?" Vesey grinned evilly as he reminded his wife of her earlier, confident words when they had first heard that General Streathern was on his deathbed.

Personally, Lord Vesey had never admired his wife's looks. He had married her because she was the only woman he had found in the Ton who was utterly indifferent to his little peccadilloes and quite happy to let him go his own way…as long as she was allowed to go hers. Other men fell all over themselves to get at those swelling breasts of Leona's, but he found such lushness rather grotesque. He much preferred a lither, slimmer silhouette…such as the one on that Gabriela chit. Unconsciously he licked his lips as he thought of her. Leona was far too old, as well. It was the sweet bloom of youth that he preferred, and there was nothing quite like the joy of being the first to pick the fruit.

He relished Leona's look of chagrin so much that he went on. "That is the second one, you know. First you bungled that affair with Devin last summer, and now you couldn't even rouse the interest of an old man. I fear you are losing your touch, my dear. Or is it your age showing, do you think?"

Flame leaped in Leona's eyes, and her face screwed up in an unattractive snarl. She wanted to leap on him, claws out, and damage him. But she knew that Vesey was such a coward, he would probably start wailing and shrieking, and then someone would come running. It would be thoroughly embarrassing to have everyone in a common inn see what a pitiful, mewling creature her husband was. So she contented herself with saying, "As if you would know what a real man wanted! You are nothing but a degenerate!"

"My, my, and to think you know such big words." Vesey widened his eyes in mocking amazement. "Have you been bedding down with a man of letters?"

Leona sneered at him. Vesey was hardly a man. He had come to her bed a few times when they were first married, making a feeble attempt to get her with an heir—as if either one of them cared about that! She had soon set him straight in that regard. She had no intention of growing fat with anyone's child, and she took pains to prevent that occurring. His lovemaking she regarded as pathetic, nothing like the passion that Devin had been able to give her. Her eyes glowed a little even now as she thought about his skillful caresses. No other man had been able to make her shudder and moan as Dev had, and she had missed him sorely during the past few months. No matter how many men, from lord to common laborer, she had tried to replace him with, none had proved to have his stamina or skill…or inventive mind.

What rankled the most was the fact that Vesey was right. She had indeed bungled the whole thing with Devin. She had overestimated her power over him. She had been the one to suggest that he marry the American heiress. But how was *she* to have known that the whey-faced, social disaster of a woman whom she had envisioned would turn out to be a cunning beauty? Instead of Devin's taking the woman's money and spending it on Leona and their pursuit of pleasure, he had settled down with the doxy at that stupid estate of his in Derbyshire, and Leona had been left both penniless and sexually frustrated. The whole thing had made her permanently cross.

"It doesn't matter now, anyway," she said in disgruntlement. "We got nothing in the General's will, and the best thing we can do is go home. I can't wait to get away from here. I cannot conceive how anyone can stand to live in the country."

"Ah, but we still have a chance to gain something, my dear—quite a lot, in fact, if we only have the courage to seize the moment."

"Seize what moment? What nonsense are you babbling?"

Vesey sighed exaggeratedly. "Are you really so

short on wit? We may have been cheated out of our inheritance, but Gabriela is only fourteen. Her fortune will be handled by her guardian. If I was her guardian, we would have a tidy sum at our disposal. And I would be quite willing to take it upon myself to, um, look after the girl's proper education."

Leona rolled her eyes. "You are a pig, Vesey. Not only that, you're stupid. She already has a guardian. And the Duke of Cleybourne is not a man you want to cross."

Vesey shrugged. "You are thinking of the duke as he used to be. The truth is, for the past four years he has been a shell of a man. You know what a recluse he turned into when his wife died. You think someone like that will welcome an adolescent girl into his household? He doesn't need her money—he's as rich as Croesus. Besides, he's far too noble to think of using her money for his own benefit. No, she will be nothing but a bother to him, and I am willing to bet that he will be happy to lay the burden off on someone else."

"Not if that someone is you."

"I'm not saying I would be Cleybourne's first choice. He and I have never been friends—he is far too dull. But if I am already in the house, if I am in possession of the girl, so to speak, and he sees it will be a battle in court to regain her, well, it will be a far easier matter to hand the guardianship over to me."

"What makes you think you will be in possession of her? They won't even let us in the door."

"Really, Leona, who will stop us? The servants

won't have the nerve to deny me admittance. The old man is dead now, after all. They no longer have his authority behind them. They won't dare say no to a lord, especially since they know that if the girl does not reach her majority, I would inherit the place as her only relative. Believe me, they will not risk offending me.''

"The girl can tell them not to let you in.''

"A fourteen-year-old female? She wouldn't have the courage or the wit.''

"Her governess is a dragon.''

"She may be, but she is merely a governess. She won't stand up to a lord, either. When I show up at the door, they won't know what to do except stand back and let me enter. Once we are in the house and have actual control of the girl, we will be in the cat-bird seat. I will sue to be named her guardian. As her only living relative, I have a good case for it, and, besides, I don't think Cleybourne will contest it. What will he care? He doesn't even know the chit.''

Leona looked at her husband doubtfully. The whole thing seemed far less sure than Vesey made it out to be. On the other hand, they were teetering on the edge of financial ruin. Indeed, they had been slipping down the side of it for quite some time. Their creditors were becoming increasingly insistent, and the last time Leona had been to the dressmaker, the blasted woman had flatly refused to make another garment for her until Leona paid her bill. Any possibility that would alleviate their situation would be worth a try.

"Oh, all right," she agreed testily. "Let's go over to the bloody house. At least if they slam the door on your nose, it will be somewhat amusing."

There was a knock on the door, and without waiting for permission to enter, the innkeeper opened the door and backed into the room, carrying a large tray. "Good afternoon, my lord. My lady. Here's your luncheon."

His wife bustled in behind him, carrying another tray, and together they unloaded a vast array of food on the table. Leona cast an eye over the fare, plentiful but, she felt sure, as bland and plain as every other dish the inn had given them in the past few days. Never, she thought, had she appreciated her cook in London so much.

"Ah, Sims, tell them to have my carriage brought 'round after we eat. Lady Vesey and I are going to transfer to the General's house."

"Of course, my lord. Goin' over there to see to things, are ye? I warrant they'll be glad to see ye after that theft last night."

"Theft?" Vesey looked blankly at the portly innkeeper. "What are you talking about?"

"Why, at the manor house, my lord. I thought ye knew. I supposed that was why ye was goin' over there, to make sure the house is safe and all."

"What happened?" Leona asked. "What did they steal?"

Sims shook his massive head. "That's just it. They didn't take much. The safe was broken into, and things inside it were all scattered about, but Pierson didn't know exactly what the General had in there.

Some jewelry's gone, they think. All the drawers in the old man's desk were opened, and papers all over—the General's will, ye know, and all kinds of business papers. Couple of things broken. The place is a right mess, is what me nevvy told me. He were makin' a delivery there, ye see, and the cook told him about it. He says the butler near had a fit, ye know, seein' that. What with the General barely cold in his grave.''

He sighed lugubriously. '''Tis a sad, sad thing. No respect for the dead anymore. Ah, well, at least the girl was safe away. Reckon it would have scared her somethin' awful.''

"Safe away?" Lord Vesey repeated in hollow tones.

"Why, yes." The man looked at Vesey closely. "Didn't ye know? The young lady and her governess left yesterday afternoon, after the funeral and all. Gone to her guardian's, Will says, some duke in Yorkshire. I woulda thought ye'd know all about that.''

"Yes, of course. I was merely distracted by your tale. I do know that. She has gone to Castle Cleybourne.''

"Aye, that's the place." The innkeeper nodded. He stepped back from the table, giving Lord Vesey a cheerful grin. "Well, there ye are, my lord. Enjoy your meal.''

"What? Oh, yes, of course.''

"And I'll tell them to bring up yer carriage.''

"Oh. Uh, yes, do that.''

The innkeeper followed his wife out of the room,

closing the door behind him, and Vesey sank with a sigh into his chair. Leona regarded him with a malicious little grin.

"I would say that knocks your plans all cock-a-hoop," she said with no discernible sympathy.

"Bloody hell! Whatever possessed that girl to go running off to Cleybourne like that?"

"Mmm. Perhaps she suspected what you were planning?"

"Don't be absurd." Vesey, who counted himself quite clever, sent his wife a nasty glance. "I didn't even know it until a few minutes ago. How could she?"

Leona shrugged. "Well, whatever caused it, you certainly won't be able to lay hold of her now. At least we shall be able to return to London."

She walked over to the table and looked down at the array of food. Vesey remained in his chair, thoughtfully tugging at his upper lip.

"Perhaps not…" he said after a moment, rising and sauntering over to the table, looking pleased with himself.

"What are you talking about?" Leona asked crossly. "Not return to London? I trust you are not thinking of going to the manor house still."

"No. Especially not with people popping in and out, taking things. I was thinking more of going to Yorkshire."

Leona stared. "You can't be serious. Yorkshire? Cleybourne? You think you can wrest the girl away from the duke?"

"Wrest? Of course not. Don't be nonsensical. But

it would do no harm to ask. I told you—what use does Cleybourne have for the girl? He'd probably love to get rid of her. If we were to go by there on our way to London..."

"A little out of the way, don't you think?"

Vesey waved this objection aside. "I could offer to take the chit off his hands. Blood relative and all. He might be swayed by the argument."

"I sincerely doubt it." Leona had little faith in her husband's ability to sway anyone. "Cleybourne's always been an honorable sort—not a prig like Westhampton, of course. He did like to have a little fun back before he married Dev's sister, but marriage ruined him."

She paused, looking thoughtful. "But he has been living like a monk ever since Caroline died."

Vesey looked over at her. "What are you saying?"

"Well...he might not be immune to a little feminine persuasion. What has it been since Caroline's death—three, four years? That's a long time. I've heard no rumor of his having an affair with anyone, even a light-o'-love, in that time."

Lord Vesey smiled. "You think he might be ripe for the plucking?"

Leona's golden eyes were alight with anticipation. "A lonely widower...winter evenings around a cozy fire...that's almost too easy a target for one with my talents."

The more she thought about it, the more Leona liked the idea. Cleybourne was a handsome man, tall and broad shouldered, and wealthy. Seducing him into her bed would be no hardship on her, and it would be pleasant to have a new, indulgent lover. She didn't know whether he would turn the girl over to Vesey, but that was entirely secondary to Leona. Of first importance was the prospect of acquiring an infatuated lover eager—and able—to ply her with expensive gifts.

"I don't know, Leona," Vesey warned. "He is quite friendly with the Aincourts, and you know in what esteem they hold you."

Leona's eyes flashed. "I don't care if he is as thick as thieves with the loathesome Lady Westhampton. She is Dev's own sister, and her opinion of me never kept Devin out of my bed. Trust me, a few hours with Cleybourne and he'll be panting after me. A few days and he will be willing to give me whatever I want."

Lord Vesey smiled. "Well, then…eat up, and we're off to Yorkshire."

Jessica awoke the next morning in a much improved mood. A good night's rest was often the best antidote to one's fears and doubts. Looking out the nursery window at the rolling Yorkshire countryside, washed with the pale light of a wintry sun, she believed the reassuring things she had said last night to Gabriela. This morning, she was sure, the Duke of Cleybourne would follow the honorable course and accept his guardianship of the girl and welcome her into his house. He had simply been caught by surprise last night.

She breakfasted with Gabriela, talking about how

they would explore the house today, and later in the morning, when a servant came to the nursery with a summons from the duke, she followed him downstairs with a light step.

The footman ushered her into the same study where she had spoken to Cleybourne the night before, then bowed out of the room, closing the door behind him. The Duke of Cleybourne was seated behind his massive desk, more formally attired in a jacket and snowy cravat than he had been last night. He rose at her entrance and with a gesture indicated a chair in front of his desk.

"Miss Maitland."

"Your Grace."

"Please, be seated."

Looking at his face, some of Jessica's good mood evaporated. He was by daylight as handsome as he had appeared last night in the dimmer candlelight, but his expression was, if anything, even grimmer. She wondered, briefly, if this man knew how to smile.

"I have given a great deal of thought to this situation," Cleybourne began in a heavy tone. "And I have come to the conclusion that it would not be in Miss Carstairs' best interests to be my ward."

Jessica stiffened, and her hands curled around the arms of her chair, as if to keep herself from vaulting out of it. "I'm sorry. Perhaps I misunderstood you. Are you saying that you are sending us away? Are you going to turn Gabriela over to Vesey?"

Her mind was racing even as she spoke, thinking how she could flee with Gabriela before he could give the girl up to Vesey. *Where could she go? How could she protect her?*

Cleybourne flushed faintly, and his mouth tightened. "Good God, no, I don't intend to turn her over to that roué! How can you even ask that?"

"How can I not?" Jessica retorted heatedly. "I know nothing of you except that you refuse to be her guardian."

"It is not that, exactly. It is just…well, when her father wrote his will, my circumstances were different. My wife was still alive, and my—" He stopped abruptly and rose to his feet, pushing back his chair. "But mine is a bachelor's household now, Miss Maitland," he went on, pacing away from her. "Scarcely a good place for a young girl. She needs a woman's guiding hand, someone who can plan her debut and introduce her to society, teach her all the things a girl on the edge of womanhood needs to know. I would be at a complete loss at any of those things."

"She has me, sir," Jessica said, rising to her feet as well. "I may be only a governess, but I did make my coming-out in London. I was brought up as Gabriela should be brought up. And when the time arrives for her to come out, surely you have some female relative, a sister or mother or aunt, who would be willing to guide her through the waters of London society."

"Makeshift remedies, Miss Maitland," he said in a clipped tone, facing her from across the room. "No doubt you are an excellent teacher. However, she needs more than that. She should have the close guidance and company of an older woman, one experienced in the ways of society. I cannot provide that, and neither can you."

"She needs comfort and strength right now, and that is more important than what she will need four years from now. She needs a home, a place where she belongs, where she is wanted. She lost both her parents six years ago, and now has lost the man who was a grandfather to her. She has no family because I will *not* consider Lord Vesey her family."

"Of course not. But *I* am not her family, either."

"No, but you were her father's friend. You are the man her father would have wanted to be her guardian. Because of that, she places her trust in you. And you are the man the General wanted to be her guardian. He placed his trust in you. Did you not read his letter? He feared that Vesey might try to—"

"I will not let Vesey have her. I already told you that. It isn't as if I am turning the two of you out into the street." Cleybourne scowled at her blackly. "Damn it! You are the most infuriating woman. I told you, I will find a suitable place for her. My sister-in-law, perhaps. I will write Rachel and see if she and her husband would raise her. Of course you will stay here until I find the proper place, and I assure you that if Vesey should pursue the matter, I will take care of him."

Jessica started to argue again, but she stopped and pressed her lips tightly together, controlling her anger. She had to stay with Gabriela; that was the most important thing, especially if this man was going to shuffle the girl about. She had already pushed him as much as she dared. She must not offend him so much that he let her go. "Very well, Your Grace."

The duke's eyebrows rose in faint surprise at her capitulation. "Yes. Well, that's settled, then."

"Shall I bring Miss Gabriela to meet you now?"

"What?" An odd look, one almost of fear, crossed his face, and he shook his head quickly. "No. I—it would be best if we did not meet, I think."

"What?" Jessica was too astounded not to stare at him. "You will not even meet her?"

"It would be better for her."

"How is it better for her?" Jessica demanded, anger boiling up too fast and hard for her to be prudent. "To know that you will not even see her? That you cannot be bothered?"

"That is enough, Miss Maitland!" His dark eyes flashed. "I am her guardian, if you remember, and that is my decision. She should not become attached here. This will not be her home. It will be easier for her to leave this way."

"Easier for you, you mean!" Jessica retorted hotly.

Richard's eyes widened in astonishment, and Jessica realized then how far she had overstepped. But, in the next moment, to her surprise, the duke let out a short bark of laughter. "I cannot imagine how you managed to be a governess, Miss Maitland, given that razor of a tongue of yours."

Jessica lifted her chin a little. "General Streathern approved of straight speech."

"I would not think he brooked insubordination."

Looking Cleybourne straight in the eye, Jessica

said evenly, "The General was not a man to use his power unwisely."

Cleybourne looked at her for a long moment. Finally he said, "Thank you. That is all."

Jessica, resisting the impulse to give him a sarcastic curtsy, merely nodded and left the room.

Inside she was seething. *The man was unfeeling!* She stalked down the hall, scarcely noticing where she was going, and scowling so blackly that a maid, dusting a table, quickly stepped out of her way.

She knew that she could not return to Gabriela in this mood. She must come up with some way to present Cleybourne's decision to the girl without hurting her, and right now all that would come spurting out of her would be the furious, unvarnished truth. She decided a walk would be the only way to burn off her ire, so she went down the back stairs and out a door into the pale winter sunshine.

Immediately she realized her mistake; it was far too cold to be outside without a wrap. But she could not go back upstairs for her coat without running into Gabriela. She decided one quick turn around the garden would have to do.

She had walked halfway down the center aisle of the garden when footsteps on the stone behind her made her pause and turn. A small woman, bundled up in a cloak, was walking toward her, and over one arm was draped another cloak. She smiled as she neared Jessica.

"Miss Maitland, I thought you might find it a wee bit cold out here, so I brought you a cloak."

Jessica took the wrap from her gratefully. "Thank you, Miss…"

"Brown. Mercy Brown. I am the housekeeper here." Her eyes twinkled merrily, matching her smile. "And I must confess it was curiosity more than kindness that sent me out here. I have been wanting to meet you ever since Baxter told me about your arrival with the wee one."

Jessica smiled back at the woman. "It is a pleasure, Miss Brown, whatever the reason. But Miss Gabriela is scarcely a wee one."

"Ah, well, she was but a baby the last time I saw her. She was a pretty thing then, and Baxter tells me she still is."

"Yes. She is very pretty. And good-natured, as well."

The housekeeper's smile grew even broader. "I'm glad to hear that. It will be so good to have a young person about the place again. It will be good for the master, too."

"The duke? Not much. He plans to ship her off somewhere as soon as he can," Jessica told her sourly.

"No!" Miss Brown looked dismayed. "He never said that."

"Close enough. He says it's not the 'proper place' for a child, him being a bachelor. He is the most arrogant, irritating man—I cannot imagine why the General thought he would take care of Gaby. He was obviously deluded about the duke's sense of honor and duty."

"Oh, no, he is an honorable man!" the older

woman protested. ''And he would not shirk his duty.''

''Mmm,'' Jessica replied on a note of disbelief. ''So long as it did not put him out, I suppose.''

''You must not judge him so harshly,'' the housekeeper told her earnestly. ''The duke is a good man. He really is. You have to understand—he has had a sad history. Things have happened to him that have made him, well, a bit of a recluse, but there isn't a wicked bone in his body.''

''What else would you call it when he rejects an orphaned girl whose last relative has just died, who has been entrusted to him by a man who was his friend? Her father and General Streathern trusted him to take care of Gabriela, but he cannot be bothered. So he plans to ship her off to whoever will take care of her for him.''

Jessica glanced at the housekeeper and saw a look of great sadness on her face. The woman shook her head, saying, ''Ah, poor man. It must be because of Alana. No doubt he cannot bear to be around a child again.'' She looked at Jessica. ''Why don't you come back to my sitting room and warm up with a cup of tea? I will tell you about His Grace and why, well, why he is as he is.''

Jessica agreed readily, curiosity as much as the cold impelling her inside. The two women turned and retraced their steps to the house, where the housekeeper hung up their cloaks and led Jessica along a back hall and through the kitchen into a cozy little sitting room beyond that was the housekeeper's domain. A word to a maid as they passed brought her to the room a few moments later with a pot of tea and cups, and a dish of scones, on a tray.

The scones were delicious, and a few sips of the strong sweet tea warmed Jessica up almost immediately. She settled back into the comfortable chair to listen to Miss Brown.

"I have known His Grace since he was a little boy. So have Baxter and most of us older servants," she began, her brown eyes alight with fondness. "He was always a wonderful boy. And as he grew into manhood, well, you could not ask for a kinder or better employer. Almost ten years ago he married Caroline Aincourt, the daughter of the Earl of Ravenscar. An excellent marriage—old family, good name—but far more than that, His Grace was madly in love."

Miss Brown let out a little sigh, her eyes taking on a faraway look. "Oh, but she was a beauty. Every inch a duchess, she was. Tall and striking, with black hair and green eyes. Good-looking lot, the Aincourts, whatever else they might be. There's a portrait of her in the Great Hall. They were very happy. And, oh, the times we had at the castle then! There were often guests—for weeks at a time, sometimes. Balls and dinners and all sorts of entertainment. His Grace was a sociable man."

"The duke?" Jessica asked in disbelief.

The other woman nodded. "Oh, yes. I am sure you would not credit it, to see him now. But he enjoyed company. He wasn't one of those who was irresponsible or wild, you understand. He always did his duty and took an interest in his affairs, but he liked a party as well as the next man. And the duchess! Well, she fairly glowed at a ball. She was always the center of attention. They had a daughter, Alana.''

"A daughter? He said nothing about her. He said that his wife had died, but…''

Miss Brown nodded, her eye darkening a little. "Oh, yes, he had a daughter.'' She smiled to herself. "Ah, she was a corker, that one. Lively as could be, always into everything, but no one could get mad at her, because she had the sunniest disposition. All she had to do was smile at you and say she was sorry, and you would forgive her anything. After she was born, they spent even more time here, only going to London for the height of the season. The duke felt it was better to raise a child here in the country, you see. Miss Alana didn't even sleep in the nursery. His Grace thought it was too far away: they could not hear if she cried out. She stayed right down the hall from her parents, and her nurse slept on a bed in her room.''

"What happened? I mean, what changed everything?''

"They were in a carriage accident. The duchess and the little one were killed.''

"Oh, how awful.''

The housekeeper nodded, her eyes filling with tears as she remembered. "His Grace was riding outside the carriage. It was winter, before Christmas, right about this time of year, in fact.'' She sighed. "They were probably driving too fast. Anyway, the carriage overturned as they took a corner. It rolled down an embankment, and the duchess was thrown out. Her neck was broken, and she died instantly. But the carriage, with the wee one inside, rolled on down into the pond.''

Jessica drew in her breath sharply in horror. ''Oh, no! How awful!''

''There was a thin layer of ice on the top of the pond, but of course the coach broke right through. His Grace went in after her. The coachman said it was a pitiful sight, how he dived again and again into the cold dark water. Finally, he brought her up and carried her onto land, but it was too late. The poor sweet child was dead.''

Sympathetic tears welled in Jessica's eyes as she thought about the horrific scene—the frantic parent, the frozen pond, the dark, icy night. She could imagine the overturned carriage, the frightened horses, the beautiful woman dead on the ground, and the duke throwing himself into the icy water in a desperate search for his child, emerging at last with her still form.

''He carried that child in his arms all the way home, and when he walked through the door, holding her—I'll never forget his face that night. I've never seen anything as bleak. We could hardly pry the child out of his arms and bundle him off to bed himself. He came down with a terrible fever—it was no wonder, him being in that icy water and then in freezing weather all the way home—and he nearly died himself. His valet, Noonan, and Baxter and I took care of him. For days we thought we were going to lose him, too, and then it was still more weeks before he was well. He was so gaunt you would hardly recognize him, and that's a fact. He aged years in those weeks.''

''Poor man.'' However much he had angered Jessica, her heart was wrung with pity for him. He had suffered terribly—the loss of a beloved spouse was sad enough, but to have had his adored daughter taken at the same time seemed almost too much to bear.

''Yes.'' The housekeeper heaved a sigh and leaned forward to replenish their cups with tea. After a moment, she went on. ''After that he changed. Not just the way he looked. The way he *was*. At first he just sat in his chair and stared out the window. Didn't seem to care whether he lived or died. He would hardly see anyone—wouldn't let the vicar anywhere near him, and he barely tolerated the doctor. The only one who had much luck with him was Lady Westhampton, his wife's sister. He would see the duchess's brother, as well, Lord Ravenscar. The only place he would go was to the graveyard. It was terrible…terrible…. We were all so worried about him. Finally, one day, he told us he was going back to London. We were happy, thinking he had decided to get on with his life.'' She paused, and tears glinted in her lively brown eyes.

''But he had not?'' Jessica prompted gently after a moment.

The housekeeper shook her head. ''Later he told his valet that it was just that he could not bear to live in this house any longer. It's his ancestral home—it has been the seat of the Dukes of Cleybourne since

1246. And he lived in it his whole life. But he hasn't been home for almost four years.''

"But surely he has gotten out more, living in London. He has lived a fuller life, even if he could not face this house.''

"No. I only wish he had. Baxter writes to me every month with news about His Grace and the household. You see, only a skeleton staff and I stayed here. Most of the staff went with him, so we are always eager for news of the rest.'' She smiled. "We are close, a kind of family, you see. So I write to Baxter and he to me, and we share the news with the others. The sad truth is that for all that time His Grace has been a recluse in London as much as he ever was here. He sees his relatives and friends every once in a while—if they come to visit him. He never calls on others, and he does not attend parties. Baxter says he never even visits his club. He has shut himself off from the world. And Lady Westhampton, the Duchess's sister, is worried about him. She has told Baxter that lately he has seemed even more melancholy. Of course, this time of year is the worst for him.''

"But he came back here,'' Jessica pointed out. "Surely that is a good sign.''

"We hoped so. I was very cheered. But he—well, he is as polite and nice as ever, but there is a a sadness to him that just hurts my heart to see. Sometimes I worry about why he came home now.''

"What do you mean?''

The other woman frowned. "I'm not entirely sure,

miss. But it being this time of year and all…I can't help but think, maybe he's come home to die.''

"To die!" Jessica raised her eyebrows in surprise. "But he is still a young man. He can't be forty yet."

"No, miss. He's thirty-five is all. But…"

"Surely you don't mean—" Jessica looked shocked. "Do you actually think he might intend to…to harm himself?"

Her companion looked even more troubled. "I don't know. I don't want to think so. He's a strong man, but sometimes I fear that he has given in to despair. I think perhaps he hoped that one day, being in London, away from here, he would begin to heal his sorrow. Maybe he has become so heartsore that he fears he never will. I think Lady Westhampton feared it. She cautioned Baxter to look after His Grace carefully. Not, of course, that he would ever have done any less than that, and her ladyship knows it. It was a sign of her worry about him."

She sighed, then shook her head firmly. "No, I will not think that. But, you see, that is why I was so happy to hear this morning that you and the young miss had arrived. I thought, a child in the house is just what he needs. She will bring life to the place again, and laughter. But when you told me that he would not keep her, would not even see her…" Again she sighed. "Ah, me, it's a sad, sad thing. I think he must feel that he cannot bear to see a child here. Miss Gabriela is older than his own little one would have been, but still, it would be a reminder to him of all that he has lost."

"Then that is why he wants to find someone else

to take her guardianship from him. I am sorry. I misjudged him.'' Jessica frowned. ''Poor man. I thought him simply grim and unsociable. I had no idea such loss lay at the base of his actions.''

She thought back to the duke's sharply carved face—the jutting lines of cheekbone and jaw, almost gaunt in their severity, the dark, brooding eyes, the taut lines of his body—and she could see now the sorrow that lay behind those things.

''It is too bad that he has decided to turn Gaby away,'' Jessica went on. ''I think you are right. She might be just the thing he needs in his life.'' She sighed. ''Ah, well, I shall just have to explain it to Gaby as best I can.''

After Jessica left the housekeeper's room, she walked into the Great Hall, the large area that ran back through the middle of the house from the front door, centered by the staircase. It was two stories high and had been the main room of the castle back in its early days. It was here that the housekeeper had said the late duchess's portrait hung.

Obviously the first few pictures were not of her, for they were of men in the attire of Tudor and Stuart times. She came upon a painting of a woman in a high white-powdered wig, and then, just beyond that, was a portrait of a young woman in modern dress. Jessica stopped, sure that this must be the duke's Caroline. She was beautiful, even allowing for the flattering nature of most portraits. Tall and slender, she smiled invitingly out at the viewer. There was a dimple in one cheek, and her green eyes twinkled. She stood beside a chair, one slender hand resting upon its back, and at her feet sat a toy spaniel, its black-and-white coloring reflecting the coal-black of the woman's hair. She was dressed in green velvet that emphasized her large eyes, and a magnificent emerald ring glowed on her finger.

It was easy to see why Cleybourne had been so in love with her. She looked like the sort of woman who had men falling at her feet, declaring love. Jessica gazed at her with a certain fascination. She had never possessed the sort of charm that it was clear this woman had had. A gawky adolescent, Jessica had grown awkwardly into womanhood, and her blunt tongue and forthright manner had put off many a would-be suitor. She had never had the gift that women like the duchess seemed to possess naturally—the ability to flirt and beguile, to beckon men with a look or a smile. Her aunt, who had introduced her into society when she was eighteen, had often despaired of her, declaring that she would never catch a husband if she persisted in talking to men about the war in Europe instead of smiling and simpering like the other girls. Aunt Lilith, she remembered, had been both ecstatic and amazed when Darius offered for her. Jessica gave a small, wry smile as she thought that she, too, had been rather surprised.

Shrugging off her memories, she turned away and started up the stairs. It was useless to think of the past. She would not know the sort of married happiness she had dreamed of as a girl, but thanks to the General's generosity, she would be well able to live without having to scrimp and save, or depend on others. She had her independence, and she had Gabriela, and she would have a very pleasant life.

Jessica turned over in her bed, sighing. It was late, and Gabriela had gone to sleep at least an hour earlier. Sleep, however, had eluded Jessica.

It was not for lack of physical weariness. Baxter had offered to show them around the house, and she and Gabriela had spent the majority of the day tramping all over with him. Surprisingly tireless for a man his age, the butler had shown them the entire castle, even poking into the unused wings and the cavernous cellars that had once held the castle's dungeons and storerooms. Gabriela had especially enjoyed the latter visit, shivering with obvious delight at Baxter's ghoulish stories of the dungeons. Afterward, he had turned them over to the head gardener, who had given them an equally detailed tour of the gardens and outlying areas. By the end of the day, even Gabriela was thoroughly worn-out. Jessica had been grateful for the exercise for both of them, after almost two days spent in a carriage, and she had thought she would sleep easily.

Instead, as soon as her head touched her pillow, she had started to think of all the problems and pitfalls that lay before them. She had tossed and turned for almost an hour.

Finally, she admitted to herself that she was not going to fall asleep any time soon. Jessica got out of bed and pulled her dressing gown on over her nightgown. She decided that she would read for a while in the hopes that that would encourage her to sleep.

She thought that she remembered the way to the library, which Baxter had showed them earlier.

She checked on her charge, who was sleeping soundly, then slipped out of the nursery and down the stairs to the library. As she approached it, she saw that light spilled out from the duke's study, which lay a few doors before the library. She hesitated for a moment, not wanting to see Cleybourne again. She thought about going back upstairs without a book, but instead, she tiptoed, hopeful that he would not even notice her passing.

He would not have, she realized as she glanced inside the room, for he was not looking out the door, but what she saw pulled her to a stop. She stared into the study.

Cleybourne was seated at his desk, leaning his head on his hands, elbows propped on the desk. To one side sat a decanter of liquor and a half-empty glass. In front of him lay an open case of dueling pistols. As Jessica watched, he reached into the case and took out one of the pistols. A chill ran through her. *The housekeeper had been right. The duke was going to kill himself!*

4

Jessica was so shocked that for a moment she did not know what to do. Her first instinct was to rush in, crying out to him not to do it. But something held her back, told her that was not the way to snap the Duke of Cleybourne from his black mood. She hesitated, remembering her two conversations with the man. Then she went forward, crossing her fingers that her second impulse was correct.

"Well," she said coolly as she stepped into the study. Behind the desk, the duke's head snapped up in surprise. "So this is why you are rejecting Gabriela. She would interfere with your plans to do yourself in."

Richard scowled, his eyes narrowing. "I wasn't...bloody hell."

He had spent the evening in his study, drinking more than he should. The arrival of this damnably irritating woman had ruined all his plans. Obviously he could not do what he had come home to do until he had arranged for Rachel or someone to take over the care of the girl who had been suddenly placed in his charge. He had already written to Rachel, but it could be days, even weeks, before he heard from her. After that, it would be still more time before she could arrive and take the girl in hand—*and what if she and Michael did not want to take responsibility for her?* Then he would have to search for someone else. It was clear that he might have to stay in this damnable place for months, surrounded by reminders—hearing Alana's laugh, seeing her face, sleeping in the same bed where Caroline had once lain with him....

He had started drinking, hoping to ease some of the pain. He had *not* been about to kill himself. *He was not that irresponsible.* He had taken out the case of dueling pistols simply to look at them. He had thought he ought to clean them, but before he could move to do so, this wretched woman had come into the room. *She, of course, would put the worst possible interpretation on his actions.* Richard could not think when he had met anyone as irritating.

From the first moment that Richard had seen her, when she had come striding down the hall, shouting his name imperiously, as if he were a recalcitrant servant, he had disliked her intensely. She was rude and abrupt, and she looked at him with a cool contempt, even dislike, that he was unaccustomed to, especially in a woman. He had never been one to stand on ceremony, to demand the respect that was due his station. He knew that he was an easygoing sort. His mother had often complained of his laxness with the servants and his general lack of the self-importance that was proper in a duke. But with Jessica Maitland, he found himself wanting to remind her of his rank, to wipe the look of contempt from her face.

"What the devil are you doing here?" he growled. "Every time I turn around, there you are, sticking your nose into my study."

"Hardly that, since this is but the third time I've seen you. To answer your question, I could not sleep and was on my way to the library when I saw you in here, contemplating your guns."

Jessica came up to his desk and looked down at the pistols, keeping her face cool and her voice light. "Beautiful workmanship."

"Yes. They were a gift from my father."

"Ah. I am sure he would be pleased to know what you intend to do with them."

"I was *intending* to clean them," Richard responded. "Not that it is any of your business."

"It *is* my business, I'm afraid. The fact that you are Gabriela's guardian makes it so. Otherwise, I frankly would not care whether you put a period to your existence. Some people simply do not have the courage to face life. That is the way they are made; I suppose there is little they can do about it."

Anger shot through Richard with such force that he jumped up, shoving his chair back. "How dare you imply that I am a coward!"

The woman was an absolute harpy—poison tongued and hard as nails. The fact that she was beautiful, with skin as white as cream and that wild tumble of hot red curls falling loose around her shoulders, somehow made her sharp nature even worse, he thought. Seeing her there, her curves softly encased in a dark blue dressing gown that turned her eyes a deep, pure blue, her hair loose and wild, she looked the sort of woman who made a man think of only taking her to bed—and then she opened her mouth, and all he wanted to do was shake her.

It increased his bad temper to realize that she made him think of sex. He had not wanted another woman since Caroline's death—not in a specific way. It was both annoying and ironic that this acidic woman should cause a stirring of his loins.

Jessica, watching the anger that lit up the man's face, felt pleased with her plan of attack. Pleading and reasoning would not deter him, she had thought, knowing that his loving servants and no doubt his family and friends had done plenty of that. Angering him, however, worked like a charm—jolting him right out of his melancholy.

She shrugged. "Well, it is scarcely the act of a brave man—to take the easy way out, leaving all his loved ones to mourn him."

"The easy way? You know nothing about it! You don't know me or what my life has been like."

She raised her eyebrows. "Yes, I am certain it must have been a burden to you—being handsome and wealthy and possessing one of the highest titles in the land. I can see why you should go spinning into despair."

His dark eyes flared with a red light, and Richard had to curl his hands into fists to keep from grabbing her by the shoulders and shaking her. "You don't know what you're talking about. You know nothing about me.''

"Perhaps I do not. But I do know about my life. I know that until I was eighteen, I lived a happy and privileged existence. I came from a good family. I had a loving father. I had that coming-out that you spoke of for Gabriela. I was even engaged to a dashing young lieutenant. Then suddenly that life was cut off when my father was cashiered out of the army. Perhaps you don't recall the scandal, as we did not move in the exalted circles of a duke. My father was Major Thomas Maitland, and he was an upstanding and honorable soldier all his life. Then he was thrown out, stripped of his title, his honor, his very livelihood. We were no longer received by anyone. My fiancé broke off our engagement. His family, you see, could not ally itself to one so tainted by scandal. My father, the best of men, changed before my eyes. He took to drinking and bad company. He was killed three months later in a fight in a common tavern, and, as my mother had died, I was left alone—without money, without prospects, without even my good name anymore. I lost everything. I became a governess, and as you have pointed out, I am not highly successful at bending my knee to others, so as a consequence, I was close to starvation. Only the General's kindness saved me.''

"Good Lord. I'm sorry. I didn't know.''

"And I know Gabriela's life,'' Jessica went on. "She has seen a great deal more sorrow than anyone her age should have to see. She was orphaned when she was but eight, and now her only real relative, the man whom she loved as a grandfather, has been taken from her. She has been turned over to a stranger, but even he does not want her and cannot wait to give her away to some other stranger, because she is too much trouble.''

''Damnation!'' Cleybourne roared, and his face, which had softened with sympathy during Jessica's recital of the events of her life, turned hard and angry once again. ''That is not the case at all! I am not rejecting the girl. It is not because she is too much trouble.''

''Oh, no, that's right. I forgot. It is because she would put a crimp in your plans to do away with yourself. And no one must be allowed to do that, must they?''

''You overstep yourself, Miss Maitland.''

''Do I? I am so sorry. I know that you are used to dealing with servants, loving servants, who would gladly do anything for you, who worry themselves silly about you—until they almost had me convinced that you must be a better man than I thought for them to care so much for you. Well, I am not your servant. General Streathern hired me, and when he died, he entrusted me with Gabriela's welfare. However little you may want responsibility for her, I accept it gladly, and I don't intend to let you damage her life still further by killing yourself while she is in your house. If you haven't the courage to accept life and its troubles, if you care so little for your servants that you will let them stumble upon your bleeding and lifeless body some morning, that is all right with me. But pray do not do so until Gabriela is gone.''

"Enough!" Cleybourne's face was white and stark, his eyes glittering with fury.

There were many who would have quailed at the sight of his rage, but Jessica stood calmly, facing him, her hands linked in front of her. He was a little frightening, but she had provoked him deliberately, seeking such a reaction. She was not about to back away from it now.

"You are a poisonous, razor-tongued witch, and I want you out of my study this minute," Cleybourne went on, his voice low and furious. "Indeed, Miss Maitland, were it not for the impropriety of a girl of Miss Carstairs' age residing here without a governess, I would turn you out of the house immediately."

"No doubt you would, but as I said, my charge to take care of Gabriela came directly from the General, and I will not shirk that duty, no matter how little you like it."

"Leave my study now. And pray let me see as little of you as possible in the time that you and Miss Carstairs are here."

"My pleasure, Your Grace." Jessica inclined her head slightly, then turned and swept out of the room, head high, back straight. Behind her, she heard the crash of something heavy on the Duke's desk, followed by a series of curses, cut off by the slamming of his door.

There would be no further thoughts of killing himself tonight, Jessica knew. Cleybourne would be far too busy thinking of delightful ways to do *her* in. Smiling to herself, she started back toward her room, all thoughts of reading forgotten.

* * *

The book Richard slammed down on his desk after Miss Maitland left his study did little to relieve his bad temper, nor did the crash of his study door as he closed it. In fact, it left him feeling a trifle childish. He strode aimlessly around his study for a while, but that did not bring him much peace, either, and finally he gave up and went upstairs to his bed. There Noonan managed to annoy him further by clucking over the bit of port that he had spilled on his coat sleeve, but of course he could not take out his bad temper on the man. Noonan had been with him since he was barely out of short pants, and his look of wounded dignity made Richard feel like the worst sort of monster.

Baxter, of course, was almost as bad. Caroline had laughed and told him he was the only man she had ever met who was hag-ridden by his servants. But he could not be severe with either of the old men—or Miss Brown, either. The three of them had practically raised him, far more so than either of his parents had. And Nurse, of course. He had set her up in her own little cottage with a niece to care for her; she was so far gone in her mind now that she scarcely recognized anyone, but she still knew him.

It took him over an hour to fall asleep. He kept thinking of the things he should have told the venomous Miss Maitland. He wondered what her first name was, then told himself that by all rights it should be Medusa, to fit her nature. He thought with great glee of firing her. He would find another woman to look after the girl, and then he would tell Miss Maitland, quite calmly and coolly, that he would not need her services anymore. He smiled to think of the look upon her face then.

But he knew, even as he thought it, that he would not do so. Miss Maitland had been with the girl for some time, and the poor child had had enough to bear without losing her companion of the past few years. He felt guilty enough as it was to be sending the child to someone else. He could not stop thinking about the fact that Carstairs had entrusted the child to him, and he knew that he was, in effect, letting his friend down. At the time Roddy had died, he would have taken the child gladly and raised her with Alana, but her great-uncle had been the proper choice, of course. And now...well, it didn't bear thinking of to have a child in the house again. True, she was older than Alana, but he knew that she would be a constant reminder of what he had lost.

She would, anyway, be better off with Rachel and Michael. They had no children of their own, and he suspected that Rachel felt the absence of them keenly. Rachel would welcome Gabriela. They were good people and would be much better at raising the girl than a widower sunk in sorrow. He was doing the right thing, he knew—no matter what that harpy of a governess might say.

Thinking of her made him grind his teeth again. It occurred to him once again that a governess should not look as Miss Maitland did, either. Governesses did not have manes of curling red hair that invited a man's touch, nor wide eyes as blue as a summer sky—nor sweet curves beneath soft velvet dressing gowns. A proper governess, in fact, would never have intruded upon a man in her dressing gown, any-way!

She was, in short, a most improper person to be a governess, and he wondered if he ought to look into her suitability further. She had spoken of her father's scandal; he faintly remembered it, though he had been recently married then and far too wrapped up in his new bride to pay attention to military scandals. But Major Maitland had come from a good family; his brother was a baron, if Richard remembered correctly, and the family had never been stained with scandal before. He thought perhaps there had been whispers of treasonous matters, and then, when the man had died, there had been a consensus that it was not surprising, the sort of end one might expect for a man who had been cashiered out of the army a few months before. No doubt the brother had done his best to cover it up.

Of course, Richard thought, he would not hold a father's misdeed against his child, though many would have. No doubt her life had been very hard after the scandal. He knew the poisonous tongues of society matrons, and he had little doubt that she had been ostracized. To have had her fiancé jilt her would have been an added blow. It was no wonder that she had become hardened and embittered. It was a difficult life for a woman with no means of support. She would have had to depend on the generosity of her relatives, and that could be a cruel existence. The only way a woman could respectably make her living was by becoming a governess, but it would have been a bitter come-down for one who had once moved in high circles. Nor, he imagined, had it been easy for one who looked as she did to get or keep a job. Not many women were willing to introduce a flame-haired beauty into their house.

But even as he felt pity for her stirring in him, he recalled the look of contempt she had visited on him this evening, the scornful way in which she had accused him of rejecting Gabriela. She had as much as said he was a coward! Pity quickly vanished before another spurt of anger.

And so it had gone, his thoughts circling round and round, until, finally, he had fallen into a restless sleep.

Then he dreamed of her.

In the dream, he was walking down a long hallway. He did not recognize the place, but in his dream he knew that it was part of the Castle. A woman stood in front of a tall window at the end of the hallway, light streaming in through the glass. She was tall, silhouetted against the window, and her white dress, with the sun pouring through it, plainly revealed the soft curves of her body. His pace quickened.

She turned as he approached, and as he drew nearer, he saw that it was the girl's governess. Her red hair tumbled down past her shoulders in a fiery fall. Her blue eyes were lambent, and her face was soft and beckoning in an expression that he had not seen on it before. She smiled, slowly, and he felt it in his gut.

Then, somehow, they were no longer in the hall, but on a bed, and she was beneath him, naked and yielding. Her breast filled his hand, supremely soft, her nipple in hard contrast pushing against his palm. She moved beneath him, her voice a low moan. He knew that she wanted him, and that knowledge spurred his own desire. He was hot and hard, aching for her.

She spread her legs, and he moved between them, groaning as he thrust himself home inside her.

The sound of his own groan awakened him. His eyes flew open and for an instant he stared in confusion at the tester above his bed. His body was damp with sweat, his lungs laboring, and he was stiff with desire and painfully unsatisfied.

Sweet Jesus! What a rude jest—could he actually desire that redheaded witch?

Richard sat up, plunging his fingers back through his hair. *The governess!* He could scarcely believe he had actually dreamed about her—and such a hot, lascivious dream, at that. His veins were pulsing, his loins aching—and all for a woman the very sight of whom raised his ire.

She was irritating, infuriating. He scarcely knew her—he did not even know her given name—but what he did know he disliked. She was overbearing, opinionated, unwomanly. Richard paused. He had to change that thought: she was unwomanly *in manner*. In appearance she was deliciously curved, even in the plain, dark sort of dresses she wore. In appearance she was...*beautiful*.

He sighed, flopping back on the bed and staring sightlessly above him. For a moment he gave himself up to thinking of the way she looked—the springing flame-colored curls, the vivid blue eyes, the pale skin as lustrous as satin. He thought of her as she had appeared in the dream, the warmth in her eyes that he had never seen, the softening of her mouth in desire. He remembered the feel of her beneath him, the trembling excitement of touching her....

Cursing, he sat back up. *What the devil was he doing? How could he think of her? Dream of her?*

It had been years since he had had that sort of dream about any woman but his wife. From the moment he met Caroline, he had been faithful to her. It had not taken a tremendous effort; quite frankly, he had not wanted any woman but Caroline. And after her death, he had no longer cared about anything or anyone. No woman had stirred him, and the few times he had felt desire, it had been merely an animal instinct, directionless lust, or, sometimes, like now, a dream. But in those dreams, it had been Caroline to whom he made love, and he had awakened, not only sweating, but crying, too.

Guilt twisted through him. He loved only Caroline, desired only Caroline. Even putting aside the bizarre fact that it was the governess who was the subject of his imagination, it shocked him that he had dreamed about another woman. But he knew that if he were honest, he would have to admit that he had had lustful thoughts about Miss Maitland even when he was awake and rational. He knew that others would tell him his wife had been dead for four years, that it was only natural for him to find another woman attractive, even to think of the pleasure of bedding her. Less than a year ago, he remembered, his brother-in-law Devin had pointed out to him that it had been Caroline who had died, not Richard, and that no one expected him to never look at another woman.

But, as he had told Dev at the time, he felt as if he had died, too, that night four years ago. Without his wife and daughter, his life was ashes, and every day held the same empty, lifeless round of activities, worth nothing except to say that he had made it through another day.

How, then, could he now feel desire for another woman? Caroline was the only woman he had loved, could ever love.

The dream had been an aberration, he told himself. It was bizarre and unreal and clearly the opposite of what he really felt. After all, he disliked the woman intensely. The desire, he thought, must have been spawned in some strange way by the intense anger he felt for Miss Maitland. He did not understand it, but that had to be the reason. It was the same sort of thing as the way one laughed sometimes when what one really wanted to do was cry or scream. It had to be. Anything else was impossible.

With a sigh, he lay back down, turning onto his side, and set his mind to thinking of something, anything, besides Miss Maitland. Sleep, he found, was a long time coming.

Richard sat in lonely splendor at the dining table the next evening. He looked down the length of the gleaming mahogany table and thought, not for the first time, how foolish it was to sit here by himself to eat at a table and in a room meant to accommodate a small army of people. A huge silver epergne graced the center of the table, filled with fruit, and silver candelabras, each as ornate as the epergne, were spaced down the length of the table, candles ablaze. Two footmen stood at the ready, should Richard require something not on the table.

It would make more sense, Richard knew, to put a table in one of the small rooms downstairs and eat there, but Baxter, of course, would be horrified at the idea of his not dining formally. There were, after all, certain standards to maintain when one worked for a duke.

Richard began to spoon up his soup. He wondered idly where Miss Maitland took her meals—in the nursery with her charge, he supposed. It must be difficult for her, he thought, living in that odd limbo occupied by governesses, where one was neither a servant nor a member of the family, especially for someone like her, who came from a good family and had even had her season in London. Surely she must miss the life she had once had—doubtless that was one reason she had turned so sour!

He grimaced, wondering why he had allowed her into his thoughts. Up until then, he had been in rather good spirits. When he awoke this morning, he had still felt disgruntled, and he had decided that a good, hard ride would be the only way to rid him of the pent-up anger he felt. So after breakfast, he went to the stables and rode out on his stallion, Poseidon.

He had ridden hard and fast at first, which was exactly as the horse wanted it. The rides he took in London were far too tame for Poseidon, and he often thought, guiltily, that he should sell the animal to someone who would give him longer rides, but he loved the horse and could not bear to give him up. It felt good now to be on him again, to tear down the road or to take a fence. After a few minutes, a certain peace began to settle on Richard, and he slowed the horse to a more sedate pace.

It had been the first time he had ridden over his lands in over four years, and he had begun to look around him with interest, noticing the changes in the farms, where new fences stood and walls had fallen, what houses were there that had not stood there before, where a stream had altered course. The weather was cold, but invigoratingly so, and even though the sky was winter gray with clouds, the land was beautiful and rolling beneath it. It was his home.

He had run into Jem Farwell, one of his tenants, who had insisted on his coming into the house to see his family, then stay with them for lunch. It would have been rude to refuse, so he wound up staying and eating with them, and then chatting with neighbors who had seen him go by. He was warmed by their obvious delight in his return to Castle Cleybourne, and it was nice to sit by the fire in the neat little house and hear about the things that had happened in the past four years—births and deaths and marriages.

By the time he was able to tear himself away, it was late afternoon, and he rode home in a pleasant mood, his former irritations vanished. He wished he had not thought of the governess, for it spoiled the mood. Worse, as if his thoughts had conjured her up, he thought he heard her voice somewhere down the hall.

With a sigh, he set down his spoon and gestured for the soup to be taken away. One footman sprang to take the bowl, and the other followed deftly with the next course, a platter of fish, poached and elegantly dressed by the cook. Just as he laid the platter down on the table in front of Richard, the sound of the front door knocker clanged, muted by distance and walls.

Richard frowned. *Who the devil would come calling at this time of night?* He remembered Miss Maitland's late arrival the other night, and he sighed again, suspicion seizing him that this, too, was somehow her fault.

He dished up a piece of fish, determined to ignore whatever was going on at the front door, but the sound of voices was impossible to avoid, even though he could not understand what was being said.

Then, ringing out clearly, came the governess's voice, saying in tones of shock, "Lord Vesey!"

"The devil!" Richard exclaimed, jumping up and throwing his napkin down on the table. He strode out of the room and down to the Great Hall.

Miss Maitland stood at the foot of the stairs, staring at the group gathered in front of the door. There, though Richard would scarcely have credited it, stood Lord and Lady Vesey, handing their cloaks to a hapless footman.

"Bloody hell!" Richard exclaimed, with something less than hospitality, and he shot Jessica a look as though she were responsible for the couple's presence. "What the devil are you doing here, Vesey?"

Vesey, who was in the process of smoothing down his jacket, turned toward Richard with a thin smile. "Ah, there you are, Cleybourne. Thought this was your place. Got rather lost, you see. Knew you wouldn't mind putting us up for the night."

Richard stared, bereft of speech. Beside her husband, Leona smiled in a warm, intimate way. "Hello, Richard."

Richard turned to look at Jessica, who was standing still and white on the stairs, looking at the Veseys as if she had seen a ghost. She turned to him, her eyes wide, and for once she had nothing to say.

"Oh, the devil," Richard said ungraciously. "Well, come in, then. I was just sitting down to supper."

"Ah, just the thing," Vesey said with a smile, starting forward. "I'm famished."

It occurred to Richard then that he was going to be stuck eating his meal with Lord and Lady Vesey, and, surprising even himself, he turned back to the stairs.

"Why don't you join us, Miss Maitland?" he said smoothly, and his smile told Jessica that he knew how little she would like the prospect of doing that.

Jessica frowned. "Oh, I couldn't possibly."

As she spoke, Lady Vesey said, "The governess? Really, Richard, how droll. You can't be serious."

Richard looked at Leona without expression. "I am."

Leona's words were enough to propel Jessica forward despite her previous disclaimer. "Thank you, Your Grace, I should love to join you."

Leona shot her a look of active dislike, and her gaze swept down Jessica's plain dark dress significantly. "You do not dress for dinner?"

"We are very informal here in the country," Richard put in.

"Fortunate, isn't it, Lady Vesey?" Jessica said in a bright voice. "For I am sure you must be rather travel stained."

"Yes," Leona said absently, then turned a brilliant smile upon Richard, sweeping forward, hand extended, forcing Richard to offer her his arm to escort her to the dining room. "Richard...it has been ages since I've seen you. You're looking very well."

Richard gave her a perfunctory smile. "And you, Lady Vesey, but, of course, that goes without saying."

"Ah, but I like it so much better when you say it." Leona smiled, giving Richard an arch look.

"I am surprised to see you away from London," Richard commented as they walked into the dining room, where Baxter, ever efficient, had set the footmen to laying several more place settings. "It is hard to imagine you in the country."

"Nor you. It is well-known that you rarely leave the city," Leona replied, sitting down in such a way that it afforded Richard a full view of her swelling breasts. Jessica, watching, thought sourly that it was a wonder the woman's breasts did not completely fall out of her dress, so low cut was the neckline.

"What brings you this way?" Richard looked over

at Leona's husband, who strolled into the room after them and sat down on Richard's other side.

Jessica took a quick look around, unsure which was the lesser of the two evils—sitting beside Vesey or his wife. One of the footmen decided it for her by pulling out the chair beside Vesey.

"I am sure the governess has told you, hasn't she?" Vesey replied casually. "Came up for General Streathern's funeral. Great-uncle, you know."

Richard found that the way Vesey referred to Miss Maitland as "the governess" grated on his nerves, the obvious inference being that she was not important enough to know her name. Richard, who knew the names of all his servants and tenants had always despised such snobbery.

"Miss Maitland," he said pointedly, "did tell me that you were related to my ward."

"Yes. Cousins. Darling girl," Vesey drawled. "Where is she, by the way? Why doesn't she dine with us? Would even the table, don't you see?"

"She has already eaten," Jessica said flatly. She did not add that she had eaten, too. The prospect of courses of food in this company was not appealing. She wondered if she could plead illness and escape the table. However, she wanted to hear everything that was said between the Duke and Vesey, so she rejected that thought.

Vesey looked at Jessica as if amazed to find that she could talk. "Indeed? Well, perhaps I can pay my respects to her after we eat."

"She will be asleep."

"Never knew you to be so familial, Vesey," Richard commented as the footman whisked away the now-cold fish platter.

"Well, you know…I'm the only relative she's got now."

"Sad," Richard murmured.

"Yes," Vesey went on, unaware of the irony of the duke's comment. "No one on her father's side."

"Of course, Lady Vesey and I would have been happy to take the girl ourselves. No children of our own, you see."

"Not, of course," Leona put in, "that I am old enough to be her mother. But, still, I would enjoy helping her navigate the shoals of the season, when it comes time."

"Oh, but I am sure that is too much trouble for a woman as lovely as yourself, Lady Vesey," Richard said. "I shall take care of it when the time comes."

Leona's full lips curved up in a seductive smile. "It would be no trouble, Richard. I place myself entirely at your disposal." There was little mistaking the double entendre of her words, but Cleybourne blandly ignored it, turning his attention to his plate.

The conversation continued in the same way throughout the seemingly interminable meal, with Vesey bringing it around at every opportunity to the matter of Richard's ward and Leona flirting madly with Richard, and neither of them addressing a remark to Jessica. If the Duke had hoped to use her to deflect the Veseys, Jessica thought to herself, he had failed miserably. As far as that couple was concerned, she didn't exist.

Leona found every possible opportunity to touch

Cleybourne's arm, and she frequently put her hand on her chest as she exclaimed about one thing or another, thus drawing attention to the lush curve of her bosom. At one point, Jessica was sure that she saw the woman surreptitiously tug down her neckline even farther. Richard, she saw, with amusement welling up inside her, seemed not to notice any of Lady Vesey's little ploys. By the end of the meal, Jessica could see that Leona's luscious mouth was growing tighter and tighter with irritation. It was a sight that made sitting through the meal almost worthwhile.

"Good of you to put us up," Vesey commented at one point.

"Am I? Good of you to tell me."

Vesey let out a little chuckle. "You were always fond of a jest, Cleybourne."

"And exactly why would I put you up, Lord Vesey?" Richard went on.

"Well, we are lost, you know."

"I'll be happy to set you on the right path."

"We can hardly travel now. It's dark."

"There is an inn in Hedby."

"Full up."

"I see."

"Yes. 'Fraid we're stuck here."

"Apparently." Richard glanced over at Jessica, who was gazing at him in dismay. He gave her a slight shrug.

When the meal was finally over, Cleybourne turned the Veseys over to his butler, smoothly suggesting that they would no doubt like to rest now. Leona, with a significant look at Richard, opined that she doubted she would go to sleep any time soon, and Vesey once again asked about Gabriela. Richard, however, smiled and blankly ignored their hints, directing Baxter to care for them.

"You cannot let them stay here!" Jessica snapped as soon as the Veseys left the room, swinging around to face Cleybourne.

Richard lifted his eyebrows. "I cannot?"

"Oh, I know you're the lord of all you survey and all that, so you can do whatever you please. But it's foolish. It's dangerous. You should not allow that man anywhere around Gabriela."

"I don't know what Vesey hopes to accomplish here. But I can assure you that he is not going to go up against me," Richard said, a faint smile on his lips. "Vesey is a well-known coward. Besides, what could he do? Kidnap her? From under my own roof?"

"I wouldn't put anything past him. General Streathern didn't trust him, and he was his own nephew. That is why he had me rush Gabriela here, because he feared what Vesey might do. He is—well, it's not just Gabriela's money. He is also…there are other reasons why he should not be around a girl of Gabriela's age…." Jessica stumbled to a halt, blushing.

"Yes. I am quite aware of Vesey's predilections, although I must say, it is a trifle odd for you to know about such things."

"One has only to see the way he looks at her to know that there is something wrong with him," Jessica retorted. "Besides, the General felt I should know, so I would understand how very dangerous he really is.''

''Vesey is scum,'' Richard agreed. ''But he would never dare to try anything with a girl under my protection. You, my dear Miss Maitland, obviously have no qualms about crossing me, but as a rule, other people do. They are a nuisance, but that is all. There is no need to worry, I assure you. Now, if you will excuse me, having just had to spend the evening with Lord and Lady Vesey, I would very much like to lock myself in my study. Alone.''

As if she had forced him to put up with the Veseys all evening! Jessica watched him stride out of the room. Well, however much the Duke of Cleybourne prided himself on Vesey not daring to cross him, Jessica was not about to let Gabriela's life depend entirely on Cleybourne's inflated opinion of himself. Turning, she started for the nursery, where she intended to lock herself and Gabriela in tonight.

5

Richard spent the rest of the evening in his study, looking over the estate's accounts. His manager had brought him the books as soon as he returned to the castle, but Richard had not bothered to look at them. They had scarcely seemed to matter, given his plans. But today, riding over the land and talking to his tenants, he had grown a little curious about the farms. Since he meant to spend the rest of the evening alone in his study, he supposed he might as well look at the accounts.

After an hour or so, there was a tap on the door, and before Richard could answer, it opened and Lord Vesey stuck his head inside the room. "Ah, there you are, old chap. Knew you must be hiding yourself away somewhere."

Looking pleased with himself for that deduction, Vesey sauntered into the room and closed the door behind him. Richard let out a groan. "Did it not occur to you that I might be hiding myself away for a reason?"

"Are you? What reason?"

"I was looking for a little solitude."

"Really?" Vesey replied indifferently as he plopped down in a leather wing chair on the other side of the desk from Richard. "Never cared much for that myself."

"Only one of the many ways in which we differ." He sat, looking at Vesey, who was glancing about the room. Finally, after a long silence, he prompted, "Well?"

"Well, what?"

"What are you doing here? I know you are not here for the pleasure of my company, and since I have none in yours, it would seem more efficient for you just to say why you are here and then leave. Why are you at the castle? Why are you sitting here right now?" He was sure of the answer, of course, but he reasoned that the most expedient course of action would be just to face it head-on and get it over with.

"That's what I like," Vesey said with an attempt at a jovial smile. On his pale, thin-lipped face, it was a bizarre expression. "A man who goes straight to the heart of the matter. The reason I'm here is to offer to take the girl off your hands."

"Who?"

Vesey looked at him oddly. "You know. My, ah, cousin."

"What is her name?"

Vesey's face was blank. "Name? Oh, well, um, Carson, no…Carstairs. That's it!"

"Her first name."

"How the devil should I know?" Vesey scowled

at him. "What difference does it make what her name is?"

"It rather makes one wonder why you should want to take someone who is apparently a stranger to you 'off my hands,' as you say."

"Oh, well, as to that, she's my cousin, you see. Second or third, of course, can't remember which. Doesn't matter. I'm her only family."

"She has my condolences."

His companion looked faintly puzzled but plowed on gamely. "Yes, well, of course. Sad about the old man and all that." He paused, then added, in case Cleybourne wanted that information, "General Streathern, you know."

"Yes. I know."

Vesey's face cleared. "Yes. Well, anyway, blood's thicker than water. Girl should be with her relatives, and of course I'll do my duty."

"Ah, your duty. I see."

"Yes. Can't be something a man in your position wants to take on—young girl to raise. No wife to take care of her. Just a burden to you. So..." He raised his hands, spread them in a gesture of generosity. "That's why I'm willing to take her, you see. Too much to ask of someone who isn't family."

"And I'm sure her rather large fortune has nothing to do with the decision," Richard said in a silken voice that would have warned anyone less thick than Lord Vesey.

Vesey looked at him uncertainly. "Ah, well..."

Richard rose from his chair, leaning forward and planting his fists on the desk before him. "Let me make myself clear, Vesey. I would not put a dog into your care, let alone a young girl. Your vices are well-known to me, and your wife has less maternal instinct than a wolf. There is no way in hell that I am giving up my guardianship of *Gabriela* to you! The fact that you think I might be willing to do so is an insult to me, and should you approach me about it again, I promise you that I will call you out. Do I make myself clear?"

Paler than usual, Vesey rose from his chair. "No need to shout, dear fellow. Only a suggestion. Can't think why you should care."

"Because I have some scruples. But I wouldn't expect you to understand that. Now kindly remove yourself from my office before I give in to my baser side and throw you out on your ear."

Vesey sidled around the chair, casting a cautious glance back at Cleybourne. "No need to get in a taking. Out of here in a trice."

Vesey opened the door and slipped into the hall. Richard grimaced and sat back down in his chair, congratulating himself that at least that ordeal was over. He had known Vesey would be bound to make an effort to persuade him to turn over Gabriela, but now the scoundrel knew where Richard stood on the matter, and he would give up and leave tomorrow.

But his hopes that he was through with the Veseys were dashed a few minutes later when the door opened without even a warning knock and Lady Vesey glided in. For a moment all Richard could do was stare. Leona had changed dresses and was now wearing a pale muslin thing so sheer that he could see the pink-brown circles of her nipples beneath the material. The high-waisted gown cupped her full breasts, pressing them up so that they looked as if at any moment they might spill out entirely. Her hair lay in artful curls, one long tress falling across the white expanse of her chest and onto the swell of her breast.

"Richard!" she exclaimed, feigning surprise. "I did not know you were still up. I came in search of a book." She strolled across the room toward him, her hips swaying provocatively. "I was having trouble sleeping...."

"Were you?" Richard rose and walked over to the bellpull and tugged at it vigorously. "I fear that I use the study more for business than reading pleasure. Most of the books are down the hall in the library. I will have one of the footmen show you the way."

Leona's chuckle was low and throaty. "You are such a tease, Richard." She walked over to him and laid her hand against his chest. "I don't need a footman. I'd much rather you showed me."

"Yes, well, I happen to be going to bed right now."

"Really? That sounds interesting." Leona gazed up into his face, her golden eyes full of sexual promise. "Wouldn't you like some company?"

"I am used to sleeping alone, Lady Vesey."

At that moment the door opened to admit his valet, coming in answer to Richard's tug at the bellpull. "Your Grace?"

"Ah, Noonan. Lady Vesey is apparently having some trouble sleeping. Fetch her a glass of warm

milk, would you? Oh, and show her where the library
is.''

''Certainly, Your Grace.''

''There. No doubt now you will have more luck
sleeping. I shall bid you good-night, my lady.'' He
sketched a bow toward Leona, then turned and
walked out the door, leaving her standing speechless
behind him.

Jessica and Gabriela spent the next morning doing
lessons in the nursery schoolroom, hoping that by the
time they finished, the Veseys would already have
left the house, bound for London. It was close to
noon, and Gabriela was growing very tired of con-
jugating French verbs, when they were startled by a
piercing scream.

Jessica leaped to her feet and ran out of the schoolroom, Gabriela on her heels. As Jessica ran, she
heard a man's voice shout, ''Help! Help me here!
Leona, my pet, are you all right?''

His only answer was a moan. Jessica glanced at
Gabriela, suspicion blossoming in her. The two of
them descended the staircase more slowly. When
they reached the landing and looked down on the
Great Hall below them, they saw Leona Vesey lying
at the bottom of the stairs. Her husband knelt beside
her, holding her hand in his and patting it.

Two footmen had just arrived at the scene, and as
Jessica looked on, the duke strode in, saying, ''What
the devil is going on? Who screamed?''

The gathering servants all stared in fascination at

Leona's prone form. At that moment she let out a moan and raised her head a little.

"What—what happened?"

"You fell, my dear," Lord Vesey supplied her with an answer. "We were about to leave, and you were going down the stairs, a trifle too fast perhaps, and your foot slipped and you fell. Thank God, you're still alive."

Richard moved forward, frowning, and squatted down beside her. "Can you move, Lady Vesey?"

"I—I think so." Leona lifted a hand to her head in a gesture worthy of the stage. "Oh, dear, I'm a trifle dizzy. Richard, help me up."

She reached for him, and when he extended his arm to her, she artfully leaned into him, so that he was half-holding her as she sat up. Rising from his crouch, he pulled her up with him. Once again her hand went to her head, and she slumped against him with a moan.

"Just a moment," she murmured, and looked up at Richard with wide eyes. "Everything is twirling. I must have hit my head."

Jessica rolled her eyes in disgust and exchanged another glance with Gabriela, who looked equally suspicious. They continued down the steps until they were almost even with the others.

Leona, eyes closed and face pale, leaned against the duke's chest. He stood stiffly, looking profoundly uncomfortable. "Are you able to walk, Lady Vesey?" he asked, pulling his arm from her.

"I shall try—if you will help me." She grabbed his arm with her hand as he pulled away and leaned on it while she took a hobbling step forward. She let out a cry and crumpled, and Cleybourne grabbed her to keep her from falling.

"Oh, no!" she wailed, leaning her head against his broad chest. "I cannot walk! I fear I have broken my ankle."

Her words brought such a dark scowl to Cleybourne's face that Jessica had to smother a giggle.

"Oh, no!" Vesey exclaimed. "Oh, dear, we must send for a doctor. My dear Cleybourne…"

"Yes, yes!" Richard snapped, turning to one of his servants. "Blake! Send one of the stable boys for Dr. Houghton." He turned back with a sigh, still supporting Leona's clinging form.

"Best go back to bed, my dear," Lord Vesey announced mournfully. "And to think we were just about to set off on our journey."

"Yes," Richard agreed dryly. "An amazing coincidence."

Vesey gazed back at him blandly. Leona took the opportunity to curl her arm around Cleybourne's neck.

"Carry me, Richard, please." Her eyes were huge and pleading, their color brightened by the sparkle of unshed tears. "It hurts too much to walk."

"No doubt." Richard glanced again at his servants. "Hobbs, Williams. Here, carry Lady Vesey upstairs to her room." He handed her off to the two footmen, saying to Leona, "I will send one of the maids up to help you."

Jessica bit back another giggle at the astounded

expression on Lady Vesey's face as Richard all but shoved her into the hands of the two servants.

"No doubt you'll want to sit with her until the doctor comes, Vesey," Richard went on.

"What? Oh. Yes, I suppose so." Lord Vesey did not look too happy at the idea, but he turned and followed the two footmen up the stairs as they locked hands and carried Lady Vesey away.

Leona's eyes locked with Jessica's as the group passed them on the stairs, and her gaze was full of venom. Jessica was not entirely sure whether the spite in her eyes was directed entirely at her or was simply a generalized fury at the brusque way the Duke of Cleybourne had gotten out of carrying her up the stairs. Jessica turned back to the foot of the stairs. Cleybourne looked at her.

"I suspect our guests will be staying with us a trifle longer than expected," he said with an obvious lack of delight.

His gaze slid past Jessica to Gabriela, standing on the step above her. His eyes moved quickly away, and he turned, saying, "Baxter! Send up one of the maids to Lady Vesey."

"You had better make it someone who doesn't mind being slapped," Jessica said crisply, irritated by the fact that he had just snubbed Gabriela.

"I beg your pardon?" Richard swung back around.

"Lady Vesey looked to be in something of a temper—no doubt it's the pain of her 'broken ankle.' And I have observed that she is apt to take her temper out on the servants."

Richard looked at her for a moment, then said to Baxter, "Send Katy, and tell her if Lady Vesey slaps her, she has my permission to break her other ankle."

With those words, he strode off rapidly.

Jessica turned to Gabriela, trying to think what she could say to lessen the sting of Richard's not speaking to her. Gabriela was standing looking after Cleybourne's retreating form, and there was an aching loneliness in the young girl's gray eyes that tugged at Jessica's heart.

"I am sorry, Gaby," she began, reaching out to take her arm.

"Why does he dislike me?" the girl asked, turning to her mentor and friend.

"It isn't that. Please believe me."

"Yes. It has to be. He has not met me. He hasn't spoken to me. That was the first time I have seen him except at a distance."

"It was very rude of him. But he is not a sociable man. He is used to a solitary life. I understand that for the past several years he has lived almost like a hermit, never going out, not seeing anyone but a few people."

"I don't require that he converse with me a great deal," Gabriela explained earnestly. "It is just—he was my father's friend! I wanted—I thought he would want me because of that. That he would want to raise me. I thought, in a way, that it would be a little like having a father again. I mean, I know what it must be like, at least a little, to have a mother, because you have been very like a mother to me.

And I thought that he might be like a father. Or at least *something* like a father.''

Touched, Jessica slipped her arm around the girl's waist and hugged her. "You are very like a daughter to me. But perhaps the duke simply is not capable of being that way with you. The housekeeper told me that he has had a great deal of sorrow in his life. His wife and daughter died four years ago, and apparently he has never recovered from the blow. I think it is that which causes him to avoid talking to you. I think it is painful for him because his daughter is dead, and he misses her.''

"Oh." Gabriela looked at Jessica, and though there was still sorrow in her face, there was also a measure of relief. "Then it is not just me that he doesn't wish to have around—it would be any girl.''

"I think it is not so much what he wishes as what he is afraid of—the hurt he would feel. But yes, I am sure he would be the same about any young person, boy or girl. And he is thinking of you, too. However rude and stubborn and thoroughly hardheaded he might be, I do think he wants to do what is best for you. He knows that he never goes out, that people do not visit here. It would be a very lonely life for you and would ill prepare you for your future. I am sure he is right, that it will be better for you to be with a couple. A father and a mother. When your father made his will, the duke was married. No doubt your father intended for you to be brought up by a man and wife, not by a widower.''

"I suppose.''

"And he is right that in a few years, when you are

eighteen, you will need the expert guidance of a lady who moves in the highest circles of the Ton. A man would never be able to manage it, nor can a governess. I can tell you about some things, but you need an experienced woman there at the parties with you, helping and watching over you.''

"But I don't care about some stupid old parties!''

"Not right now, you don't. But, believe me, in a few years, they will be the center of your existence. I'm sorry. I know it is difficult for you right now. You want to have a home, to be where you belong, to have a family again. But it will be better to wait a bit and get a proper home, and not have to leave and go to someone else in a few years so that you can make a proper coming-out. The duke mentioned his sister-in-law, and from what the housekeeper told me, she seems to be a good woman. So that might turn out to be a much better thing.''

"Maybe," Gabriela admitted grudgingly.

"Now, then, I think we've had all the excitement we are likely to receive today. It's time we returned to our books.''

Gaby sighed and nodded, and the two of them turned and walked up the stairs.

It did not surprise Jessica that, throughout the rest of the day, Lady Vesey managed to disrupt the household. She kept the servants busy running up and down the stairs to her room to answer the ring of her bell. She wanted food; she wanted drink; nothing that was served was quite right; she needed her

pillows fluffed; the bed linens had to be changed—
the list seemingly went on forever.

Finally Leona realized, after several boring hours
stuck in her bed all alone, that while she might have
managed to remain in Castle Cleybourne, she was
also completely unable to work any of her wiles on
the duke. She had expected him to come to her bedside to check on her, which he had not done even
once. When she inquired after him, the maid replied
that he was busy in his study, going over the books
with the estate manager.

By the middle of the afternoon Leona decided that
she needed a change of scenery and had the footmen
carry her back downstairs. She lay half-reclining on
the blue velvet chaise longue in one of the drawing
rooms, her skirts arranged attractively about her legs,
with just the hint of bare ankle showing as she
propped that injured appendage on a small pillow.
Daylight was not her favorite lighting, as it tended
to reveal all sorts of tiny lines that the kinder candlelight left hidden, but at least the drapes of the tall
windows opened on a south prospect, and no direct
sunlight fell upon the chair where she sat.

Still, she found, the duke did not come to visit her,
and she grew more bored and irritable by the second.
She was, finally, reduced to talking to Vesey, who
wandered in to see how she was doing. He came up
with the idea of sending one of the maids up to fetch
the governess and the girl.

"It would be quite natural, you know, for the
child's cousins to take an interest in her. Children are

always being trotted out to speak to boring old relatives.''

"And you are lumping me in that class?'' Leona asked in a chilly voice.

"Not at all, my dear. Just saying I wouldn't mind seeing the chit. Might give us a chance to make friends with her, so to speak. Be bound to make her feel important, talking to us.''

"Well, what does one say to a child?'' Leona whined. "I have spent my entire life avoiding them.''

"Not your entire life,'' her husband pointed out. "You once were a child. You were around other children then, bound to have been.''

"And I am sure they were deadly dull. Vesey, you are of no help at all. And what about the governess? I don't want to have to sit and chat with *her*.''

"Well, who else are you going to talk to, then? The servants? At least that redhead comes from a decent family. Uncle's a peer.''

"And she is making a living as a governess? What twaddle.''

"No, it's true. Some scandal about her father several years ago—everyone dropped her, of course. But a bit of scandal shouldn't bother you, love.''

Leona grimaced. "I am sure it was not an interesting scandal. She is Miss Prisms-and-Prunes.'' She sighed, thinking of spending the rest of the afternoon in Vesey's company. "Oh, go ahead and send for them.''

Vesey was happy to comply, and a few minutes later Jessica and Gabriela walked into the room. They looked, Leona thought, neat as a pin and just as boring, but perhaps it would provide some amusement to watch Vesey make a fool of himself trying to win over the girl.

Jessica and Gabriela sat down on the love seat across from Leona, Jessica positioning herself between Gabriela and the chair in which Vesey had been sitting when they entered. She had considered not responding to Vesey's arrogant summons. Gabriela had been frightened at the thought of having to be in the same room with him. But, Jessica reasoned, she and Gabriela could not avoid him for days on end. And if they did not go down to make their formal visit now, Vesey was all too likely to come up to the nursery to call on her. And she certainly did not want to have to be stuck with him there, where she could not take Gabriela and leave whenever she wanted. So, in the end, she had brought Gabriela down to the blue drawing room.

Apparently Baxter had taken it upon himself to inform Cleybourne of their impending conversation with the Veseys, for within two minutes of their entrance, the duke himself strolled in.

He cast a glance around the room. Lord Vesey, who had been about to move to a chair closer to Gabriela, quietly stayed where he was. Jessica straightened in her chair, facing Cleybourne with an almost defiant air, and beside her on the sofa, Gabriela cast a nervous glance at her governess. Leona, oblivious to everyone else, smiled at Cleybourne and adjusted her position on the chaise longue a little, just to emphasize the lovely, lush line of her reclining figure.

"Richard," she said in a low, intimate voice, "what a naughty boy you've been, leaving me here by myself all day."

"Hardly alone, Lady Vesey," Richard replied, looking significantly at the others. "Miss Maitland. Miss Carstairs. Vesey."

Gabriela turned to Jessica. "May I be excused now? I should go finish my lessons."

"Yes, of course, my dear."

Jessica stood up, too, as Gabriela jumped to her feet and hurried from the room. "I should go, too. Please excuse me."

"No, wait, don't leave," Cleybourne said. "Stay here. I, ah, I wish to talk to Miss Carstairs."

Jessica stared at him, too dumbstruck by his words to do anything but nod and sit back down.

Cleybourne turned and followed Gabriela out into the hall, catching up with her at the foot of the stairs. "Miss Car—Gabriela! Wait."

Gabriela froze, one foot on the first step, and turned. Remembering her manners, she gave him a little curtsy and said, "Yes, Your Grace?"

"It seemed to me that you left the room because I had entered it," Cleybourne began.

"I'm sorry. Was I rude?" Gabriela looked at him uncertainly. "I did not mean to be. It was just, well, I thought that you would not like it if I were there."

A look of chagrin crossed Cleybourne's face. "I was afraid that was your reason. I am very sorry I have given you that impression." He paused, then went on a little stiffly. "I followed you out here because I wanted to apologize to you."

"You did?" Gabriela looked at him in amazement.

"Yes. I realized that I—that I behaved very rudely to you this morning. It was just that I was startled to see you, and I—I didn't know what to say. I have been thinking about it ever since then, and I feel, well, as though I have been something of a monster to you."

"Oh, no," Gabriela reassured him. "At first I thought that you did not like me, but Miss Jessica explained to me."

So that was her name: Jessica. It suited her. *Jessica...* He tried the name out in his mind.

"Did she? And what did your Miss Jessica tell you?"

"She told me that you were giving me away because it is in my best interest—that I should have a married man as my guardian, so that his wife can bring me out."

"Exactly." Richard let loose a little sigh of relief, somewhat surprised that the governess had adhered to his story. "You will need a woman who can introduce you to society properly."

He stole a quick glance at Gabriela. He had not yet really looked at her, merely catching glimpses in the distance. He had not wanted to see her. Yet he could not keep from looking at her now.

She was older than Alana would have been if she had lived. Alana would have been only seven, half this child's age. Still, he could not look at her, or even think of her, without it bringing his own dead child to his mind. Alana would have been this age in seven more years; he tried to imagine what she would have looked like.

It was harder all the time to summon up Alana's image in his mind. She had disappeared from his life more years ago than she had lived before she died. She had been lost to him longer than he had known her. Yet she had made a greater impact on him than anyone else had ever made—or ever would make now, he supposed.

Gabriela's coloring was different. Alana's hair, like her parents', had been coal-black, and her eyes had been hazel. Her merry little face, with its chubby, rosy cheeks, had been far different, too. This girl looked up at him solemnly, gray eyes wide in her heart-shaped face, a frame of straight, light brown hair falling around it.

"But I told her I knew that was nonsense," Gabriela went on, shattering his hope that she understood and accepted his reasons for seeking a new guardian. "It is bound to be easier to find a suitable lady to guide me through society in four years than to persuade someone to take over my guardianship for the next seven."

"It would be better for you to stay with the same person," he began persuasively, but his voice trailed away as Gabriela leveled a look of skepticism at him.

"And is that the reason you have not met me? That you are never anywhere I am? You have not even spoken to me."

Though she spoke in an even tone, she could not completely dispel the note of hurt from her voice. Richard's heart twisted within him.

"I am sorry," he said again. "I was acting very selfishly. I—I did not stop to think how it must look to you. I assure you, my not seeing you had nothing to do with you or not wanting you."

"Miss Jessica told me that you had a daughter, and she died. She said it was because of that. Is it? Because I'm not like her?"

"No. It is nothing about you. The fault is all in me. I was…I guess I was afraid of how I would feel, seeing you, being around you. Do you understand what I mean?"

"It would make you unhappy to see me?"

He nodded. "That is what I feared. That the sight of another child, even one of a different age, would remind me of Alana. And the pain would be worse."

"I'm sorry. I don't want to make you feel bad."

He smiled faintly. "You don't. The truth be told, it is not Alana you remind me of. When I look at you, I can see your father."

"Really?"

"Yes. His eyes were quite like yours. He used to look at me in that quiet way when I suggested some idiotic scheme or other. He was generally more sensible than I. But then he would smile, and there would be a little twinkle in his eyes, and the corner of his mouth would go up—yes, just like that."

Gabriela chuckled, her eyes shining. "Really? Am I truly like him?"

"Your eyes are very like his. Otherwise, in looks, you are much more like your mother. Who was, I might add, a very attractive woman."

"Yes, she was," Gabriela agreed, a note of pride

in her voice. "But I wasn't sure I look like her. The General said I did, but I couldn't see it. I thought perhaps he just said it to be polite."

"Well, you need not worry about that with me," Richard assured her, "since we both know I am frequently not polite."

Gabriela laughed. "I like you."

"Do you? Then you are a most forgiving person, for I fear I have acted abominably where you are concerned."

"You are sad about your daughter. I understand about that. I'm sad about the General."

"I'm sorry."

"Sometimes, when I wake up in the morning, I forget and think I need to tell Gramps something. Then I remember that he's gone." She paused. "Do you ever do that?"

"Yes. I did it frequently right afterward. I would wake up and think, 'I'll take Alana for a ride this morning.' Or, 'I must tell her about the new puppies down at the kennel.' Then I would remember that I could not." He looked down at her and added, "But it got better after a time. Now it almost never happens."

He said it to comfort Gabriela, but then he was struck by the truth of his words. He had become so accustomed to grief that he had scarcely noticed the ways in which it had gotten better.

"Good." Gabriela gave him a smile and moved a step away. "I—I'm glad I met you."

"So am I." He started to turn back, then paused and said, "Perhaps…"

"Yes?" Gabriela looked at him eagerly.

"I had been about to take a walk around the garden when Baxter told me about the conclave in the drawing room. I am sure they won't miss me if I take it now. Perhaps you…might accompany me. I could tell you about your father. Would you like that?"

"Oh, yes!" Gabriela clapped her hands together, her eyes shining. "I would like that above anything!"

Richard smiled. "Right. Then run get your coat, and we'll sneak out the back door."

6

The minutes crawled past as the three occupants of the formal drawing room sat stiffly, saying little, each thinking their own thoughts. Jessica could not imagine where the duke had gone. It had appeared that he intended to follow Gabriela and speak to her. There were a few faint tendrils of hope inside Jessica that he had decided to accept the girl. She knew that even though Gabriela had taken Cleybourne's avoidance of her with a good deal of grace, the girl would dearly love it if he paid a little attention to her. On the other hand, she could not help but reflect sourly that he had managed to leave Jessica with the burden of enduring the Veseys' company.

Vesey said little, clearly bored, and though Lady Vesey made some conversation, it was invariably about herself, primarily the dreadful inconveniences of being laid up in bed with a sore ankle.

"The doctor says it isn't broken," she told them, her raised eyebrows bespeaking how little she trusted his expertise. "But I cannot imagine how it cannot be—a mere sprain could not cause such pain."

Jessica cast a glance at Leona's ankle, raised up on a pillow, the hem of her dress sliding away to reveal the fetchingly bare appendage. "Remarkable, how little your ankle is bruised or swollen," she commented dryly.

Leona's eyes narrowed as she looked at Jessica. "Yes, isn't it? I am very fortunate that way."

"Well, country doctors are not always the best," Jessica commiserated. "Perhaps you should go to London—so that you can see a much better doctor."

Intense dislike sizzled in Leona's eyes. "And perhaps you should learn to keep your mouth shut when you are in the company of your betters."

"Oh, I do," Jessica replied smoothly.

It took a moment for Leona to understand the insult Jessica had just handed her. Then, before she could make a furious reply, there was the sound of footsteps in the hall, and Duncan, one of the footmen, walked into the room, beaming with delight.

"Your Grace! Lady Westhampton has arrived." He came to a stop, looking about the room in a puzzled way.

A tall woman entered the room after him. She wore a black wool mantle, trimmed in sable, the hood pushed back to reveal her face. She was a striking woman, with bright green eyes and hair as black as her cloak. "Rich—"

She too stopped as she saw that Cleybourne was not in the room. Her gaze fell on Jessica, puzzled, then traveled on to Leona. She stiffened, one elegantly arched eyebrow flying up in astonishment.

The surprise she felt upon seen Lady Vesey was patently not pleasant.

"I beg your pardon, my lady," Duncan apologized. "I thought the duke was in here. I—I will find him and tell him you are here. May I take your coat?"

"Thank you," the woman said with a gracious smile, taking off her mantle and handing it to the man before she turned back to face Leona. Her fashionable dress was a vivid emerald that made her eyes seem even greener.

"Well, Lady Vesey." Her voice was as brittle and colorless as winter leaves. "I must say, it is something of a surprise to find you here." She gave a short nod in the direction of Leona's spouse. "Lord Vesey."

She turned to Jessica, saying in a carefully neutral voice, "Hello. I am Rachel, Lady Westhampton. I am Cleybourne's sister-in-law."

"How do you do? I am Jessica Maitland."

"She is a governess," Leona said dismissively.

"A governess?" Rachel repeated blankly.

"Yes. My pupil is the duke's ward."

The other woman looked even more at sea. She glanced at Leona, as if for confirmation, and Lady Vesey shrugged.

"Yes. The girl is a relative of Vesey's."

"I see," Lady Westhampton responded, though it was clear from the tone of her voice that she did not. "It is a pleasure to meet you, Miss Maitland. I'm sorry. I am a little startled, I confess. Cleybourne had not told me that he had a ward."

"Thank you. I am honored to meet you, as well. His Grace speaks very highly of you. And Miss Carstairs, my charge, just recently became his ward."

"Then that is why he came to the castle—to meet his ward." Rachel looked faintly relieved. "He sent me a note saying where he was going, but he did not tell me why."

"He was not expecting us," Jessica explained. "The duke and Gabriela's father were friends, and her father died."

"Oh! You mean the child is Roddy Carstairs' daughter?"

"Yes."

"But Roddy died some years ago."

"Yes. When Gabriela's parents died, her father named Gabriela's great-uncle, General Streathern, as her guardian, with the Duke of Cleybourne as guardian if her great-uncle could not serve as such."

"I see."

"I have been Gabriela's governess for the past six years, all the while she has been living with General Streathern. Unfortunately, the General himself passed on a few days ago."

"Oh, I'm so sorry." Rachel walked over and sat down beside Jessica on the couch, her face sympathetic. "That poor child."

"Yes." Jessica nodded, thinking that she liked Lady Westhampton. "It has been a very sad time for her. Her great-uncle was more like a grandfather to her." She went on to explain the General's designation in his will of the Duke of Cleybourne as Ga-

briela's guardian and his instructions to Jessica to
bring the girl immediately to Castle Cleybourne.

"Then Richard is to be her guardian?" Rachel
looked pleased. "How nice. I mean, well, that will
be good all around."

"I hope so," Jessica answered equivocally.

The other woman caught her tone and frowned a
little. She started to say something, then stopped,
glancing from Jessica to the Veseys. "Then...the
four of you traveled here together?"

Leona let out an unladylike snort. "No, of course
not. We came in our own carriage."

"Got lost and wound up here, you see," Vesey
explained.

"It was a great coincidence," Jessica added.

"Yes. I imagine it was."

Jessica went on. "Lady Vesey fell and injured her
ankle this morning."

"So of course we had to stay here," Vesey told
her. "Couldn't make poor Leona travel with her ankle in bad shape."

"Of course not." Rachel looked somewhat skeptically at Leona's propped-up ankle.

Irritably Leona twitched her dress down to cover
her ankle. "I am in a great deal of pain," she announced. "Vesey, ring for the footmen. I think I
must go upstairs and rest again."

"Of course, my dear." Vesey rose quickly to do
as she bade.

Jessica felt sure that since Gabriela was no longer
here, Vesey had as little desire to linger in the room
as Leona did to stay there without the duke. Lady

Westhampton and Jessica watched with a mixture of amusement and annoyance as the grand production of removing Lady Vesey from the room played out before them. It required two footmen, a maid to carry Lady Vesey's pillow and smelling salts, and Lord Vesey to direct the entourage, and it went on for several minutes, ending on a final note of silliness with the maid scurrying back into the room to retrieve the shawl Leona had left behind.

When at last they were gone, Rachel turned to Jessica. "I am very glad to meet you, Miss Maitland. It pleases me terribly to hear that Cleybourne has a ward. It will enliven his life, I think, give him a…a…"

"A reason to live?" Jessica said, without stopping to think.

Lady Westhampton's eyes widened, and she drew a sharp breath. "What do you mean?" She reached out and wrapped her hand around Jessica's arm. "Has something happened? Is Richard—"

"I'm sorry," Jessica said quickly, mentally cursing her unbridled tongue. "I should not have said anything. I didn't think. I don't want to alarm you."

"I would rather be alarmed than unknowing. Please tell me why you said that."

"I talked to the duke's housekeeper the other morning, soon after we arrived. I was upset because the duke does not wish to be Gabriela's guardian."

"You mean he refused?"

"He said that he would find someone else to do it. In fact, he mentioned your name."

"Mine?" Lady Westhampton looked surprised,

then thoughtful. "Well, I suppose I could...but it would be much better for him if he did it."

"That was Miss Brown's thinking. She explained what had happened to him four years ago and why he might not want a child around."

The other woman nodded sadly. "Yes. Richard has never recovered from my sister's and niece's deaths. He loved them dearly."

"He would not even meet Gabriela. He said he thought it would be better for her, given that she would be going to another home."

"Oh, no!" Rachel looked stricken. "I'm not sure who to feel sorrier for, Richard or that poor young girl."

"Miss Brown said you had told Baxter that the duke was...well, she seemed to think that you feared he would do himself harm."

"Yes, I did," Rachel said candidly. "I love Richard very much. He is like a brother to me. The past four years have been hard for him. And recently, he seemed to get even worse, as though he had finally given up hope of his life improving. Then, when my servants forwarded that note from him, I was terribly worried. He hasn't lived here in so long, I didn't know why he had decided to come here—and at this time of year, the anniversary of Caro's death. It gave me chills. That is why I came. I was visiting my brother Dev and his new bride, and I had planned to travel on to Westhampton House for the holiday. But I was so worried..."

"May I speak to you candidly, Lady Westhampton?"

"Yes, I wish you would."

"I think that your fears were not unjustified."

A spasm of pain crossed the other woman's lovely features. "He plans to kill himself?"

"I went to the library the other evening to get a book to read, and I passed his study. He was sitting at his desk, drinking, with a case of dueling pistols on the desk before him. He said that he was merely cleaning them. But the way he looked at the gun in his hand, and with what Miss Brown had told me…"

"Oh, no! I was afraid of this. There was something about that note—I felt as if he were saying goodbye, and not just for the holiday."

"I think that may be why he is refusing the guardianship. Perhaps even why he would not meet her. It would indeed be kinder to her not to know him at all if he will be dead within a few weeks."

"Or days." Rachel looked infinitely sad. "Oh, dear, poor Richard. I don't know what to do. I thought to invite him to Christmas with us, but I am certain he won't come. And if he has his mind set on self-destruction…"

"I don't think he will do anything like that with Gabriela in the house."

"Yes, he is a very responsible man."

"I think he will put it off at least until she and I have gone on. When he finds another guardian."

"I can influence that. If he asks me, I shall just say no, and then he will have to find someone else. Or perhaps…" Her face brightened. "I shall tell him that it is a rather large thing, and of course it would involve my husband, so I must ask Lord Westhampton's opinion. I can put him off until after Christmas that way. Then, if I refuse, he will have to look for another, and that will take another bit of time.'' She sighed. ''I only wish we could stop him instead of just delaying it.''

''I would not give up hope, my lady. The other evening, when I thought he might be about to do himself in, I was able to distract him.''

''Distract him?'' The other woman looked slightly puzzled.

Jessica nodded. ''The duke and I—well, I tend to annoy him somewhat.''

''Richard?'' Rachel looked amazed. ''But he is an affable man. Not very sociable anymore, I will admit, but he has never been one to be cross.''

''No doubt he is not with other people, but he dislikes my manner. My outspokenness. We wind up arguing every time we talk.''

''Oh. Well.''

''That is how I distracted him. I criticized him for trying to do away with himself, and he grew quite angry, and we had a somewhat heated discussion. He wound up slamming the door.''

''My goodness.''

''But it turned him away from his thoughts about death.''

Rachel regarded Jessica for a long moment, the faintest hint of a smile beginning to form at the corners of her mouth. ''Is that your strategy, then—to keep him angry all the time?''

Jessica chuckled. ''I am afraid that even I am not capable of doing that. Still, he did go riding about the estate yesterday, which Baxter seemed to think was a very good sign. It was the first time he had done it since he returned home. If he can be made to participate in life more, it seems to me that it would be good for him. Sometimes, when you are surrounded by loving people, they can try too hard, take away too much of one's burdens, be too sympathetic, so that one never has to just pick up and keep on with life."

"Perhaps you are right. He is a well-loved man. Perhaps we have all kept him too protected."

"And if he will only get to know Gabriela, it might help them both tremendously." She paused, then added with an impish grin, "Besides, now that Lady Vesey is here, I will have plenty of help in keeping him aggravated."

Her words startled a laugh from Rachel. "What is that woman doing here? I know that Richard cannot stand either one of them. He cannot have invited them to stay here."

"It is more that they invited themselves," Jessica explained. "They arrived here yesterday evening, claiming to have gotten lost driving from Norfolk to London."

"They went through Yorkshire?"

Jessica shrugged. "I didn't say that Lord Vesey was clever at making up stories. However, here they were, and it was late, and the duke finally allowed them to spend the night. They were to have left this morning, but on the way down the stairs, it would appear that her ladyship fell and hurt her ankle. 'Broke her ankle,' as she would have it."

Jessica then proceeded to describe the scene she had witnessed at the bottom of the stairs that morning, imitating the Veseys to such perfection that Lady Westhampton was soon laughing helplessly.

"That woman's gall knows no bounds," Rachel said at last. "But I don't understand why they are doing this. Surely she cannot expect to snare Richard. I mean, I am sure she is looking for a wealthy man to help support her ways now that Dev is gone, but... Richard? Doesn't she know that he despises her? Everyone in the family does."

Suddenly some of the gossip that Jessica's good friend Viola had written clicked into place. Viola had told her that Lady Vesey had carried on an almost public affair for years with the Earl of Ravenscar, Devin Aincourt, and that she had lost him several months ago to an American heiress. The entire Ton had been abuzz with gossip about it. Now Jessica realized that the "brother Dev" of whom Lady Westhampton spoke was the Devin Aincourt who had been under Lady Vesey's spell for so long—and his bride would be none other than the selfsame American heiress whom much of London society would like to congratulate for besting Lady Vesey.

"I think that Lady Vesey would have difficulty conceiving that any man might not succumb to her charms," Jessica replied. "Certainly she has been flirting madly with him every moment that he is around." With a grin she added, "I have noticed that the duke has made himself scarce around here today."

"I shouldn't wonder," Rachel said feelingly.

"Still, why would she have chosen Richard, of all people? It cannot simply have been an accident, their stopping here. And who would take her husband with her on a seduction attempt?"

"Oh, no. It was no accident. I am not sure exactly what Lady Vesey hopes to gain by this, but I know why Lord Vesey is here." She explained the loathesome Vesey's relationship to Gabriela, as well as his desire to be her guardian instead of Richard. "So I think when they found out we had come here immediately after the funeral, he decided to follow us. Perhaps he thinks his wife will be able to charm the duke into giving him Gabriela."

"As if Richard would ever think of such a thing!" Rachel exclaimed indignantly. "However much he might not wish to be her guardian, Richard would never turn anyone over to a snake like Lord Vesey."

"I know. I was afraid at first that he might, when he did not desire to be Gabriela's guardian, but I have come to realize that he is far too honorable to do that, and too aware of Vesey's true nature."

They were interrupted by Baxter, who carried in a large silver tray containing a teapot and cups, as well as the plates of sandwiches and cakes necessary for afternoon tea.

"I thought you might welcome a little refreshment, my lady," he said, beaming at Rachel.

"Thank you, Baxter. You are right, as always. It is so good to see you."

Baxter set the tray down on the low table in front of the sofa. "And you, Lady Westhampton. I know His Grace will be happy that you are here. I sent one of the footmen to get him. He was walking in the garden with Miss Gabriela.''

''Gabriela!'' Jessica exclaimed in astonishment.

Baxter turned to her with a smile and a significant look. ''Yes, miss. Exactly.''

His words were confirmed a moment later when the duke himself entered the room, Gabriela on his heels. ''Rachel!''

For the first time since she had met him, Jessica saw Cleybourne's face lit by a smile. It was amazing, she thought, how very handsome the man was when he smiled. Happiness altered his features subtly, softening the rather stark lines of his cheeks and jaw. Jessica's stomach did a curious little flip-flop at the sight of him.

''It is wonderful to see you,'' he said as he crossed the room to Lady Westhampton, who had stood up when he entered the room. He placed his hands on her shoulders, beaming down at her, and bent to kiss her cheek.

Another feeling, far less pleasant, sizzled through Jessica. It occurred to her suddenly that the duke might harbor feelings for Lady Westhampton that were not precisely brotherly. Lady Westhampton clearly resembled her dead sister quite a bit; even Jessica, who had not known the duchess, could see the similarity in the two women's features. Lady Westhampton was perhaps not as striking as Cleybourne's wife had been. Rachel's features were softer and somewhat more subdued. But their hair and eyes were the same color and their faces enough alike that anyone would have guessed they were sisters. And being so closely related, there were bound to be other similarities, mannerisms and tones of voice, even laughter.

Loving his dead wife the way Cleybourne had, it seemed reasonable to Jessica that he might have been drawn to this woman who must remind him of her. *Did he harbor feelings for her?*

He turned, and his gaze fell upon Jessica. She stood up, feeling suddenly awkward. He must be disappointed to find her here, she thought, and was surprised by the fact that the thought hurt.

"I'm sorry. I am sure the two of you would like a chance to visit alone. If you will excuse me…"

"No, don't leave," Lady Westhampton protested. "We haven't even had our tea yet. Tell her to stay, Richard."

"Yes. Of course you must stay, Miss Maitland. We shall all have tea." Cleybourne seemed almost jovial. He turned and held his hand out toward Gabriela, motioning for her to step forward. "Rachel, you must allow me to present Gabriela Carstairs to you. She is Roddy Carstairs' daughter. Do you remember her?"

"Yes, of course. Miss Maitland was just telling me about you, Gabriela." Rachel smiled warmly. "It is nice to meet you."

"Pleased to meet you, my lady," Gabriela responded, giving her an excellent curtsy.

"You look very much like your mother," Rachel went on. "But there is something of Roddy Carstairs about your eyes."

"That is just what the duke said," Gabriela rejoined happily.

"Come, sit down and let us have tea." Rachel began the ritual of pouring tea for all of them. "I hope you are enjoying it here at the castle, Gabriela. It can be a trifle medieval, I've found."

"You wrong it, Rachel. It is a cozy enough place," Cleybourne said.

Rachel laughed. "Yes, if you find a great pile of stones cozy."

"It reminds me of a castle in a book I once read," Gabriela piped up. "Except that one was in France, and there was a wicked count who lived there."

"It is precisely the sort of place where one would expect to find a wicked count," Lady Westhampton agreed with a twinkle in her eye. "And perhaps a ghost or two."

"Oh, yes. And dungeons. There are dungeons here. Baxter showed them to us."

"Cellars," Cleybourne said firmly, but there was a smile lurking about his mouth. "They are merely cellars. A few times there may have been some prisoners kept there, but they were not dungeons."

He glanced over at Jessica, who was watching him. *Jessica...* Knowing her name now, he found himself wanting to say it. Her eyes were clear blue and steady as she gazed at him, and there was something about them that always made him feel as if she could look right through him. Richard suddenly remembered the dream he had had the other night and the way those eyes had looked, gazing up at him in the heat of passion. He flushed and turned away quickly. "I...I am most surprised to see you here, Rachel. I had thought you were going back to West-hampton for Christmas."

Rachel blinked at the abrupt change of subject. "Why, yes, I am. But, as you know, I stopped first at Dev's to see him and Miranda. That is where I received your note telling me of your intention of coming to Castle Cleybourne. So I thought it was a perfect opportunity for me to drop by on my way to Westhampton and see if I could persuade you to come have Christmas with Michael and me."

"It seems a long way round to go from Derbyshire to the Lake District by way of Yorkshire," Cley-bourne commented dryly, smiling a little to take the sting out of the words.

"Well, you know me. Michael says I have no sense of direction," Rachel responded lightly.

"It is very kind of you to offer. However, I am afraid that I must decline."

"Yes, I see now that you have guests. Or, rather, new residents, I should say. And of course it is im-portant for Gabriela to have Christmas at her new home."

Jessica wondered if he would tell Lady Westhamp-ton that he did not intend to keep Gabriela. It was a perfect opening for it. She watched with heightened interest as the duke nodded then glanced away with-out saying anything. Jessica felt her heart lifting in her chest. *Did he mean not to ask Lady Westhampton to take Gabriela, after all?* Seeing him coming in the door with Gabriela had given her hope. Had he actually walked with her in the garden? Surely that meant he had softened toward the girl.

"Uh, yes." Richard shifted a little uncomfortably in his seat. He had spent most of the morning writing and rewriting a letter to Rachel asking if she and Michael would take over guardianship of Gabriela. It had been difficult to find the right words to explain why he could not take the child. Now he found that it was equally difficult to explain the matter in person.

Of course he could not say anything about it with Gabriela herself in the room. He would wait until later, and perhaps then the words would come more easily to him.

They finished their tea, engaging in the social small talk that one generally had among a group of relative strangers, discussing Lady Westhampton's trip from Derbyshire and the conditions of the road and whether the cold, gray winter skies would produce snow any time soon. Cleybourne inquired after Rachel's brother and his new wife, and Rachel smilingly revealed that Miranda, Lady Ravenscar, was expecting a great event in the spring.

"So of course she could not travel. Otherwise, I would have tried to get them to come with me to Westhampton for Christmas, too," Rachel explained. "But, then, I don't think they would have. It is their first Christmas together at Darkwater."

"Darkwater!" Gabriela exclaimed. "Oh, I'm sorry. I didn't mean to interrupt. It is just—that is such a gloomy name. Is it foreboding as well?"

"You mean like Castle Cleybourne?" Rachel

teased. "No, it isn't at all gloomy. The name comes from a tarn nearby, where the water looks black as night. But the house itself is a light, warm stone, and quite welcoming and beautiful. I grew up there, and I love it dearly. However," she added with a smile, "it does have a curse upon it."

"Really?" Gabriela looked entranced.

"Oh, yes. Really."

"What sort of curse?" Jessica asked, almost as intrigued as her pupil.

"Oh, a family sort of thing. It happened during the Dissolution of the Abbeys under King Henry VIII. A nearby abbey was torn down and the lands given to our ancestor, the Earl of Ravenscar, to repay him for his loyalty to the king. It was said that the abbot had to be dragged out of the place, and he put a curse on it, saying that no one of our family, no one who lived 'within the walls of these stones' would ever know happiness."

"Since the sixteenth century?" Jessica could not hide the note of skepticism in her voice.

Lady Westhampton chuckled. "It does seem a rather long time for a family to be unhappy, doesn't it? Anyway, it would seem that Dev has broken the curse. He and Miranda are very happy. I daresay no curse would stand a chance against the new Lady Ravenscar."

Richard smiled faintly. "Dev tells me that she is something of a dynamo. I gather she keeps him on the straight and narrow."

"She is breathtakingly energetic, and quite efficient and practical, as well. But she understands Dev and loves him dearly. He has taken up his art again.''

''I know. He sent me a portrait of Miranda. Apparently one of many he has painted. It was masterfully done, as his work always was. But more mature now.''

''Yes. There is a new depth of emotion in him. Thanks to Miranda.''

''Well, she will always be a saint to you,'' Richard said with a faintly teasing tone, ''since she vanquished the dread Leona.''

''She saved Dev,'' Rachel said simply.

''Yes, I rather think she did. And for that we must always be grateful.''

''As for Leona,'' Rachel went sternly, ''I cannot believe that you would let her in the house. Or Vesey, either.''

''I wish to God they were not here,'' Richard replied in a heartfelt tone. ''But Miss Maitland will attest that I could not get out of it. Their sheer audacity carries them far. I know that she faked her fall.''

''You mean you don't think she hurt her ankle?'' Jessica asked, her eyes dancing.

Cleybourne shot her a sardonic glance. ''I am sure that her ankle is no more hurt than her heart was over Dev, but I cannot prove it. The doctor said it wasn't broken, but she moaned and got great tears in her eyes—no doubt having unbuttoned the first few buttons of her bodice—and he decided that it must be a sprain.'' He grimaced. ''Well, one can have a sprained ankle only so long. Hopefully she will get so bored that they will leave soon. I cannot think what they are hoping to accomplish. I already told Vesey I'd never let him be Gabriela's guardian.''

"Of course not. It's absurd," Rachel agreed.

Jessica glanced at Gabriela and saw the pleased surprise on her face—and more than a touch of hero worship. She could only hope that Cleybourne did decide to remain her guardian. She could see that Gabriela would be crushed now if he shunted her off to someone else.

They had finished their tea, and Jessica excused herself and Gabriela, saying it was time they returned to their lessons. Lady Westhampton bade them goodbye, stating the usual polite pleasantries with obvious sincerity.

"I like Miss Maitland," Rachel told her brother-in-law. She watched him carefully as she went on. "Though she hardly seems like a governess. She is far too beautiful. Don't you agree?"

Richard, whose gaze had remained on the doorway through which Gabriela and Jessica had walked, glanced at Rachel. "What? Yes, I suppose so," he said with studied casualness. "I never much cared for redheads myself."

"She seems genteel, as well."

"Genteel? I don't know whether I'd term her that, exactly. But she comes from a good family, if that is what you mean. Uncle's a lord, but her father was involved in some sort of scandal several years ago, lost all their money and position."

"How sad."

"Yes. It is why she became a governess."

"Well, I like her," Rachel reiterated. "She has a forthright manner, but she is quite pleasant, too, and rather humorous."

Richard snorted. "Oh, she is certainly forthright. She is the most damnably forthright woman I have ever had the ill fortune to meet."

"You do not like her?"

He grunted. "She says whatever she thinks, without the slightest regard to politeness or tact. She is argumentative and stubborn in the extreme. I cannot imagine how she ever kept a position as governess. General Streathern must have been the most patient and undemanding employer in the country."

"You don't think she is a good governess?" Rachel asked innocently. "Perhaps you should get rid of her, then. You wouldn't want your ward having an unsuitable or ill-prepared governess."

"I can't do that," Richard protested. "She has been with the child since she was eight. Gabriela has had enough people taken away from her already. I could not take away Miss Maitland, as well."

He hesitated. Now, he knew, was the time to tell his sister-in-law that he did not plan to be Gabriela's guardian. It was, after all, one of the main reasons he was reluctant to let Gabriela's governess go. Surely Rachel would understand why he did not want to have a child around, a constant reminder of his own loss. Of course, it had not hurt as much as he had thought it would to meet Gabriela and talk with her. There had been some pain, inevitably, but she was so different from Alana in age and looks, so much her own entertaining person, that after he had been around her for a few minutes, he had found himself no longer thinking of her in relation to his dead daughter but simply as herself. It might not be the horror he had dreaded to have her around day after day.

But, he reminded himself, there was still the problem of carrying out his plans. He could not take his pistol and seek his own quiet peace until he had gotten Gabriela and Miss Maitland away from the house. It would be far too cruel a thing to do to the young girl.

And here Rachel was, presenting him with the perfect opportunity to ask her and Michael to take over the task for him, yet he could not bring himself to do it. It was too abrupt, he thought; that was the reason for his reluctance. He should give Rachel more time to get to know and like Gabriela. She would readily accept her as her ward if she had already come to like her. That reasoning made sense, even if there was a niggling doubt inside him.

For her part, Rachel watched her brother-in-law struggle with some inner turmoil. She was very fond of him, and she would have liked to help him, but she was sure that right now it would be better for her not to. She was not sure if Miss Maitland was right that they had coddled Richard too much, that he needed to be challenged. But she suspected that what he needed just might be Miss Maitland. She had seen him looking at the governess in a different way from the way she had seen him look at any other woman. Miss Maitland might irritate him, but Rachel thought that she intrigued him, also. And she did not for a moment believe that disinterested pose of his, as if he had not noticed what a stunner the woman was. There was a decided undercurrent of something in his tone when he spoke of the woman—or *to* her, for that matter.

There was that thing about the scandal, of course, but, frankly, Rachel did not care if Miss Maitland herself had been in a scandal if she could help Richard out of the deep well of pain he had been living in the past four years.

She almost wished she were not committed to go to Westhampton for Christmas. It might be quite interesting to stay here and watch what happened.

7

Upstairs, Gabriela was bubbling about her visit with the duke.

"He was ever so nice, Miss Jessie, and he told me stories about my father. He even apologized! He said he had been rude, and that it was wrong of him. Can you imagine?"

Jessica smiled at her charge, enjoying the unabashed happiness on Gabriela's face. Her cheeks were flushed, her eyes sparkling, and she was talking with her old vivacity. It was heartening to see the weight of her sorrow lifted for the moment. "It was very good of him," she said now. "Exactly what he should have done."

"He wasn't at all high in the instep, either. You would think a duke would be, wouldn't you? But he didn't seem proud or self-important. Just sad. He explained about his daughter and how he thought it would hurt to see me, because I would make him think of her. But then he invited me on the walk anyway. Do you think he will change his mind and let us stay now?'' Gabriela looked at Jessica hopefully.

Jessica shrugged. ''I don't know. Lady Westhampton is here, and I think it is she—and her husband—who he hopes will take over your care. He might go ahead and ask her.''

''She seemed very nice,'' Gabriela admitted. ''But I would rather stay here. Wouldn't you? I liked the duke.''

''Well, I imagine that Lady Westhampton would have to ask her husband about the matter before she gave him any answer, and perhaps in the next few weeks the duke will change his mind.''

''I hope so.''

Jessica decided that it was pointless to try to continue any lessons with Gabriela that afternoon, so she allowed her to read until it was time for their supper. Jessica knew that she should probably use the time to work on her plans for Gabriela's studies this week, but she was having a little difficulty concentrating this afternoon, as well. Finally she settled down to do some mending, which would leave her mind free to ponder the events of the afternoon.

She was surprised when one of the maids knocked on the door and handed her a note stating that her attendance at supper that evening was requested by the duke. She had assumed that since Lady Westhampton had arrived, Cleybourne would not feel the need to use her as a buffer against the Veseys again.

She understood it better, however, a few minutes later, when Lady Westhampton breezed into the nursery with her maid in tow. The lady's maid carried three dresses in her arms, which Lady Westhampton directed her to spread out on Jessica's bed.

"You are coming to supper tonight, aren't you?" Rachel asked Jessica.

"Yes. It seems I am expected to. But I really don't see why it is necessary."

"You jest. Safety in numbers, you know. That is important when Leona is around. And you can be sure that she and her 'broken' ankle will manage to make it down to the dining room. She will spend the whole time monopolizing Richard. That is how she always is, which will leave me with no one to talk to except Lord Vesey. You have to come so that I can have some decent conversation."

"I see." Jessica smiled, but she could not help but feel a certain letdown at the realization that it had been Lady Westhampton who wanted her there, not Cleybourne.

"And I assumed that you probably had not brought any dresses suitable for formal dining," Rachel went on.

Jessica thought glumly of her best black dress. She would feel like a crow beside Lady Vesey's bright beauty.

"So I thought I would lend you one of mine."

"Oh, I couldn't...."

"It would be no bother. Frankly, I am rarely able to lend my clothes to anyone because of my height. But you are a tall woman, too, and they should fit you. And since you are coming down to suffer through a meal with Lord and Lady Vesey in order to help me, it only seems fair that I should help you.''

Jessica hesitated, torn. The sight of the lovely jewel-toned gowns laid out on her bed was tempting. One was a deep royal-blue velvet, low necked as formal gowns usually were, with long sleeves, puffed at the shoulders, then fitting closely the rest of the way down. She knew at once that it would suit her coloring immensely, bringing out the deep blue of her eyes. The other two were no less beautiful. It was clear that Lady Westhampton had a good eye for fashion and just as clear that she had picked out dresses that would look good with Jessica's red hair and milky-white skin.

''Try them on. Tilly will help.''

''Oh! How gorgeous!'' Gabriela exclaimed from the doorway. Curious about Rachel's visit, she had abandoned the novel she was reading and drawn closer to them. Now she walked to the bed and looked the dresses over admiringly. ''These are beautiful.''

''Thank you,'' Rachel responded. ''I am lending them to Miss Maitland to wear at supper, since she will be dining with us tonight.''

''Really?'' Gabriela smiled at Jessica. ''How exciting. Which one are you going to wear?''

''I—well, perhaps I could try on the blue one.'' Jessica could not bear not to see how it looked on her.

''Excellent. Gabriela and I shall be judges. Why don't we retire to the schoolroom and have a nice chat, Gabriela, while Tilly helps Miss Maitland dress?''

Jessica took off her own plain dress and let Rachel's maid help her into the blue velvet gown. It fit almost perfectly, and the feel of it was luxurious against her skin. Rachel's and Gabriela's reactions were everything she could have hoped for, but she could not see it herself. The mirror above the chest in her room was very small—governesses, after all, were not expected to indulge in vanity—and no matter how she twisted and turned or where she stood, she could see only bits and pieces of it. Even Gabriela's room possessed no large mirror, so Lady Westhampton swept them all downstairs to her room, where a long oval mirror stood.

''Oh...'' Jessica breathed, gazing at her reflection. She knew there was no way she could refuse to wear the dress now. For this moment, she was the girl she had been ten years ago—no, even better, for such deep rich colors were never allowed on girls just out. *Or perhaps it was that there were depths in her face that had not been there at eighteen.*

Her fair skin was lustrous against the dress, and its color turned her eyes even bluer. High waisted, it emphasized the full curves of her breasts, and the neckline dipped low enough to allow a glimpse of their swelling tops.

Rachel smiled, knowing that Jessica would not protest against wearing it anymore. ''Why don't you let Tilly put your hair up? She is an absolute wizard with hair.''

"She hasn't tried mine," Jessica retorted ruefully. "It has a mind of its own."

"Now you've offered her a challenge. Sit down here at my vanity, and let's see what she can do."

So they sat in Lady Westhampton's room, Gabriela and Jessica and Rachel, and talked and giggled like schoolgirls, while Tilly worked her art on Jessica's hair. When she was finished, Jessica had to admit that Tilly was indeed an artist. With a narrow blue ribbon and strategically placed pins, she had coaxed and smoothed and twisted Jessica's hair into a charming confection of curls.

"I cannot wait to see Leona's face," Rachel said with delight.

They had that pleasure not long afterward, when they went downstairs to supper together. Cleybourne was waiting in the small drawing room with Lord Vesey, looking about as pleasant as Jessica would have expected for a person who had been forced to endure Vesey's company for the past several minutes. Vesey was engaged in a monologue concerning the properties of Madeira, a particularly good bottle of which he had recently consumed at Lord Bashersham's house, a discourse that, from the look on Cleybourne's face, had apparently been going on for some time.

When they entered the room, Cleybourne jumped up gratefully. "Rachel. Miss Mait—" He turned toward her as he said her name, really seeing her for the first time, and his words died in his throat. He stared at her for a moment, then seemed to realize that his mouth was still open and closed it sharply.

He cleared his throat. "Miss Maitland. How charming you ladies look this evening."

Beside Jessica, Rachel smothered a smile and said casually, "Why, thank you, Richard. Good evening, Lord Vesey." Her greeting to the other man dropped in temperature noticeably.

"Lady Westhampton." Vesey bowed to her and gave Jessica a perfunctory nod of the head.

Richard turned toward Vesey. "Are you certain your wife is joining us, Vesey? It seems a great deal of effort for someone who feels as poorly as she does."

"Ah, well, you know Leona," Vesey replied vaguely.

"Not really," Richard replied shortly. "Why don't we wait for her in the dining room? It will be easier for the footmen to carry her straight there."

They spent the next fifteen minutes waiting idly in the dining room for Lady Vesey to make an appearance. Lord Vesey started to expand his discourse to include the wonderful qualities of brandy.

Richard grimaced and moved quickly to cut him off. "Hardly the topic to discuss with ladies present, Vesey. Rachel, do tell us about Ravenscar's progress with Darkwater. I understand they are intent on bringing it back to its former state."

Rachel obliged him by describing the renovations going on at her ancestral home. Vesey slumped in his chair sulkily, lifting his spoon to study his reflection in it. Jessica tried to keep the conversation going by asking questions, but she was rather distracted by the fact that Cleybourne was looking at her through-

out the discussion. She could feel his gaze all through
her, and she wondered what he was thinking. She
wondered what she wanted him to be thinking.

Finally Lady Vesey arrived, looking, Jessica
thought, rather silly being carried between the two
footmen. She was wearing a filmy gold dress that
accentuated her coloring, more appropriate, in Jessica's mind, to a fancy London ball than to a quiet
dinner in the country. Unlike Jessica's and Rachel's
long-sleeved velvet dresses, suitable for the colder
weather, her dress covered as little of her arms and
chest as was possible. The sleeves were little puffs
of sheer material through which one could see
Leona's shoulders, and the scoop neckline was so
low as to be almost indecent. Jessica also saw, faintly
shocked, that it was obvious Leona wore no petticoat
or even a chemise beneath her dress, for one could
see the dark circles of her nipples. She had heard
from her friend Viola that such was the extreme of
fashion among the faster set of ladies in London,
some of them even going so far as to dampen their
dresses so that they clung more provocatively to their
figures, but this was the first time she had seen someone dressed this way.

"Lady Vesey," Rachel said innocently, "I am
afraid you will catch cold in such a summery dress.
Shall I ring for a servant to bring you a shawl?"

Leona smiled at her with a sweetness as false as
Rachel's concern. "No, that's quite all right, Lady
Westhampton. Perhaps you are cold, but I am afraid
that I am a very warm creature." She cast a sideways

glance at Richard as she said this, and the sexual connotation of her words was clear.

Richard ruined the effect by saying pragmatically, "Well, I hope you don't regret it, Lady Vesey. You are not accustomed to a Yorkshire winter. You're likely to come down with a head cold."

Jessica bit back a smile and said agreeably, "Yes. Nasty things, head colds—all that sneezing and coughing and red noses."

Leona shot Jessica a dismissive glance, then froze, her eyes widening in surprise, and her gaze was transformed into one of pure dislike. She turned back to Richard, smiling brightly.

As Rachel had predicted, Leona monopolized the conversation during their meal. But Jessica had the satisfaction of noticing that even while Leona was talking to him, Cleybourne's gaze kept sliding over to herself. That—and Leona's increasingly sour glances at her—were enough to make the evening a success.

She excused herself when the meal was over—no matter how much she liked Rachel, Jessica refused to subject herself to Lady Vesey's malicious presence all evening—and made her way upstairs.

Gabriela wanted to know all about the supper and how Jessica's dress had gone over, and they chatted as Gabriela helped unbutton the elegant gown Jessica had worn. Jessica changed into a nightgown and put on her dressing gown against the chill, then went to Gabriela's room to tuck Gabriela into bed and read to her for a few minutes, a nighttime ritual for the past six years, which they found equally satisfying.

Afterward, Jessica went to bed herself. She was accustomed to rising early, having taken care of a child for six years, and as a consequence she was usually in bed early. But tonight she had trouble going to sleep after she lay down. She kept thinking about the way Cleybourne had been looking at her throughout supper—and the way his gaze had made her feel, the tingling awareness of her body. He was an impossible man, of course, but there was something about him....

It was a long time before she fell asleep.

A noise intruded on Jessica's unconscious, and she opened her eyes. For a moment she lay there, confused and still half-asleep. Then there was another noise—the scrape of a chair leg across the floor, as if someone had bumped into it. *Someone was in the nursery!*

She remembered then that she had not locked the door to the nursery tonight, as she had last night. She had been too preoccupied with her thoughts about Cleybourne and the evening.

Silently cursing her own inattention, she slipped out of bed and crossed the room on tiptoe. Carefully Jessica turned her doorknob and eased the door open an inch, just enough to put one eye to the door and peer out. What she saw there made her breath catch in her throat. A large dark form was standing on the other side of the nursery, right outside Gabriela's door.

Jessica reached back, and her hand fell on the pitcher beside her washbasin. That seemed a good enough weapon, and she curled her fingers around it. Then she flung open her door, screaming out Gabriela's name, and charged forward, raising the pitcher above her head to strike the intruder.

The figure at the door whirled around to face her just as she was almost upon him. Instinctively he threw up an arm, and the pitcher Jessica brought down sharply crashed into his wrist. He let out a grunt of pain and staggered backward. Jessica gasped as the water spilled out of the upended pitcher, dowsing her own front.

The intruder shoved away. She hit the table with the back of her legs and fell onto it. The man turned and ran from the room. Jessica was after him in a flash, screaming for help. She could see that he had too much of a head start on her; she would not be able to catch up with him. So she heaved the pitcher after him in a last desperate attempt to stop him, and it hit him with a resounding thunk, then bounced off and shattered on the floor.

The man stumbled but recovered his footing and pounded on down the hall and into the darkness of the back staircase. Jessica started to go after him, but at that moment Gabriela tumbled out of the nursery door, eyes wide with fear, calling Jessica's name. Jessica turned and went to reassure her instead.

"What is it? What happened?" Gabriela cried.

"I'm not sure. There was—I surprised someone."

"In the nursery?" Gabriela's voice vaulted upward, ending on a hysterical note. "Why? Who?'

They heard the pounding of feet, and a moment later Cleybourne burst out of the staircase and ran toward them. He was clad in only his breeches and an unbuttoned shirt, obviously hastily donned. At some distance behind him came Lady Westhampton, wrapped in her dressing gown and carrying a lamp.

"What the devil's going on?" Cleybourne cried as he reached them.

Jessica turned, saying, "There was an intruder in the nursery. I chased him away. I—"

She broke off abruptly. The duke's eyes had dropped down to the front of her gown, and he was staring, looking like a man who had just been struck a heavy blow on the head. Jessica remembered in that moment that the front of her nightgown had been soaked by the water from the pitcher. It was clinging wetly to her full breasts, molding to their shape and revealing the dark circles of her nipples through the white cotton, rendered almost transparent by its dampness.

"I—uh—" Cleybourne could not seem to tear his gaze away from her gown, and for one frozen moment, Jessica could not move, either.

"He went that way!" Gabriela cried, unaware of the sudden tension in the air, and pointed toward the back staircase.

Jessica recovered her senses enough to pull the damp gown away from her skin, blushing furiously as she said, "I, uh, I had better change."

She turned and hurried into the nursery just as Rachel reached them. Behind her, she heard Cleybourne leave in a hurry, heading for the back stair, and Rachel saying to Gabriela, "Oh, you poor thing. You're shaking like a leaf! What happened?"

Jessica ran to the safety of her own room, closing the door behind her, and hurriedly stripped off her wet gown. She was sure her face was bright red; she felt as if it were on fire. She threw the gown onto the floor and pulled on the dressing gown, which she had thrown across the chair before she went to bed. Oh, why hadn't she thought to put it on before she went out to attack the intruder?

She knew she must have looked like a brazen hussy, standing there before the duke, as good as naked to his eyes. She closed her eyes, feeling weak in the knees as she remembered the way he had looked at her, the sudden burst of hunger and heat in his dark eyes. He had looked at her in a way no other man ever had—his eyes so fierce and fiery. Of course, she reminded herself, he had certainly seen more of her than any other man ever had, either.

And the way he had looked at her had made her feel so, so...

She shivered, remembering the warmth that had invaded her loins, the sudden fullness and tenderness in her breasts. She blushed all over again, just thinking about it. She could only hope that he had had no idea of the sensations his look had aroused in her.

How could she face him again? She knew that she had to; in fact, she had to go right back out there now. He would want an explanation for what had happened. And she had to take care of Gabriela, as well. She could not hide here in her room the rest of the night, hoping it would all go away.

Jessica tightened the sash on her dressing gown and straightened her shoulders. Firmly overriding her reluctance, she opened her door and stepped out into the main room of the nursery. She stopped short. Cleybourne was standing in the middle of the room, looking about. He had lit an oil lamp and set it on the table. He turned at the sound of her entrance.

Richard thought he had braced himself to see Jessica again. He was embarassed at the way he had acted before, stunned into incoherence by the sight of her breasts, naked beneath the wet gown. A man had broken into her room, no doubt scaring her tremendously, and all he could do was stand there and gape at her, lust roaring through him. She must think him a cad, a lecher, to have reacted in that way.

He had returned to speak to her, determined to quell his desire, to be calm and in command, and show her that he was not the lustful creature she must think him. But one look at her had destroyed all his good intentions. She had taken off the wet gown and put on a dressing gown. She was fully covered now, except for the small V of skin that showed above the robe. However, that little expanse of flesh where the white cotton gown would normally be was enough to tell him that she was naked beneath the dressing gown. Just the thought sent heat spearing down through him. His mouth was suddenly dry, and for a moment he could not speak. All he could think of was untying her sash and pushing back the sides of the robe.

"Well, um, Miss Maitland." He struggled for words.

"Yes, Your Grace?" Jessica tried to still the tingling that started in her at the sight of him. In her embarrassment before, she had scarcely noticed Cleybourne's own state of dress. His shirt hung outside his breeches, open, a wide strip of his skin showing all the way down to the waistband of the trousers. She was aware of the hard ridges of bone and muscle, and the tan smoothness of the skin lying over them, the narrow line of dark, curling hair that crept down toward his waist. His hair was tousled from sleep, thick and black, and her fingers itched to reach up and smooth it back.

"What...what happened here?"

"I am afraid I know little more than you," Jessica replied, fighting to keep her voice even. "I heard a noise and awoke. I heard more noise, and I went to the door and looked out. I saw...someone standing outside Gabriela's door."

"What was he doing?"

"I'm not sure. Nothing that I could see. Listening, perhaps? Or maybe he was about to open the door. I don't know. All I thought was that Gabriela was in danger. So I grabbed the pitcher from the washbasin and ran out at him and hit him."

His brows rose. "You hit him? You ran toward him?"

"Yes, of course. Where else would I have run?"

"Well, away, one would think."

"And leave Gabriela with him?"

"You could have gotten help."

Jessica looked back at him levelly. "Would you?"

"Of course not."

"Then why would I?"

"Because you are a woman. You might have been hurt."

"Anyone might have been hurt, including you. Being a woman does not make one a coward."

"I didn't say—" His mouth tightened. "You are remarkably adept at twisting my words, Miss Maitland. I was—oh, blast! Never mind."

"Where is everyone?" Jessica asked. "Where's Gabriela?"

"Rachel took her downstairs to the kitchen for a soothing cup of hot chocolate. I sent the servants out to look around the house, see if they could locate where he went in or out. Provided he came from outside."

"And do you think he came from outside? Or in?"

"Meaning, was it Vesey? I don't know. I sent servants to his room, ostensibly to check on his well-being, but even if he is there, it won't prove that he wasn't the man in here. During the commotion, he could easily have slipped back to his room and pretended to be asleep before the servants got there. You struggled with him. Do you think it was Vesey?"

"I'm not sure. It might have been. He was taller than I, but not as tall as you. He might have been Lord Vesey's height. I could not see his features. It was dark, and he had something tied around his face, hiding his features." She shivered a little. "It was awful, as if his face were blank, nothing, except the little holes for eyes. I think that was the scariest thing about him."

He came forward. "I'm sorry. I—it's inexcusable that this should happen while you are under my protection." His face darkened. "If this was Vesey, he will regret it, I assure you. Whoever he is, he will regret it."

He stopped, looking down at her. He raised his hand as if to touch her cheek, then let it fall back to his side. "Are you all right? Did he harm you in any way?"

"No. Actually, I think I did more harming than he did."

A smile flickered across his lips. "That does not surprise me. One would have thought Vesey would have known better than to cross you."

Her eyes were huge and blue, her pale skin luminous even in the dim light. Bright curls tumbled down around her head. Richard thought about touching one of those curls, of sinking his hands into the springing mass. He could almost feel them winding around his fingers, soft as silk, clinging.

With great effort, he tore his gaze away. "I'll just check your rooms."

He walked to Gabriela's door and looked in, then turned and went across to the open door of Jessica's room and went inside. Jessica trailed after him. Richard glanced around the room, taking in the small, barren place, the narrow bed, the small chest and hard chair. He had not remembered the governess's room as being so small and spare. He resented the fact that she had to live in such a room, and it bothered him even more that he was responsible for her being there.

"Tomorrow I shall have the servants make up rooms for both of you closer to me." He stopped, then added hastily, "So that you will be safer. It's dangerous, the nursery being so far from everyone else. I can't think why they put you here to begin with."

Jessica felt relatively sure that they had been put here precisely because Cleybourne wished them as far away from him as possible, but she refrained from pointing that out.

"Tonight I shall put one of the footmen outside the nursery door to make sure nothing else happens," he went on.

"Thank you. That is very kind of you."

"I am not really the ogre you think I am." He hesitated. "I—"

Cleybourne reached a hand toward her, and this time, almost as if it moved without his volition, his hand touched her hair. It was as soft as he had imagined, and the feel of it beneath his fingertips made his loins tighten. He swallowed, trying to assemble some sort of coherent thought. He did not know what it was about this woman. She seemed to be able to rob him of all thought, no matter what the situation, to leave him floundering in a morass of emotions and sensations.

She looked up at him, her blue eyes wide and faintly surprised. Her lips parted a little, soft and pink. His gaze fell to her mouth, and his mind was filled with kissing her. Hunger swelled in him, hard and throbbing, as he thought of tasting those lips, touching her…. He tried to look away, tried to take his hand from her silken curls and move back, but he could not. Instead he leaned forward, his fingers curling into her hair, crushing the curls, and his mouth came down to hers.

He could feel the little intake of air that moved across her lips before his own lips touched hers. He could smell the sweet scent of lavender that clung to her. Richard trembled a little, his body racked by opposing forces, torn between guilt and the fierce desire that snaked through his loins. Then his lips brushed hers, and he was lost to all else but that hunger.

8

His lips pressed into hers, gently at first, tasting and teasing, experiencing the velvety softness of her mouth, the honeyed taste. Then he shuddered, rocked by the force of need pouring through him, and he wrapped his arms around her, pulling her up hard against his body, burying his lips in hers. Urgent and hard, his mouth merged with hers, demanding all that he desired.

Jessica went limp against him, stunned by the flood of sensations rushing through her. No man had ever looked at her that way or kissed her so. She had never felt a man's hard body pressed against hers all the way up and down, so that her breasts were flattened against his chest and her abdomen cradled his masculinity. His mouth consumed hers, his tongue arousing her in ways she had never imagined. She trembled and clung to him, lost in a tumultous world of pleasure.

A low, animal noise sounded deep in his throat, and his hands moved around and up her front, easing between their bodies and cupping Jessica's breasts.

He stroked her breasts through the material of her dressing gown, moving the satin against her skin. Jessica's nipples hardened and tingled, and her breasts felt swollen and aching. Another ache was growing deep inside her, hot and tender, and she squeezed her legs together, trying to ease it. She was aware, faintly shocked, that she wanted to feel his hands upon her naked body, yet she knew instinctively that that would not ease the ache between her legs, only make it grow more.

Richard's mouth shifted on hers, bringing another wave of pleasure to her, and one hand slid over her breast and beneath the dressing gown. His fingertips moved lightly over her bare breast, arousing the tender skin, exploring the heavy, luscious globe and finding the hardening center. He took the little nub between his thumb and forefinger and squeezed gently. Jessica jerked in surprised pleasure, and a little moan escaped her. She had never felt anything like this, never dreamed of it, yet she found herself hungry for it, eager....

He tore his mouth from hers, kissing his way across her face and down her throat. His hands went beneath her dressing gown, pushing away the sides so that it opened, the sash slipping apart and uncurling. He nibbled at her throat, kissing and laving it tenderly with his tongue, while his hands roamed down her body, gliding over breasts and stomach and hips, curving back over her rounded buttocks. His fingertips dug into the firm cheeks, startling a gasp from Jessica, and pressed her up into his own hardness.

Raw hunger seized Jessica, and she trembled. She wanted something desperately—she wasn't sure what—and she let out a low groan. "Please…oh, please, don't…"

She was not sure what she was asking for, whether it was for him to stop the pleasure so intense it was almost pain or to give her a chance to pause for a moment and gather her scattered, wild emotions, or simply for him not to stop what he was doing until she had reached the unknown thing her body sought so achingly. Whatever it was, the word struck him like a blow. He went still, then pulled back with a sharp, indrawn breath.

"Sweet bloody hell!"

Cleybourne took a long step backward. He stared at her for a moment, his chest rising and falling with harsh, ragged breaths. "Oh, God, what am I doing?"

Abruptly he turned and strode out of her room.

Jessica stared after him for a moment, trembling all over. With shaking hands, she pulled the sides of her dressing gown together, wrapping her arms around herself to keep it closed. She sank down onto her bed, her knees suddenly too unsteady to stand.

She knew she must pull herself together. Gabriela and Lady Westhampton would be back at any moment, and she must not let them find her in this state. But neither could she imagine how she could possible resume a normal air. What had just happened was too startling, too bizarre. Jessica could not remember feeling anything this intense, even with her fiancé many years ago. It was not love, she told herself; after all, she didn't even know the man. It was lust, she supposed, nothing more, but never before had she realized that lust could be so powerful.

Whatever it was, at this moment, she felt as though her life would never be the same.

Seething with sexual frustration, guilt and self-hatred, Richard stormed down the stairs and along the hall straight to Vesey's bedroom.

"Vesey!" he roared, turning the knob of Vesey's door and charging in.

Only Leona was in the bed, and she sat up with a shriek at Richard's entrance. When she saw who it was, she smiled, saying, "Why, Richard, what a pleasant surprise. I had not expected you to visit me in quite such a forceful way."

"Where the devil is—" Richard began, looking around the room, then spotted Lord Vesey, lying on the couch, clutching a blanket to him, with a terrified look on his face. "I should have guessed she wouldn't let you in the bed with her."

He stalked over to where Vesey lay and reached down, grasping him by the front of his nightgown and jerking him to his feet. There was something decidedly comical about the look of Lord Vesey in a nightgown that revealed his spindly calves and with a silk nightcap on his head, but Richard was too upset to see the humor.

"Damn you, Vesey! I ought to tear your heart out!"

"B-b-but why? What have I done to you?"

"Did you think I wouldn't care if you sneaked into that child's room? Did you think I would just look the other way if you tried to have your perverted way with her? Or did you think that you could actually steal her away right from under my nose?''

''In your own house?'' Vesey sounded genuinely shocked. ''You must be mad! I'm not stupid, you know.''

''That's debatable.'' With a sigh of disgust, Richard pushed him back down onto the couch. ''That is the only reason I haven't torn you apart already. Usually you are too inclined toward self-preservation to try something like that.'' He paused, then went on. ''The hell of it is, if it wasn't you, who could it have been?''

Vesey shrugged. ''I don't know. Some servant, maybe, who took a liking to that governess. She was something of a looker tonight, wasn't she?''

Richard swung back to Vesey, his face black with rage. ''I don't even want to hear mention of her on your tongue again. Do you understand me?''

Vesey's eyebrows went up. ''I say, Cleybourne, don't tell me you've developed a tendresse for the wench yourself.''

''Damn you!'' Richard curled his hand into the front of Vesey's nightshirt and hauled him up again, twisting his hand so that the collar of the shirt bit into Vesey's throat. ''You are skating on the edge, Vesey, I warn you. Not everyone is the sort of selfish, disgusting lecher that you are. Miss Maitland is under my protection, just as Gabriela is. And I am telling you, if you do anything to either one of them— anything—I will not rest until I have hunted you down and broken each and every one of your bones separately. Am I clear?''

''Eminently,'' Vesey squeaked out.

''All right, then.'' Richard opened his hand, and Vesey plopped back onto the couch.

Richard turned and strode out of the room without a backward glance, slamming the door shut behind him.

''Well,'' Vesey said, rubbing his throat gently, ''I seem to have struck a nerve there, haven't I?''

''Of course you did, you imbecile,'' Leona said from the bed. ''Intimating that a man like Cleybourne would be interested in that dowdy governess. What an idiotic notion.''

Lord Vesey cast his wife a sardonic glance. ''Yes, of course, my dear. How foolish of me.''

Immediately after breakfast the next morning, a pair of maids arrived at the nursery and began carrying down Jessica's and Gabriela's things to the floor below, where all the main bedrooms were located. Baxter had given Gabriela a lovely, cheerful room that looked out over the driveway to the castle. It had three tall windows that let in plenty of light, and its furniture was daintier than most pieces in the castle, done in white and gold. There was a secretary on which Gabriela could do her schoolwork, and a small sofa against the opposite wall, not to mention a wardrobe, chest and vanity that were more than enough for her needs.

Jessica's room, across the hall, was smaller and contained less furniture, but it was quite cozy and welcoming, with a comfortable chair beside the window that looked like a perfect spot to curl up and read a book. There was a vanity table with a nice, large mirror above it and, best of all, a lovely fireplace with a fire burning merrily in it.

"It's beautiful," she told Baxter honestly. "It is very kind of the duke to put me in here."

"His Grace is the kindest of gentlemen, you'll find," Baxter said with a smile. "Oh, I almost forgot. He asked me if I would tell you that he wishes to see you in his study this morning."

"Oh." Jessica's pulse picked up its pace. "Of course."

After the butler left, Jessica rushed to her new mirror. She straightened her hair and pinned a few recalcitrant curls that had already managed to escape. She smoothed her dress down. There was nothing she could do about it, she thought, and sighed. As long as she was a governess, she could hardly go about in finery. What she had worn last night had really been too attractive and expensive to wear even for a formal dinner. Only the fact that Lady Westhampton had urged it on her had made it acceptable.

Sternly she shook off her thoughts. She should not be worrying about how she looked, she reminded herself. She was a governess here, that was all. The fact that Cleybourne had kissed her last night meant nothing. She could not allow it to mean anything. What had happened last night had been wildly abnormal behavior. She never should have let a man kiss her like that, especially her employer! Granted, it had been more pleasurable than anything she had ever experienced, or that she had ever imagined experiencing. She had been taken completely, overwhelmingly, by surprise.

But it would not, could not, continue.

Yet she could not quell the leap of hope and excitement within her chest as she went down the stairs to Cleybourne's study. The door was closed when she approached it, so she rapped lightly and waited for Cleybourne's invitation to enter.

She found him standing behind his desk, as if he had just risen from his chair, and his fingertips touched the desk, as if bracing him. His face was drawn in stern lines, and the anticipation inside her fluttered to its death.

Jessica came to a stop in front of his desk, facing him with all the calm she could muster.

"Miss Maitland, I, ah, I have asked you here this morning because I feel that I—" He half turned from her, fixing his gaze on a spot across the room. "I must apologize to you for my behavior last night. It was inexcusable." He swung away, as if he could no longer bear to stand still, and began to pace back and forth across the room, talking as he went. "What I did was terribly wrong. You are my employee. Living in this house under my protection. I cannot tell you how sorry I am that I—I, took advantage of our situation."

Jessica went cold, the chill spreading from the center of her being outward. She could not even have said what she had been secretly hoping would happen. She was not naive enough to have thought he would declare his undying passion for her. Still, to see him so stern and controlled, so cool toward her, pierced her to the quick. Of course a gentleman would apologize for having grabbed her and kissed her like that, but this...she knew that this was something far more than an apology. Cleybourne did not just regret having acted in an ungentlemanly manner. She could see in his drawn face, in his inability to even look her straight in the eye, that he regretted, too, the emotions, the desire, that had caused him to behave so. He hated the fact that he had wanted her, despised his passion for her.

"I promise you that it will not happen again," he went on.

Jessica linked her hands together. They were as cold as ice. She could think of nothing to say. She lowered her eyes, unable any longer to look at him, to have to witness him steadfastly refusing to meet her gaze. What they had done last night obviously disgusted him. Perhaps she disgusted him, too, for the wanton way she had responded to his kisses and caresses. She remembered thinking only minutes ago that she had acted in a way no lady should. She wondered if now he no longer thought she was a lady, if he found her promiscuous and bold.

She thought, too, of the way he had called her his "employee." That rankled, as well. He did not think of her as an equal, but as someone who worked for him. Of course, she was not his equal in rank, and she could see now that it had been wrong of her to let Lady Westhampton's easy friendlines deceive her into feeling that she was on the same level as they were.

She was not, and she never could be. And, of course, it had been entirely foolish of her to let herself dream that last night had meant something. Cleybourne was a man still in love with his dead wife, and even if he were not, there could never be the hope of anything between them, at least anything honorable. Though her own family was good enough, she was only a governess, scarcely someone a duke would marry. And, even worse, her good name was stained irrevocably by her father's scandal. So the passion of last night, if allowed to continue, could lead to nothing but being his mistress, and she could not live as that. Nor was Cleybourne the sort of man who would turn an unsullied female into his mistress: he was too much of a gentleman.

It had been unbelievably foolish of her, she told herself, to have given way to her desire last night, and she should be grateful that the duke was too much of a gentleman to take advantage of her moral laxity.

A heavy silence settled on the room, and Jessica realized that he must expect her to say something, to leave the room. Their business was over. "Yes, of course," she said in a colorless voice. "Thank you, Your Grace."

She forced herself to raise her face to look him in the eyes. His expression was unreadable. She hoped her words had been appropriate; she scarcely knew what she had said. She wanted only to get away now and be by herself for the next few hours. "If you will excuse me..."

"Certainly."

She turned and walked to the door, curling her fingers into her palms until the nails cut into her skin. She kept her stride slow and regular, too proud to appear to run like a rabbit, as she felt like doing.

Cleybourne watched her go, wondering why, when he had done exactly what he should, he felt even lower than he had.

Jessica begged off joining the other adults for supper that night, claiming that she was not feeling well. She felt sure that her starkly white face and shadowed eyes had convinced Lady Westhampton that she was indeed ill. Rachel told her she must indeed lie down and rest; she was probably done in from the fright she had received the night before.

As soon as Richard saw that Jessica was not at supper that night, he was certain she had stayed away because of him and his abominable behavior the night before. He had hoped his apology would make things all right between them, but the whole thing had been so stiff and awkward that he felt almost as if he had made things worse.

He had acted in a way completely unlike himself last night. Never had he felt so much at the edge of his control, so unable to govern his actions. He had taken advantage of the situation, seducing—no, practically forcing himself upon—her when she was at her weakest. It had not been the act of a gentleman, and he felt even guiltier at acting the cad toward Jessica than he did about desiring a woman other than Caroline.

Richard had stayed awake much of the night thinking about it, and the more he thought about what he had done, the worse it seemed, until this morning, when he made his apology to Miss Maitland, he had felt so low he had barely been able to make himself look her in the eyes. And she had been so subdued. So unlike herself. He would not have been at all surprised if she had lashed out at him in anger, telling him exactly what she thought of him for his unwelcome advances. Indeed, he had rather expected it. Instead she had looked down and spoken softly, clear indications of how badly he had wounded her trust.

He felt sure there had been other men who had tried to take advantage of her powerless position as governess in their household—and now she would think he was like them. The idea made him slightly nauseated.

Leona, of course, was as irritating as always, smiling at him archly and preening, frequently letting her hand stray to her throat or chest, trying to draw attention to her overflowing bosom. Looking at her in her flimsy dress, Richard wondered how the woman managed not to catch her death of cold in the winter.

After the meal, Richard made his escape to his study, but he disliked being alone with his thoughts there as much as he had all day. He left the study and walked aimlessly down the hall, pausing at the end to part the drapes and look out into the night. The sky was leaden, clouds obscuring the stars and moon, and with the drapes open, cold seeped through the glass. Baxter had told him earlier that the gardener said he could smell snow in the air. Richard was not sure exactly how the wiry old man's nose could warn him of snow, but he had never known one of Calhoun's weather predictions to be wrong. His bones told him of impending rain, the phases of the moon dictated his plantings, and his gardens were the most-admired for miles around.

He dropped the heavy velvet drape back into place and started up the stairs toward his bedroom. He was not sleepy yet, but he hoped that a little time spent quietly reading might induce that state. Turning the knob of his bedroom door, he stepped inside and took several steps across the floor before he stopped dead still and stared.

"Bloody hell!"

Leona was sitting on his bed, pillows propped up behind her supportively, and her legs curled under her. She wore nothing.

"Cat got your tongue, Richard?" she asked in her sultry voice, raising her arms above her head in a languid stretch that showed off her large, unhampered breasts to their best advantage. "Why don't you come over here and take a closer look?"

"Have you run mad?" Richard exclaimed. "What the devil do you think you are doing?"

"Well, you wouldn't come to me," she said, pouting provocatively, "so I decided that I would simply have to come to you."

"Didn't you think that maybe there was a reason I didn't come to you?" he asked harshly, striding toward the bed. "Where the hell are your clothes? Don't tell me that even you came down the hall completely naked."

Leona chuckled. "No. Although no doubt it would

have brightened some footman's day.'' She rose up onto her knees, planting her hands on her hips and tilting her head to one side. ''Well? See anything you like?''

She crossed her arms under her breasts, cupping the full white globes, then brushed her forefingers across the nipples so that they pointed sharply. ''Come on, Richard, wouldn't you like to touch me? Or maybe here...'' Her hands slid down her body, caressing her abdomen and gliding over her hipbones and down onto her thighs.

''For pity's sake, Leona, get out of that bed right now and put on some clothes. What if someone walked in?''

''Who would do that?''

''Well, my valet, for one,'' he retorted sharply, looking about the room for whatever she had worn when she came in.

He found the sheer piece of cloth lying across the footboard of the bed and tossed it to her. ''Here. Put this on. Now.''

Leona tossed the gown aside and got off the bed, walking toward him seductively. ''Don't be scared. I won't bite.'' She grinned. ''Well, maybe just a little. Look at me, Richard. Can't you feel yourself getting hard? In a minute you'll be like a rock, I promise.''

She reached out her hands to the top button of his shirt and began undoing it. Richard jerked back quickly, and the button popped off. Leona's eyes darkened.

"Is that what you want?" she asked huskily. "For me to tear that shirt off you?"

"No!" Richard felt embarrassed and more than a little foolish. "Leona, you will regret this in the morning."

"I rarely regret anything."

"You will regret making a fool of yourself," he retorted grimly. "And that is precisely what you are about to do. I am not bedding down with you tonight, and if you continue in this way, it will simply be embarrassing for both of us."

"Don't be so stuffy," Leona said, running her forefinger teasingly around one nipple. "Come on. We can do whatever you want. How long has it been, Richard, since you've been inside a woman, felt her tight and squeezing around you? I can guarantee that you've never felt anything like me."

She reached out and took his hand in hers, pulling it to her breast. Richard jerked it back, cursing. He swung around and marched to his wardrobe, opening it and pulling out one of his dressing gowns. Then he turned and went back to Leona and wrapped it around her shoulders, pulling it together in the front, and clamped one of her hands around the lapels to keep it mostly closed.

"Goodbye, Leona," he said flatly, taking her elbow firmly in his hand and steering her toward his door. "Since you are persisting in this idiocy, I must tell you—I am not interested in bedding you. I feel no desire for you. It is a fool's mission, and whatever you hope to accomplish by it is not going to work. Now leave."

He jerked open the door and pushed her out into the hall. "By the way, I notice that your ankle is miraculously healed. I think it would be a good idea for you and your husband to leave first thing in the morning."

Leona gaped at him in astonishment, her hands falling to her sides, letting the too-large dressing gown slip open. For a long moment they stood there looking at each other. Richard reached for her arm, thinking he was going to have to propel her bodily down the hall to her room.

Just at that moment there were footsteps at the top of the stairs, and both Leona and Richard whirled toward the staircase. Jessica stood there, just turning down the hall toward the bedrooms, frozen in place. She was dressed in one of her plain dark gowns, but her hair had been taken down and brushed for the night and lay caught back loosely at the nape of her neck in a ribbon. In the crook of her arm, she held a book.

She stared at the couple down the hall from her, Richard's hand reaching out toward Leona, who was dressed in a man's robe that was hanging open down the front to clearly reveal her nakedness.

Jessica could not even find the air to gasp. *He had turned to Leona with his passion!*

She turned and ran away from them, not knowing where she was going, desperate only to get away from the scene she had just witnessed. She could not have gone to her room, for it would have meant moving toward them instead of away, as her room lay only one door down from Richard's. She fled instead to the one place she knew, running down the hall, then up the narrow back stairs to the floor above.

"Jessica!" Richard exclaimed. He started for her, then turned back to Leona. "I want you out! Tomorrow!" he rasped, his face thunderous. "Now get back to your room!"

Leona nodded, too frightened by the look on his face to do anything else. She scampered back to her room, and Richard strode off down the hallway after Jessica. He guessed she would go to the nursery, and when he reached the next floor and saw its door closed, he was sure he was right.

Striding down the hall to the door, he grasped the doorknob and turned, but the door would not open. She had obviously locked it from the inside. He rattled the knob. "Jessica. Open the door. I have to talk to you. Jessica! It wasn't what it looked like. Damn it, open this door!"

"Go away. I have a right to my privacy," Jessica said from the other side of the door.

"Let me explain."

"There is no need to explain to me. What you do is your own business."

She was right, he knew. He had no obligation to explain anything to her. But he knew that it was unbearable for her to think him a randy lord of the manor who tried to bed a different woman every night. Even worse for her to think that he had wanted Leona tonight the way he had longed for her yesterday.

"I have to talk to you. I am not leaving until you open this door," he warned.

"Then I am afraid you will look rather foolish, spending the night in the hall," Jessica replied crisply. "Good night."

He heard the sound of footsteps inside, then the firm clunk of the inner door to her bedroom closing. Richard stood for a moment, looking at the blank door. Then, with something like a growl, he swung around and stalked off back down the hall to the stairs.

9

Jessica awakened the next morning to snow. It was falling in great puffy flakes, and already the ground below was almost covered in white. Gabriela came bounding into her room before Jessica had finished dressing, babbling about the snow.

"Isn't it beautiful, Miss Jessie? Can we go out and take a walk in it later? I just love the snow, don't you?" She went over to Jessica's window and looked out, enraptured by the scene. "It makes everything look so pretty, all white and…and sort of mysterious, too. Don't you think?"

"Mysterious?" Jessica questioned, twisting her hair into a knot at the nape of her neck and securing it with pins. "Why do you say that? It's so clean looking, I think. Pure."

"Yes, but it's the way it covers everything up that makes it mysterious. You know, all the bushes and walls and everything that's outside are just white lumps, and you're not sure what anything is. Or where it's safe to walk. What if you tramp across a snowy piece of ground, only to discover that it covers an icy pond and you fall straight through. Or what if there is a hole, but it looks solid because of the snow, but then, if you step in it, you sink right down.''

''What appallingly morbid thoughts you have. I think you are reading too many of those novels with mad monks and wicked counts.''

Gabriela laughed, unoffended. ''No. They never have snow in those. It's always stormy and raining. Or they live on a cliff above the sea, which pounds at the rocks below.''

''That's true. And it's always nighttime and dark.''

''With the candles guttering.''

There was a knock on the door, startling them, and they jumped, then looked at each other and began to laugh. ''Come in,'' Jessica called.

Rachel opened the door, smiling. ''Well, everyone seems to be in high spirits this morning.''

''It is the snow. It makes me happy,'' Gabriela told her.

''It's lovely, isn't it? But, I fear, not good news for me,'' Rachel said, advancing into the room. ''I came to make my goodbyes. I was planning to leave later today, but I think now I must go as soon as I can.''

''No!'' Gabriela cried in disappointment. ''Please stay. Miss Jessica and I are going to take a walk in the snow later.''

''Yes, you ought to stay,'' Jessica seconded. ''You should not travel in the snow.''

''Lord Westhampton is expecting me before Christmas,'' Rachel explained. ''I delayed going there to come see the duke. What if a great deal of snow falls, and I cannot leave? Michael would be worried.''

''I see. Well, we shall be very sorry to see you go,'' Jessica said. ''Oh! Your dresses! You will need to pack them. They are in my wardrobe.''

Rachel smiled. ''Oh, no, don't bother. Tilly has already packed my things, and they are loading them onto the coach. And I have plenty of dresses at home. I shall get them when I visit next time.''

Jessica protested, feeling guilty at the thought of keeping the other woman's dresses for an indefinite period of time, but Rachel insisted, shrugging off Jessica's protests with a smile.

''Here is some news that will make you happy,'' Rachel said after a moment, changing the subject. ''I am not the only person leaving today. I understand that Lord and Lady Vesey's carriage is being brought around, also.''

''Really?'' Gabriela asked, delighted.

''Yes. Richard is insisting on it. I think he may have had a fight with them last night. He is cross as a bear this morning.''

Jessica thought about asking what was different about that, but she bit back the sharp words. Lady Westhampton was very fond of her brother-in-law, and Jessica did not want to offend her.

Gabriela and Jessica walked with Rachel downstairs to the Great Hall, where Richard stood waiting. He turned at the sound of their approach, and his eyes went to Jessica. She looked back at him coolly, and he scowled, then faced Rachel.

"Your bags are secure on the coach," he told her. "Are you certain you want to leave in this storm?"

"Scarcely a storm, Richard," Rachel said with a smile. "It is merely a snowfall."

"Baxter tells me Calhoun thinks it will get worse, and he is never wrong."

Rachel smiled. "That is why I must leave now, before it does. Goodbye, dear Richard. Take care of yourself."

She went up on tiptoe to kiss him on the cheek. Then she addressed Jessica and Gabriela, standing a few feet behind her. "Promise me that you two will look after him, as well."

Jessica saw the significant look the other woman directed at her, and she nodded. She understood that Lady Westhampton was entrusting her with keeping the duke from doing away with himself. Rachel gave her hand to Jessica, and Gabriela gave Rachel an impulsive hug, which seemed to please her considerably.

She tied on her hat and put on the gloves her maid handed her, then let Baxter help her on with her heavy wool coat. Tilly handed her a fur muff to keep her hands warm, and they left, Richard walking Rachel down the front steps and handing her up into her carriage. Gabriela and Jessica braved the cold to stand at the open front door and wave to her as the carriage pulled away.

Jessica noticed before they went back inside that another coach was approaching from the stables. It was the Veseys' carriage, and it lightened Jessica's mood a little to see that Rachel had been right—

Richard was making Lord and Lady Vesey leave. She knew they would not be doing so on their own.

Cleybourne walked back to the house as the carriage proceeded down the long driveway, and Jessica and Gabriela turned back to the stairs.

"Miss Maitland," Cleybourne said as he closed the door to the cold. "I would like to talk to you."

Jessica turned around, keeping her demeanor cool. "I am sorry, Your Grace, but I must oversee Gabriela's lessons now."

Gabriela cast a surprised glance in her direction. Their doing lessons was scarcely unusual, but it was strange, indeed, for a governess to turn down her employer's request for an interview.

Cleybourne's mouth tightened impatiently, but he said only, "And at what time will you be through with those lessons?"

Jessica was saved from answering by the less-than-dulcet tones of Lady Vesey as she and her husband clattered down the stairs. "There you are! Cleybourne, I cannot believe that you would be so cruel as to toss us out in the storm like this." She gestured dramatically toward the front of the house. "What if we freeze to death?"

"You will not," Cleybourne replied shortly.

"Really, Cleybourne," Vesey chimed in, "it *is* rather dreadful out there. Not good weather for traveling."

"It will be worse later," Cleybourne assured him. "That is why you are leaving immediately. I won't have you snowed in here for days."

"I cannot believe you are being such a monster," Leona pouted prettily.

"I don't see why not. It isn't as though I have ever been particularly nice to you." He turned aside, saying to one of the footmen, "Duncan, Lord and Lady Vesey need their coats."

The footman had anticipated him, for he stepped forward almost immediately to put a cloak around Leona's shoulders. Her eyes flashed with anger as she looked at Cleybourne. She was not accustomed to men turning down her favors, much less to one rushing her out the door like an embarrassing relative.

"You are a fool, Cleybourne," she seethed as she stalked past him, pulling on her gloves with fierce jerks of her fingers. "You will live to regret this day."

"I already regret it," he assured her, following the Veseys to the front door.

Jessica took the opportunity to slip away up the stairs, taking Gabriela's arm and pulling the girl with her. Gabriela cast her an annoyed look, protesting, "I wanted to see them leave!"

"We can watch from upstairs in your room. It looks right out on the yard."

They hurried to Gabriela's room and stood at the window, gazing down through the increasing flakes of snow at the yard below. Lord and Lady Vesey climbed into the carriage, with Leona casting a last burning glance back at Cleybourne, who stood just outside the front door, and the carriage rolled slowly away up the driveway.

Jessica whisked Gabriela to the nursery for her lessons after that. She knew she would have to talk to the duke at some point; he was, after all, her employer. However, she was hoping that if she put it off long enough, she would reach the point where she would not feel as if she were on the verge of bursting into tears when she looked at him. She did not want to have to struggle for control while he pointed out to her that he paid her salary and that she was merely there to look after Gabriela, that she had no right to question his behavior or condemn what he chose to do or with what woman he chose to do it. *God knew, she had told herself those things often enough last night.*

The morning dragged as they worked their way through geography, history and French. Gabriela was bored and restless, eager to go outside. It was fortunate, Jessica was sure, that the windows in the nursery were all small and high, or she would have been jumping up every few minutes to go over and look out at the snow. Finally, when Gabriela was beginning to complain of an empty stomach, Jessica closed her book and pushed it aside.

"All right. Why don't we have a little tromp through the snow before lunch?"

It took some time to put on their outerwear for the snow, but then they hurried down the stairs and out the rear door. What they saw there made them gasp. Snow blanketed the whole back garden and was falling in a much more furious fashion than before. Rails and hedges carried ridges of snow several inches thick, and it piled in drifts around the bottoms of the shrubs. Everything glistened whitely, and the falling snow limited their vision to only a few yards.

"Isn't it beautiful!" Gabriela exclaimed, turning her face up and sticking out her tongue to taste the snowflakes.

"Yes, it is. The gardener was right. The snow is growing deep."

They made their way around the side of the house, following the garden path. It was difficult walking; they had to lift their feet out of each deep depression they made. When they reached the front and looked out across the property, the usual vista of rolling hills blurred into a sea of white: sky and ground and everything in between blending.

They heard the carriage before they saw it, but in a moment the dark shape of a coach became clearer and clearer through the snowfall as it made its way up the driveway.

"Oh, no," Jessica groaned.

"What? What is it?" Gabriela asked, looking at Jessica, then back at the carriage. "Is that—"

"Yes," Jessica answered disgustedly. "That is the Veseys' carriage."

The coachman atop the carriage was almost covered with snow, as were the bags and trunks on the carriage roof. He pulled the horses to a stop and started to climb down, but before he could, Lord Vesey erupted from the carriage, cursing. He strode straight toward the house, not even turning around to help his wife down.

Just as he reached the steps, the door opened and a footman came out, looking astonished. Vesey

growled something at him and pushed him out of the
way as he charged into the house.

Jessica trudged through the snow to extend a hand
up to Lady Vesey to help her, and though she grimaced at Jessica, she took her hand and stepped
down out of the carriage. Without a word of thanks,
she dropped Jessica's hand and hurried into the house
after her husband. Jessica, Gabriela and the footman
all followed curiously.

By the time they got inside and closed the door,
Cleybourne was striding across the marble floor in
their direction. Vesey, taking off his hat, threw it
onto the ground in a paroxysm of fury.

"You nearly got us killed!" he shrieked at Cleybourne. "The road is closed. We saw a carriage that
had slid off into the ditch. The bridge below Trysdale
is closed. We had to turn around, a pretty iffy thing
on a snowy road, I must say. I thought we would
never make it back here."

"I want to go to bed," Leona wailed. "I'm cold
clear through, and it will be a wonder if I don't catch
my death of pneumonia."

"And if you think it isn't bad enough driving three
hours through the snow on treacherous roads, then
try doing it with *her* in the carriage with you, complaining the whole time!" Vesey shot his wife a venomous look. "For God's sake, go ahead and go to
bed, Leona, and stop moaning about."

"Yes, Duncan, see her to her room," Cleybourne
said grimly. "Bloody hell."

For the first time he noticed Gabriela and Jessica

standing behind Lord Vesey. "What the devil are you two doing?"

"We were walking in the snow," Gabriela explained.

"Walking? In weather like this?"

"Just around the house. I had promised Gabriela we would go out into the snow for a little while after her lessons."

"For God's sake, why?"

"Because it is fun!" Jessica retorted. "You do remember that concept, don't you?"

"Yes, I remember it. I just did not connect it with getting your feet soaked and cold, and breathing in freezing air."

Jessica opened her mouth to reply, then stopped, suddenly remembering something. "Cleybourne!"

"What?" He looked at her intently, his attention caught by the sudden note of fear in her voice. Neither of them noticed that she had addressed him as an equal, not a servant.

"What about Lady Westhampton?" Jessica asked with rising alarm. "Isn't the road north from here just as likely to be blocked?"

"Yes. I suppose it is." Worry flickered in his eyes. "Then why hasn't she arrived back here, too?"

"What if her carriage has gone off the road like the one Lord Vesey saw? Or broken a wheel or something? She could be stranded in the cold."

"I'll find her," Richard said shortly and turned, calling, "Duncan! Baxter!"

Another footman hurried in at the bellow. "Yes, Your Grace?"

"Send round to the stables. I need my horse saddled. And I'd better have one of the grooms saddle up, too. I may need his help. I shall change into my riding boots and I'll be right there."

He turned back to Jessica. "Will you—"

"I will see to everything here, " Jessica assured him. "I'll have her room made up again and the bed warmed. Everything."

He nodded and trotted up the stairs.

Gabriela turned to Jessica with wide, frightened eyes. "Do you really think she is in danger?"

Jessica gave her a reassuring smile. "I imagine she would be more cold than anything else. The carriage wouldn't have been going very fast in this weather, so even if it slid off into a ditch, it wouldn't have harmed Lady Westhampton. And they had a carriage rug and were dressed warmly. I'm sure they will be fine, and the duke will reach them soon."

Inside, she did not feel as sanguine as the words she had expressed. If the roads were as bad as Vesey had said—and however little she trusted him, he had seemed genuinely upset—then there were many opportunities for a carriage to have an accident or get hopelessly bogged down in the snow. And even though Lady Westhampton was warmly dressed and had a carriage rug, it would get very cold, especially after the sun set. What was really worrisome was the possibility that she might have gone quite some distance before anything happened, in which case it might be too far for Cleybourne to find her.

Jessica knew, too, that the possibility of her having a carriage accident must weigh heavily on Cleybourne's mind, given the tragedy that had befallen him four years ago in just such an accident at this time of year.

She was also worried about Cleybourne's safety. He was apparently planning to ride, which would make him much more mobile and faster, but it would also expose him fully to the elements. And how easy it would be for his horse to stumble and fall—perhaps step into a hole hidden by the snow, as Gabriela had been talking about! Then he would be out in the elements on foot, an even more dangerous proposition. It was some reassurance that at least he was taking a groom with him.

With those thoughts preying on her mind, Jessica went to the housekeeper to apprise her of the events of the past few minutes and to tell her to set the maids to warming a bed for Lady Westhampton and the cook to have a pot of hot soup ready.

She accomplished this task quickly enough and also said a few soothing things to the servants about the return of the dreaded Lady Vesey. She then went back to the Great Hall, where she met Baxter, who was looking pale and suddenly older than he usually did.

"It's a terrible thing, miss," he told her, shaking his head. "He's gone out after her, looking like Death was riding on his shoulders. I know he's thinking about the duchess and the little one. So am I. In two days it is the anniversary of her death. And this is so like it."

"But it isn't the same. There is nothing to say that the consequences will be the same," Jessica reassured him. "You must be strong for the duke's sake. He will need you when he comes back. You are who keeps the household running."

Baxter gave her a wan smile. "Thank you, miss, for saying so. You are—"

They were interrupted by a sudden banging on the knocker of the front door, so loud and unexpected that both Jessica and the butler flinched. Baxter hurried to the door, worried, and Jessica trailed after him.

On their doorstep stood two men, one thin and small with a nervous manner, and the other a sturdy soul dressed warmly but not stylishly in an old greatcoat, boots and gloves, a cap pulled low on his head and a woolen scarf wrapped around his neck and the lower part of his face.

"Good day to ye, sir," the sturdy one said, giving a tug of his cap. "I'm from the mail coach. Seems we've had an accident and overturned—couple of fine gennelmen in a carriage taking up more than their share of the road, that's wot it was, and we started to slide, and well, next thing you know, we're on our side, like, and their carriage is off in the ditch."

"Oh, my!" Baxter said, looking even frailer than he had a moment before. "What a terrible thing. Well, His Grace is not at home. I—uh—"

"We will send someone to help you," Jessica said crisply to the man. "Why don't you come inside while Baxter sends down to the stables and has the carriage and a wagon brought round, as well as some men? I am sure the duke would want to help, aren't you, Baxter?''

"Oh, yes, of course, miss. You are quite right.'' Baxter straightened and assumed a more proper butlerish face. "If you men would like to follow me, you can wait in the kitchen while they bring up the wagon, and Cook will see that you get some warm food and tea in you.''

The sturdy man broke into a grin, saying, "That sounds like just the thing, that does.''

The other man smiled uncertainly, straightened the lapels of his coat again and stuck his hands in his pockets. "Yes, miss, sir. Thank you very much.''

"That's settled then. Baxter, I will inform Miss Brown of what's afoot.''

"Thank you, miss.''

Baxter led the two men back through the hall to the kitchen, and Jessica followed, then veering off from them and heading for the housekeeper's room. She heard Miss Brown's voice before she got to her sitting room and followed it down the hall to the large linen closet, where Miss Brown was handing out bed linens and instructions to two maids.

As soon as she sent the maids on their way, she turned to Jessica, who smiled apologetically and said, "I am afraid that we may have more visitors on our hands, Miss Brown.''

She explained what had happened and the probability that, with the roads impassable, they would wind up having to house the victims of the accident. Miss Brown was at first surprised, then worried about the staff's ability to prepare for such a large group, but by the time she finished mulling it over, Jessica could see from the grim determination on her face that she had accepted the onslaught of visitors as a personal challenge.

Jessica and Gabriela pitched in to help, opening up several of the bedrooms and dusting, even once or twice finishing up the beds by arranging the coverlets on top. But neither of them could put on the linens in as smooth a fashion as Miss Brown's exacting standards required.

While his household buzzed with activity, the duke was cutting across his fields, taking a shortcut to the road north. It would pare a good fifteen minutes off his time, even though he had to dismount and go through a gate instead of taking the fence because of the difficulty of riding through snow. And he didn't worry about not searching that stretch of road, because he felt certain that had they gotten stuck so close to the castle, Rachel's coachman would have waded through the snow to get them by now.

It was slow going, and Richard was driven by fear. Why had he let Rachel leave this morning? He should have realized that it was far too dangerous. He had been distracted by what had happened the night before. Instead of thinking about the danger, he had been thinking about how he would explain to Miss Maitland that he had not bedded—or even wanted to bed—Leona, despite the incriminating circumstances in which Jessica had found them.

It would be his fault if something happened to Rachel. Once again it would be his fault.

He could not keep from remembering the night almost four years ago and the sickening sight of the carriage taking the corner too fast, rocking onto its right two wheels and then crashing over, rolling in a seemingly endless descent to the iced-over pond. He had lived years in that moment, watching his life tumble to an end.

Desperately, he pushed the memories away and continued at the fastest pace his horse could keep up along the road. A racking hour passed without any sign of Rachel's carriage—or, indeed, any sign that a vehicle had even passed this way. The snow was clean and fresh, any ruts that might have been there earlier already filled in.

Then, as he rode over the crest of a small hill, he saw in the distance a black form. He stiffened, leaning forward and squinting through the still-falling snow to see what it was. It was moving, he thought, gradually becoming larger, and soon it resolved itself into several distinct blobs of movement. Finally he could make out that there were four horses plodding toward him, three of them ridden and the fourth carrying an inert bundle. Carriage horses, he saw with a smile, without bridles or saddles. Rachel's rather portly coachman rode one, while Rachel sat ladylike in a sidesaddle position on another, and her poor maid bounced along on the third, clinging wildly to the horse's mane or harness or neck, whatever presented itself. The fourth horse of the team had some of their bags strapped on its back.

Gleefully Richard waved both arms at them and started forward.

Jessica watched in some dismay as the duke's carriage pulled into the yard, followed by the wagon, and a group of people emerged from the two vehicles and tromped into the house. Cleybourne had not yet returned, and she was growing more worried by the moment. Now it occurred to her that she probably needed to worry about what the duke would say when he did return and saw that she had invited a number of complete strangers into his home.

The wagon carried the luggage from the coach, as well as the servants who had gone to help the passengers. The two men who had come to the house to report the accident had ridden in the wagon with them.

Three more people climbed down from the carriage. The first one out was a slender man dressed in the simple black suit and white collar of an Anglican priest. He turned to help down the two women who were inside. The group hurried inside, the minister solicitously helping the elder of the two women up the steps.

"Thank you, madam," the minister said when they were all inside and the door closed against the cold. He gave Jessica a small bow. "It is most kind of you to let us take refuge in your house. I fear the elements did not favor traveling today."

"No, I think not," Jessica agreed. "Welcome to Castle Cleybourne. I am afraid that the Duke of Cleybourne is not here at the moment, but I expect him shortly.''

''Oh, dear,'' the priest said softly. ''Out in this weather? It is most inclement.''

''Yes. It was an emergency.'' Jessica introduced herself, then Gabriela, who was standing beside her, watching all their new guests with interest, and Miss Brown.

The minister responded by saying, ''Pray allow me to introduce myself, Miss Maitland. Miss Carstairs. I am the Reverend Borden Radfield. I am on my way back to my parish.''

He was a nice-looking man, Jessica thought, rather young and handsome for a priest. Since he appeared to also be single, Jessica suspected that the young women of his church probably chased him assiduously.

He then went on to introduce the other passengers. The thin, rather twitchy man was a Mr. Goodrich, the other man who had come to the house to seek help was the coachman. The older woman was Miss Pargety. She was small, with a pinched-looking face and a thin, slightly hooked nose that gave her, Jessica thought, the look of a bird. A crow, Jessica decided, given the unrelieved black of her coat, hat and gloves. Her graying hair was done up in tight corkscrew curls that fell on either side of her face, a rather too girlish style for a woman her age. Whenever she talked, the curls jiggled and bounced.

''I don't know what we are going to do,'' Miss Pargety said querulously, looking at Jessica as if she were responsible for inconveniencing her. ''I am traveling to my sister's for Christmas. I really must get there.''

"I am afraid that it looks as though you will be here for the present time, Miss Pargety," Jessica replied. "I am sure your sister will understand, given the weather."

"Well, I don't know how she will handle it all without me," Miss Pargety said in tones of gloom. "She will be most put out."

"I am sure that she will simply be relieved to know you are safe and out of the weather," said the other woman, who then turned, smiled at Jessica and introduced herself as Mrs. Woods.

Mrs. Woods was an attractive woman in her thirties, with a smooth olive complexion and thick black hair. She had a low, faintly husky voice, and there was a trace of an accent to her speech. She looked, Jessica thought, a trifle exotic for such a plain name as Mrs. Woods. Her coat and hat were a dark hunter-green, plain but expertly cut, and as Baxter relieved her of her coat, Jessica saw that the brown wool traveling dress beneath was also fashionable and expensive.

"We wouldn't have had any problem," Miss Pargety plowed on, undeterred by Mrs. Woods' attempt to soothe her, "if it hadn't been for those two young men. They were reckless. Absolutely reckless."

"No doubt they were unused to handling their horses on such a road," the minister told her, with a faintly apologetic glance toward Jessica and Gabriela.

"Where are the two young men?" Jessica asked.

"I assumed they would be coming, also. The roads are impassable, surely."

"Oh, yes. They were not so foolish as to think they could travel on," Reverend Radfield told Jessica with a faint smile. "But the men you sent were able to get their carriage out of the ditch. It had only had a wheel slip off the road, and it was in a good enough state to drive, so they are following us in it."

"I see."

"That must be they," the reverend said, turning toward the door at the sound of voices outside.

The front door opened, and in strode Cleybourne, his arm around Lady Westhampton, who sagged against his side. They were followed by the lady's maid and the coachman. Rachel was pale and shivering, and Jessica hurried toward them, followed by Gabriela.

"Lady Westhampton! You must be chilled clear through. Let us get you upstairs."

"Thank you. I am all right. It has been quite an experience, but I am sure that I will be none the worse for wear. Thank heavens Richard came, though. I fear we would have gotten lost trying to return."

"Who the devil are all these people?" Cleybourne exclaimed rudely, glancing around the entryway.

"Passengers on the mail coach. It broke down on the road not far from here." Cleybourne scowled at her, and Jessica looked back blandly at him. "I felt sure that, had you been at home, you would have insisted they come here."

"Yes, yes," he said impatiently. "That's all very

well. But right now Rachel needs to go to her room and get warm."

"Of course. Gabriela and I will take her. Miss Brown will see that our other guests are taken to their rooms."

At that moment there was a knock on the door, and the footman opened it. Two young men, the "gennelmen" of the coachman's description, Jessica was sure, strode into the entryway. They were obviously young men of the Ton, dressed in greatcoats sporting double rows of bright brass buttons and several capes at the shoulders, their boots polished to a mirror shine, and if their clothes had not given away their status, their arrogant demeanor would have.

"Lord Kestwick," the one in front said, immediately picking out the duke as the important person in the room and bowing to him.

The other man stepped around to Kestwick's side, saying, "Mr. Darius Talbot."

Jessica stiffened, her eyes widening in shock. It was all she could do to not gasp. *Darius Talbot!* Lord Kestwick's companion was none other than the man to whom she had once been engaged—the man who had thrown her over at the first sign of scandal.

10

It was all Jessica could do not to duck behind the duke so that Darius would not see her. However, she clenched her fists and managed to remain standing where she was. Darius did not even glance at her.

The duke unenthusiastically greeted the two men, then introduced Rachel, Gabriela and Jessica. Kestwick hardly spared her a glance, but Darius's head snapped around at the sound of her name, and when he saw her, his eyebrows shot up. He stood, staring at her blankly.

Jessica decided to forestall his saying anything to her by slipping her arm through Rachel's and turning to Cleybourne to say, "I think I had better help Lady Westhampton to her room now."

"Yes, yes, of course." Cleybourne handed Rachel over to her, his face creased with worry. "I shall be up in a moment to see how you are doing, Rachel."

She smiled at him. "I shall be fine, I'm sure."

But Jessica noticed that Rachel leaned on her rather heavily and was still shivering. Jessica swept her up the stairs and along the hall to her room, doing her best to concentrate on Rachel's condition and not on the presence of her former fiancé in this house. It seemed the worst sort of luck that he should wind up here—and it looked as though the whole group would be stuck here for several days.

Inside Lady Westhampton's room, Jessica quickly helped her off with her coat and boots, both rather sodden from the snow. Next she whisked away the rest of Rachel's clothes and wrapped her in a warm towel, then urged her into bed. A maid had warmed the sheets with a warming pan, and there was a hot-water bottle, as Jessica had requested, on the bed. Jessica positioned it at Lady Westhampton's feet and pulled the covers up about her shoulders.

Now Lady Westhampton was shuddering almost uncontrollably, and her teeth chattered. "I'm so sorry. I—I didn't even realize how cold it was until we came inside."

"You'll be fine now. Just give it a little time." Jessica rang for a maid, meaning to order hot tea for her patient, but right after that, a maid bustled in carrying a tray with a teapot and cups, as well as a bowl of warm stew.

The lady's bags had not been brought up to her room yet, so Jessica went quickly down the hall to her room and pulled out one of her own warm flannel nightgowns and her dressing gown. She returned to Rachel's room and helped her into the clothes, then warmed her up further with a cup of tea, followed by a bowl of the hearty stew. Gradually Rachel's shivering stopped.

"The snow was terrible," she told Jessica. "I

should have told Stephens to turn back sooner, but I am afraid I am afflicted with the Aincourt stubbornness. I had delayed too long already, and I was worried that Lord Westhampton would be upset. He was probably expecting me there today. Now I cannot even send him a note.''

''Well, I am sure that your husband would much rather you were here safe than risking your life trying to get home in time.''

''Yes. No doubt. And Michael is a very calm man,'' Rachel said, with what Jessica thought was a faintly wistful note in her voice. ''He will probably realize that I am staying over because of the snowfall and not worry. He is quite pragmatic.''

She told Jessica how they had finally turned the coach around and were headed back toward the castle when her carriage had drifted off the road and gotten mired down in the ditch. Unsure anyone would happen by, the coachman had unharnessed the horses, and they had set out, riding the animals.

''I was greatly afraid we were going to get lost. It was all so featureless out there, with snow covering everything. Thank goodness Richard came looking for us.''

''He was very worried about you.''

Rachel smiled. ''He is a good brother-in-law.''

But Jessica could not help but wonder if the duke's feelings for Rachel were something more than those of a brother-in-law.

Gabriela came in to see how Rachel was doing, and then the two of them left in order to give Lady Westhampton a chance to sleep. They returned to the schoolroom, Gabriela chattering about the excitement of the visitors and the snow.

Jessica sank into a chair, and though she managed to respond to Gabriela's conversation, her mind was largely occupied by the fact that Darius Talbot was in the house. *What a bizarre twist of fate!*

She rarely thought of the man, and certainly whatever feelings she once had for him had long since burned away. Indeed, she sometimes thought that the hurt and betrayal she had felt after he threw her over were actually stronger feelings than the love she had had for him during their betrothal. But seeing him here had jarred her. It was, to say the least, an awkward situation.

But, she reassured herself, it might be possible to avoid being around him. With all these people, the duke would surely not feel the need to have her as a buffer between him and the Veseys, and Rachel was, at least for the day, going to take her supper on a tray in bed. So she herself would be free to eat with Gabriela every day in the nursery. She wished now that they were still sleeping up there, for then she would have been even more isolated from Talbot. She was much more likely to run into him since their rooms were on the same floor. Miss Brown might put some of the uninvited guests on the third floor, but Jessica knew that she would not put Kestwick and Talbot there, as they were too obviously members of the upper class.

She would simply have to keep to her room as much as possible until they left, Jessica decided, even though it galled her to think of literally hiding from the man. But it would be the most uncomfortable situation to have to speak to him! Anything, she thought, would be better than that.

Of course, she reminded herself, Darius would have just as little desire to talk to her—perhaps even less. If he tried to avoid her, too, perhaps they might be able to keep from meeting.

Her thoughts were interrupted by Baxter, who came to her with the thorny problem of where to seat all their visitors at the dining table. Jessica understood the dilemma he faced. She felt sure that most of the passengers of the mail coach would never, in the ordinary course of their lives, be seated to eat with a duke. Only Kestwick and Talbot were of any sort of rank to be seated with Cleybourne, the Veseys and Lady Westhampton, and Jessica frankly was not sure enough of Kestwick's rank to know where to place him among that group of people.

The coachman and his assistant would eat with the servants. But that left the other mail passengers to be sorted out. One could scarcely expect a man of the cloth to be seated with the servants, so he must go to the duke's table. And Jessica could tell from the spinster's demeanor that she would be horrified to be seated anywhere but at the main table. Mrs. Woods had seemed genteel and was certainly well dressed. Goodrich, the man who had arrived with the coachman's assistant, would by his attire fit better with the servants, but it would be a terrible thing to make a mistake and put him there if he did not belong. Jessica had felt too many stings of embarrassment as a governess to subject anyone else to them.

"And there is another one now, miss," Baxter put in, looking frazzled.

"Another? Who?"

"A man who arrived a short while ago on horseback. Cobb is his name, and I am sure I don't know where he belongs, either. A rather rough-looking sort, though he is dressed well enough."

"Have you asked the duke? It is, after all, his table."

"Of course. He says only, 'I am sure you will do what's best, Baxter.'" He heaved a little sigh. "His Grace is sometimes too egalitarian, I'm afraid. I really do not think he cares where any of them sit."

"Then I would say put them all at the main dining table and rank them as seems appropriate to you. My guess is that Kestwick is of higher degree than the Veseys, but even there, I am not sure. Mr. Talbot obviously has no title, and I am sure that he would not sit as high as the others. The rest—just put them farther down the table. If they are offended, it can't be helped."

"Yes, miss, thank you." Baxter smiled at her, relieved, and hurried off.

Next it was Miss Brown who came to her to confide her worries about the rooms she had had made up and how she had allotted them, and Jessica did her best to mollify her fears, assuring her that whatever she had decided would not reflect badly on the duke. Jessica was not entirely certain of that statement, but she was sure that the duke would not care, anyway.

Lady Westhampton, when she awakened, invited

Gabriela to dine with her in her room that evening, assuming that Jessica would be dining downstairs. Jessica decided that, to save the maids an extra trip, she would wait to eat until after the main meal had been served downstairs and would then just slip down to the kitchen and make up a tray herself.

She was sitting in her room, reading and trying to ignore her empty stomach, when there was a sharp rap on her door. She opened it, expecting to find Miss Brown or Baxter with another etiquette question, but to her surprise it was the Duke of Cleybourne himself who stood in front of her door.

"Your Grace! I—" She stopped, having no idea what to say.

"What the devil are you doing up here?" he asked ungraciously.

"And where else would I be?" Jessica bridled.

"You are supposed to be downstairs, eating with everyone else."

"Governesses generally do not eat with the family, Your Grace, especially when there are guests."

"They aren't *my* guests," Cleybourne pointed out. "You invited them in. This is a fine time to appear subservient to me, I must say. Where is the Miss Maitland who takes it upon herself to run the household and send out my servants to rescue mail coaches?"

"What would you have had me do?" Jessica flared. "Leave them out in the snow to freeze to death?"

"No, of course not. I just—damnation, they are a nuisance. One of them is forever twitching or blinking or clearing his throat, and that Cobb fellow is a rum sort, as well. You cannot expect me to put up with that lot of gudgeons by myself.''

"You are scarcely alone."

"I know. That is the problem. It was bad enough when it was just Lord and Lady Vesey. But now there is that sparrow of a woman twittering away, and Kestwick droning on about boot polish, of all things, and that other fellow, what's his name, is a perfect dolt." He broke off with a sigh, then looked at her with raised eyebrows. "Well?"

"Well, what?"

"You need to dress and come down to dinner."

"You aren't serious."

"I most certainly am."

Jessica thought with panic of having to sit at the same table with Darius. "But I—it will take me a while."

"We'll wait dinner."

"You don't *need* me. I don't know how I can make them any less annoying."

Cleybourne looked at her for a moment, nonplussed, then said, "Perhaps not, but it will improve my mood immensely if I know that you are having to suffer them, as well. Now, get dressed. I shall wait for you out here."

"You do not need to wait."

"I do if I expect you to join us."

Jessica grimaced and shut the door, then went to her wardrobe and pulled out another of the dresses that Lady Westhampton had lent her. She decided on the rich brown satin, which contained a hidden depth of red that seemed to reflect her hair and warm her pale skin. She left her hair in the same simple style in which she had worn it all day, a heavy knot twisted and pinned low on her neck. She had neither the time nor the skill to do up the elaborate curls she had worn the other evening.

When she opened the door, Cleybourne, who had been lounging on a decorative bench across the hall, jumped to his feet, and there was something in his eyes, a sudden flash of light, that made her insides curl with heat. She reminded herself that she was nothing to him but an employee, that he regretted the impulse that had led him to kiss her the other night, that he had been dallying last night with the licentious Leona.

He took her arm, and they went down the stairs to the sitting room, where everyone else was waiting. The furious look on Leona's face when Jessica entered the room at Cleybourne's side was enough to make her glad she had come, even if it did mean having to spend an evening with Darius Talbot.

It was a strange meal. As Cleybourne had said, Mr. Goodrich could not seem to sit in stillness. He gazed at the vast array of silverware with some trepidation and kept checking with little sideways glances to see what utensil everyone else was using. Across from him sat a man Jessica had not seen before, whom she took to be the Mr. Cobb that Baxter had told her had arrived later than the others and alone. He was a short, squat fellow with a thick trunk and heavy shoulders and arms. A scar decorated one cheek, giving him an odd, constant half smile, and his eyes were as flat and emotionless as rocks. He said nothing, just ate with a methodical slowness, looking around the table at all the others. She had to agree with Cleybourne that he looked to be a "rum sort."

Leona, as always, wore a gown that was as close to nothing as she could find. Most of the men's eyes remained on the neckline of her dress throughout the evening, hoping, Jessica supposed, that it would eventually slip that final inch and reveal her nipples. The spinster who was traveling to visit her sister, Miss Pargety, spent most of the meal staring at Leona, too, with fascinated horror. Mrs. Woods seemed unshocked by Leona's manner or attire. She ate her meal with quiet dignity, watching everyone else and saying little herself, though once or twice Jessica was sure she caught a flash of contempt in her face when she looked at Leona.

Leona seemed to have abandoned her pursuit of the duke, at least for this evening. With a tableful of men to perform for, she was at her most sparkling and provocative. She flirted with all of them, including the Reverend Radfield, who seemed to mind not at all the fact that her bosom threatened to spill over her dress at any moment. Her throaty laugh had an intimate quality, as though she were alone with whoever heard it. She smiled and dimpled and declared the men all naughty creatures, until Jessica wanted to throw something at her.

Only one man besides Cleybourne seemed immune to Leona's charms. Darius kept his eyes on Jessica most of the evening. She carefully avoided looking at him, not wanting to make eye contact, but she could see out of the corner of her eye that his gaze kept returning to her face.

Jessica tried politely to carry on a conversation with Mrs. Woods and Miss Pargety, since Leona was occupying the attention of most of the males at the table. Mrs. Woods smiled and answered Jessica politely whenever Jessica directed a remark to her, but she offered nothing more than that. Jessica was certain there was an accent to her speech, and, given her thick black hair and olive skin, she wondered if the woman was perhaps Italian, despite her very English sounding name.

Miss Pargety, on the other hand, was quite ready to talk, and she did so through much of the meal without stop, complaining about the mail coach, the snow, the cold, and now this delay, interspersing her complaints with digressions on her sister and that woman's inability to prepare for Christmas without her expert help. By the time the meal was over, Jessica suspected that the woman's sister would probably rejoice that Miss Pargety had been delayed in visiting her.

As soon as the meal was over and the guests rose from the table, Jessica made good her escape. She had absolutely no intention of being stuck sitting in the music room or a drawing room with the other women while the men retired to smoke and drink brandy. With a general smile at the people around her, she slipped out the door and started toward the stairs.

"Jessica!"

She stopped, recognizing the voice, and turned slowly. She would have liked to keep on hurrying away, but she knew that she might as well face him now and get it over with. At least there was no one else around; all the other guests were still dawdling just outside the dining room.

"Darius."

"Please. I want to talk to you." He came over to her and took her arm, propelling her into the nearest room, the smaller and less elegant drawing room.

Jessica resisted her instinct to shake off his hold. She looked down pointedly at where his fingers bit into her arm, and he dropped his hand, backing up a few steps.

"I—I'm sorry. I just—" There were beads of sweat dotting his forehead, and he cast a rather haunted look around the room, as though something in it might tell him what to do next. "I could scarcely believe my eyes when I saw you this afternoon."

Jessica waited, looking at him. She wondered vaguely what she had ever seen in the man. He was handsome enough, she supposed, in a rather ordinary way, but there was a decided weakness to his mouth, and she wondered why she had not noticed that when they were engaged. His hair was medium brown, his eyes hazel. Neither short nor tall, thin nor fat, he was, she decided, a very nondescript sort.

"I—I—uh, I was glad to see you. I've been... wanting to see you for ages, really. I know that I behaved badly before, and I've been wanting to apologize to you. To let you know how wrong I was. I see that now. And I do hope you can find it in your heart to forgive me." When Jessica said nothing, just continued to look at him coolly, he went on in a rush. "I behaved like a...like a cad to you. I have no excuse except that I was young and foolish. I was afraid that your father's scandal would taint me, too, and that my career in the army would be finished."

"Of course," Jessica replied. "One would expect you to think of yourself first."

He hesitated, looking at her uncertainly, as if he were not sure how to take her statement. "I—I felt that I had no choice. I had to give up love for my family's good name, for my own hopes in the military. Looking back on it, I see now what a fool I was for placing my career before you. I hope that you can find it in your heart to forgive me. I would appreciate it if you could do so.... If we could be friends again."

"I have no interest in being friends with you, Darius," Jessica said in a flat voice. "And, quite frankly, I imagine that after this, it will be extremely unlikely that we will ever run into each other again. We have not done so in ten years, after all. We do not move in the same circles any longer."

He had the grace to color a little at her remark. "I know. I am so sorry that you have had to—to—"

"Seek employment?" Jessica suggested. "It's all right. I do not try to hide the fact that I work. There is actually something rather satisfying and freeing about knowing that one controls one's own fate, rather than relying on a father or brother or husband to provide one with sustenance."

He blinked, seemingly at a loss as to how to respond to her candid words.

"Darius...I suppose you must feel awkward being in this situation. I do, too. But there is no need to pretend to some sort of caring that neither of us feels, just because we want to make the situation less uncomfortable. It was bad luck that we ran into each other this way, but the only thing to do is simply to make the best of it. With any luck, the roads will be clear in a few days, then you and your friend can leave, and we won't ever have to have anything to do with each other again. In the meantime, I suggest that we try to stay out of each other's way. It will make it much easier to get through."

With that she turned on her heel and strode out of the room.

"Jessica!" Darius started after her, but stopped in the doorway, watching her walk away.

Jessica looked neither to her left nor right, but headed straight for the stairs. She had almost reached them when the duke's voice stopped her.

"Miss Maitland!"

Reluctantly she paused and glanced to the side. Cleybourne approached her, casting a look at Darius Talbot, who immediately popped back inside the drawing room.

"Was that fellow bothering you?" Cleybourne asked as he stopped in front of her.

"No. It's nothing. I was just going up to bed. I am not used to late hours."

Cleybourne frowned. "I saw your face when Mr.

Talbot introduced himself this afternoon. And right now you don't look as if 'nothing' just occurred. Perhaps I should speak to him.''

"No. It isn't necessary. I have taken care of it myself.'' She sighed, realizing that she could not get out of this without telling the duke something. He obviously took his duties to protect those in his household very seriously. "Mr. Talbot is someone I used to know, many years ago. He—I—I believe I told you about the scandal concerning my father, and that after it was I was no longer received in society and the man to whom I was engaged broke it off, not wishing to have his name associated with mine.''

"Yes.''

"Mr. Talbot is that man.''

"Your fiancé?'' Cleybourne's eyebrows soared upward, and his first words were not what she expected. "What the devil were you doing being engaged to that popinjay?''

A giggle escaped Jessica's lips. "I wondered that myself this evening.''

"Well, I pegged him for a fool,'' Cleybourne went on. "I had not realized that he was also a man without honor.'' He looked toward the drawing room. "I shall ask him to leave.''

Jessica warmed a little at his championing of her. "Thank you, Your Grace. But you cannot do that. It would be tantamount to killing him in this weather. He could not make it the village or even another house.''

"Yes, you're probably right,'' Cleybourne replied

in a tone of regret. "What did he want tonight? Was he importuning you? Shall I speak to him?"

Jessica shook her head. "No. Though I thank you again. He—" She shrugged. "He told me that he wanted us to be friends. He offered an apology for how he treated me."

"I see." Cleybourne watched her face closely. "And what did you say?"

Jessica grimaced. "I told him I did not wish to be friends with him, and that I thought it would be best if we avoided each other. So, you see, it is all taken care of. Good night, Your Grace."

"No, wait, it is *not* all taken care of. I have been trying to speak to you since last night."

"There is no reason why you should explain anything to me," Jessica said stiffly, remembering the moment when she had seen him with Lady Vesey, in the hall and the piercing blade of anger and hurt that had stabbed through her. "I am merely your employee. It is not surprising to me that you should choose to…be with…a woman of your own station."

"My own sta—" He frowned in puzzlement. "Bloody hell! Is that what you think I was saying the other morning? That you were not high enough for me? That you were not good enough? Good God, woman! I wouldn't have thought you were that bloody foolish."

"Foolish?" Jessica quirked an eyebrow, her voice growing icier.

"Yes, foolish," he retorted in a low, furious voice. "You live here. You work for me. It would be taking advantage of you for me to—to force my attentions on you. That is what I was talking about, not your status. I don't give a rap about my position or whether you are a governess or a bloody washer-woman, for that matter. But the other night, in the nursery, when I—when you—damn it, I was taking advantage of you and the situation. I acted like a cad.''

"So you turned to Leona. It makes perfect sense."

"I did not turn to Leona!" His voice was rising with anger, and he stopped, reining himself in visibly. He continued in a lower voice. "That is what I am trying to tell you. Nothing happened between me and Lady Vesey."

Jessica arched one eyebrow in delicate disbelief.

"Yes, I know it looked terrible. She was wearing my dressing gown and nothing else, but I had nothing to do with that. Well, not with her lack of clothing. I found her in that state when I went into my room last night. She was lying in wait for me,'' he said in such an aggrieved tone that Jessica almost had to laugh. "Sitting there on my bed, wearing nothing. So I gave her my dressing gown and hustled her out into the hall. I never touched her—well, I mean, except to take her outside.''

Richard looked down at Jessica. It bothered him that it mattered so much that she believe him. It bothered him that he kept thinking about the other night when he had kissed her. It seemed a betrayal of Caroline—as if he had stopped loving her, as if he no longer belonged to her. Yet, even as he told himself that he should not feel this way, that he should not care what Jessica Maitland thought of him, he knew that he *did* care.

"Damn it," he said in exasperation, his voice tinged with bitterness. "Don't you know that seeing Leona naked didn't make me want her? Not the way one kiss made me want you."

Jessica's head snapped up, and she stared at him, shocked by his words. She saw the truth in his eyes, and she saw, too, how much he disliked feeling as he did. She gazed into his dark eyes, unable to look away, scarcely able to breathe. He wanted to kiss her again, she knew, and she knew that she wanted him to. Every nerve in her was suddenly alive and thrumming, and unconsciously she leaned a little closer to him.

There was a burst of laughter from down the hall, heavy masculine laughs, followed by Leona's teasing voice. Both Jessica and Richard jumped, glancing guiltily toward the sound. There was no one in the hall; the guests were all still in the formal drawing room, but they were aware of how many people were about, how little privacy they had here in the middle of the Great Hall.

Jessica looked back at Richard, her heart pounding. Then she turned and hurried away, almost running up the stairs.

11

Jessica stopped by Gabriela's door on her way down the hall to her own bedroom and turned the doorknob quietly. It was locked from the inside, as she had instructed Gabriela to do each night. She went next door and rapped lightly on Rachel's door, and at the sound of Rachel's voice, she stepped inside.

Rachel smiled at her from the bed, but it was not a very strong smile. Her eyes were watery, and she admitted that both her throat and her head hurt a little. "I think I am coming down with a head cold," she admitted mournfully. "I am so sorry. I'm sure you will need help with the extra company."

"Yes, I suppose we must do something to keep them from growing bored. What an odd lot they are, too." Jessica kept Rachel entertained for the next few minutes describing Mr. Cobb, Miss Pargety and the others, and she was glad to see that Rachel's spirits rose during her visit.

After a while she left Rachel to get some sleep and walked across the hall to her own bedroom. She glanced at Cleybourne's door, just one door down the hall from hers, and wondered if he was in there yet. She shook off the thought, reminding herself how unproductive it was, and began to get ready for bed.

Pulling on one of her plain white flannel gowns, she took down her hair, sighing with relief, and brushed out the thick red curls. She climbed into bed, shivering a little in the cold room, the fire in the fireplace banked for the night. She had thought that she would have difficulty falling to sleep, for lately her mind seemed to whir on for ages, usually concerning the Duke of Cleybourne. But it had been a tiring day, and she fell asleep quickly.

She had been asleep for a while when a noise brought her awake, eyes flying open and heart pounding. She sat up, trying to remember what had awakened her. *Had it been the sound of her doorknob turning?* She wasn't sure. She had been dreaming, and the dream and reality were blurred.

Jessica slipped out of bed, putting on her bedroom slippers, then wrapped her dressing gown around her and tied it. She walked quietly across the floor and listened, her ear against the door. She could hear nothing. Unlocking the door, she eased it open a crack and peered out into the hall. There was nothing there, only the dark corridor, lit dimly with moonlight from the windows at either end of the hallway.

She stood for a moment, looking. Then, furtively, a dark form slipped from the shadows on one side of the hallway and across to the top of the staircase, then disappeared down the stairs. Jessica's heart began to knock crazily in her rib cage. *Who was steal-*

ing down the staircase at this time of night? Her first thought was of the intruder who had broken into the schoolroom the other night. *Was it Vesey?* She could not imagine why he would be sneaking around at this time of night.

She knew, however, that she was going to follow that secretive form. She thought of taking a candle or lamp with her since the moonlight from the two hall windows provided little light. However, a lit candle would obviously draw notice from the man she was following, so she did not. She did, however, pick up the heavy candlestick, weighing it in her hand. It would do for a weapon, she thought. She took the candle out, slipped it into her pocket, and, wrapping her hand firmly around the stem of the candleholder, she opened the door wider and slipped out into the hallway.

She moved as fast as she dared, given the dimness, and soon reached the stairs. Grasping the rail, she started down slowly, fearful of slipping. About halfway down, she heard a thud somewhere below her in the Great Hall, followed by a brief and blasphemous exclamation. She hesitated, then went on as silently as she could.

When she reached the bottom of the stairs, she paused, looking carefully around her. The Great Hall was even darker than the hallway above had been. She crept through it, afraid of knocking into something, the way the person she was following apparently had. She reached the hallway down which Cleybourne's study lay, and she started along it. It was Stygian in its darkness here, where there were no windows with drapes open to the night, and she did not see the darker shapes of a table or bench against the wall until she was practically on them. She was concentrating on the immediate space in front of her when there was a loud cry from down the hall, followed by a crash.

Jessica's head flew up, and she searched the dark shadows of the corridor in front of her. There was a grunt, followed by a thud, and an instant later a dark form burst out of a door farther down the hallway and tore down the corridor straight at her. She stepped back, but not quickly enough, and the man slammed into her left shoulder, knocking her aside. She hit the wall, grabbing at the edge of the table to keep from falling.

Another man tore out of the office after the first, running past her with a single, startled glance before he sped on. This man she recognized as Cleybourne, and it was then it struck her that she had seen nothing of the first figure's face, only darkness, the same way she had not seen the face of the man who had broken into the schoolroom.

Even as these thoughts raced through her mind, she was pushing away from the wall and taking off after the two men. The first man had reached the front door and thrown it open, followed a moment later by Richard. Heedless of her delicate bedroom slippers and the inadequacy of her dressing gown for the cold outdoors, Jessica ran out after them.

The mystery figure had a lead on Cleybourne, but Richard was closing quickly. The snow slowed all of them down. The man in front went around the side of the house, slipping and falling as he made the turn, then picking himself up and hurrying on through the snow. Jessica plowed along after them, cursing the added disadvantage of her gown and robe. She was shivering in the cold, but she paid no attention to it, intent on pursuing the two men.

Richard caught up to the other man before he reached the back garden, jumping the last few feet, slamming into him and knocking him to the ground. The two figures rolled around in the snow, grappling with each other, hitting and wrestling. They struggled to their feet, still locked in battle.

By this time Jessica was almost upon them. She gripped her weapon, the heavy, ornate candleholder, more tightly, watching for a break in the fighting so she could wade into the fray and use it. However, in the shadow of the house, in their dark clothes, the two men were difficult to tell apart. She could not get a good look at either face. She circled them anxiously, trying to discern Cleybourne's features. One of them stumbled over a small stone figure buried under the snow, and the two of them went down again.

Jessica hovered over them uncertainly. The one on the bottom managed to roll over, pulling the other one under him. His hands closed around the throat of his opponent and he squeezed, bearing down. The side of his face looked dark. Fear shot through Jessica. *The other man had the upper hand, and Cleybourne was being strangled!* Grasping the candlestick with both hands, she swung it down hard on the back of the upper man's head.

He made a noise and crumpled to the ground. The other man pulled himself out from under, and Jessica saw his face for the first time. It was covered by a dark scarf, his eyes the only thing visible. *She had hit the wrong man!*

"Richard!" she cried out, dropping down on her knees beside the limp body and frantically rolling him over.

The other man took off into the back garden. Jessica scarcely noticed. Her heart was in her throat, looking down at Richard's still form.

"Richard!" She grabbed his shoulders and shook him a little.

He groaned, and his eyelids opened. His eyes rolled around a bit, then his lids closed again.

"Oh, God!" A little sob escaped Jessica. She smoothed back his hair, struggling not to cry. How could she have been so stupid? she wondered frantically. She had struck without thinking, scared that Richard was being killed. "Please wake up. Oh, please."

A thought struck her. She picked up a handful of snow and rubbed it over Richard's cheeks. The shock of the ice-cold wetness on his face woke him up again, and this time, though his eyes wavered a little, they steadied.

"Jessica?" he asked faintly, looking puzzled.

"Yes. Can you stand up? Are you all right?"

"I—I think so." His hand came up to his head. "Where the devil am I? What ha—" Suddenly his face cleared, and he barked, "Where is he?"

He sat up, but the movement was too sudden, and

he swayed. Jessica wrapped her arm around his shoulders to keep him up.

"He is gone. He ran away. I am so sorry. I hit you."

Richard let out a curse. "I might have known." He gingerly touched the crown of his head. "Why the devil did you do that?"

"I was trying to help you!"

"Well, next time, please don't."

"I thought it was he!" Jessica retorted indignantly. "I thought you were the—the robber, or whatever he is. He was—I mean, *you* were choking him, but I thought he was you. I thought he was killing you. So I hit him," she finished lamely. She lifted the candlestick up to show him.

"Sweet Christ! I shall have a knot there in the morning." A shiver ran through him, then another, and in that instant Jessica, too, realized how cold she was out here, kneeling in the snow.

"Come. Get up. We need to go inside and see to your head. Are you hurt anyplace else?"

"Isn't a head wound sufficient for you?" Cleybourne asked sourly.

"There's no need to be surly about it," Jessica said, standing up and reaching down to help him rise. Even in the dim light, she could see that there was a gash above one eyebrow, and blood had poured down from it, covering much of one side of his face. Jessica realized one reason why she had assumed that he was the intruder. The side of his face that she could see had been dark with blood, and she had thought it was the intruder's mask.

He shook off her hand and rose to a crouch, swayed, then steadied and stood up the rest of the way. His knees almost buckled, and Jessica jumped forward to put her arm around his waist.

"Lean on me," she ordered. "You're hurt. We need to go inside and tend to that wound."

He did not argue, for once, just draped his arm around her shoulders. They walked back inside, Richard not leaning on her so much as using her to keep himself balanced. They walked slowly but finally reached the front of the house and went up the steps.

Inside, it was brighter than it had been when they left. Several people holding candles were standing at various places along the staircase, watching them. Two footmen, still in their nightshirts, had come in through the hall from the back staircase, and they, too, stood stock-still, gazing incredulously at Jessica and Richard.

Jessica took in the faces of those on the stairs. Gaby was there, looking both scared and excited, as well as Mrs. Woods, her thick black hair tumbling loose down over her shoulders, and Miss Pargety, one hand to her throat and a horrified expression on her face. For a long moment everyone stood, staring at one another. There was the sound of heavy feet on the staircase from the third floor, and a moment later Mr. Cobb joined the others on the staircase.

"What's going on here?" he asked gruffly. "What was all that noise?" He looked down at Richard and Jessica. "Are you hurt, sir?"

"Yes, he is," Jessica said. "I will need bandages and something to clean the wound with."

"It's all right," Richard said shortly, dropping his arm away and straightening. "I shall tend to it later. Right now I have more important things to do." He turned to the gaping footmen, saying, "Go knock on all the doors and look in the bedrooms. See if any man is wearing clothes that are wet from being out in the snow or if discarded clothes are lying around anywhere."

"Yes, Your Grace," one of the footman replied, looking somewhat doubtful.

"There's them as won't like it, sir," the other servant cautioned.

"I know. Apologize profusely, but tell them it cannot be helped. Tell them there has been an intruder in the house, and I have ordered you to check all the rooms to see if he is hiding anywhere."

On the stairs, the spinster let out a little shriek. "There is someone inside the house!" She cast a frightened look around her, as if some terror might pop out at her at any moment.

"I do not know, Miss Pargety. The odds are that he is some distance away from here already. But we must make sure."

"What happened?" Gaby asked breathlessly. "Was it the same man?"

"You need to go back to bed, Gabriela," Jessica said firmly.

Since the duke now seemed able to stand on his own, she left him and crossed over to the stairs, intent on keeping the women from succumbing to hysteria. She went up the stairs, hooking one arm through Gaby's and the other through the spinster's thin, trembling arm.

"Come, I will take both of you back to your rooms," she told them, giving Miss Pargety what she hoped was a reassuring look. Mrs. Woods' pretty face, she noticed, was pale but calm. It would take more than an intruder, Jessica thought, to shake her. Nor did Mr. Cobb look startled or upset; she had the feeling that bleeding head wounds were not an unfamiliar sight to him. Or perhaps his lack of surprise came from the fact that he had been the one fighting with Cleybourne outside. She wondered if he had had time to enter the house through another door and go up to his room. She glanced down at his trousers and noted that they were dry all the way down; he would have had to change, because Cleybourne's opponent would have been as wet from the snow as he. Could he have done all that and appeared on the stairs as soon as he did?

Jessica glanced up and saw that he was watching her. She turned away, propelling Gaby and Miss Pargety up the stairs with her. Both of them were full of questions, Gaby about all the details of what had happened and Miss Pargety about whether there was someone in the house waiting to harm her. Jessica did her best to reassure Miss Pargety, going into her room with her and looking all around, even in the wardrobe and under the bed, to prove that there was no one hiding there.

"Just lock your door now, and you will be fine," she told her.

She left and heard the click of the key in the lock after her. Gaby was somewhat harder to satisfy, but Jessica managed to answer enough questions to hold her for the moment.

"I have to get back downstairs to talk to the duke. I will know much more after that," Jessica pointed out.

"All right," Gaby agreed somewhat reluctantly. "But you have to promise to tell me tomorrow."

"I will. Now lock your door again. Promise."

Gaby nodded and Jessica left, waiting in the hallway until she heard the key turn in the door. Then she hurried across the hall to her own bedroom, closing the door and whipping off her dressing gown and nightclothes. They were soaked from the snow and clung chillingly to her legs. She dressed with haste, throwing on stockings, a petticoat and a warm woolen dress, afraid that Cleybourne might go to bed before she had a chance to talk to him. She did not bother to put up her hair. She knew that she probably looked like a wild woman with it down around her shoulders and curling everywhere, but she didn't care. She wanted to find out exactly what had happened earlier.

After lighting a candle from the embers of her fire, she stepped into the hall and glanced toward the duke's room. No light showed beneath his door. She hoped that meant he was still downstairs. She hurried down the stairs toward his study. Several of the sconces were lit in the hallway leading to the study, and there was ample light in that room.

When she reached the doorway, she found Cley-

bourne standing in the center of the room, looking
about him. She noticed that he, too, had apparently
changed into dry clothes. He turned at the sound of
her approach and looked unsurprised to see her.

"I thought you'd be back," he said simply, then
returned to his survey.

A small table had been overturned, the things that
had been on it now lying beside it on the floor, and
a few papers had fallen from his desk. Several pictures were askew, and the doors of a low cabinet
stood open, revealing the face of a safe.

"There is where I found him," Cleybourne said,
gesturing at the low cabinet. "We struggled, and I
think that is when the table got overturned and the
things fell off my desk. Nothing else seems disturbed." He waved a hand toward one of the pictures. "Looking for the safe, I think."

"That would make sense." Jessica eyed the cabinet. "What do you think he was looking for?"

Cleybourne shrugged. "I have no idea. Something
in the safe, or something he thought would be in the
safe."

"A common thief, do you think?"

"Perhaps. But not, I think, a thief from outside the
house."

"It would seem unlikely," Jessica agreed. She had
thought the same thing herself. "It would be much
easier to break in if one did not have to struggle
through deep snow. It must have been someone in
the house. But who?"

"I don't know. I am not even sure about his size.
It was so dark, and he had something over his face.

I think he was slighter than I, shorter, but not a great deal.''

"That description would rule out Mr. Cobb.''

Cleybourne nodded. "I don't think it was he, although otherwise he would certainly be my first suspect. But, as I said, it is all supposition. I cannot be sure.'' He bent down to close the cabinet. "Why were you down here?''

"Oh. I heard a noise. It awakened me. I wasn't sure what it had been, so I looked out into the hall and saw someone slipping furtively down the stairs. Apparently that was you.''

"Yes. I couldn't go to sleep. I kept hearing noises—doors opening and closing. I swear, I think half the people in this house were slipping in and out of their rooms tonight. Finally I went out in the hall to investigate, and I saw a light downstairs. I was curious, so I extinguished my candle and went downstairs. He must have heard me because by the time I reached my study, the light had been doused. I saw him crouched here by the safe, and I charged at him. We struggled, but he got away...and the rest you saw.''

"Who do you think it was?''

"I don't know. Baxter and the other servants checked all the rooms. He just reported to me when I came back down here. Everyone was in his or her room. They saw no wet and discarded clothes lying about. Whoever it was got rid of them somehow or hid them well enough that the servants didn't see them.'' Cleybourne grimaced. "It's a damnable thing. I am certain that it must be someone in this house, but I have no idea who."

"It seems particularly odd—given the other intruder."

"Yes. Too coincidental. I would think it was the same person, but I was sure that was Vesey, trying to take Gabriela away from here. Why would he break into my study? What could he hope to find in there?"

"I don't know. Perhaps he might think that if he took the papers making you Gabriela's guardian..."

"But it would still be in the original will, which has already been filed and read."

"Yes. I cannot see how it would do him any good. Besides, he has always seemed like too much of a coward to break into one room, let alone two. I would not have thought he had the courage to do it."

"Neither would I. And I warned him after the first incident. I told him what I would do if he tried anything else. It does not seem like him to have crossed me in the face of a clear warning. He is a fool, but he has a good sense of self-preservation."

"I would have thought so. But perhaps he is desperate enough to try anything. The General did tell me that he would put nothing past him, no matter how despicable. And he told me once that Vesey was on his last legs financially. He said he owes a great deal of money."

"So I have heard. He would not care about his creditors, but he is an inveterate gambler. He would be very eager to pay whatever gambling debts he had, else he would be cut off from his games. His is an expensive lifestyle, and Lady Vesey is as profligate as he—and she lost what she thought would keep her in clothes and jewels when she lost Devin last summer.''

"Well, I suppose there is nothing more that we can do about it tonight," Jessica said reluctantly. She looked at him. "I ought to clean that wound, you know."

He cast her an amused glance. "Are you a doctor, then, as well, Miss Maitland?"

"No, but I have tended a few cuts and bruises in my time—both as a governess and as a soldier's daughter."

"All right. I will admit your expertise," he said with a faint smile. "Baxter brought a tray of things to apply to it, but I wanted to check things out down here first. The dressings are upstairs."

He turned out the lamp, and they went upstairs, using the candle Jessica had brought with her. Cleybourne strode down the hall to his door and opened it. Jessica, beside him, hesitated for an instant. She had rarely been inside any man's bedroom—certainly no one's besides her father's or the General's. It seemed far too intimate a place to be alone with a man.

Cleybourne lit the lamp on the table beside the door. Jessica squared her shoulders and walked into the room. There was nothing wrong with her being here to tend to his cut, she told herself; she refused to be missish about such a silly thing.

Baxter had left the tray of bandages and pots of ointment on a low table beside a chair. Cleybourne walked over to it and sat down so that she could reach the cut. Jessica wet a cloth in his washbasin and squeezed it out, then began to wipe away the crusted blood on his face.

It made her feel strangely breathless to stand this close to him. She looked at his cheek, where she was washing away the blood, refusing to look into his eyes, but she knew he was watching her. She put a hand under his chin to steady his head as she dabbed at the blood, and her fingers trembled slightly at the brush of his stubble-roughed skin on her fingertips.

She cast about quickly in her mind for something to say, some subject to take her mind off the fact of her touching him. "What if it were not Vesey? Why would any of the others have broken into your study?"

"To steal something, I would presume. It seems the most likely reason."

"But they could not run away with what they stole," Jessica pointed out. "The snow is too deep outside. They must have known they would get caught."

"It makes little sense. Perhaps they were looking for something very small. But what? And none of them were here before. Only Vesey. The whole thing makes no sense."

Jessica rinsed out the washrag in the basin, then began to clean the cut itself. Cleybourne flinched and let out a sharp, short noise. "That is a wound, you know, not a spot of dirt."

"I am aware of that," Jessica retorted acidly. She added a little hesitantly, "I am sorry I hurt you."

The corner of his mouth quirked up. "Don't tell me you are having pangs of guilt."

"No, of course not. I did not mean to do it. And I—well, I am very sorry, though." She frowned a little worriedly.

He cut his eyes toward her. "I should probably let you suffer over it, but I won't. Your apology is accepted. I don't believe your blow would have knocked me out if he had not already hit me with a paperweight while we struggled in the study."

"No wonder you were so woozy after I hit you."

Cleybourne looked up at her. It occurred to Jessica then how close she was standing to him, how alone they were—and where they were. He was so close to her that she could feel the heat of his body, his head only inches from her breasts. Less than two feet away from her on the other side was his bed, wide and ornate, dominating the room. Her mind went involuntarily to his kisses the other night, to this evening, when he had leaned against her in his momentary weakness, his arm warm and heavy around her shoulders. Jessica could not deny that she had been stirred both times.

If she bent a few inches, her lips would be on his. She recalled quite clearly how they tasted. Abruptly she pivoted, going to the tray that Baxter had set on the small table.

"What are these pots?" she asked, though she had to clear her throat and ask it again when her first attempt to speak cracked.

Reluctantly Cleybourne pulled his gaze from her face and looked at the small pots. "Something to put on the cut, I gather. Miss Brown makes them from herbs. Woundwort?'' He shrugged. ''I've used whatever they've slapped on me for years and seem none the worse for it.''

''All right.'' Jessica opened one pot and smeared a dab of the gooey dark jelly inside it on Cleybourne's cut. Then she applied the dressing plaster and wound a bandage diagonally around his head to hold it.

Cleybourne glanced in the mirror. ''I look as if I had been in a war,'' he said critically.

''It is a difficult place to bandage,'' Jessica pointed out a trifle defensively. ''At least leave it on for the night.''

She washed her hands at the basin and dried them. She should leave now, she knew. There was no further reason to stay.

''Your Grace—''

''You could at least call me Cleybourne, now that you have knocked me in the head. I think we are past titles, don't you?'' He stood up, his eyes on her face. ''It might even be all right to use first names.''

Jessica's chest was suddenly tight; it was hard to look into his eyes this way and still remember to breathe. ''I—it—it would not be proper.''

''And you are always so proper.'' His smile was slow and warm. It licked like fire along Jessica's nerves. ''You have called me a coward and a fool, if I remember correctly. 'Richard' seems mild compared to those.''

He raised his hand to her cheek. His touch was light, his skin searing in its heat. His gaze went to her mouth, his eyes darkening with passion, and his thumb softly traced the curve of her bottom lip. "Jessica."

Jessica's knees went weak. This was what they meant, she thought, when they said someone swooned with ecstasy. It was this constricted airless feeling in the chest, the trembling all over that made one buckle at the knees, the fire in the stomach turning everything below it into flames—and all because of the overwhelming nearness of one person. How could her name on his lips affect her so?

Why did she feel as if the world might end if she did not have his kiss?

His face loomed nearer, and she closed her eyes, engulfed by a thrilling, terrifying eagerness. Then his mouth was on hers, and it was even sweeter than her memory, more tantalizing. Soft, then hard, seeking, then demanding, the pleasure intensifying and spreading with every moment.

Jessica let out a soft animal moan and pressed herself up into his hard body. There was a need in her that she had not known existed until now, a need so intense it was almost frightening. She wanted him to love her, to know her, to claim her with his mouth and hands and body.

Richard wrapped his arms around her tightly, his body jolted with passion at her unfettered response, and he pressed her even harder into himself. He could not remember when he had last felt this wild, this needful. He wanted to sink into her, to thrust deep into her until there was nothing else but this pleasure, no thought or feeling but her.

He sank his hands into the cloud of her hair, gathering the soft, fragrant mass and squeezing it in his fists, feeling it slip like silk through his fingers. He thought of her lying naked on his bed, her hair spread out gloriously around her, all fire and light and softness, and at the thought, desire shuddered through him.

His hands swept down through her hair and over the curve of her buttocks, and he lifted her up into him, grinding her against the hard, aching staff of his desire. He hated the clothes that lay between them, wanted to feel her flesh against his.

Jessica felt the hard length of him and knew instinctively what it meant. There was an answering, throbbing ache between her legs, and she wanted to open them to him, to take him inside her and ease them both.

He walked with her the few feet to the bed, and they hit the edge of it, tumbling back onto the mattress, sinking down into it. The luxurious softness cupped her body. His leg was between hers, tantalizingly touching the hot, throbbing center of her desire. Jessica arched up against his thigh, rubbing against him to ease the ache. He jerked as if someone had touched a red-hot poker to his flesh, and a groan escaped him. His fingers dug into the bedclothes, for he feared that he would bruise her if he touched her now, so powerful was the need to take her, subdue her, crush her beneath him.

He moved against her, unable to remain still, and his mouth left hers to kiss her face, her throat, her ears. His fingers fumbled at the line of buttons down the front of her dress, pulling, unfastening, even tearing at the more recalcitrant ones. His breath rasped in his throat, heavy and animalistic, and he could hear Jessica's ragged breath, arousing him even further. She moaned, moving her pelvis against him.

Something was building in her, something powerful, unstoppable. She wanted him, wanted him inside her, easing the ache, wanted him to *do* something to her, she wasn't sure exactly what. Jessica had never experienced such fevered, desperate, pleasurable sensations. They thrilled and amazed her, creating new and ever-more-hungry desires. With every delightful thing Richard did, the need built in her.

He opened her dress, and his hand slipped beneath it, curving over her breast, caressing and stroking, taking her nipple between his fingers and teasing it into hard, hot life. Jessica sobbed with desire, pressing herself against him, and her hands dug into his hair—painfully, if he had not been too far gone in his hunger to feel the pinch of pain. He cupped one breast in his hand, his hard, callused flesh curving enticingly around hers, so soft and sensitive, and, startling her, he softly kissed the rosy bud of her nipple.

Jessica let out a little sound of something, part need, part satisfaction. Then, amazing her even more, his tongue traced over the button of flesh, teasing it into hardening and prickling. She shivered, wanting more, afraid he would stop, but he did not. Instead, with a sigh of pure pleasure, his mouth settled down over her breast, pulling her nipple into the warm, wet cave of his mouth, stroking and caressing it with his tongue as his lips suckled gently at her breast.

She arched her back, groaning at the sensation of pure, almost unbearable pleasure. As his mouth tugged gently at her breast, moving in a sweet, un-hurried rhythm, his leg pressed firmly into her. Jessica moved against it, the pressure inside her multi-plying, expanding, swelling into something so huge that she was panting and desperate. Her hands dug into her shoulders, and she moaned his name, moving her hips in a mindless, instinctive rhythm.

And then something burst within her, so hard and bright and powerful that she cried out, her eyes flying open with surprise.

Richard raised his head and looked down at her, seeing the astonished pleasure in her face, the faint flush rising up her chest and throat. He knew that she had climaxed, and it filled him with a rush of pride and triumph, and at the same time sent such white-hot desire jolting through him that it was all he could do not to lose control. He looked at her, filled with a jumble of emotions and sensations, aroused almost past bearing at the thought of her passionate nature, her innocence, her untutored, honest response.

But Jessica saw only his stillness, his surprise, and she knew in a rush that she had done something wrong. She let out a little gasp, her hand flying up to her mouth. "Oh, no! I should not!"

She had not behaved as a lady should; she had felt something no lady was supposed to feel. Never in her aunt's talk to her when she was going to marry Darius, never amongst all the words of duty and submission and a man's lower needs, had there ever been any mention of this heady rush of pleasure, this delightful, joyous burst of ecstasy. The marital bed, she had assumed from that one brief, embarrassed lecture, was a place of, at worst, pain and embarrassment, and at best, a necessity quickly over.

Only the depraved, lower sorts of women must feel this, she reasoned, the kind of women who men set up as their mistresses or who, like Leona Vesey, engaged in illicit affairs. Quite frankly, at that moment, Jessica did not care that she was not the sort of woman she should be; that had often seemed to be the case. What she really wanted was to feel that wondrous sensation again, to see what else she could feel, what other tingling sensations awaited her—for there was more to it, she was certain of that. She wanted—oh, a hundred things. To see his naked body, to feel his skin upon hers, to have the tender ache between her legs filled, to see the same sort of pleasure burst in him.

But, looking at Richard, she was sure, with a sudden, horrid sinking sensation, that he was appalled by what she had just done. She had little doubt that his wife would never have been so low, so common, as to moan and rub herself against his leg, all but begging him to take her. Hot anger at the precious Caroline stabbed through her. Caroline would not have shuddered with such wanton, pleasurable release—much less have thought of wanting more… and again….

With a little noise of hurt and embarrassment, Jessica rolled to the side, pulling out from beneath him.

Richard, thrumming with passion, struggling for control, groaned, digging his fingers into the bed to keep from reaching out and grabbing her and pulling her back under him. He wanted to take her, thrust into her, ride out his raging desire until he was spent and quivering in release.

But he had seen the horror leap into her face as Jessica realized what she was doing, what she was about to do. He would be a cad to take her, to rip the remaining shreds of her innocence, to use her passionate nature against her and, in so doing, ruin her name and reputation.

So he stayed, fighting back the desperate hunger, as she slipped from his bed and ran out the door. With a groan, he rolled to his side and cursed long and softly.

12

Richard cursed the snow the next morning. It kept him from spending the day as far away from the house as he could, and that was really the only thing he wanted to do. His head pounded from the blows he had taken the night before—and from the fact that he had not fallen asleep until it was almost dawn. There had been no possibility for sleep when his head was filled with thoughts of Jessica lying in her bed on the other side of his bedroom wall. It seemed to him that Baxter must have placed her there solely to torment him.

It was wrong, he told himself, to feel this way about Gabriela's governess, to want to do with her the things he wanted to do.

However passionate her response had been last night, it was equally clear that she was inexperienced. Virginal. Just as his wife had been when he first brought her to his bed on their wedding night. The fact that Jessica had not reacted with fear as Caroline had did not mean that she would be able to accept lovemaking without regrets or qualms. The distress on her face when she had realized what had just happened to her told him that—and she had not even really known a man yet, had just felt the passion inside herself.

And, Good Lord, what passion it had been! Simply thinking of it brought his blood to a boil all over again. She had been so natural, so untamed, so unwittingly seductive… He could not keep from thinking what her response would be to his undressing her, caressing her, parting her legs and driving deep within her.

He reminded himself that he could not afford to think this way. She was an innocent woman under his care. His desire should be to protect her, not take her into his bed and seduce her. She was not someone like Leona, the sort of woman one could bed and then forget, nor the sort that he could make his mistress, exposing her to the scorn of the polite world. Even if he provided well for her, so that she did not ever have to work for anyone again, she could not live that way, knowing that she was a kept woman, a scandal. No, Jessica was the sort of woman who should have love and a devoted husband—a marriage and children and everything a woman desired.

Richard knew that he could not give her those things. He would never love again. He could not replace Caroline, and marrying a woman who meant any less to him would seem a sacrilege, an insult to Caroline. He felt low and guilty enough that he could feel such desire for another woman—but to marry again? It would be impossible.

So that morning he locked himself in his study and

tried to immerse himself in the account books his manager had brought by. He did not succeed, but at least it gave him an excuse to stay shut away from everyone else all day…even though hardly an hour passed that he did not wonder what Miss Maitland was doing.

What Miss Maitland was doing most of the day was trying to keep a large group of bored and diverse visitors happy—or at least not quarreling. Normally Rachel would have taken over the hostess duties, being the duke's sister-in-law, but the head cold that had threatened the day before had arrived in full today, and she felt feverish, stuffy nosed and generally miserable, so that instead of helping with the guests, she had to be looked after, as well.

Jessica was in and out of her room all day, making sure that Rachel did not need anything and was taking the nostrums that Miss Brown had prepared for her and generally alleviating the boredom of illness. Jessica was fortunate in that Gabriela liked Rachel and did not like the other guests, so she was happy to sit with Rachel through much of the day, talking and sometimes reading to her. Still, keeping a sick person company was not enough to keep Gabriela occupied all the time, and cooped up in the house as she was, she frequently turned to Jessica with complaints that she was bored or restless.

Leona, not surprisingly, seemed to delight in shocking Miss Pargety and tried to get the same sort of rise out of Mrs. Woods, but with little success. Lord Vesey spent most of his time trying to get up various games of chance with the other men, but he, along with the others, began drinking far earlier in the day than was wise, and Jessica was afraid that trouble would result from it. She had had ample experience with men drinking too much in close quarters from being around military men all her life, and she certainly did not want them getting in their cups and starting fights with one another. She wished with some bitterness that the duke would come out of his isolation in his study and tend to the men, at least.

But he did not. She was sure he was too busy regretting his actions of the night before and trying to avoid her to ever emerge from that hideaway. She had known as soon as she realized what she had done that he would turn away from her. She felt sure he was appalled by her wanton behavior, no doubt very unlike that of his wonderful wife. Jessica cast the duchess a dirty look every time she walked past her portrait. The woman was far too lovely for any other woman ever to hope to compete with her, and Jessica was sure that she had not been outspoken or high tempered or shockingly lustful.

Indeed, many times through the day Jessica wished that she herself were not so shockingly lustful, or at least that her memories of Cleybourne's kisses and caresses were less clear. It tortured her, thinking about the way his hand had felt on her or the taste of his mouth…or how fire had shot through her just at hearing the sound of his labored breathing. He had wanted her; she knew it. But she also felt sure that he would not admit it—and certainly would not act on it again. He had made it clear the last time he had

kissed her that he was later horrified at the notion
that he desired her. She knew that he did not want
her, and it was stupid of her to want him. She could
never have him in any way except as his mistress.
He was too in love with his dead wife to remarry,
and if he ever did, it would certainly not be to someone like her, below his station and tainted by scandal.
All he felt for her was lust, and if at times throughout
the day she toyed with the idea that that might be
enough for her, she knew that ultimately it would not
be. However wild her desire might be, she knew herself well enough to know that her emotions lay not
far behind it. She wanted him, and she knew she
wanted him in every way.

Was that love? She wasn't sure. It seemed absurd
to think of loving a man she had known no longer
than she had known the duke, a man, moreover, with
whom she was so frequently in strife. A faint smile
touched her lips as she thought of their arguments.
There was always something compelling about their
rows. They left her feeling strangely invigorated.

She leaned against the wall beside one of the windows, looking out at the cold, white landscape. But
in her mind's eye she was picturing Cleybourne, his
eyes flashing, cheeks flushed with temper as they exchanged words. It made her think of the way his dark
eyes had lit with fire last night. Her breasts felt heavy
and tender as she thought of him on top of her, an-
choring her to the bed. She closed her eyes, wondering what it would be like to feel the full extent
of his hunger, the depths of his passion. There was

the faint echo of that throb again between her legs, the hint of that tender ache.

Grimacing, she opened her eyes and moved away from the wall, irritated all over again by her own weakness and by Cleybourne's undeniable power over her. She strode out of the room, determined not to think about him anymore. Walking down the hall, she stepped into the sitting room, where she found Leona looking amused, Mrs. Woods bored, and Miss Pargety sitting straight in her chair, cheeks pink, whether with anger or embarrassment, Jessica was not sure.

Reverend Radfield was there, too, she noticed, carefully examining his fingers, his face expressionless. He looked up as Jessica entered, and his smile was one of great sweetness. "Miss Maitland. How nice of you to join us. We were just discussing how close it is to Christmas and whether any of us will be able to get to our destinations for it. I personally shall be most sorry if I must miss my first Christmas with my new congregation."

His voice was smooth and educated, his face kind, and for an instant when Jessica looked at him, she thought she detected a faint glint of humor in his eyes, as well. It would be a good thing, she thought, for a man of God to have a sense of humor, especially when dealing with his flock. He was also, she suspected, a liar, since she did not think that Leona was looking sly and Miss Pargety shocked over any discussion of the Christmas holidays. But, she supposed, men of the cloth must also have to be skilled in the art of diplomacy, since she imagined most con-

gregations also contained people who liked each
other as little as Lady Vesey and Miss Pargety did.

"Yes, it would be very sad to miss Christmas,"
Jessica agreed, and it was then that the idea struck
her. "Indeed," she said, "it has just struck me that
we are so near Christmas, and we have not even put
up any Christmas decorations. If you will excuse me,
I must go talk to Baxter."

She found the butler in the main dining room,
checking on the placement of the silverware by one
of the undermaids. "Baxter…"

"Yes, miss." The butler turned to her with a
smile. Though he had been somewhat startled by her
forthright manner at first, he had come to like and
rely on Jessica a great deal, particularly over the past
couple of days, with the bothersome problem of their
many uninvited guests.

"I could not help but notice that there are no
Christmas decorations in the house."

The butler's smile fell away. "No, miss."

"I would not want to add to the servants' burden
at a time like this, but it occurred to me that adding
some Christmas decorations might just lift everyone's spirits. You could send the gardeners and
grooms out to cut down some fir boughs. It isn't far
to the spruce trees in the garden. They would not
have to trek very far through the snow. There are
some holly bushes right by the back door. And the
men are idle, anyway, with the snow. I think everyone would feel better just to smell the scent of them,
don't you? And it would keep the female guests occupied, too. We could make bows from red ribbon

and fashion a mistletoe ball, decorate the mantels and doorways with garlands. Perhaps some of the men could help hang them.''

Baxter looked at first eager, then wistful. ''Oh, yes, miss, it would brighten up the place, and it would, as you said, give people something to do. But…well, we haven't celebrated Christmas here for many years now.''

''Not at all?'' Jessica asked, amazed.

''Oh, His Grace does not deny us our own dinner and Christmas festivities. He gives us gifts on Boxing Day, of course. But he does not want the house decorated. It…hurts too much, you see. There were decorations all over the house when the accident occurred.''

''Oh. That is too bad. Miss Gabriela will be terribly disappointed. Children are so fond of the Christmas celebration.''

''Yes, miss.'' His eyes grew sadder. ''Our own little Alana loved the holidays. I know Miss Brown told you about the tragedy.''

''Yes, she did.'' Jessica paused, then asked, ''Did the duke forbid you to put up the decorations this year?''

''Well, no,'' the butler admitted, looking thoughtful. ''He did so the first year after the deaths, of course, and then the next, when I asked him, he refused in no uncertain terms.''

''Four years have passed,'' Jessica pointed out. ''Perhaps he has simply grown used to not having them. But that does not mean he would object to a few garlands being hung here and there, a few touches of holly and mistletoe. Miss Gabriela and I decorated the General's house every year at this time, and I was thinking how happy it would make her to do so here. It is a very sad time for her, you know, having just lost her great-uncle,'' Jessica added. ''And I am sure the other guests must be feeling a trifle blue, as well, knowing they may miss Christmas with their loved ones.''

''It would be nice for her,'' Baxter mused. ''I suppose it might be all right if I asked the gardener to cut a few branches.'' The older man smiled, and Jessica could see anticipation beginning to shine in his eyes. ''I'm not sure what His Grace would say,'' he hedged, looking torn.

''If he says anything, just tell him that I asked you to,'' Jessica suggested. She was not at all sure Cleybourne wouldn't fly into a taking about the decorations. But she did not think that he would blame Baxter. He would bring his complaints straight to her. And, frankly, right now she did not mind the thought of a little row with the duke at all. It would be far better than his locking himself in his study all day, ignoring her.

''I am sure he will tell me about it if it displeases him,'' she went on confidently.

''Of course, miss.'' The butler turned and hurried off, smiling with anticipation.

It did not take long for the servants to get into the holiday mood. The gardeners and grooms brought in armloads of fir boughs and strands of ivy, and Jessica, Gabriela and Miss Pargety were kept busy most of the day, making bright red bows and knotting them into the garlands, and intertwining holly leaves and ivy, showing clusters of shiny red berries. Even Leona deigned to help, wrapping wire with a ribbon to form an open ball in which to hang mistletoe, which was, she told Lord Kestwick with a sly smile, her favorite holiday plant. Mistletoe was hung in the doorway to the formal drawing room, and garlands were wrapped around the banisters of the stairway and hung over mantels. Soon the air was filled with the refreshing scent of the garlands, and the house took on a festive air. Miss Brown brought out a supply of red wax candles, which they placed about the house, sometimes wrapping a wreath of holly or ivy around the bottom of the candle.

Rachel, waking from an afternoon nap, heard some of the hubbub and came out of her room to find the upper hallway being decorated. She gazed around delightedly at the red candles on the hall tables, the garlands decorating the tops of door frames. After that she insisted on sitting up in bed despite her cold and helping Gabriela twine holly leaves and berries into small wreaths for the candles.

"It's lovely," she told Jessica with a smile. "I cannot believe that you convinced Cleybourne to let you do it."

"I didn't ask," Jessica admitted, a trifle too breezily.

Rachel stared. "He doesn't know?"

"No." Jessica shook her head.

"You are a brave woman."

At that moment there was a bellow from downstairs. "Miss Maitland!"

Rachel and Jessica looked at each other.

Jessica shrugged. "I think he has discovered it."

Looking not the slightest bit worried, she got up and strolled out of the room.

It did not strike Cleybourne right off that the house had been decorated. He had made it almost to the stairs when the scent of the garlands finally sank in on his consciousness. He stopped and for the first time took a hard look around him.

There were garlands of greenery wrapped around the railings, dotted here and there with clusters of holly leaves and berries, and anchored to the fine wood with bright red bows.

He looked at the front door, then the open doorway into the drawing room, where a bundle of mistletoe hung in a wire ball. He swung on his heel and strode back into the Great Hall, through which he had just passed. Garlands of spruce festooned the huge fireplace at the other end of the hall, the one where they had always placed the Yule log. Fat red candles sat atop the mantel of the fireplace, encircled by holly and ivy leaves.

He turned at the sound of footsteps and saw Baxter approaching, looking at him with some trepidation.

"What is the meaning of this?" Cleybourne asked sharply.

"Good afternoon, Your Grace. Would you care for tea?"

"No, I would not. And don't try to distract me. What the devil is all this greenery doing about the house? Did I not tell you I wanted no reminder of

Christmas?'' His voice was cool, but all the fiercer for it, his eyes dark and glittering in a too-white face.

''Ah, actually, no, sir, not this year. It has been some time since you said that, and I thought, especially seeing as we were back here at the Castle, and with the young miss and the other guests—''

''*You* thought?'' Cleybourne's voice deepened with suspicion. ''The devil you did. Why did this thought not occur to you until that bloody governess arrived here? It was she, wasn't it, who put this idea in your head, this mockery of—''

''No, Your Grace! No!'' Baxter cried in a shocked voice. ''No mockery, sir, I would never...''

''I know you would not. Just as you would not have ordered this without my say-so. Somehow that she-devil convinced you to do it.'' When his servant looked uneasily about, not answering, he snapped, ''Answer me! Didn't she?''

The butler was several shades paler as he said, ''Miss Maitland did say as how the young lady would miss the decorations, sir, and her being so sad and all, for her great-uncle. And she thought the decorating might give the, um, guests something to do to while away the hours.''

''Where is she?''

''I—I—the last I saw her, she was upstairs, Your Grace, with Lady Westhampton.''

''She is a fool if she thinks she can escape me by hiding behind Rachel's skirts.'' Cleybourne turned and shouted up the stairs, ''Miss Maitland! Come down here this instant!''

* * *

Jessica did not linger, but neither did she hurry down the stairs. She walked at her usual pace, her face settled into lines of calm, her hands folded together. When she reached the wide staircase, she saw the Duke standing at the bottom of it, hands on his hips pugnaciously, his eyes glittering and dark with fury. Her heart began to beat faster, but she made herself walk down the stairs without haste.

"Did you wish to see me?" she asked collectedly as she neared the bottom step.

"No!" Cleybourne lashed out. Her calm infuriated him. And it was even more infuriating that as he watched her approach, all he was able to think about was reaching out and jerking the pins from her hair, destroying the prim knot at the nape of her neck and sending the fiery mass tumbling down over her shoulders as it had been last night.

"I would much prefer not to see you ever again," he went on. "But you force me to do so. You are everywhere, disrupting everything."

"I am sorry that you think so." As he stood on the first riser of the stairs, Jessica's face was level with Richard's. If she leaned forward, their lips would touch. The thought alone was enough to send a little flicker of desire sizzling through her blood. She hoped that what she wanted was not written on her face.

"Perhaps we should go to your study to discuss this calmly," Jessica continued, turning her gaze upward significantly, to where Mr. Cobb, Miss Pargety and Mrs. Woods were standing at the top of the stairs, watching interestedly. "I think you may be alarming your guests…and servants."

Cleybourne glanced into the Great Hall and saw a knot of servants clustered to one side, looking anxious. "Oh, bloody hell!" he muttered, and stalked through the Great Hall and down the corridor into his study.

Jessica followed him, closing the door after her. She turned to face him. "Perhaps you would like to sit down."

"No, I wouldn't. Damn it, woman, what is the matter with you?"

"Nothing, Your Grace. I am feeling quite well. It is you who seem to be disturbed."

"Yes, I am disturbed. Have you no sense? Have you no shame?"

"Yes, Your Grace, I think am amply endowed with sense. As for shame, I—"

"Damn it!" he roared, cutting her off. "You come here, poking your nose into everything, giving orders with no authority, changing things…."

"I am sorry if I have overstepped my bounds, sir."

"No, you're not. You are not sorry at all. Overstepping your bounds is precisely what you *like* to do. You do it at every turn. Telling my servants what to do. Telling *me* what to do. Damn it, we were all doing very well before you got here!"

"I beg to differ. This house when I arrived was a gloomy, disheartening place, where the servants were worried and sad, and the master of the house was contemplating doing away with himself."

"I was not—" Richard shouted, then cut himself

off abruptly, clenching his jaw and balling his hands into fists. It astonished him how much he wanted to grab Jessica and shake her. Why did she have to be so difficult? So stubborn? So infinitely desirable?

He took a moment to pull himself back under control, then went on in a lower voice. "What I did or did not plan to do is really none of your business, Miss Maitland. Nor are the state of my house and the feelings of my servants, who, by the way, are well treated and quite loyal."

"Indeed, they are," Jessica agreed. "And that is precisely why they are so sad and concerned. They worry about you and your sorrow. They know how low you have been, and how near to—"

"Nonsense!"

Jessica gazed back at him blandly. "How do you think I leaped so quickly to the conclusion that you planned to shoot yourself the other night? It was because of the concern of your servants."

He stepped back, his brows drawing together. "No, they could not know."

"Of course they know. Servants know everything. This house is their world, and you are at the center of it. Their very livelihood depends upon you. Of course they know your moods, your feelings. Moreover, your servants are quite fond of you."

"Not fond enough, apparently, to follow my orders," he retorted. "They knew I did not want these abominable decorations all over the house." He cast a black glance at the holiday greenery over the mantel.

"I would have said cheerful, rather than abominable. However, the fact is that they did not ignore your orders. When I questioned them, it turned out that it was fully two years ago that you had told them not to. So I pointed out that if it were still important to you, you would have told them this year, and since you had not…''

"Miss Maitland, I will thank you not to be educating my servants on ways to get around my orders."

"I merely pointed out that it would be unreasonable to expect people not to celebrate Christmas for years upon end."

"You are treading on dangerous ground here."

"Indeed? Well, Your Grace, unlike your servants, I do not live in fear of you or your moods. And I am certainly not going to pretend that you are reasonable about this whole Christmas issue when you clearly are not."

"My people are not afraid of me."

"No, they are afraid of hurting you. They are afraid of pushing you over the edge. They are afraid—"

"All right! I understand your point. But I am master of this house. I do have the right to decide what will or will not be put up in it."

"You have no right to deny everyone else the joys of the Christmas season. There are your guests to think of, stuck here far from their homes during Christmas."

"I did not invite them. They are a damned nuisance, and I wish they would all leave."

"I am sure you do, but they cannot. So they must

make the best of it, and I would think you could do the same. You certainly do not have the right to deny Christmas joy to Gabriela. She has been through enough. She should not have to spend her Christmas sunk in a black mood simply because you are too selfish to let anyone around you be happy.'' Jessica was warming up to the argument now, her blood pumping fiercely through her, energy flooding her.

"How dare you?'' Cleybourne took a long step toward her, light flaring in his eyes.

Jessica drew herself up, meeting his ire head-on instead of stepping back, and said, "I dare because it is the truth. The sight of Christmas things makes you unhappy, so you forbid them to everyone else in the house. Not just for one year or even two, but for four years.''

"I do not forbid them Christmas. They are welcome to—''

"Where? How? Your servants live here, they work here. There is church, I suppose, where they could find some little bit of cheer and happiness. Otherwise, their only choice is to leave your employ, and they are all far too fond of you for that. However, Gabriela does not work for you, and neither do I. Why should she have to endure the same restricted life that you and your servants do? I see no reason for Gabriela to miss what joy she can find in the Christmas season because you are too coldhearted to allow a few bows and bits of greenery to be hung about the house.''

"A few bows and bits of greenery? The place is covered in them!'' Richard growled. He felt ready to explode with rage. This woman was the greatest damn nuisance he had ever met, and all the time he was looking at her, he kept remembering bits and pieces of the night before—how soft the orb of her breast was beneath his hand, and how her breath had caught in her throat when he toyed with her nipple. He could imagine her legs locked around his back as he sank deep inside her.

Richard whipped around, pacing away from her, struggling to control his voice. Finally he turned and said in a lower tone, "And, may I remind you, while I may not employ Miss Carstairs or you, I am her guardian."

"You have given up your guardianship."

He fixed her with a piercing glare. "Until I have turned it over to someone else, I am her guardian. And you are both residing in my house."

His words hung on the air as Jessica said nothing, merely regarded him for a long moment. Richard began uncomfortably to realize that what he had just said sounded overbearing, even faintly like a threat.

"I realize that we are here on your sufferance," Jessica replied, looking at him in a way that spoke of anything but submission. "And, of course, if you choose to have your servants take down the Christmas decorations, there is nothing Gabriela or I can do to change it. I will, of course, explain your position to Gabriela. However, if you want the *vast* amount of greenery and bows taken down, it is your servants you need to speak to, not me. As you pointed out, I have no control over them. I suggest *you* tell them to take everything down."

Jessica looked back at him challengingly. She thought she knew the Duke of Cleybourne well enough to know that he would not, in the end, have the heart to disappoint his servants by telling them to take down the decorations.

He looked at her narrowly, aware of the pounding in his blood, knowning that if he stayed here much longer, his rage would burst its bounds, and then he would grab Jessica and kiss her and God only knows where it would stop. "The devil with it! Keep your bloody bows and twigs!"

He wheeled and marched across the room, flinging open the door. There, without much surprise, he found a cluster of servants. He gave them a grimace and said, "Oh, finish hanging the damned things!"

He strode off down the hallway, leaving the servants babbling excitedly.

13

It took Jessica a few moments to compose herself enough to leave the study. She knew all the servants would be studying her covertly, and she was determined to look unaffected by her encounter with the duke.

Walking along the corridor into the Great Hall, she nodded to one of the maids dusting a table and continued up the stairs to her room. Once inside her bedchamber, she let out an enormous sigh and sank down on her bed. She thought about the scene that had just taken place, but even as she was remembering just how Cleybourne had looked, her mind was taking in the fact that something was different. Finally the uneasy thought penetrated her consciousness far enough that she stood back up and glanced around the room. Something seemed wrong, but what was it?

Her gaze fell upon the dresser and moved on, then back to the dresser top. *Her jewelry box was not there.* She scanned the room, turning all the way around and coming back to the dresser. It was still empty of any small boxes.

Jessica strode over to the dresser and began to open all the drawers and look inside to see if perhaps a maid, while cleaning, had put the jewelry box away. But she could not find it in any drawer or behind the dresser or under the bed or wardrobe, or anywhere else she could think to look.

It occurred to her that perhaps Gabriela had taken it into her room to play with her jewelry. She had not done that sort of thing in over a year, but it had been one of her favorite pastimes when she was young. She had liked to take out the locket Jessica had inherited from her mother and read the inscription inside, and she had liked to put on Jessica's bracelets and necklace and brooch, or fasten one of her hair combs, decorated with mother-of-pearl, in her own hair.

Jessica went across the hall to Gabriela's room and rapped on the door. When there was no answer, she opened it and looked around. There was no sign of her missing jewelry case. Next she walked down the hall to Lady Westhampton's room, where she found Gabriela sitting in a chair beside Rachel's bed, reading to her. Both of them turned and smiled at Jessica as she walked in.

"Good, you are here," Gabriela said, jumping up. "Lady Westhampton is quite enjoying the book, but I have to go help Miss Pargety with the holly wreaths. I promised her I would come back soon."

"That's fine. I will read to Lady Westhampton, if she likes," Jessica said with a smile at her charge.

"It is very good of you to spend some time with Miss Pargety."

"She's awfully fussy, isn't she?" Gabriela said candidly. "But she is all right, as long as you don't listen very carefully to what she says."

"Gaby…did you take my jewelry box out of my room for any reason?"

Gabriela looked surprised. "No. Why? Is it missing?"

"Yes. I cannot find it anywhere. I thought perhaps you wanted to try on my locket or something."

Gabriela shook her head. "No. I'm too old for that sort of thing nowadays, you know."

"Yes, I know. I just cannot imagine…oh well, I shall look through my room again. Run along and help Miss Pargety. I will sit with Lady Westhampton."

With a grin, Gabriela left the room. Jessica walked over and sat down in the chair beside Rachel's bed. "How are you feeling?"

Rachel heaved a sigh. "Aside from the fact that I cannot breathe without opening my mouth, I suppose I am all right."

"Oh dear, I'm sorry."

"Miss Brown's concoctions help some. Hopefully by tomorrow I will feel better." She paused, frowning a little. "You are certain that your jewelry box is not there?"

Jessica nodded. "Yes. There are not that many places for it to be. I had hoped it was just Gaby borrowing it. But…"

"I cannot imagine any of Richard's servants taking it. They are all good, honest people, and they have worked for him a long time.''

''I know. I have trouble thinking it was any of the maids, too. But there are a number of other people in the house right now, and I am not so sure about them. One or two of them are, frankly, a little havey-cavey.''

''Really? I met only Miss Pargety, when she came in to pick up the bows I made this afternoon.''

''Well, there is a very rough looking man named Cobb. I could believe him capable of almost anything. And Mr. Goodrich is exceedingly nervous all the time. It makes one wonder exactly *why* he is so jumpy. Mrs. Woods is something of an enigma. We don't really know any of them. I suppose one of them could easily be a thief. The thing that is odd, though, is why would anyone have chosen my little box of jewelry? It has a great deal of value to me. It contained a brooch made with my father's hair, and my mother left me a locket that her mother gave to her. It is a heart, and inside it has my grandmother's initials. To me these things are priceless, and I cannot bear to think of losing them. But the case is small and not terribly expensive, and my jewelry is worth almost nothing in monetary terms. I feel sure that any of the other women in this house right now would have more and better jewelry than I.''

''It *is* odd,'' Rachel agreed. ''You ought to speak to Richard about it.''

''I am not sure the duke would be willing to talk to me about anything right now,'' Jessica said wryly.

"He did not take the Christmas decorations well?"

"No, he did not. He was in something of a rage."

"Oh dear." Rachel looked worried. "Perhaps we should have pretended that I told the servants to put them up."

Jessica shrugged. "I can live with his rages. Anyway, I am sure that he would have known I was behind it. You are much too considerate of his feelings to have done it. But he did not cast me out, and he did not tell the servants to take down the decorations, so I suppose it came out all right."

"Really?" Rachel's expression brightened. "Well, that is good, isn't it? He has been in pain for so long, I—" She broke off, then said in a low voice, "Sometimes I feel that we really are a cursed family, and that we bring pain to the lives we touch."

"Oh, no, Lady Westhampton! I cannot believe that."

"Please, call me Rachel. There cannot be formality between us when you have sat here with me all red nosed and watery eyed."

Jessica smiled. "All right, then, Rachel. And I am Jessica. But you cannot believe that your family is really cursed."

"Most of the time we treat it as a jest, but..." Rachel shrugged. "We Aincourts have never been a happy lot. Who knows, perhaps it does all come from that ancestor who drove out the abbot. Or maybe it is just the sin of pride passed down from one generation to the next, beginning with him."

"Pride? Excuse me, but you do not seem one

puffed up with pride. You have been quite kind to me, and you must know that I—"

"What? That you were so misfortunate as to have a father who involved himself in a scandal? It is scarcely your fault, any more than it was mine that my father was a puritanical tyrant who cut his only son out of his life. But it is pride, don't you think, when a family always marries for advancement, never love? We have always made 'good' marriages, you see, in the eyes of the world. Marriages for wealth, for position, for land or name—or almost anything other than for the heart. As a consequence, we have never been happy."

"But your sister—"

"Richard loved her. I know that. I am not as certain that she loved him. Or perhaps I should say I think she found it easy to love a duke. Had Richard been a baron or, God forbid, had no title at all, I am not so sure she would have loved him."

"Oh." Jessica looked at the other woman, pale, her eyes shadowed, looking into a past that obviously brought her little joy. "I am sorry."

"My husband and I have a...a pleasant marriage, I suppose most people would say. He is all that is kind, and he does not deny me anything I wish. I am free to live my own life in London, and he remains on the estate with his books and correspondence and...all the things that matter to him."

"Rachel—" Impulsively Jessica leaned forward, putting her hand comfortingly on top of Rachel's.

Rachel smiled at her a little sadly. "I'm sorry. I am burdening you with our lives much more than I should. It must be the illness. It makes me silly and weak. Michael and I entered our marriage knowing what it was. I loved another man, someone unsuitable—not that there was anything wrong with him, but he had no money, no future of any consequence. My family needed, always needed, money. So I did my duty. Michael did his. And we have been... satisfied with our life.''

Jessica, looking at the sadness lurking in the other woman's eyes, did not believe for a moment that Rachel was satisfied. But she did not dispute it, just squeezed her hand gently.

''I guess that none of our lives turn out as we had thought they would, hoped they would,'' she said. ''We simply make the best of what we get. What else can we do?''

''You are right, of course.'' Rachel gave her a sweet smile. ''And sometimes things turn out even better. Dev married for the family, to keep Darkwater from going under, and they have turned out to be gloriously in love.''

''Well. There you are.''

''Yes. Sometimes miracles happen. And I am very glad one happened to Dev.'' Rachel paused, looking at Jessica intently. ''I hope that a miracle will happen for Richard, as well.''

''I hope so, too,'' Jessica agreed. But she knew, with an inward stab of regret, the if that miracle of love came to the duke again, it was very unlikely that it would involve her.

Supper that evening was no more enjoyable, Jessica found, than it had been the night before. However, it was livelier, since this evening there was the fracas the night before to discuss. There were opposing opinions as to whether the intruder had come from outside or inside the house, as well as to what he had been seeking.

Miss Pargety was certain that it had been an outsider—more from wishful thinking, Jessica guessed, than from any reason—who had come to rob the duke.

"Last night?" Lord Kestwick replied with scorn, raising an aristocratic eyebrow. "Really, what sort of thief would come traipsing through all that snow, knowing it would equally impede his getting away?"

"Yes, my lord, there is that," Reverend Radfiel said pacifically. "But why would anyone staying here rob His Grace, either, knowing he would be stuck here for who-knows-how-many more days? It would seem awfully dangerous to me."

"Ah, but he did not take anything, did he?" Kestwick drawled in his supercilious way, dabbing at the corner of his mouth with a napkin. "Isn't that true, Cleybourne?"

"What?" Richard, who had been watching Darius Talbot sending Jessica long looks, turned blankly to the man at his right.

"The man last night. He did not steal anything, correct?"

"No. I could find nothing missing."

"Well, if he wasn't a thief, then what was he after?" Lady Vesey asked, irritated that tonight she was not the center of attention. No amount of exposed bosom could match the excitement of an intruder.

"I did not say he was not a thief, my lovely Lady Vesey," Kestwick told her with a thin smile. "My theory is that he was searching for what he would like to steal right before he leaves. I feel sure he did not plan to get caught and tip everyone off to what he was doing. What do you think, Mr. Cobb?"

Everyone turned toward Cobb, sitting at the other end of the table. "About what, my lord?" he replied phlegmatically.

"Why, my theory, sir, about the thief."

"Aye, it might be a thief, my lord. As to what he was thinking, I'm afraid I've no idea of that." Cobb's face, while not exactly challenging, was not deferential, either.

"I, uh, I don't like all this talk of thieves," Mr. Goodrich spoke up, surprising them all. Jessica could not remember his saying anything at all the night before at the table; his attention had seemed to be fully occupied by the array of silverware before him. "After all, we do not know it was a thief."

"Very true, Mr. Goodrich," the minister said in his mellifluous voice. Though Jessica had not found that he usually said anything particularly striking, she supposed that his parishioners must enjoy listening to his sermons simply because of his lovely voice. "We do not really know why he was there, and doubtless we should not cast aspersions on the poor man."

Jessica glanced at the duke and saw the corner of his mouth tighten. She suspected that Cleybourne would like to cast a few aspersions—and other things—at the intruder for the nasty gash over his eye.

"Funny thing, all these people breaking into houses," Vesey said idly.

Cleybourne looked at him, his eyes narrowing. "What do you mean?"

"Well, there's been a rash of them recently, hasn't there? I mean, didn't someone break in here a few nights ago? And then there was that night at the General's house."

Jessica frowned. "What are you talking about? When did someone break into the General's house?"

"Oh, 'twas after you left," Vesey said casually.

"What happened? Who was it?"

Vesey shrugged. "Don't know. Do you remember what the innkeeper said, Leona? He was the chap who told us about it."

"I don't really recall," Leona said, her tone expressing a vast disinterest in the matter.

Vesey frowned, obviously exerting his brain. "I think he said they had been in the study or the library or some such place. You know, I think he said nothing was missing there. Odd, don't you think?"

"Definitely odd." Cleybourne's brows were drawn together in a dark scowl. He looked at Vesey, then glanced down the table at Jessica.

Jessica lifted her brows a little, conveying her own puzzlement. She would have named Vesey as the most likely candidate for both the incidents here at the castle. But it seemed bizarre that he would then call attention to the connection between the two—

and to another at the General's house. *What could be the meaning of it? What could he hope to achieve?* On the other hand, she reasoned, given Vesey's apparent mental powers, perhaps he had no purpose at all but was merely blathering. Still, she could not deny the possibility that he brought them up because he had not had anything to do with them and that what he said was simply what had gone through his mind—the oddity of someone breaking into this house twice and the General's, as well, all in a fairly short span of time.

If that were the case, then there was something else entirely going on, and Jessica had no idea what it was. Disturbed by the idea, she continued to mull it over during the rest of dinner, not paying much attention to what else was said. Afterward, as she left the dining room, she was surprised when someone grabbed her arm and whisked her into the music room, quickly closing the pocket door after them. She looked up into the face of her companion, startled.

"Darius! Whatever are you doing? Why did you pull me in here?"

"How else was I to get to talk to you? You have been avoiding me all day," he said almost petulantly. "Whenever I enter a room, you leave. You scarcely speak to me. You will not look at me."

"I thought we agreed to stay out of each other's way," Jessica said, irritation lacing her voice. "That will be the easiest for both of us."

"Not for me. I don't want to avoid you," Darius

protested. "Jessica, when I saw you again…I knew what a fool I had been to let you go."

"Let me go?" Jessica asked, astonished. "As I remember, you tossed me away."

"I know I hurt you," Darius said. "And you have every right to be angry at me. But I am asking you to give me a chance to redeem myself."

"Redeem yourself? Darius, it is a little late for that. It is in the past; there is nothing that can be done about it. You cannot change what happened."

"No, but I can try to make up for it. If you will but give me another chance, Jessica…"

He took a step toward her, and Jessica backed up. "Another chance! Have you gone mad?"

"No! No, I think rather that I have come to my senses. I have missed you all this time, thought about you, wanted you."

Jessica gaped at him. "For ten years?"

"Yes."

"This is nonsensical. I don't know what maggot you've gotten into your head, but the whole thing is absurd. We don't even know each other anymore. I don't want you to 'make up' to me for anything. Yes, I was angry once, but that was long ago. I am not angry still. I—I don't feel anything for you now."

"No! That cannot be true!" Darius exclaimed, surprising her by moving forward swiftly and grabbing her arms. "You can't have forgotten how it feels. Deny it all you want, but you must remember the sweetness of our kisses."

All that sprang to Jessica's mind at his words was how Richard had kissed her last night, and she would hardly term his kisses sweet—searing, perhaps, or stunning, fiery and fierce and hard, branding her very soul, it seemed, but nothing so insipid as "sweet." She blushed a little at her thoughts.

"There!" Darius said triumphantly. "I knew you remembered them."

"No!" Jessica protested, realizing too late what he intended.

He pulled her to him and kissed her. His lips pressed hard into hers, pushing them back against her teeth. Jessica put her hands between them, shoving at him, trying to pull away, but his fingers dug into her arms, holding her still. Finally, in exasperation, she kicked him sharply in the shins.

"Ow!" Darius raised his head in surprise.

"Damn you!" a masculine voice roared behind them, and the next thing Jessica knew, Cleybourne was beside them. He grabbed Darius by the arm and flung him away from Jessica. Darius stumbled, his arms flailing wildly, and fell backward over a sofa, rolling onto the seat and then to the floor in front of it.

"Richard!" Jessica exclaimed in astonishment.

Cleybourne was not listening to her. His eyes fiery, he ran around the side of the couch to reach down and haul Darius to his feet, then swung his right fist flush into Darius's jaw, knocking him down again.

"Richard!" Jessica cried, hurrying around the couch and grabbing his arm before he could punch the man again. "Stop it. Please. You are creating a scene!"

"You think I care?" he asked. "I'll kill this bastard."

"Well, I care," Jessica pointed out, exasperated. "It will hardly do my reputation any good to have the whole household come in here and find you two brawling. Everyone will know what happened."

Richard hesitated, then let his arm fall to his side. "All right." He looked sharply at Darius. "You can thank her for saving your worthless skin. Get up and get out, and if I see you around Miss Maitland again, I won't stop next time. Understood?"

"Yes, yes…" Darius was scrambling away from him as he got to his feet. "Sorry. My mistake. I didn't realize she was your—that you were—"

As Richard's eyes flashed red and he started after the man again, Darius broke off and ran from the room. Richard stood for a moment, still facing the door pugnaciously. Then he made an obvious effort to relax, shaking out his arms, and turned back to Jessica.

"Are you all right?"

"Yes, I am fine. I had no idea he would—I—how did you know?"

"I saw him pull you into the music room. Didn't take much intelligence to know that he was up to no good. I would have been here sooner, but that bloody Pargety female trapped me, whining about the intruder, and I couldn't let her follow me in here."

He strode quickly over to the door and closed it, in case anyone had seen Darius's hasty exit and came to investigate. When he turned around, Jessica had difficulty meeting his eyes, embarrassed by what he had witnessed.

"Thank you," she said stiffly.

"You are welcome. Frankly, it was rather nice to hit something. I have been wanting to for the past three hours."

Jessica could not suppress a smile. "I see. I am sorry."

He shrugged. "You needn't be. I—I should not have yelled at you this afternoon. I am—having these people around tries my temper sorely."

"And here I thought I was the one who tried your temper."

A smile flickered briefly across his mouth. "So you do."

"I am sorry that you had to witness this scene."

"You needn't be. I should have thrown the scoundrel out into the snow as soon as you told me who he was. Do you suppose he might have been the intruder last night?" Richard's expression was suddenly hopeful.

Jessica chuckled. "I am sorry to disappoint you, but I cannot imagine Darius having the nerve to do it. Besides, why would he have been snooping around your study? To steal something? He was not an enormously wealthy man, but he was well enough off."

"Yes," Richard agreed regretfully, "he is too big a fool to have any sort of scheme, to plan a robbery."

"A fool?" Jessica's lips curved up in amusement. "You are, perhaps, a trifle harsh. You scarcely know the man, after all."

The duke grunted. "Don't need to. It's obvious. He broke off his engagement with you because he was frightened by the scandal. Only a fool would do that."

Jessica's eyes flew up to his, startled. "I would have imagined you would not find him foolish to disconnect himself from me. I am, as you may recall, the 'most annoying female' you have ever met."

"Don't turn my own words against me," he said in a mock-stern voice. "You are immensely aggravating. You are also beautiful and passionate." He stopped, his mind going, unbidden, to the night before and the unchecked passion that had flowed through her at his touch, and suddenly he was hot and hard. His eyes darkened involuntarily, and he turned his gaze away from hers.

Jessica saw the look in his eyes before he turned away, and it sent a sizzle through her even as she reminded herself that he had rejected her for that very passion. "He had his career in the army," she said colorlessly. "He could not very well permit himself to be tied by blood to a disgraced officer."

"Any man who chooses a career over a woman's love is a fool," Cleybourne replied shortly. "One has nothing without that." He shifted a little, still not looking at her. "Obviously he has regretted doing it."

"I don't know." Jessica shook her head. "I—it baffles me a little. I have not seen him in ten years. I cannot believe that he has been regretting his action all this time. Why would he never have gotten in touch with me before?" She shrugged. "I think he is probably just bored, stuck in a house with strangers and nothing to do.''

Cleybourne's eyes flashed. ''So he tries to compromise a lady? To reengage her affections? Out of boredom? You should not have stopped me.''

''I don't know,'' Jessica replied honestly. ''But I find it hard to believe that he loves me still.'' She looked at Cleybourne, adding, ''He is not the sort of man you are.''

''Thank you. I would hate to think I resembled Talbot. The man is a worm.''

Jessica smiled faintly. ''Yes. But what I meant, specifically, is that he is not a man of depth. Of loyalty.''

Her words warmed Richard. He had not felt today much like a man of deep feelings and loyalty. He had felt like a man of pure need, hanging on to his control by a thread, guilty and mentally unfaithful. To hear the respect in Jessica's voice was soothing and—as everything about her seemed to be to him right now—also arousing. His hands curled into fists as he said stiffly, ''Thank you.''

He could not understand why every time he was around this woman he dissolved into a mass of confused and scattered emotions, why all his nerves seemed to have risen to the surface, raw and exposed, vulnerable to sensations. For years he had felt cut off from the world, deadened by sorrow, and now suddenly he was all too alive, aware of every passing pain or pleasure.

He spoke, more to remove himself from his

thoughts than anything else. "I do not remember the scandal concerning your father, at least not clearly."

Jessica shrugged. She had talked to almost no one about the scandal that had ripped her life apart. Everyone had shied away from the subject, whether from fear of hurting her, as Viola and the General had been, or from sheer distaste. The ones who had wanted to talk about it with her had been gossipmongers, their eyes bright with curiosity, wanting to dabble in her pain in order to have more grist for their rumor mill. It had remained a hard knot of pain inside her, buried beneath years of living.

She looked at Cleybourne uncertainly, but there was in his face no eagerness, only the understanding of life's pain. For a moment she could not speak, emotion welling up in her throat and closing it. She took a breath, then said, "It was not a very clear thing. He—" She looked away, a little surprised at the pain that pierced her after so many years. "He was cashiered out of the army after years of service. No one said why. Rumors abounded, of course, the favorite being that he had been engaged in treasonous activities."

Her eyes flashed fiercely as she went on. "But he would not! I know he would never have done anything to betray England. He was a man of surpassing loyalty. A soldier through and through. He would never have done anything to hurt his country." She blinked back tears. "He would not tell me why. I asked him. I was hurt and furious about what people were saying. I wanted him to reveal the reason, to prove to everyone that he was not a traitor, that he had done nothing wrong. He swore to me that he had not betrayed the army or the country. He—he told me he was sorry, that he would not have hurt me for the world. And he looked so sad, so stricken, that I could not pressure him more. I told him I believed him, that I trusted him. I did, you see. I still do. I know that, whatever happened, he did not do anything wrong. They were mistaken. They had to be.''

Jessica stopped, her voice choked by emotion. She struggled for control, and as she did, Cleybourne reached out, laying his hand gently on her shoulder. The gesture of comfort was too much for her, and suddenly the tears overwhelmed her. She began to cry, and it seemed as though the more she tried to stop, the more she could not. She sobbed, her shoulders shaking, long-buried emotions pouring out.

''Jessica...'' Instinctively Richard wrapped his arm around her shoulders, pulling her gently against him. She laid her head against his chest and wept, her hands curling into his jacket.

His arms were loose around her, warm and comforting, and he bent his head to hers. She thought she felt the brush of his lips against her hair, but the touch was too brief and soft to be sure. Finally, exhausted by her tears, she stood for a moment longer, leaning into him, supported by his strength, surrounded by his warmth.

Then she pulled back, wiping her tears away with her hands, embarrassed at her own weakness. ''I am sorry. That was silly of me.''

''No. It wasn't silly at all. There is no reason to apologize.''

Jessica shook her head, unable to bring herself to meet his gaze. He had been kind to her, and it had felt so good, so safe and easy, to lean on him. It was, she knew, much too easy, and it was a mistake to indulge herself this way. It would be sheer folly to come to rely on Cleybourne, just as it had been folly last night to give in to the pleasure of his kisses.

"It was so long ago," Jessica said, smoothing back her hair and straightening her dress, fussing over nothing to give herself time to recover. She straightened and looked Cleybourne in the eye, hoping that she appeared once again calm and under control. "It is foolish to even think about it still. And even more foolish to bother you with it."

"You did not bo—"

"I am feeling quite tired," Jessica went on quickly, interrupting him. "If you will excuse me, I think I will go up to my room now."

Cleybourne looked at her, frowning, then gave her a little bow. "Of course. As you wish, Miss Maitland."

Jessica turned and left the room, her steps moving faster as she went, until by the time she reached her room, she was almost running. Inside, she knew, she *was* running—from the very real danger that the Duke of Cleybourne represented. If she was not alert, if she was not careful, there was the very real possibility that she would find herself falling in love with Richard. And that would be the greatest folly of all.

14

Jessica awoke with the sort of headache that she got from crying herself to sleep, which, she supposed, was only natural, given that that was what she had done. She dipped a washrag in cold water and lavender, and lay for a few minutes with it on her eyes to bring down the puffiness. Then she arose and dressed, feeling that she would like nothing so much as to return to her bed and lie in it all day, wallowing in self-pity, but she was determined not to. She refused to live her life in regrets and what-ifs. Her life was as it was, and she could not change the fact that she would never be considered a proper candidate for a duchess any more than she could change the fact that the Duke of Cleybourne was still in love with his dead wife. All she could do, she told herself, was go on with her life, enjoying it as it was and making sure that she did not make the mistake of allowing herself to fall in love with Richard.

To that end, she avoided him most of the day, spending the bulk of her time in the schoolroom with Gabriela or in the sickroom with Rachel. When she unavoidably came face-to-face with him because she was in Rachel's room playing a game of cards with her and Gabriela, and he entered the room to check on Rachel, she quickly turned her hand over to him and excused herself, saying that she had to check on the guests.

She caught the odd glance he sent her way, but she pretended not to notice as she slipped out of the room and made her way downstairs. To avoid having lied, she did look into the various public rooms to make sure that none of the visitors needed anything. She soon wished that she had not. Except for Darius Talbot, who turned pale and left the room as soon as she entered it, everyone seemed to have something to say.

Miss Pargety had had trouble sleeping because, as she put it, people had been parading in and out of their rooms all night, closing the doors. Lord Kestwick was petulant and bored, having grown weary of playing games of chance with Lord Vesey and, Jessica presumed, of flirting with Lady Vesey. Mr. Goodrich wanted to know when they would be able to leave, and Mr. Cobb, as always, seemed vaguely threatening. Mrs. Woods was restless, drumming her fingers on the arm of her chair and turning peevish when Jessica tried to engage her in conversation. Even Reverend Radfield, usually a person one could count on to supply pleasant conversation, seemed subdued. Only Leona, oddly enough, had no complaints. She looked like the cat who had got into the cream, which led Jessica to believe, cynically, that she had spent the night with someone other than her spouse.

Jessica was glad to leave the uninvited guests and return to her room. She was surprised when she walked into her bedchamber to find one of the maids there, a freckle-faced girl named Flora, sitting on the edge of a straight chair, a small sack in her lap. Flora jumped to her feet as soon as Jessica entered, and the worried look on her face grew deeper.

"Miss Maitland," she began. "Baxter said as I was to bring this to you." She extended the bag to Jessica, looking apprehensive. "I found it in the music room, tucked down behind a chair. This is the way I found it."

Her curiosity aroused, Jessica took the sack from the girl and opened it, peering down into it. There were several pieces of wood inside, broken and splintered, as well as bits of metal and pieces of jewelry. She stared, then let out a little cry of distress. "My jewel case!"

Flora nodded unhappily. "Yes, miss. I recognized it from cleaning your room, but I don't know what it was doing there or why—why it's all to pieces like that."

Jessica reached inside and pulled out a handful of the objects inside—a brooch, a necklace, an earring, two or three pieces of wood that had once been part of the decorative box. She walked over to her bed and dumped the rest of the contents out onto the mattress. She bent over the pieces, separating her meager jewels from the broken bits of the box. It did not take long to see that only one earring was missing.

"I don't understand...."

"Nor me, miss. I'm right sorry that happened to the little box. It was a pretty thing."

"Yes." Tears filled Jessica's eyes. "My father gave it to me when I was Gabriela's age." She sighed. "I noticed yesterday that it was gone from my room, and I could not imagine what had happened to it." She looked back at the mess on the bedcover. "I still cannot. Obviously no one took the jewelry, or at least nothing but one earring, and I suspect that just got lost somewhere. Why would anyone steal a jewelry box and then take none of the jewelry? And why did they smash it up like this? It was not even locked."

"I don't know, miss. It's that strange. I couldn't understand it, neither—or why it was in the music room like that. I took it straightaway to Baxter, it being so odd, but he couldn't make heads nor tails of it, so he told me to bring it to you."

Jessica turned back to the box, trying to arrange the pieces of wood back into a recognizable form. It was impossible. The thing had been smashed beyond repair. It made her shiver to think of what anger had lain behind the destruction of such a small and innocuous thing.

"I suppose that someone must have stolen it and then, when they found out how little of value was in it, they were furious and smashed it," she mused. *Or had it been destroyed out of sheer hatred for her, taken and broken for no other reason than because it was hers?* That idea made her feel decidedly uneasy.

"Mayhap, miss," Flora replied, then added, "'twasn't none of us, miss. All the servants like you, they do, and none of us would steal anything, anyway."

"No, I never thought it was one of you."

They looked at each other, considering the alternative, that it was one of the guests. Finally Flora said, "It was a wicked thing, miss."

"Yes, I am afraid you are right."

The maid bobbed her a curtsy, reiterating how sorry she was, and left the room. Jessica sat down on the bed and looked thoughtfully at the remnants of her jewelry box. There were some decidedly odd things going on around here. She could not help but wonder what lay behind it all. She remembered Miss Pargety's words about people going in and out of their rooms the night before. The duke had said something similar to that the night he had found the intruder in his study. She did not understand what any of it had to do with the rest of it, including her destroyed jewelry box, but she would certainly like to find out who had entered the schoolroom that night, as well as who had ruined the jewelry case that was dear to her heart.

The first thing to do, she decided, was to sit up tonight and keep watch, see exactly who was leaving their rooms and where they were going. She could sit at her door with it cracked open, but then she decided that she would be able to see better if she was farther down the hall. There was a spot near the stairs where she might be able to hide well enough between a large potted plant and a table, and she would have a better view of all the rooms from there. She would wear a plain dark blue dress, she thought, and soft slippers, so she would be neither seen nor heard. If only there was some way she could keep her pale face from showing. She thought a little wistfully of tying a dark scarf over her face as the intruder had, then discarded the idea. If someone found her, she might be able to explain being in the hall; if she was found with her face masked, it would be rather difficult.

The more she thought about it, the more she liked the plan. Jessica was always one who preferred to take action rather than sit around waiting for things to happen to her. She spent the evening in anticipation, doing all the things she normally did with her mind only half on them and the rest of it on what lay ahead. She listened to Gabriela's chatter about the day and Lady Westhampton and how much fun it had been to play cards with her and the duke, then dressed for supper and stopped by to look in on Lady Westhampton before she went downstairs.

The meal was much the same as always: the food excellent and the dinner guests less than pleasing. But tonight Jessica paid more attention than usual to the conversation, studying each of the guests and wondering what, if anything, they had to do with the mysterious events. She could feel the duke's eyes upon her now and then, but she did not look at him, for fear he might read something in her face that gave away the fact that she had something planned for tonight.

Afterward, she slipped away and went to her room, where she tried to lie down and catch a little sleep before the others went to bed and she could begin her watch. However, she was too excited to be able to sleep, and after a while she got back up and dressed in the darkest dress she had. She brushed her hair out and left it hanging loose about her shoulders, reasoning that if she kept her head down and let her hair fall around her, she could keep much of her white face hidden behind the darker curtain of her hair.

Once she was ready, she sat down in the straight-backed chair close to the door and opened it a crack to keep an eye on the hallway. It was silent out there, and before long she saw one of the footmen walk by on his evening round, snuffing out the candles that lit the hallway during the evening. The corridor grew dark behind him. Jessica continued to wait, leaning her head against the wall and peering out through the crack of the door.

She opened her eyes, blinking, and realized, with some chagrin, that the sleep which had evaded her so successfully earlier had come upon her. She was not sure how long she had dozed or exactly what had awakened her. The hall outside her door was dark and still, with no sign of anyone moving through it.

Jessica opened her door wider and stuck her head out, looking up and down the hall. She saw no sign of anyone, so she stepped out of her door and closed it silently behind her. Head down to hide her face, she glided noiselessly down the corridor. She had almost reached her hiding spot when she thought she heard a noise behind her. Just as she started to turn her head to look, an arm went around her tightly from behind, pinning her arms to her sides and pulling her hard against a man's body, and a hand clamped down over her mouth.

Fear shot through her, and she stiffened. In the next instant she felt someone's breath against her ear, and a low voice murmured, "It is I, Richard. Don't scream."

Jessica sagged against him in relief and nodded her head. He released her and took his hand from her mouth, and she turned to find him watching her with a wry expression. He was dressed all in black, his usual white shirt and ascot replaced now by a simple black shirt, collarless and open at the throat. Taking her by the hand, he pulled her back a few steps along the hall and into an alcove. There was a padded bench stretching across the width of the alcove, almost filling it, and above it in the wall was a narrow window set with the thick opaque glass popular in Tudor times. Moonlight filtered in through the glass, lighting the small recess dimly. Cleybourne gestured toward the bench, and Jessica sat down on it. He sat beside her and reached out to either side of the doorway in front of them and pulled two pocket doors out of the walls, closing them across the open doorway of the alcove. The doors were made of open woodwork, creating a grill through which one could see, but which kept the alcove hidden.

Jessica glanced around her in surprise. "I didn't

even know this was here,'' she whispered. She had walked past the wooden grillwork many times but had not realized that anything lay behind it.

Richard nodded and leaned closer. ''It was part of the castle's defenses originally, a place for an archer to stand and fire out.'' He indicated the narrow window above them. ''Later they filled it in with glass and made this embrasure a place to sit. Later, some secretive soul put in the doors.''

Jessica nodded. She glanced at him; he was looking back at her. He raised his eyebrows questioningly. ''Are you going to tell me what you were doing?''

Jessica sighed. ''I was going to hide close to the stairs, by the potted plant, and keep watch.''

''For what?''

Jessica arched one eyebrow at him. ''For the same thing you are watching for, I imagine. There is something strange going on, and I want to find out what it is.''

''I suppose there is no way I can convince you to go to your room and allow me to keep watch.''

Jessica could not hold back a grin as she shook her head. ''I have something at stake here.''

He raised an eyebrow, saying, ''And what might that be?''

Before she could answer, there was the sound of a door opening in the hall, and both Richard and Jessica leaned into the screen, gazing through its carved curlicues, first one way and then the other. Two doors down, a woman dressed in a dark dressing gown stepped out quietly into the hall and closed the door behind her. It was Leona Vesey, her tawny hair loose and curling invitingly over her shoulders.

She looked up and down the hall, then moved quietly along it, stopping at a door and tapping so softly that Jessica could not hear it, only see the movement of her hand. The door opened to reveal a man dressed in breeches and a shirt, the shirt open and hanging outside his pants. The man was the Reverend Radfield.

He reached out, smiling at Leona, and took her by the wrist and tugged her inside. Leona went willingly, with a little giggle, coming up against his chest. He closed the door behind her.

Jessica turned, astonished, to Cleybourne. He looked back at her, then shrugged. They returned their gazes to the hallway. For the next few minutes, nothing happened. Jessica, keeping her eyes straight ahead toward the doors, was very aware of Richard's presence beside her. His large body filled the little room, his shoulder so close to hers they were almost touching. She could feel his warmth, smell the scent of shaving soap and male body that was uniquely his, hear the sound of his breath.

It occurred to her that being with him like this was hardly in keeping with the decision she had made to avoid him. Sitting here together in the darkness was far too intimate. Whenever he leaned closer to whisper in her ear, his breath brushed her hair and skin, sending little tendrils of desire snaking through her. She could not keep her mind from turning to his kisses of the other night and the delightful sensations that had flooded her at his touch. Jessica told herself that she should go back to her room; she was putting herself right in the path of danger.

A noise in the hall made her jump. She peered out and saw Lord Vesey close his door and saunter down the hall. He was moving toward Gaby's room, and Jessica felt Richard tense beside her as Vesey stopped outside Gabriela's door. He reached out, took the doorknob in his hand and turned it. Richard and Jessica rose to their feet, ready to burst through the door and down the hall.

The doorknob turned and stopped. It was locked. Jessica let out a sigh of relief and sank back to the bench as Vesey shrugged, letting go of the knob, and strolled back down the hall. He turned onto the stairs and disappeared down them.

"Where is he going?" Jessica whispered.

"I have no idea. Perhaps I should follow him. You could stay here to watch and—"

He broke off, for another door had opened. He and Jessica turned once again to look. This time it was Mrs. Woods who had left her room. She, like the others, glanced up and down the hallway, then started off.

"This is like a French farce," Jessica muttered.

Mrs. Woods stopped in front of a door only two doors away from them. Because the door lay on the same side of the hallway, they could not see who opened it, but they heard the sound of it opening, and Mrs. Woods passed through it.

"Who was it?" Jessica asked.

"I don't know. I couldn't see him. But that door belongs to Kestwick's room."

"So Lady Vesey has an assignation with the minister, and Mrs. Woods is rendezvousing with Lord Kestwick. I wonder if Lord Vesey was meeting someone downstairs."

"There is no one young enough for him except Gaby, and he already failed there." Richard sighed. "Unfortunately, I cannot see how a few romantic assignations could have caused someone to break into the study. Which makes it more likely that it is Vesey."

He glanced out into the hall. "I am half-afraid that if I go in pursuit of him, I shall run into someone, there has been so much traffic in the hall," he said dryly, then stood up. "Well, I shall venture downstairs after him. You keep watch."

Jessica nodded, and Richard slipped silently out the door. He was gone from sight in a moment. She waited, watching the dark corridor, but nothing happened. She wondered what Richard was doing, if he had found Vesey. Minutes inched by. Just as she was beginning to think of going after Richard, a dark shape appeared at the top of the stairs. Her heart began to pound violently, but then as it turned and made its way stealthily down the hall, Jessica recognized it as Richard.

He came down the hall toward her. There was the crack of a door opening. Richard whirled and looked over his shoulder, then quickly took a few more steps and ducked down between the potted plant and the table, where Jessica had originally intended to hide.

Jessica watched as Mrs. Woods once more came into view. She walked to her door, which lay almost directly across from where Richard was hiding. Jessica held her breath, afraid that the woman would glance over and see him.

But she did not, merely went to her door, opened it and walked inside. Richard stood up and hurried the rest of the way down the hall to the alcove. He opened the door and stepped in, flopping onto the bench beside Jessica.

"Thank God," Jessica said in a low voice. "I thought you were caught."

"So did I. I was wondering how I was going to explain to Mrs. Woods what I was doing in my own house, hiding behind potted plants and spying on people."

Jessica smiled. "It does seem somewhat absurd." She leaned closer, whispering, "But what of Vesey? Did you find him?"

"Yes." His tone was filled with disgust. "The fellow's lounging in one of the chairs of my study, drinking my port. Insolent bastard." He glanced at Jessica. "Beg your pardon."

"No need," Jessica replied absently. "It doesn't seem likely, does it, that he would be there so coolly now if he had been ransacking it in the dark two nights ago."

"God knows what Vesey would do." He was silent for a moment, then said softly, "Why were you avoiding me today?"

"What?" Jessica glanced at him, then away. "I was not."

"Everywhere I went today, you were not there." Richard had spent much of the day drifting about the house, not even realizing that he was looking for her until he walked into Rachel's room and his chest had felt suddenly lighter upon seeing Jessica there. Then she had left immediately, scarcely giving him a look.

Jessica looked at him coolly. "I was doing what I am employed to do—instructing Gabriela."

"I see. Yet that scarcely explains why you would not look at me at supper tonight." He leaned closer to her, and when Jessica turned to answer him, she found his face only inches from hers.

She froze, unable to move, unable to think, aware of nothing but how intensely she wished he would kiss her. Heat blossomed in her abdomen, just thinking of it. "Please…"

There was a faint tremble to her voice, a vulnerability, that stabbed him with lust even as it made him want to wrap his arms around her and protect her. "Jessica…"

He laid his forefinger against her cheek, slowly sweeping it down over her silken skin. Jessica closed her eyes as pleasure washed through her. She knew she should stop him, should protest, but her tongue seemed stuck, her lips unable to move.

"You are so beautiful." He spread out his hand, cupping her cheek. "So passionate. The other night, I—"

"No," Jessica choked out, flushing at his words. "Please, don't. I know I was—I am so ashamed that I—"

"No! Don't say that. Don't think it. You did nothing wrong," he said, his voice low and fierce. "*I* was the one who was wrong. I was a—a cad to act as I did, to kiss you when I had no right. You did nothing wrong. You were lovely...desirable...you were everything a man could want.'' His hand slid caressingly back into her hair.

Her curls twined around his fingers, clinging and soft, catching against the rougher surface of his skin, sending desire slithering along his nerves. Jessica looked up at him, her eyes dark pools, and he had trouble remembering the thousand reasons he must not kiss her. All he could think of was how soft her breasts had been in his hands, how delicious her skin had tasted on his tongue, how trustingly she had given herself up to him, dissolving in passion when he had barely begun to pleasure her. He thought of what she would be like when he explored her body fully, when he showed her how much more awaited her, of how she would shake, her skin like fire, and cry out her release.

''Jessica...'' His voice was thick with desire as he bent and kissed her.

He heard her little sigh, felt her breath in his mouth, and he shuddered, burying his lips deeper in hers. His hands went to her shoulders, digging in, pulling her to him. Jessica's arms went around his neck, and she kissed him back, her tongue twining with his. The blood thrummed through her veins, pounding in her head. Her breasts felt fuller and tender, and she knew that she wanted to feel his hands on them. She was aware that she was acting shamelessly, that she must be a horribly wanton woman, but at the moment she did not care. The only thing that mattered was the desire coursing through her.

Her hands caressed his back, exploring the hard muscles beneath his shirt. She slipped her hands over his shoulders and down his chest. She heard his quick indrawn breath of pleasure as her fingers caressed him, and the sound aroused her even further. Jessica remembered his lips on her skin, and suddenly she wanted to taste him the same way, to kiss and caress him. Her fingers went to the top buttons of his shirt, unfastening them, and her hand slipped in under the material, gliding over the bare skin of his chest.

Richard jerked, a low moan escaping him, and Jessica hastily started to withdraw her hand. But he clamped his hand over hers, stopping the movement. ''No,'' he murmured, his breath coming raggedly. ''Don't stop.''

He kissed her cheek and ear and throat as Jessica explored his chest. Her fingertips slid over the smooth skin, padded by muscle, and dipped down to find the flat masculine nipples. She circled one with her fingertip, pleased by the discovery that it tightened and hardened with desire just as her own did. Her fingers raked through the triangle of curling hairs that centered on his chest and moved lower, following as it narrowed into a single line going down to his stomach. His shirt impeded her movements, and she stopped, frustrated, but he quickly unbuttoned it the rest of the way, allowing her hand to drift farther down.

Richard let out a soft groan as Jessica placed her hands on his stomach and moved them apart, opening

the sides of his shirt. She pushed at his chest, and he
gave in easily, leaning back until he touched the wall.
She moved in, bending over to place her lips lightly
against the center of his chest. He made a soft noise,
his hands curling into fists, but he did not move
away, so Jessica was emboldened to continue. She
kissed her way across his chest until she reached his
nipple, and there she ran her tongue around it as he
had done to her. He dug his hands into her hair,
squeezing handfuls of it. Softly Jessica began to
suckle. He stiffened, but when Jessica started to lift
her head, he held her down.

She smiled against his flesh, aroused by his response to her, and moved to the other side to begin
to work on that nipple. She teased him with her
tongue, delighting in the way his breath caught and
his skin flamed when she touched some point that
particularly aroused him. Her hands went around him
and up his back under his shirt as her mouth finally
fastened onto the nipple. He shuddered, groaning her
name, and he reached down, undoing the buttons of
her dress and thrusting his hands beneath her chemise, gathering her breasts in them.

Suddenly he pulled her over on his lap so that she
straddled him, and he buried his face between her
breasts. Cupping the full white orbs in his hands, he
feasted on them. Moisture flooded between Jessica's
legs. She could feel the length of his desire pulsing
against her through their clothes, and she moved instinctively against him, seeking to ease the ache that
grew there, hot and soft and vulnerable. His hands
went down to her skirts and moved up under them,

gliding up her thighs until they reached the curve of her buttocks, and his fingertips dug into the soft flesh.

It was at that moment that a scream ripped through the air.

15

Jessica and Richard sprang apart at the sound, and for an instant they stared at each other, stunned.

Richard jumped to his feet and threw the doors open, running out into the hall. Jessica was right on his heels. They ran toward the staircase, where it seemed the sounds had come from, Jessica hastily buttoning up the front of her dress. All around them, up and down the hall, doors were opening, and there was the excited buzz of voices. Richard reached the top of the stairs and stopped, and Jessica jerked to a halt beside him. Both of them looked down the long flight of stairs to the bottom. Jessica's stomach turned, and her head was suddenly light.

A dark-haired woman lay at the bottom of the stairs, her navy-blue gown tangled around her. Her head was turned to the side at an unnatural angle. It was Mrs. Woods.

Richard's hand went around Jessica's arm, his finger biting into her flesh. "Don't you faint on me now."

Jessica nodded slightly. "I won't. I'm all right."

Richard started down the stairs, Jessica behind him. At the bottom of the stairs, he knelt beside the body and, unnecessarily, took the woman's wrist in his hand and felt her pulse. It was clear her neck was broken. Jessica stood, looking down at Mrs. Woods' lifeless body. She was so pale in death.

There was a wordless cry above them. Jessica turned and looked up. The guests were crowded together at the top of the staircase, all gazing down in stunned astonishment. It was Reverend Radfield who had made the noise. He stood frozen, staring, his face white and stamped with horror.

"Reverend Radfield…" Jessica said.

For a moment the man did not move; then he turned and looked at her blankly. Jessica nodded significantly at Mrs. Woods. His eyes turned back to the body and returned to Jessica, still uncomprehending.

"A prayer?" Jessica suggested.

"What? Oh! Yes. Yes, of course." He started down the stairs, holding on to the banister for support.

Jessica supposed that he had never seen anyone die a violent death before, given the way he looked. Surely a minister would have seen dead bodies before, but they were, no doubt, tidier than this.

He sank down onto his knees beside Mrs. Woods and picked up her hand, holding it between his. He began a stumbling recital of the Lord's Prayer, then sat back on his heels, wiping at his cheek with the heel of his hand. "'She should have died hereafter,'" he murmured, and laid the woman's hand back on her body. He stood up and walked over to the side, sitting on one of the steps and leaning against the railings.

Lord Vesey came around the stairs from the Great Hall, carrying a candle, and stood, swaying slightly, looking down at the woman. "Good Gad," he said blankly. "What the devil happened here?"

"Did she fall?" asked a woman's voice from the top of the stairs. Jessica turned to look. It was Rachel, standing with her arm comfortingly around Gabriela.

"I don't know." Richard rose to his feet, frowning. "She obviously took a tumble down the stairs, but I don't know if she slipped—or was pushed."

There was a collective gasp from the top of the stairs.

"The devil!" Lord Kestwick snapped. "Why would you say that? Who would have pushed her? Why? Clearly she tripped and fell."

"At this hour of the night? It is a little late for her to be traipsing down the stairs." Richard walked over to Lord Vesey and took the candle from him, bringing it back to the body and once again crouching beside her. "There is a cut here on her cheek, and it is red around it. It seems to me that might have been made when someone hit her, sending her backward down the stairs."

Miss Pargety began to wail, and Lord Kestwick said pettishly, "Now see what you've done."

"That's nonsense!" Leona exclaimed. "Richard, you are being melodramatic. Why couldn't she have hit her cheek as she tumbled down the stairs and cut it?"

"It is possible, I suppose…" Richard looked up at the group on the stairs. "Did anyone see her fall?"

He was met with intense silence. He nodded shortly. "All right. I think we have to treat this as if it might have been done deliberately. We are snowed in. We cannot reach the village to fetch the magistrate. Therefore, for the time being, I am going to take charge of the matter."

He raised his head and looked around him, catching sight of Baxter and the other servants, who had gathered in a small huddle at some distance from them. "Baxter, give us some light. Get blankets and wrap up the body." He paused. "For the time being, given the weather, the best thing would be to place her body in one of the outbuildings. Lock it securely."

"Yes, Your Grace."

"We need to get down all the facts we can right now," Cleybourne went on, speaking to the guests. "I am sure that none of us would be able to go back to sleep now, anyway. All of you go into the drawing room." As one or two of them started to turn away, he added quickly, "Don't go back to your rooms, just down to the drawing room. Baxter—" he turned to his butler "—send a couple of the footmen up. They can escort everyone to the formal drawing room by the back stairs."

"Very well, Your Grace." Baxter spoke to the servants, and two of the burlier footmen started up the stairs toward the knot of people, carefully skirting the body lying at the foot of the steps.

"Now see here, Cleybourne," Lord Kestwick

snapped, his face flushing. "Just what do you think you're doing? I don't intend to be shuffled around by your servants. I am going back to my chamber, and—"

"No!" The word cracked through the air like a whip. Cleybourne faced Kestwick, his face like stone, and he was suddenly every inch a duke. "No one is to return to their room. You are all going to the drawing room to wait, and I will speak to each of you in turn. There has been a death in this house, and I do not intend to let that go without investigating it. As long as you are in my house, you will do as I say, and I don't believe there is much possibility of your leaving here right now."

"How dare you!"

"Do you intend to challenge me, Kestwick?" Cleybourne asked softly, and he took a step up the stairs, his hands knotting into fists.

Kestwick's gaze went to Cleybourne's fists, then cut away. He pressed his lips together and inclined his head slightly toward the duke. "No. Of course not. It is, as you say, your house."

"But, really, Richard, is this necessary?" Leona whined.

"Yes, my lady, it is." Mr. Cobb spoke up suddenly, surprising everyone. He came forward through the crowd. "The duke has the right of it. There's something odd about this death, and that's the God's truth of it."

"What do you know about it?" Darius Talbot asked scornfully.

"Quite a bit, as it happens," Cobb replied calmly.

He looked down at Cleybourne. "I'm a Bow Street Runner, Your Grace, and I'm offering my services to you in this matter."

"A Runner!" Goodrich squeaked.

Miss Pargety gasped and put one hand to her throat dramatically. Gabriela looked at the man with new interest. Jessica felt an urge to let out a faintly hysterical giggle. Of all their guests, she would have guessed that the most likely to be a criminal was Mr. Cobb, and he had turned out to be an officer of the law!

Cleybourne assessed the man for a moment, then said, "Very well, Mr. Cobb, I accept. If you will go with the others to the drawing room, then escort them one by one to my study, you and I will question them there."

Cobb nodded. "Done, Your Grace."

He turned and started to herd the guests before him along the hall toward the back staircase, assisted by the footmen. Lord Kestwick looked as though he was about to protest again, but Cleybourne quelled him with a look.

Jessica walked over to where the Reverend Radfield still sat on the steps, leaning against the railing and staring down at his feet. Jessica leaned over and touched his shoulder, saying quietly, "Reverend..."

He looked up at her vaguely.

"You need to go with the others." Jessica pointed up to the top of the stairs, where the other guests were trailing along toward the back stairs.

"What? Oh." He grasped the banister and pulled

himself up, then turned and started up the stairs after them.

Jessica turned back to Cleybourne. His eyes softened a little as she walked up to him. "I suppose now you are going to challenge my authority, as well," he said without rancor.

"Oh, no, I would never do that," she replied, smiling up at him.

She knew it was probably quite wrong of her and showed that she lacked the sensitivity a genteel woman should have, but, however sad and upset she felt about Mrs. Woods' sudden death, she could not keep from feeling warm, even happy, when she looked at Richard's face. Was that love? she wondered. Had she already fallen into the trap she had sworn she would avoid? Or was it merely the leftover glow of the lust she had felt in his arms just a few minutes ago in the alcove? Whatever it was, she noticed that he smiled back at her.

"I was just going to point out," Jessica went on, "that you would need someone to take down what the others say to you. So you will have something to show the authorities once we are able to get out."

"Yes, you are right." He paused, then said, "And I don't suppose that you know anyone who is adept at writing things down quickly and accurately?"

"As it happens, I used to help the General write his memoirs. He would tell me what he wanted to say, and I would write it down. I developed a few little codes to make my writing quicker."

"Very well, then." He surprised her by taking her

hand and squeezing it briefly. "To tell the truth, I would value having your judgment."

Inside, Jessica could feel the glow his words brought to her. She was unaware of how it lit her eyes, but Richard saw it and was struck all over again by her beauty. He wanted suddenly and quite fiercely to pull her to him and hold her for a moment, but he was well aware of the presence of the servants at the foot of the stairs, so he did not.

"Perhaps you would prefer to go to the study by the back stairs, also," he suggested. "I am going to place a footman on guard at the door to Mrs. Woods' room. I think it might be a good idea for us to look it over after we talk to everyone else."

A few minutes later they were set up in the study, Jessica at Cleybourne's desk with paper in front of her and a sharp pen in the inkwell, and Richard seated in front of the desk in one of the two chairs. The guest of the moment would sit in the other chair, facing him, while Mr. Cobb had been allotted a chair by the door, apart from the others but with a good view of the face of the person being interviewed.

Mr. Cobb started toward the door to bring in the first person, but Richard stopped him. "Wait. Mr. Cobb, before we start, I think we should clear up something first."

"Oh. You'd be wanting to see my credentials, I warrant." The man reached into a back pocket and brought out a paper, which he handed over to the duke.

Richard perused it and handed it back to him. "I

think, considering the circumstances, I have a right to know exactly what you are doing here and why. You did not arrive on the stagecoach. Did you plan to come to this house before the snow came? Who are you working for?''

The Bow Street Runners, Jessica knew, were hired by private citizens to find out who had committed a crime.

''I don't mind telling you, Your Grace,'' the thickset man answered easily. ''It were a Mr. Joseph Gilpin that hired me, a rich cit in London. He had some expensive jewelry stolen from his home, and he set me to find it. He suspected the theft was done by a middle-aged dancing master he had hired to teach his daughters. I had reason to believe he had taken the mail coach to York, so I was following him.''

''You mean—the very coach the other guests arrived here in?'' Jessica asked.

Mr. Cobb glanced at her and shrugged. ''Mayhap, miss. I had reason to think so. He couldn't have got away much earlier. If he was on the coach, then he's here in this house. Personally, I've got a notion it might be that Goodrich chap. He's a nervous sort. Always does his best to keep as far away from me as ever he can.''

''I see.''

''Course,'' Cobb went on philosophically, ''if the fellow did happen to catch a coach the day before, then I've lost his trail right proper, what with the snow stopping me.''

''A thief…'' Richard mused. ''Then do you think Kestwick might have been right the other night at supper when he said it was a thief in my study that night? That he was looking it over to decide what he might steal?''

"Well, he's an audacious one, he is,'' Cobb said. "If Mr. Gilpin's right, he lived with them for a couple of weeks, then stole the jewels right out from under their noses. Not the usual thing of slipping into and out of the house under cover of darkness. If I was a thief, sir, and I found myself in a house like yours, I think I'd be tempted to see what I could find to take with me. Especially if I thought I was a crafty one.'' He tapped his temple. "That's what brings ones like that down, I'll tell you that. Thinking they're so much smarter than anyone else. Trips them up, that pride.''

Mr. Cobb left to bring in the first of the guests to be interviewed. After he walked out the door, Jessica said, "Do you think that Mr. Cobb's thief has anything to do with what happened to Mrs. Woods? Even if he is who you surprised in your study?''

Richard shrugged. "It's all a tangle. I am not even sure that Mrs. Woods didn't simply fall, as everyone would obviously like to believe. It is just that cut on her cheek, and the lateness of the hour...''

The door opened to admit Lady Westhampton. The interview was brief, as she had gone to bed early, nursing her head cold, and had neither seen nor heard anything until Mrs. Woods' scream awakened her. Gabriela's interview was much the same, and Richard sent the girl and Lady Westhampton back to their rooms to seek whatever rest they could. Next came Miss Pargety, who was eager to talk. Indeed, they soon discovered that she was difficult to stop.

"I knew that woman was trouble," she said, bobbing her head to emphasize the point. "Right from the beginning. Foreign looking. Up to no good, I'll warrant. Popping in and out of her room at all hours of the night."

"Did you see Mrs. Woods leave her room?" Richard asked, leaning forward interestedly.

"I didn't see any of them. But I could hear them. It was hard for a decent body to get a wink of sleep, the ways doors were opening and closing."

"But you did not specifically see or hear Mrs. Woods."

"No," Miss Pargety admitted reluctantly.

"What about anyone else? Did you see anyone else leave his or her room? Or hear a voice you recognized?"

"I heard that Lady Vesey," she said, primming her mouth. "I heard her giggling, but I didn't see where she went."

They finished the interviews of the female guests with Lady Vesey. She came in and sat down, looking for once somewhat subdued.

"I am sure I cannot tell you anything important, Cleybourne," she said, sighing. "I did not see the woman fall. I came running out when I heard the scream."

"And where did you run out from?" Richard asked pointedly.

She cast a quick glance at him, then looked down

at her hands. "I don't see how that is any of your business."

"If you were with anyone else, it would prove that you were not the one who shoved Mrs. Woods down the stairs," Richard said.

Leona gasped with outrage. "As if I would have had anything to do with that!"

"I don't see how it would have benefited you," Richard said agreeably, "otherwise I would be more suspicious of you."

She narrowed her eyes. "There is no need for you to be insulting, Cleybourne. You know I didn't shove her down the stairs. Why would I?" She tossed her hair back, looking at him with a certain defiance. "Well, I *was* with someone. But it would be a scandal. I cannot tell you."

"I think I have a pretty good idea," Richard replied.

"I doubt it."

"The Reverend Radfield?"

Leona stared at him, bug-eyed. "How did you—"

"What I want to know is whether the two of you were still together when Mrs. Woods met her death."

"You must promise you will not tell," Leona said, making a show of reluctance, then shrugged and said, "Yes, we were in his room together when she screamed. So you know it was not he, and it was not I. Personally, I doubt the woman was even killed. It was an accident, and you just enjoy being officious." She paused and added what to her must have been the killing blow. "I cannot imagine what I ever saw in you."

"Mmm. Nor I, Lady Vesey."

Leona flounced out of the room, and Mr. Cobb turned to look at Cleybourne with a new respect.

"Well, aren't you the downy one, Your Grace. How did you know she and the good minister were..." He hesitated, cutting his eyes toward Jessica, and added, "Beg pardon, miss."

"Because I was keeping watch tonight. After all that has happened, I thought it would be a good idea." His mouth tightened. "Unfortunately, I was no longer looking when Mrs. Woods met her demise." He kept his gaze on the Runner, careful not to glance in Jessica's direction.

"Doesn't surprise me," Cobb mused. "That one's the sort that could make any man forget his collar."

They began to interview the men after that, but their questioning met with little more success. Mr. Goodrich, eyes blinking, shifting in his seat, told them that he had been in bed, sound asleep, and had seen and heard nothing. Lord Vesey explained that he had been downstairs in Cleybourne's study the whole time, drinking a bit of port, and since Richard had seen that fact for himself, there was little he could say to dispute it.

Reverend Radfield, too, professed no knowledge of what had happened. Pale and distracted, he sat lifelessly in his seat, staring most of the time at the floor a few feet in front of him.

"Where were you when you heard the scream?" Richard prodded.

"Um, in my chamber. Um, reading." He shifted.

"Was there anyone else with you?"

The man's eyes flew up to Richard's face, and he looked at him for a long moment, then turned his gaze away. "Why—why do you ask?"

"It is rather important that you tell the truth now, sir," Richard said, his gaze not leaving the other man.

"I—well, that is—" He cleared his throat and glanced over at Jessica, who was busy scribbling down his words. He turned back to Richard. "Yes," he said finally in a low voice. "There was someone with me. I—you must understand, I cannot say who it was. A lady…her name…I cannot damage her reputation."

"I see. Well, it is obvious that you do not know her well if you think that you could damage her reputation."

Radfield opened his eyes wider and gave Cleybourne a startled look. "Your Grace!" Their gazes held for a moment, and it was Radfield who gave in. With a groan, he leaned forward, bracing his elbows on his knees and sinking his head to his upraised hands. "What is the use? Of course you're right— there is nothing there to damage." He clenched his hands in his hair. "To think that I was with that trollop while *she* was falling to her death!"

The young man broke off, drawing a ragged breath.

"When did Lady Vesey leave your room?"

Radfield shook his head, not looking at anyone in the room. "After the scream. We heard it, and then we ran out into the hall like everyone else.'' He did at last raise his head then, looking at Cleybourne with a tortured expression. ''I shall regret this night all my life.''

Lord Kestwick was next, and he strode into the room in a temper. ''I say, Cleybourne, what do you mean, keeping me waiting all this time while you conversed with every—'' He stopped as his gaze fell on Jessica. He swung back toward the door and saw that Cobb had followed him into the room and shut the door and was now settling down on a chair, leaning back in it and tilting its front legs off the floor. ''What the devil! What is the meaning of this? Don't tell me you expect me to talk to you with—with these people in the room.''

The expression on his face was that of a person who had been asked to share his space with rats. He turned to Richard imperiously. ''See here, it is one thing to discuss this matter with you. You are a peer. But a governess? A Bow Street Runner?''

''Miss Maitland is here to take notes, Lord Kestwick. It seems she has had some experience with that. And I would think that a Runner would be a particularly appropriate person to have at this interview. There is, after all, the possibility of foul play.''

Kestwick rolled his eyes. ''I don't know what maggot's gotten into your head. I mean, really, Cleybourne, don't you think you are being a trifle dramatic about the whole thing?''

''I usually find that death is a dramatic event,'' Richard responded coolly.

"But I mean, all this questioning and suspicion. My God, the woman just took a tumble."

"How do you know that?" Richard asked quietly. "Did you see her?"

"Of course not! I was in my bed asleep—as I wish I were right now."

"You seem uncommonly cool about this whole thing, Kestwick," Richard said casually, "for a man who just had the recently deceased in his bedroom."

"The devil!" Kestwick exclaimed, and across the room, Mr. Cobb's chair came back down on its front legs with a crash. Kestwick stared at Cleybourne for a long moment, then said bitingly, "So you have been spying on your guests?"

"I have been somewhat cautious since I found an intruder in this room the other night." Richard paused, then went on. "Now, would you like to tell us about Mrs. Woods?"

"I most certaintly would not!" the other man shot back, his face settling into its most aristocratic lines. "It is scarcely any of your business. And a woman's reputation is concerned."

"Since that woman is dead, I doubt that her reputation really matters now. And when someone dies in my house, then it is most definitely my business. Are you refusing to explain? Is that what I shall have to tell the magistrate—that only Lord Kestwick concealed information?"

Kestwick sneered, but he said, "All right, then, *yes*. I had an...interlude with the woman. We are both adults. And she is—was—an attractive woman, a widow. It isn't as if I seduced an innocent. Besides, since you were spying on me, I assume that you also saw Mrs. Woods *leave* my room. I went to sleep after that. I never saw her again until you found her lying at the bottom of the stairs.''

He looked at the duke for a moment, his expression cool, even challenging. ''You know, Cleybourne, one is tempted to ask where you were when all this was happening. It strikes me that you were the first one to reach the foot of the stairs.''

Richard said nothing, merely nodded toward Cobb, who immediately rose to his feet and opened the door to usher Lord Kestwick out.

''Damme!'' Cobb said, stepping back into the room after Kestwick had gone. ''That one's a cold fish. When I think I was standing right next to him when he was looking down at that poor woman. I never would have guessed he'd even spoken to her, and him having just—'' He broke off, shaking his head. ''I'll never understand the gentry.''

''Unfair, Mr. Cobb,'' Richard said with a faint smile, ''to paint all of us with the same brush as Lord Kestwick. It is not his degree of birth that makes him cold, it is his heart. Unfortunately, he's right. She did leave his room and go back to her own. I saw her.'' Richard cursed softly, pushing himself away from his desk. ''If only I had continued watching!''

Cobb shrugged. ''Well, we all have to sleep, Your Grace. No sin in that.''

''No. Of course not.'' Richard glanced over at Jessica and just as quickly looked away. ''Still, it seems the devil's own luck…''

"There's just one of them left to question, Your Grace," Cobb said. "Shall I bring him in?"

"Yes. Although I doubt Mr. Talbot will have anything pertinent to offer," Richard said.

He was right in that. Darius came in, and except for one initial glance at Richard, he spent the rest of the time looking anywhere but at his interregator. He had, predictably, seen and heard nothing, and disclaimed all knowledge of Mrs. Woods or her whereabouts that evening.

"Useless," Richard said disgustedly as soon as Darius was out the door. "Well, I would say the only thing that's left to us now is to search the woman's room."

Jessica was pleased to note that he made no attempt to exclude her from this activity but seemed to assume that she would join him and Mr. Cobb. She thought that Mr. Cobb viewed at her with some curiosity, but he obviously did not dare to question a duke.

The three of them went up the stairs to Mrs. Woods' room, where one of the footmen was sitting beside the door, keeping watch. Richard opened the door, and they stepped inside, lighting the old lamp that lay on her dresser.

For a moment they stood hesitantly in the middle of the room, looking around. It seemed macabre, a violation of the woman, to be searching through her things after she was dead. Finally Richard sighed and said, "Well, it can't be helped. However little we might want to, we have to search the room. We don't even know where she came from or where she was going, or whom to notify about her death.''

Jessica nodded and went to the wardrobe, opening it. There were only a few dresses hanging in it. She had not bothered to take out more than just a few things, Jessica supposed. The trunk at the foot of the bed yielded more clothes.

''Look at these,'' Jessica said, pulling out one rose satin dress.

Cleybourne looked at it. ''Yes. Very pretty.''

''No, I mean look at how different it is from the dresses we saw on Mrs. Woods. She wore dark colors—navy, dark green—and they were very plain. These are beautiful dresses, rich fabrics, bright colors, plenty of lace and decorations. It is odd that she has such different types of clothing. And another thing...''

She shut the trunk lid and stood up, struck by a thought. ''I don't know why this didn't occur to me before. These clothes, and even the ones she wore every day, plain and dark though they are, are of nice materials and well-made. They were expensive.''

''And what was someone who could afford expensive gowns doing traveling by mail coach?'' Richard asked, finishing her thought.

''Exactly.'' Jessica moved to the dresser, pointing to the silver-backed toiletry set that sat there. ''These are expensive, too.''

''Almost anyone can fall on hard times,'' Richard said. ''She could once have had money and lost it but still have the things she owned back then.''

''That's true,'' Jessica conceded. For a time, after

the scandal, she had still had some trinkets and gowns that were much too expensive for her circumstances. "One sells the jewelry and furniture and such, but no one wants to give you money for ball gowns already worn."

Richard considered her words but said nothing, just continued opening the drawers of the dresser and pulling out objects.

"Didn't Reverend Radfield strike you as acting oddly?" she asked, picking up the various pots and jars that he was pulling from the drawers and examining them. It was obvious that Mrs. Woods had used cosmetics to enhance her appearance.

"You mean other than having illicit relations with married women?"

"Yes. He was so shaken when she died. He looked as if he were about to faint. And he said the prayer a little wrong, and that last thing he said—about her dying hereafter? That isn't religious. I am sure it's from Shakespeare—*Macbeth,* I believe."

"Perhaps he is literary. No doubt he isn't used to seeing dead bodies every day." Richard gave her a sardonic look. "You realize, Miss Maitland, that if you were a properly genteel woman, you would have fainted or had hysterics or something of that sort."

"No doubt. However, fainting and hysterics were not considered becoming behavior in a soldier's daughter," Jessica retorted, picking up a pot and opening it. "But you would think that a minister would have seen a fair number of dead or dying people."

"But perhaps not violent death."

"True. Besides, he couldn't possibly have killed her. He is one of the few people who could not have. He was with Leona at the time."

"Yes. And perhaps his discomfort came from knowing that he had just been engaged in breaking one of the Commandments," Richard added.

Jessica closed the pot of flesh-colored greasepaint of the sort used by actors on stage and opened another pot. It contained much darker greasepaint. Jessica froze, her mind skittering back to the dead woman at the bottom of the stairs. "Oh! Rich—I mean, Your Grace! Look at this."

Richard peered at the jar. "She painted her face. Yes, she has quite a few beauty aids, I see. Creams and rouges and black pencil."

"Yes, but don't you see? She wore cosmetics that made her look darker than she actually was. Don't you remember how pale she was tonight? I remember thinking how pale she was."

"She was dead."

"I know. That's what I assumed. But now, seeing this…I don't think so. That night, when you chased the man out of your study, she was standing on the stairs with the others when we came back into the house, and I remember thinking that she was very scared because she looked so pale. But what it was, both times, was that it was night, and she had taken off the cosmetics. And another thing—I saw it tonight, but I didn't think about it until just now. Her hair was darker, too!"

She pounced on another jar that he had set out on the table. "This is dye, such as some women use on their hair. I think she was trying to make herself look different. She was disguising herself. Why would she do that? Why would she travel by mail coach? Unless she was fleeing something—or someone.''

Richard frowned at her. ''Perhaps. It is true that I have not yet found anything of a personal nature among her things—no letters or books or—''

''Sweet Mother in Heaven!'' came an exclamation from the side of the bed, and they swung around to look at Mr. Cobb.

While they were talking, he had been poking into all the corners of the room, opening doors and drawers. Finally he had knelt beside the bed, and he had apparently found something under it, for a traveling bag was open in front of him.

''What is it?'' Richard asked. ''What have you found?''

Cobb reached into the bag and pulled out a smaller box. He had opened it, so the lid was standing up, revealing the contents of the box: several items of sparkling diamond and sapphire jewelry.

''I think I just found my jewel thief.''

16

"What? Are you sure?" Richard asked, going over to the other man, Jessica following.

"Oh, yes. There was a portrait of Mr. Gilpin's wife wearing this diamond necklace," Cobb said confidently, taking one of the pieces and laying it on the bedspread. "And these earrings, too."

He laid the box and jewels on the bed, then pulled more items from the bag: a leather purse containing a startling amount of gold coins, another, smaller, drawstring bag from which he spilled a handful of unset gems onto the bed, and another cloth bag containing some more jewels.

"I'd have to get my list, but I'm almost certain several of these other pieces would match the descriptions of the stolen jewels. There was a good bit of money taken, too. And these other jewels—I would lay odds that these were stolen from someone else in the past and taken out of their settings to make them easier to sell." He shook his head. "A woman! I never guessed.... Well, that disproves the dancing master theory."

"So she is—*was* the thief," Richard mused. "But it could not have been she who I found in my study the other night. That was no woman I was fighting. He was not as big as I, but he was too strong for a woman."

"That is a problem," Cobb agreed. "But we cannot deny this evidence, either, Your Grace. These are the Gilpin jewels."

"This grows more confusing by the moment," Jessica said. "Is there a second thief? And is he connected or not to Mrs. Woods? Or was the person in your study there for some entirely different reason? And we still have no idea who killed Mrs. Woods, if, indeed, anyone did."

"You are right," Richard agreed. "It is too confusing. And I don't think any of us are thinking clearly anymore. I suggest we all go to bed and leave it until tomorrow. Perhaps things will seem clearer then."

They agreed that they needed sleep. Taking the jewels and money downstairs, Cobb and Richard put them in the safe, and Richard then locked the door to his study for extra protection. They went up the stairs, where Cobb parted from them, going up to his room on the third floor. Richard and Jessica walked down the hall toward their own rooms, side by side at the other end.

Despite the late hour, Jessica felt jumpy and wound up, her mind spinning. She had gone through so many feelings this evening—the anger and hurt at what had been done to her jewelry box, the passion she had experienced in Richard's arms, then the fear

Mrs. Woods' scream had engendered, followed by the shock and horror of finding her body. She felt as though her emotions were raw and exposed.

"I don't know how I will ever get to sleep tonight," she mused aloud. "Right now I feel as if I could never close my eyes again."

"Don't tell me the redoubtable Miss Maitland is frightened," Cleybourne said with a faint smile.

"Nervous, maybe. And confused. Yet I can't stop thinking about it, wondering…. And how does my jewelry box fit into the whole thing? All of it must be connected somehow. I cannot believe in so many coincidences."

"Your jewelry box?" Richard asked, looking puzzled. "What are you talking about?"

"Oh, I'm sorry. I did not get around to telling you about that. We were distracted by something in the hall. That is the reason I decided to keep watch tonight. My jewelry box went missing yesterday."

"Missing? Why didn't you tell me about it?"

"I don't know. I guess it didn't seem very important. And I could not believe that someone had actually stolen it. It wasn't valuable. All my jewelry and the box together would have been worth no more than a few pounds. It held mostly sentimental value. I kept thinking that if someone had taken it, they would see how little it was worth and give it back— or that it had been in some mysterious way misplaced and would show up again sooner or later. Then, tonight, one of the maids brought it to me. She had found it in the music room. Nothing was missing except for one little earring, but…" Her voice faltered a little, but she shook it off and plowed ahead. "The box had been smashed to bits."

"What!"

Jessica shrugged. "It is broken into pieces. The jewelry is all there, but the box is ruined. I cannot imagine why anyone would have done such a thing." Tears sprang into her eyes, and she dashed them away impatiently. "I'm sorry. You must think me foolish to care so. It isn't important compared to something like Mrs. Woods' death. But my father gave it to me, and it is dear to me for that reason."

"Of course. And it is important. Let me see it."

"It's inside." They had reached the door to Jessica's room and stopped while they were talking. She reached out and opened the door, closing it behind them for privacy, then leading Cleybourne into the room and over to the dresser.

"Bloody hell!" Cleybourne exclaimed when he saw the ruins of the jewelry case. He strode over to the dresser and picked up one or two of the pieces, looking at them in amazement. He turned to her, frowning. "It has indeed been smashed. Why? Who would—" He broke off, his face clearing. "Of course."

"Of course...what?" Jessica gave him a startled look. "You know who did this?"

"I have a guess. Your former fiancé."

"Darius?" Jessica gaped at him. "Why on earth would Darius take my jewelry box and break it?"

"Because it is yours. Because it is precious to you. This is not the work of reason. A thief would take the jewelry from the box and leave it, or take it all to sell. But to smash the box and leave the valuables, too—that indicates a great deal of anger. Anger directed against you personally. He tried to reignite your interest in him, and when you turned him down, it enraged him. Humiliated him. I made it worse by hitting him and warning him away from you. He wants to hurt you, and he knows he cannot without suffering the consequences. But this—it is a secret thing, a way he can hurt you without anyone knowing.''

Jessica looked from him to the box. ''I suppose it does make sense, in a way. It's just…well, I can't imagine Darius caring that much, even in a bad way. It was all so long ago, and he was the one who broke off the engagement, not I. It is hard for me to believe he has loved me all these years, or that it sprang up in him again when he saw me here. I am sure that he would not like my turning him down, and certainly he would not like to be humiliated in front of you, but…'' She shrugged. ''This implies such violent emotion. Still, you are right, it does appear to be anger directed at me personally, and no one else here knows me. Well, except you, and I don't think you are the type to smash jewelry boxes.''

''Why, thank you. I am honored that you trust me so.''

''Which makes Darius the most likely one.''

''The violence of this…it seems so wild and unreasoning. It makes me wonder if whoever did this might not also have killed Mrs. Woods.''

''Darius? Oh, that seems most unlikely.''

''I don't know. This destruction seems to me to

verge almost on madness. Certainly it indicates a violent temper and lack of control. That seems to me the sort of person who very well might murder someone—if she thwarted him, say. If that is the case…if it is Mr. Talbot, then you would be in grave danger.''

''No. It cannot be Darius,'' Jessica said firmly. ''That is impossible. For one thing, he doesn't even know Mrs. Woods.''

''How do you know? You haven't known the man or what he's been doing for ten years.''

''But there has been no indication that he knew her. Anyway, Darius is not a killer. He is too weak a person to kill anyone. He might bluster or rage or even smash up a jewelry box. But he would not have the courage to kill someone.''

''Don't assume that because someone is weak they won't commit murder. Rather, I think murder is the outgrowth of weakness. The killer takes the easy way out of a situation. He kills because he doesn't have the strength to face up to something that a strong man would. He kills from cowardice, not bravery.''

''Maybe so, but we still have no reason to suppose that it was Darius. There is no evidence. The only person we know she had contact with was Lord Kestwick, not Darius.''

''Why are you defending him?'' Cleybourne frowned.

''Why are you so determined that he is the culprit?'' Jessica retorted.

''You still care for him,'' Richard accused.

Jessica stared, then began to laugh. ''I'm sorry,'' she said after a moment. ''That is just too funny. I don't care for Darius. Not at all. At first, yes, I was very hurt that he called off our engagement. But looking back, I don't think that even then it was so much love as it was wounded pride. I was more devastated by my father's scandal. And his death was much, much worse. Now, when I look at Darius, I wonder why I ever thought I was in love with him. It was much better that he broke it off. I would have been terribly unhappy being married to him. He is too weak. And I, as you have pointed out, am far too pushy and opinionated. We would soon have hated each other.'' She paused, then let out a little sigh and added, ''I am not, I am afraid, one of such deep feelings.''

''Why would you say that?''

''I got over my wounded heart fairly easily. I did not mourn as you have mourned. I did not love him the way you loved your Caroline.''

Richard grimaced. ''I am hardly a good example of love.''

''You are extremely faithful and unbending in your love for her.''

''Am I?'' There was a bitter tone to his voice that startled Jessica, and she looked at him closely. ''She died four years ago this evening. And I—I scarcely thought of her at all tonight.''

''You had quite a few things to occupy your mind,'' Jessica reminded him. ''It is little wonder that you did not think only of her and her death.''

''It wasn't those 'things' that made me forget. I was simply too busy thinking about you.''

Jessica felt as if her breath had been knocked out of her. She struggled to think of something to say.

"Hardly the thoughts of a faithful husband," he went on, his mouth twisting sardonically.

"How can you say that? You have mourned her for four years. When I came here, you were still so despairing, so sorrowful for her that you were about to end your life. And do not tell me that you were not. I saw you with that gun—I saw your face. You may not have intended to do it at just that moment. But you wanted to. You planned to."

"Yes. I did," he admitted. "I grieved for four years. I grieved for my wife, I grieved for my daughter. Most of all, I grieved for myself. I despaired. But do you know why? It wasn't pure, faithful love. It was because—" He looked away, then turned his gaze back to her, his jaw knotted as though he forced himself to speak. "I was nearly mad with grief because I knew it was my fault. I killed them."

Jessica stared at him, stunned. "What? No. I don't believe it. You killed your wife and daughter?"

"I should say, I drove them to their death. It amounted to the same thing. We were not a family leaving together, with me riding outside the carriage. Caroline had left me. She planned to run away with her lover. She was going to leave while I was away on a trip. She had the carriage loaded. She had written me a letter explaining it all. But I ruined her plans by coming home early from my trip. I missed them—I missed Alana mostly. Caroline and I—I loved her madly when I married her. Later I found out that she did not return my love in the same way. She had married me because it was the most advantageous match she could make. It was easy to decide she loved a duke, less easy to remain in love with one when she had to live with me.''

"Oh, Richard..." Jessica reached out to him, putting her hand on his arm. It was rigid beneath her touch. "I am so sorry."

"I knew she did not love me, and after that my love began to cool somewhat. Still, she was my wife, and she was the mother of my child. Alana was the light of my life. I missed her. I missed my home. So I came home two days early, and I found the carriage packed and ready to go. Caroline almost fainted when she saw me. I asked her what was happening. She made up a story about having to visit her family. I wanted her to leave Alana, but she refused. I wanted her to wait, said that I would accompany them. Finally she admitted the truth. We had a terrible row. I told her I would not let her leave. There was no way I would allow her to take my child with her. She told me she hated me, that she loved another and would never be happy here. I told her I didn't care. She could not take Alana from me. She ran from the room, crying.''

He shook his head. "At first, in my arrogance, I assumed that she had gone up to her room. I paced around the drawing room a bit, trying to calm down before I went up to see Alana. I didn't want her to see me so angry. After a few minutes I went up to her room, and I found her nurse there, crying. She told me that Alana had gone, that Caroline had not allowed her to accompany them. Then I realized that

Caroline had defied me. She had taken my daughter and left. I rode after them. It was cold, there was ice. She had, not unlike her, left it till too late to start. It was bitterly cold, and the light was fading. I shouted to them to stop. If it had been my coachman, he would have, but it was not. My coachman had been with me on my trip. She had hired a post chaise, with a hired driver. So when Caroline told him to drive faster, he did. He took a curve too fast, and the coach went off the road.''

Richard muttered a curse and walked away from her to the fireplace. He stood, looking down into the fire, leaning on the mantel. ''That is what haunts me,'' he rasped, and his eyes glittered with tears in the firelight. ''If I had not chased them, they would not have died. It was my selfishness, my arrogance, my stubbornness. I killed them…because I wanted to keep them here.''

''Oh, no, no…'' Jessica went to him. ''It was not your fault. Caroline chose to leave. She tried to sneak out and steal your daughter from you when you were not here. You had no idea—how could you not react with anger? Anyone would have. Anyone would have resisted her taking their child away. And she was the one who ran instead of staying and trying to work something out. She selfishly took your daughter away from you and ran. That was neither right nor fair. It is no wonder you reacted with anger. How could you know what would happen if you chased them? And she is as much at fault for urging the driver to go faster. It was a horrible, tragic accident. They did not deserve to die, and you did not deserve to have them taken from you. It just happened, as horrible things sometimes do. You cannot blame yourself for it. You cannot make the rest of your life miserable in penance!''

Impulsively, Jessica slipped her arm around his waist and leaned against him. Almost convulsively, he wrapped his arms around her and held her to him. His body was taut, rigid with tension. She wrapped her arms around his waist, holding him, and her hands stroked his back. Richard buried his face in the crook of her neck, making a low moan of despair deep in this throat. His shoulders shook as the sobs took him, and he clutched her even more tightly to him.

Jessica clung to him, absorbing the pain that poured out of his body, the years of unspoken guilt and blame. She was sure he had never told anyone what he had just told her; he had doubtless held it deep inside, loathing himself, eaten up with sorrow and guilt and thinking that he deserved it as his penance.

''It's all right,'' she murmured, rubbing her hands soothingly up and down his back. ''It will be all right.''

His hand clenched into fists, digging into her dress and squeezing handfuls of it as he cried. He had cried before for Caroline and Alana, and always, when he cried, he had felt as well the bitter lash of guilt, the knowledge that he deserved all the pain he felt and more, that he could never repent or repay enough to take back that precipitate chase that had led to the deaths of all he loved. Now, for the first time, he cried for himself, for the pain inside, the bitter, almost unendurable misery that had been his life for the past four years.

"Alana would not want you to blame yourself. You know she wouldn't. She loved you as only a child can love—fully, happily. She would ache to know you hurt. All she would want for you is to feel good again, to be happy again—whether she was here or not."

His arms tightened further at her words, almost squeezing the breath from her, and she heard his ragged intake of air. "Oh, God. You're right. How did you—you did not even know her. Yet you understand her better than I."

He pulled back from her, wiping the tears from his face, and looked down at her. Jessica smiled up at him.

"I know how a daughter feels about her father. My father's scandal ruined both our lives. There were times when I was so angry at him I wanted to scream at him, to pound him with my fists. There I was, ostracized by almost everyone I had associated with before, suddenly on the edge of financial ruin, not knowing what to do or where to turn, and he would go out at night, drinking and carousing. I would rage at him, beg him to tell me what he had done and why, and he would tell me that he could not. Then he would leave again. There were times when I hated him.

"But when he died, I thought I would come apart with grief. I regretted every bitter word I had ever said to him or thought about him. He was my father and I loved him, and I still to this day cannot believe that he did anything wrong. I would give anything to have him back. I would be willing to endure being ostracized time and again, if only I could somehow change those last few months and make him alive and happy. I know now that all that really mattered was how much I loved him. And I hope desperately that, wherever he is, he is happy. That's how I know what your daughter would want for you. Because I want it for my father."

Richard drew a long, shuddering breath, and he raised his hands to her face, laying them against her cheeks and gently stroking his thumbs over the ridges of her cheekbones. "Alana would have loved you."

"I think I would have loved her, too."

He smiled a little. "I am certain you would have. She was like you in some ways—fearless and honest...and blunt. And very tender of heart."

"I think perhaps she is also rather like her father in those ways." Jessica smiled and went up on tiptoe to brush a light kiss across his lips. "You are a good man. Don't destroy yourself with grief and guilt."

Richard gazed at her for a moment. "Thank you." His voice was husky with emotion. "You seem to be in the habit of saving me." He bent and returned her light kiss, then pressed his lips against her forehead, as well. "Whether I want it or not."

Jessica chuckled. "I am glad that I was there when you needed...help, I would say. Not saving."

She looked up at him. "In the end, I don't think you would have used that pistol, even if I had not been there. Even if Gabriela and I had never come here. You have too much strength, too much courage. You would not have done it.''

"I am not as sure as you."

Jessica shrugged. "That is because you don't see the whole picture of you, as I do."

He gave her a lopsided grin. "I would not think it is a very pretty picture."

"Not pretty, perhaps." Jessica's smile was warm and a little flirtatious. "But quite appealing, nevertheless."

"Really?" His tone matched hers, and his eyes fell to her lips. "Not half as appealing, I'll warrant, as what I see when I look at you."

"Flattery—" Jessica began, but her words were cut off by his lips coming down on hers. He kissed her gently, tenderly, but his mouth lingered, tasting hers at his leisure. When at last he raised his head, her heart was pounding and her cheeks were flushed.

"Jessica…" he breathed, and then he was kissing her again, his arms surrounding her, pulling her up into him.

Her whole body flamed in response to him, and she went up on her toes, her arms wrapping around his neck and her mouth avid on his. He made a noise low in his throat, and his hands roamed over her back and down onto her hips, pressing her pelvis into him. He was hard against her, and it excited her.

He pulled his mouth from hers, kissing her cheek and ear and neck. "We shouldn't…" he murmured as his lips roamed her skin.

"No," she agreed breathlessly.

"Tell me to stop," he told, taking her earlobe between his teeth and worrying it.

Heat blossomed between her legs.

"Tell me to leave." His hands were kneading her buttocks, moving her against him.

"I can't...." Jessica shivered as his lips trailed down the side of her neck, hot and velvety. "I don't want you to go. I want you to..." She released a little moan as his tongue delved into the soft hollow of her throat. "Stay..." she said, her hands digging into his shoulders. "Please stay."

His mind clouded, as it always did with her. It was difficult to think about anything but the way her skin felt beneath his fingers, or how her mouth tasted, or the silken, seductive beauty of her hair. Always before with women, even Caroline, he had remained in control, his brain working over and above the desire that ran through him. But with Jessica, it was always fire and hunger and immediacy, his brain struggling to keep up with the raging needs of his body. Reason burned away, and his thoughts seemed to consist primarily of imagining how she would look naked, or how sweet it would be to slide into her and feel her legs lock around his back.

He raised his head and put his hands on her shoulders, gently turning her around. He started on the buttons down the back of her dress, the sides of the dress separating and curling away, slowly, teasingly exposing first her neck, then her back. Her head was bent, so that her neck gently curved forward, and the sight of it, tender and vulnerable, stirred the desire in his loins. He leaned down and placed his lips upon her neck, soft skin covering the ridge of bone. Gently he kissed down the line of her backbone until his lips were stopped by her plain white cotton camisole.

Her dress was open now all the way down her back, sides sagging away from each other. He slid his hands beneath the fabric, moving around until his fingertips touched in the front across her stomach. As he moved, her dress fell farther open, slipping off her shoulders and onto her arms. Richard pressed his hands against her stomach, pushing her back until she was flush against his body. His hands moved up her front beneath the dress, gliding over the camisole until they cupped her breasts. He buried his lips in her neck, kissing and nibbling, his breath rasping in his throat, as his fingers caressed her breasts and teased the nipples into hard buttons.

Jessica gasped, pressing harder back into him, moving her hips in an untutored way that sent fire roaring through him more than any lightskirt's practiced caresses. He untied the ribbon over the front of her camisole and slipped his hands beneath the cloth, taking her bare breasts in his hands. Her flesh was soft and silken, tantalizing. He kissed the nape of her neck, her scent filling his nostrils. His lips moved over the hard line of her collarbone to her rounded shoulders and then her back, and he pushed her dress down over her arms and off, exposing more of her to his caresses. Still the loosened camisole impeded him, and with a soft oath he pulled it up and over her head, flinging it away. He explored her naked back with his lips as his hands loved the orbs of her

breasts. Jessica moaned, trembling under the assault
to her senses.

His hands slid downward, encountering her petticoats, and he untied the tapes and pushed them down.
They pooled atop her dress at her feet, and she was
clad in nothing but stockings and cotton pantalets.
His hands caressed her buttocks and moved back
around to her stomach, over the undergarment and
down between her legs. Jessica stiffened and gasped
at the touch, but she did not move away. She gave
a little shiver and leaned back against his chest, re-
laxing her legs. He slid his hand between then, caressing her through the cloth, now wet with her desire. The evidence of her passionate response to him
stirred Richard almost past reason. He wanted to sink
immediately into her and ease himself, but he held
back.

He remembered well her response to him the last
time, and he wanted to take her higher now, to show
her new and more stunning depths of passion. He
picked her up to carry her to the bed and laid her
down upon it. Then he removed the last bits of her
clothing, until she lay completely naked before him.
Richard did not think he had ever seen a sight quite
so lovely.

He gazed at her, passion pulsing thickly through
his veins, as he removed his own clothes, tugging
impatiently at laces and buttons and ripping off the
garments, throwing them aside. Jessica shivered a little, and he pulled down the bedcovers and tucked
them around her, then crawled into the bed beside
her and took her in his arms. She was small and soft

against him, and for a moment he just lay there, holding her and letting his hands roam over her body. But the feel of her rounded flesh beneath his hands soon had the blood pounding in his brain.

Jessica's hands glided over his back, learning the curve of muscle, the sharp outcroppings of his collarbone, the bumpy line of his spine. They slid along his sides and over the sharp points of his hipbones and down the sides of his hips. Her fingertips were like velvet caressing his skin, soft and seductive.

Richard rolled to his side and bent to kiss her breasts. With teeth and tongue and lips he loved her breasts, while his hand roamed lower, exploring her stomach and thighs and finally slipping teasingly between her legs. Jessica shuddered at the touch, and her hands dug into his upper arms.

Slowly his fingers moved upward, teasing and stoking her. He pulled her nipple into his mouth and suckled it, sending waves of pleasure washing through her. Then his fingers came at last to the center of her desire, delving into the slick, hot folds, separating and stroking delicately, until Jessica was throbbing and aching for release. She felt the delightful pressure building in her again, and she dug in her heels, arching up against his hand, wanting to feel the pleasure sweep through her again like a tidal wave. But this time Richard brought her closer and closer to that edge, then moved away, only to build the excitement again.

Jessica dug her fingers into him, almost sobbing, pressing her hips up against his hand. Then he moved between her legs, his manhood teasing at the gate of her femininity, until finally he pushed up into her, breaking the seal of her virginity in a brief flash of pain. For an instant he paused, then began to move within her, creating a pleasure more wonderful than any she had experienced yet. She moved with him, her body instinctively settling into his rhythm. His body was hot and slick with sweat against her, his breath labored in her ear. He murmured her name, and she thought that she had never heard a sound so beautiful.

Then, in a blinding rush, the hot, dark wave of pleasure slammed through her, and she cried out, clasping him to her. He groaned, spilling his seed into her, both of them lost in a mindless swirl of passion, joined in a primitive, seamless union. Richard buried his face in the crook of her neck until finally, spent, he collapsed against her.

Rolling over onto his back, he pulled her on top of him, holding her close, neither of them able to speak. Wrapped in his arms, surrounded by his heat, Jessica slipped into an easy, dreamless sleep.

17

The room was chilly when Jessica awoke the next morning. She opened her eyes, blinking, and was immediately aware of the feel of the sheets against her bare skin. She was naked. She remembered in a rush what had happened here the night before, and color rose in her face at the memory, part embarrassment, part a surge of desire.

She turned to look at the other side of the bed. Richard was not there. He would not be, of course, she reminded herself. He was too much a gentleman to make it plain that he had spent the night with her. He would have gotten up, dressed and left long before the servants began to stir.

Jessica sat up, aware of her body as she had never been before, feeling the differences in her, the faint tenderness and soreness, the memory of pleasure lingering sensually along her skin and filling her breasts. With a groan of sheer enjoyment, she collapsed against the mattress, spreading her arms out and grinning foolishly up at the tester above her head. She felt wonderfully young and filled with experience, all at the same time. No woman, she thought, had ever been introduced so magically to love as she had been last night.

She loved Richard. She was sure of that now, had been sure of it last night before she melted in his arms. She knew she was a fallen woman now, beyond the pale of society's standard, but, frankly, she could not find it in her to care. She could not feel shame for what they had done last night, only joy.

By seeking happiness and love in Richard's arms, she was condemning herself to the life of a mistress. No matter how much Richard might desire her, no matter what he had told her of his marriage last night, she knew that he was still in love with Caroline. She knew now that his grief had been compounded by his guilt, but that did not change the fact that he had loved and mourned Caroline for years. If he was happier now, as she hoped, if she had removed the burden of guilt somewhat from his shoulders, it did not mean that he had stopped loving Caroline. It did not mean that he loved Jessica instead. No, she was realistic enough to know that he might never love anyone as much as he had loved Caroline.

And even if, by some miracle, he should come to love her, it did not mean that he would marry her. He was a duke, one of the highest peers in the realm. Dukes married the daughters of dukes and earls; they did not marry the niece of a baron—especially one tainted by scandal. With a lineage like his, he could not marry someone whose father had been cashiered out of the army and subsequently died in a tavern brawl, someone about whom treason had been whispered.

No, there could be no possibility of marriage. In taking him into her bed, Jessica knew that she was putting herself beyond the pale of society for the rest of her life. But that weighed little against her love for Richard. She loved him too much, wanted him too much, to deny herself that love because society would disapprove. The sin of it worried her, but Jessica found it hard to believe in her heart that the love she felt for Richard was a sin. As for the regard of society, she knew that she could live without it. And, thanks to the General's generous gift, she could afford to ignore the opinion of the world. Even after their affair ended, she would be able to live comfortably and not have to depend on someone's else approval of her to earn her keep—for it would end one day, she did not fool herself in that regard. Men grew tired of mistresses; desire faded. He might someday decide to marry in order to carry his line forward. And she would be cast aside.

It was not a pleasant prospect, but she did not flinch from it, either. The love she held in her heart for him—the joy of expressing that love—those made the possibility of an empty life afterward bearable.

She pushed aside the thought and rose to face the day. Whatever came, she would face it gladly.

Two hours later, Jessica was sitting in Gabriela's room, struggling through the intricacies of algebraic equations with her, when she heard the sound of a commotion in the hall. It was one of the maids, and she was talking loudly, almost frantically.

Jessica jumped up and went into the hall, followed closely by Gabriela. She found two maids there, talking, and they turned excitedly to her.

"Oh, miss!" one of them exclaimed, as though glad to turn the problem over to someone else. "It's the minister."

"Reverend Radfield?" Jessica asked, anxiety gripping her. "Is there something wrong with him?"

"No. Leastways, I don't know. But I knocked on his door with a tray of breakfast, and he din't answer, so I pushed the door open—and he was gone. No sign of him."

"Perhaps he got up early and went downstairs."

"No, miss, he wasn't with the others what ate early at the table. And he likes his breakfast in his room, he told me." She colored faintly, and Jessica suspected the girl had formed an affection for the handsome man of the cloth. "I think somethin's happened to him. There's strange things goin' on here, miss. I never seen anything like it before."

"Let's look in his room." Jessica walked down the hall to Radfield's room and knocked on the door, followed by the maids and Gabriela.

When there was no answer to her knock, she opened the door and went in. The bed was still turned down, obviously slept in, but there was no sign of personal belongings, such as brushes or shaving kit, on the dresser. Frowning, Jessica walked over to the wardrobe and opened it. No clothes hung inside.

"Do you know—had the reverend taken out any of his clothing?"

"Oh, yes, miss, he kept some things in the dresser there."

A quick search of the dresser drawers revealed that all were empty, stripped of his belongings. Jessica glanced at the corner, where a trunk and a bag sat. "Did he have any other baggage?"

"Yes, miss, a cloth bag, smaller, like, than those."

Clearly that piece of luggage was missing.

"I think our reverend may have scarpered," Jessica said inelegantly, and left the room.

She found Cleybourne in his study, and when she entered the room, he looked up and a smile spread across his mouth, his eyes warming. "Jessica..."

He stood up, seeing now the little frown between her brows. "What is it? Is something the matter?"

"Reverend Radfield is not in his room. He seems to have left."

Richard looked at her blankly. "The house? You're saying he left the house?"

Jessica nodded. "So it appears. The maid did not find him there when she took up his breakfast this morning, and it seems that one of his bags and several items of clothing are missing. I think he ran away."

"In this weather? That's suicide! What the devil...."

It did not take long to organize a search of the house, which turned up no sign of Radfield. In the meantime, Richard had two horses saddled and set some of the gardener's men to searching around the house for tracks. Before the house search was completed, the gardener returned with a report that there were tracks of someone wading through the snow, cutting across the field toward the road.

Richard took Mr. Cobb with him to search for the man, telling Jessica tersely to keep the others occupied. She did the best she could, though her mind was on Richard and what was transpiring with the reverend. Why had he run away? It certainly seemed suspicious, as though he had run because he was guilty of a crime. Was he even really a priest?

In the deep snow, the tracks were easy to follow, and two men on horseback moved much more quickly than one struggling along on foot. It did not take Cleybourne and Cobb long to return with the minister in tow. Jessica and most of the guests were seated in the formal drawing room. Rachel was there, too, feeling well enough—and bored enough—today to come downstairs and meet their visitors.

Richard strode into the room, propelling Radfield before him, and Cobb followed close behind. Firmly Richard pushed the minister down into a chair. Radfield sat there, shivering, looking wet, bedraggled and thoroughly miserable.

"Now, Radfield, if that is indeed your name," Richard said bitingly, "I think it is time that you told us the truth. Did you kill Mrs. Woods?"

"No!" Radfield looked up at him fiercely. "No, I didn't kill her. I would never have hurt her!"

"It looks a little suspicious, your running away like that," Richard pointed out. "Why would you take off into the snow, risking your life just to get away, unless you were the killer? Unless you feared discovery?''

"Of course I feared it!" Radfield cried out. "It was clear that you and that Runner were going to pin her murder on me!" He made a sweeping gesture toward Mr. Cobb.

"Now why would we do a thing like that?"

"You knew about her! You searched her room. You are bound to have found—" He broke off and slumped back in his chair, lowering his gaze.

"Found what?" Richard prodded. "The jewels?"

Radfield raised his head and shot Cleybourne a fulminating glance. "Yes, of course, the jewels. You were circling around, waiting for me to make a misstep. And she was—she was gone!" Tears pooled in his eyes.

Jessica, looking at the handsome young man, felt something stir in her brain, some vague hint of an idea. She frowned, watching him, her mind whirring.

"She was the one who always knew what to do," he wailed forlornly. "Without her, I—I was lost. I didn't know what to do."

"You were her partner, weren't you?" Cobb spoke up for the first time, striding forward and planting himself pugnaciously in front of the slender young man. "You stole that money from Mr. Gilpin together, didn't you? It wasn't a middle-aged dancing master at all, just you and that doxy—"

"Don't you call her that!" Radfield blazed, jumping to his feet.

Cobb grinned, flexing his fingers with relish.

"Want to pop me, do you? Well, come ahead, then. I'll be happy to oblige you."

"Oh, sit down," Richard said irritably, putting a hand on Radfield's shoulder and shoving him back down into his seat. "Don't be daft. You are no match for him, and you know it." He turned and gave Cobb a look. "You don't need to beat the information out of him."

"And why are you so tender about the man?" Cobb shot back. "'Tis clear he killed her. They were partners, they had a falling-out, and he pushed her down the stairs. He's no match for a man, but he could kill a woman easily enough."

"I didn't kill her!" Radfield shouted. "Why can't you understand that?" Tears spilled out of his eyes and ran down his cheeks. He raised his shaking hands to his head, thrusting them into his hair, the very picture of despair. "She is the last person I would ever have hurt. Yes, she was my partner. The one person in the world I trusted. I loved her!"

He broke down into sobs. Richard looked at him, his face touched with sympathy. "You were married to her?"

"No!" Radfield shook his head, letting out a strangled sort of laugh through his tears. "No, we were not married. Nor was she my mistress, for I am sure that will be your next thought."

The idea that had crept into Jessica's head a moment before formed fully now, and she said gently, "Mrs. Woods was your sister, wasn't she?"

Radfield nodded.

Richard glanced at Jessica in surprise. "How did you know that?"

"I didn't know, I guessed. Just a minute ago, when he got tears in his eyes, I realized that he looked like someone, and then it came to me. Without the makeup to darken her skin, if her hair had been its natural brown instead of black, she would have looked quite a bit like Rev—I mean, Mr. Radfield."

Radfield brushed the tears from his face with his hands. "Bettina always looked after me. She was several years older than I. We were always moving about, so we hadn't any other friends. And we were on our own a lot. Children were a bother. The other members of the troupe didn't much like having us around."

"The troupe?" Rachel asked. "You were actors, then?"

He nodded. "Our parents were. Us, too, as we grew older."

"Of course!" Cobb slapped his hand against his thigh triumphantly. "It *was* the middle-aged dancing master—only that man was you!"

"Yes. We were good at disguises. It made it easier to get away, less dangerous. Who would connect the blond, well-bred lady who befriended Mrs. Gilpin with the Italianate, quiet Mrs. Woods? Or the graying, paunchy dancing master with an Anglican priest?"

He sighed, leaning back in his chair, and went on dully. "Bettina was the one who thought of the jobs, who found the marks and plotted out what we would do. I was just good at opening safes and pocketing things without anyone noticing. Sometimes, when I was younger, I'd work the audiences outside the theater to get a little extra money. It was much easier—and more fun than treading the boards. I hated that life. So did Bettina. She left when she was sixteen, came to London to make her fortune. And she did. She became a very successful courtesan, you see. The toast of London—Marie MacDonald.''

''Good God!'' Darius gasped from across the room. ''Marie MacDonald!''

Everyone in the room turned to stare at Darius, and he blushed fiery red and said, ''Beg pardon. Didn't mean to interrupt. Go on with your story.''

''Nothing much to tell,'' Radfield said. ''Marie was beautiful, celebrated, but she hated that life, too. Besides, she was getting older, close to thirty by then, and you age fast doing that. She wanted to stop, and so, after a while, she came up with this scheme. She knew a lot of wealthy men. Her parties were famous all over London and attended by some of the highest names in the country. She knew where the jewels were and who made a show of wealth and hadn't any really. So we started out…'' He shrugged. ''And we were good at it.''

He looked up at Richard in supplication, ''So you see, I would never have harmed Bettina. She was my best friend. My whole life. I'm no good without her.''

''You know, I am rather inclined to believe you,'' Richard said.

''What?'' Cobb swung around and looked at Cleybourne in disbelief. ''The man's a villain.''

"Oh, he is your thief, all right. You have found your Mr. Gilpin's jewels and the pair who took them from him. I will even wager that Lord Kestwick had it right, and you were the fellow I ran into the other night in my study."

"Yes, I was there," Radfield returned a little sullenly. "I could hardly be expected to forgo a try at the Cleybourne emeralds, could I, when I'd landed smack on them."

Richard arched one brow. "There are those who might consider robbing one's host a rather poor return for his hospitality."

"I know." Radfield sighed. "My character is weak. I hadn't anything against you. You seem a perfectly good man. But the emeralds are world renowned."

Richard grimaced and went on, "However, the fact that he is a thief doesn't necessarily mean that he killed Mrs. Woods."

"No one did, I'm sure," Lord Vesey put in. "Merely an accident."

"I agree," Kestwick added. "You are making far too much of it, Cleybourne. The whole thing is nonsense."

Richard glanced around the room at the others. "I'm sorry. But if the rest of you wouldn't mind…I need to speak to Radfield alone." He raised his eyebrows toward Kestwick and the others, looking, for the moment, every inch a duke, and with a bit of grumbling, they began to file out of the room.

"You may stay, Cobb," he said to the Runner, who was hanging about by the door, glowering.

"And, of course—" Cleybourne bowed toward Jessica "—I shall need my note-taker."

Jessica quickly hurried around to sit down behind the desk and pull out a sheet of paper. Cobb assumed a position in front of the closed door, arms crossed in front of him, as though ready for whatever escape attempt Radfield might make.

"Now, Mr.—" Cleybourne stopped. "Is that your name? Radfield?"

"Actually, it is my first name. Radfield Addison. You may call me whatever you like. Over the years I have answered to almost anything."

"All right, then, Mr. Addison. Let us say I believe you that you did not harm your sister."

"I didn't. I swear it."

"I believe that someone else may have. There have been some other odd incidents around here lately, and your sister's death strikes me as suspicious. If someone did kill her, I am sure you would like to help us find the culprit."

"Of course. I'd do anything."

"First, I want you to answer me honestly. I am trying to separate the various things that happened here. You broke into my study the other night. But before that, did you break into the nursery?"

"What? No. Why would I break into a nursery? There's nothing worth stealing there. Besides, I never saw this place before the coach broke down. Before we arrived here, I was on the mail coach, traveling from London."

"And since you have been here, did you by any

chance take a small jewelry box from Miss Maitland's room?''

"Miss Maitland?" Radfield glanced over at Jessica. "The governess? Why would I take something that belonged to a governess? That's absurd."

"I just wanted to make sure. Now, then, can you tell me if your sister was involved in something else while she was here? Something besides the jewelry theft?"

"You mean, did she help me look around your study? No. She rang a peal over my head the next day for doing so. We tried not to be seen talking much—we weren't supposed to know each other, you know. But Bets came to my room after the fight and gave me a proper tongue-lashing about it. She was afraid I had endangered us. That we'd be exposed."

"So that's why you killed her?" Cobb interjected. "'Cause she told you off? Didn't like that, did you?"

Radfield rolled his eyes. "Of course I didn't like it. But I didn't kill her over it. She's said much the same to me many times before. In case you don't have sisters, Mr. Cobb, I will tell you that younger brothers are accustomed to receiving tongue-lashings from elder sisters. Besides, she had the right of it. I shouldn't have done it. It stirred things up. Made the duke suspicious. And, of course, Bettina had figured out that you were a Runner. She was a crafty girl." His voice faltered, and he looked down at his lap.

"Why did your sister go to Lord Kestwick's room the night she died?" Richard asked. "Did she tell you?"

"Lord Kestwick?" Radfield looked at him in amazement. "What makes you think she went to his room?"

"I saw her. And he admitted it. He said that they had had an assignation."

The other man continued to stare at him. "I don't believe it. You must be mistaken. Bets hadn't been in the trade in years. Besides, the money she'd get for a night would be a pittance compared to what she had in her trunk in her room."

"Perhaps she didn't do it for money."

"For what, then? Love? She'd just met the man." Radfield sneered. "For pleasure? No. She didn't get that out of it. She did it too long for hire, you see. Bets didn't much like men, except for me. And she most certainly did not like them in that way. She once told me it was all business, not pleasure, and I have never known her to take up with a man since then." He glanced with some embarrassment over at Jessica. "Begging your pardon, Miss Maitland."

"Accepted."

"And if by some strange chance she were to take up with a man, it wouldn't be with a nobleman. She hated the lot of them. They were mainly the men she saw back then, you see, and she despised them. And Kestwick is the very worst of what she disliked— haughty, cold, full of himself, and caring for no one else. I cannot imagine anything that could have persuaded her to go to his bed."

Richard looked at him thoughtfully. "Yet she went to his room. Why else would she have gone to his room in the middle of the night? Could she have had some other scheme? Perhaps to rob him?''

Radfield considered the idea. ''She would have liked taking something from one like that. But she'd just raked me over the coals for entering your study, and all I was doing was looking. I can't imagine she would think it was worth the risk, what you'd get off one gentleman who was traveling—I mean, maybe a stickpin, some watch fobs, cuff links. Minor stuff. Lady Vesey'd be a likelier prospect.''

''Yes, well, you were already pursuing that avenue, weren't you?''

The other man had the grace to blush. ''No. Not in the way you mean. I just thought—we were attracted to each other, that's all.'' He looked down for a moment, then said, ''As I said, Bets and me, we tried not to talk to each other, to pretend to be strangers who only met on the coach. So I saw little of Bettina. But, thinking back on it, the last time I saw her, just when we were chatting a little like strangers before supper, there was something about her—she seemed a little excited or…or maybe upset. I'm not sure. But she… Bets was always a calm one. No matter what happened, she didn't get flustered. But that night, she looked a little…nervous. I asked her if she was all right, and she said that she would be. And then someone came up, and we couldn't say anything you wouldn't say to a perfect stranger.''

''All right. Well, thank you, Mr. Addison. Mr. Cobb, I presume you plan to escort Addison to London once the snow has melted enough to leave?''

''That I do. I'll take him into custody right now,

sir. Lock him in a room right and tight—not the one he's been staying in. Maybe the nursery, if that's all right with you—no windows he can climb out of, and I'll lock the door.''

"Very well. Speak to Baxter about it.''

Cobb went over and wrapped his hand firmly around Radfield's arm, lifting him up from the chair and propelling him toward the door. Radfield, however, stopped halfway there and turned back to Richard. "Are you saying Lord Kestwick killed her? Is that what you think?''

"I frankly do not know,'' Richard admitted. "All I know is that he saw her for a time before her death, but I also know that she left his room and went back to her own. I have no idea what happened after that. Where she was going or who, if anyone, was with her.''

"Will you—you won't let it rest, will you?'' Radfield asked. "I mean, because she was who she was? If someone killed her, you will keep after it, won't you?''

"Yes. I promise you.''

The other man nodded and let Cobb lead him from the room.

"Well.'' Richard looked at Jessica. "That was certainly unexpected. I never dreamed…I guess that collar makes an excellent disguise, doesn't it? I never looked past it, even when I knew he had been entertaining Leona in his room. I thought he was a bad priest, but still, I thought he was a priest.''

Jessica nodded.

"You were right,'' he went on. "I notice you have

grace enough not to say it. But you pointed out the inconsistencies in his performance—his saying the prayer wrong, quoting Shakespeare instead of the Bible.''

"Yes. But I didn't dream he was a thief masquerading as a man of the cloth," Jessica admitted. "I don't even know what it was I thought—only that he acted oddly."

"Why do you suppose she went to Kestwick's room—supposing her brother is right and she did not go there for the same reasons Leona visited him?"

Jessica shook her head. "I have no idea. It does seem a petty theft for her. Gentlemen don't usually travel with a large amount of jewels. He probably had some money with him, but, as Radfield said, it doesn't make sense, what with her admonishing her brother for attempting to steal from your study."

"Perhaps she had different standards for herself than for him. Or perhaps he is lying about the whole matter. Maybe Cobb is correct, and he is the one who killed her, and he is simply trying to throw suspicion off himself onto Kestwick."

"Even if she did go to rob him, why would Kestwick kill her over it? Why not just reveal what she had done? Have her arrested?"

"True."

They were silent for a moment, thinking, then Richard said, "I noticed that Mr. Talbot recognized her name."

"Yes. Oh, you aren't thinking it's him because of that, are you?" Jessica asked. "Why would he kill her just because she was once a famous courtesan?

Besides, he was clearly surprised when Radfield said that. He couldn't have recognized her already or he wouldn't have been surprised.''

''Perhaps it was an act.''

''Why do it at all? Why not just pretend not to know her?''

''What if Kestwick knew her, too?'' Richard mused, thinking aloud. ''What if he recognized her?''

Jessica sat up straight, struck by a thought. ''What if he recognized her and threatened to reveal who she was? She would not want all of us to know that. She would not have wanted everyone to know, to lose her status here as a decent widow. If nothing else, it would have made Mr. Cobb suspicious of her, and Radfield said that she knew Cobb was a Runner.''

''Yes, but why—ah, yes, I think I see. What if he threatened her with revealing her true identity and she did go to his room for the reason we thought— because he threatened to expose her if she did not?''

Jessica looked at him. ''Yes. That would explain it. Perhaps that was why she was nervous—she didn't want to do it, but she had to. Poor woman.'' She paused, then said, ''Well, that would explain why she would want to kill Kestwick. But I can't see how it would give him much reason to kill her.''

''True.'' Richard sighed. ''I am sorry to say it, but I fear that I cannot put Kestwick down as the murderer. I should very much like to, however, as I think he is my favorite suspect after your Mr. Talbot.''

''He is not *my* Mr. Talbot,'' Jessica protested. ''I hate to give up Lord Kestwick as a suspect, too. But

I cannot see it having been her brother, either. Obviously he is good at deception, still I cannot help but think he was telling the truth today."

"Yes. Perhaps it was nothing. Perhaps it was as Lord Vesey said, an accident and nothing more. Maybe I am jumping at shadows. Perhaps it is all coincidence. The study intruder was Radfield. Maybe the nursery intruder was Vesey, as we thought originally."

"And my jewelry box was smashed by Darius? That seems like an exceptional number of coincidences to me."

"That is true, too. My life has become quite complicated since you came into it."

"Me?" Jessica's eyebrows soared. "You are blaming this all on me?"

"My life was very dull before you arrived."

"Well, I have not had murders and thefts and intruders in my life, either, I'll have you know. It too has been quite dull. So I could as easily blame you."

"Perhaps it is the combination. We are too volatile to mix together." His voice turned husky, and suddenly it was clear that he was no longer talking about their meeting.

"Indeed?" Jessica asked, her breath catching in her throat, and she rose slowly to her feet. "Are you saying that you wish we had not—that we should not—" She was suddenly sick at heart.

"No!" He shot to his feet, too, consternation on his features. "No, that is not what I meant at all. I meant—I was saying—"

Richard came around the desk to where she stood,

and he reached out to take her hands in his. "I meant that when I am around you, there is—I feel such heat, I cannot control it. I scarcely know myself." He looked into her eyes, his own dark eyes blazing with intensity. "I should apologize for last night, for taking advantage of the situation. Of you."

"You did not take advantage," Jessica said firmly. "I knew what I was doing. I went into it with open eyes. I don't regret it."

"Honestly?" He raised her hands to his lips and kissed first one, then the other. "I am glad to hear you say so, for I find I cannot say I am sorry for what I did. I am not."

"Nor am I." She looked at him, her eyes huge and brilliant.

"I feel as if I could drown in your eyes," he murmured. He leaned down, and she came up to meet him, and they kissed, their lips gentle and searching.

"I cannot stay away from you," he said, kissing her lips, her eyes, her cheek. "I want to be with you again tonight. I know I should not—"

Jessica stopped his words with her mouth. Finally she pulled away and said, "I want to be with you tonight, too. I want you in my bed."

He drew a sharp breath. "Jessica…" He pulled her to him, nuzzling into her hair. "It occurs to me that now would be an even better time."

Jessica laughed. "I think you might be right."

At that moment there was a discreet tap on the door, and they sprang apart, turning toward the sound.

"Enter," Richard said, his voice coming out harshly.

The door opened to reveal Baxter. "Your Grace." He came into the room, his face alight with excitement. "You have a visitor. Lord Westhampton has just arrived."

Richard gaped at him. "Lord Westha—"

"Yes, Lord Westhampton." A tall blond man appeared in the doorway. He was in his middle thirties, with even, attractive features. He was bundled up warmly in a heavy caped overcoat, a muffler around his throat, and he carried a hat in his hand. He looked a trifle tired, and Jessica noticed that snow clung to his boots and the bottom of his long coat. "It is I, Richard."

"Michael! My God!" Richard let out a short laugh and strode across the room to greet him warmly, shaking his hand and clapping him on the shoulder. "Where the devil did you come from?"

"Well, home, actually," Michael replied, looking faintly embarrassed.

"The Lake District? In this snow? Are you mad? How did you get through?"

"It seemed a bit dicey at times," the other man admitted mildly. "But once I'd started, well, it would have been as bad going back, so I pressed on."

"But whatever for?" Richard frowned suddenly. "Has something happened. Is something wrong? Not Dev—"

"No, no. There is nothing wrong. At least, not with me. Not now that Baxter has assured me Rachel is safe."

"Why, yes, she has been here throughout the snow. You did not know she planned to stop here on her return journey?"

"I, well, she was much later coming home than she had said she would be, and I began to worry, so I thought I would go down to Derbyshire, just to make sure she was all right. Dev told me that she had come here to persuade you to join us for Christmas, and I felt a fool, of course. I started to go home, but then the storm came. I was afraid, you see, that she had left before and had gotten caught in it, so I decided to ride here. Just to make sure."

Jessica looked at Lord Westhampton with interest. So this was the man with whom Rachel had a "pleasant" marriage, but one lacking in love. It seemed a trifle odd to her that a man who maintained a polite but distant marriage with his wife would panic at her being a few days late and ride to meet her, let alone press on even farther through a snow so deep that the mail coaches could not run.

Lord Westhampton glanced over at Jessica. "I beg your pardon for intruding upon you, ma'am."

"It is quite all right, I assure you," Jessica replied.

"I am sorry," Richard said, turning to Jessica. "My manners have deserted me. Miss Maitland, this is my brother-in-law, Lord Westhampton. Rachel's husband. Michael, this is Miss Maitland. She is, um, governess to my ward."

"Your ward?" Michael had started forward to take Jessica's hand in greeting, but he stopped at these last words and turned to Richard, exclaiming with some surprise, "I didn't know you—"

"Michael?" There was the sound of hurrying footsteps outside in the hallway and Rachel's voice calling her husband's name.

Lord Westhampton spun around at the sound of her voice, and Jessica saw on his face a flash of something—hope, excitement?—that he quickly controlled. Rachel hurried into the room, breathless and flushed, and came to an abrupt stop. The two of them stood there looking at each other for a moment. Then Rachel swallowed and stepped forward, holding out her hand almost formally.

"Michael," she said, only the faintest tremor in her voice. "I had not expected you."

"Yes, I know," he answered with equal politeness, advancing to take her hand and raise it to his lips in a courteous gesture. "I apologize for intruding."

"Nonsense!" Cleybourne said stoutly.

"'Tis not an intrusion," Rachel told him quietly. "I was merely surprised that you had come all this way."

"I—well, it occurred to me that perhaps you had gotten trapped in the snow somewhere between here and home," he explained.

"I almost did, but fortunately Richard came after me," Rachel explained.

Jessica, watching them, decided that it was time for her to leave. These three, old friends and family, did not need a stranger hanging about. "Excuse me," she said, "I must go check on Gabriela now. It was a pleasure to meet you, Lord Westhampton. I am glad you arrived safely."

He thanked her, and she slipped out of the room, aware that Richard turned to watch her go. Her thoughts were at first on Rachel and her oddly stiff meeting with her husband. There was something strange and contradictory there, and she could not help but wonder what had happened between them. She had thought more than once that there was a hint of sorrow in Rachel's lovely green eyes. But she could not keep her thoughts on that—or, indeed, on anything—long before thoughts of Richard came creeping in. She thought about his coming to her room again tonight, and excitement leaped in her. She knew she was acting wantonly, even wickedly.

She looked in on Gabriela and found her, amazingly, absorbed in one of her books. "The little princes in the Tower," she said, explaining her interest, then returned to the macabre subject.

Jessica went on to her own room, thinking to pick up the knitting she had started the other day, before all their guests arrived, and work on it while Gabriela did her lessons. When she entered the room, the first thing she saw was her ruined jewelry box lying on the dresser. She went over to it, then began to separate the jewelry from the bits of wood.

She wondered where she would put her few pieces of jewelry now. The box was clearly beyond repair. She frowned, thinking, then suddenly brightened as she recalled the lovely inlaid wood box the General had left to her in his will. It was far too large for her jewelry, but the necklaces and earrings would fit well enough in one of its little compartments.

Jessica walked over to the trunk at the foot of her

bed, which she had left largely packed, not knowing whether the duke would ship her and Gabriela off soon. Lifting the lid, she took out the folded summery dresses that lay on top, useless for this time of year, and bent to retrieve the elegant box. It was large, over a foot long and almost that wide, though it was not as heavy as one would think from looking at it.

She set it down on the dresser, running her hand admiringly across its satin-smooth surface. She turned the little key in the lock to open it, but before she could lift the lid, a muffled grunt in the hall startled her.

She raised her head and turned, looking out into the hall. Lord Kestwick stood there, staring at her, his eyes wide in his face.

"So that's it!" he exclaimed, and he looked from her to the box. "A different box!"

Jessica gazed at him blankly. "What are—"

In that moment it struck her. It was Kestwick who had destroyed her jewelry box. She did not understand it in the slightest, but it was clear that he was galvanized by the sight of the General's box. He had mistaken her jewelry case for the one the General had given her. In the next instant other things slid into place—someone had broken in and searched the General's house, and then someone had broken into the nursery. Had the intruder been after this box?

"It was you!" she exclaimed.

"Shut up!" Kestwick strode quickly into her room, swinging the door shut behind him. His eyes flamed with a malevolence such as Jessica had never encountered. She took an involuntary step backward, but he reached her in the next instant and slapped her hard, knocking her to the floor.

"God damn you!" His rage seemed all the more terrible for the fact that it was delivered in a low voice. "Yes, I did it! So what? The whore deserved it!"

Jessica, her head ringing from the blow he had dealt her, looked up at him dazedly. The import of his words sank in, and she realized with a shiver that chilled her to the bone that Lord Kestwick had killed Mrs. Woods.

18

"**B**loody, interfering bitch!" Kestwick went on. Jessica was unsure whether he was referring to her or to Mrs. Woods. He reached down and grabbed Jessica's wrist, jerking her to her feet. He pulled her back against him, wrapping one arm tightly around her, and with the other he pulled a short, thin-bladed knife out of a back pocket and held it against her throat. "Say a word and I'll slit your throat right here."

They stood that way for a moment in front of the dresser, looking at their images in the mirror. "What am I going to do?" he mused. "I cannot let you go now. How the hell did you know?"

"I didn't," Jessica replied honestly. "I meant that it was you who tore apart my little jewelry box. Who broke into the General's house and into the nursery. I didn't know you killed Mrs. Woods until just now, when you said that."

He cursed, tightening his arm around her waist cruelly. "Well, there's no use for it. I have to do something with you."

"Why did you do it?" Jessica asked. "What do you want with that box?"

His eyebrows lifted. "You mean you don't know? You haven't found it?"

"Found what? Know what? I haven't the slightest idea what you are talking about."

He let out a laugh that bordered on hysteria. "Christ! I cannot believe it! You don't know."

"No, I don't."

"So the old fool lied to me—or maybe he hid it too well for you to find."

"Who—the General?" Jessica met his eyes in the mirror, cold and flat as a snake's eyes, and suddenly she knew with certainty that this man had murdered the General, as well. "He didn't die of a another apoplexy, did he? You were there that night, weren't you? You did something to him. Why?"

"Be quiet! You talk entirely too much. All right. We have to make this look like an accident—no! I have a much better idea." His eyes glittered evilly. "You will write a note confessing to killing Marie."

"You knew her from before," Jessica guessed. "We were looking at it the wrong way round, weren't we? You didn't recognize her and apply pressure to her. She recognized you! She knew something about you, from her days as a lightskirt. What did she do? Did she demand money not to tell?"

Kestwick sneered. "Silly bitch! As if I would knuckle under to the threats of a tart like her."

"What was it she knew?"

"I told you to be quiet!" he snapped, again squeezing her chest so tightly she could scarcely breathe. "It doesn't matter why. Now, first, you are going to write a suicide note. Let's see, why shall we say you shoved her down the stairs? Perhaps the two of you were birds-of-paradise together, and she recognized you. She threatened to tell your new employer." He smiled thinly. "Or should I say lover?"

Jessica glanced at him in the mirror, startled. "Oh, yes," he said. "I have seen how he looks at you. Were you so foolish as to think that he loves you? That he might marry you? He never will, you know."

"You are giving me romantic advice now?" Jessica asked, stung by the absurdity of it.

"Just telling you the truth of it. Men like us don't marry governesses, especially ones who are willing to let us under their skirts for nothing."

"Don't you dare classify yourself with Cleybourne!" Jessica exclaimed, rage sweeping through her. "He is nothing like you, thank God!"

"No? Well, perhaps I shall be kind and let you die with such sweet delusions in your head. Now, where is the paper?"

"You are mad! I have no intention of writing a suicide note for you!"

He pressed the knife into her throat a little, cutting a thin red line. "You will if you don't want to die."

"For what—four more minutes? And do you really think they will believe that I killed myself by slicing my own throat?"

He glared at her in the mirror, and she knew that he would have loved to kill her right there and then. But he pulled himself back under control. "Perhaps you are right. I will just write the note for you when I return.''

"Ret—" But Jessica was not able to get out the words, for he tossed the knife onto the dresser beside the box and clamped his hand around her throat, squeezing her neck tightly between his fingers until black dots swam in front of her eyes and she fell unconscious.

Jessica awoke feeling sick at her stomach. She was also bitterly cold. She opened her eyes, letting out a little groan, and saw the white snow beneath her, bouncing up and down. Her head ached, and so did her stomach, pressed hard against something. It took her a moment to realize that Kestwick must have flung her over his shoulder and was carrying her through the snow, her head hanging down on one side of him and her feet on the other. Every step he took jounced her tender head and pushed against her stomach. She closed her eyes, fighting a wave of nausea. She shivered. It was terribly cold to be out of the house without a coat, but at least the chill was making her come to her senses rapidly. If she did nothing, Kestwick was going to kill her.

She kicked him as hard as she could, twisting and struggling and drumming her hands against his back. Opening her mouth, she screamed, but she feared that the sound fell away to nothingness in the open white landscape.

Kestwick stumbled, then pitched her down on the ground, cursing. The snow cushioned her fall, so it did not completely knock the air out of her, but as Jessica struggled to her feet, she staggered dizzily.

"Shut up, damn you!" Kestwick roared, grabbing her wrist and pulling her to him, clamping his hand over her mouth.

He moved on, half dragging, half pushing her, struggling through the snow up to their knees. Jessica's shoes were quickly soaked through, as was the bottom of her dress and petticoats, and she was bitterly cold. It was small comfort to know that he was no more dressed for the elements than she, not having had the time to go to his room and put on a coat and hat.

She could not tear away from his grasp, but she made their progress as difficult and slow as possible, hoping that someone had heard her scream or would notice she was missing. She thought of Richard chatting happily with Rachel and Michael. It could be hours before he noticed she was gone. Still, she fought fiercely, determined not to let Kestwick kill her easily. She did not know what he planned or where he was taking her, but she scratched and dug in her heels, pulling back with all her weight, twisting and struggling to get away from him. They fell down more than once, but still they struggled on.

They finally reached a place where the snow lay lower than elsewhere, and Kestwick flung her out into it. She sank through it and came up against something hard and smooth. *Ice!* In that moment she realized that she was on the frozen pond. He meant to break through the ice and send her down into the frigid water to die, pulled under by the weight of her skirts and petticoats.

Terrified, she jumped to her feet and flung herself forward off the ice, thankful that it had not broken through. Kestwick let out a roar of rage and grabbed her, pulling her out onto the ice and kicking at it with his heel. Jessica clawed at his face, and he let out a shriek, grappling with her to control her arms. There was an ominous cracking sound beneath their feet.

Suddenly, behind them, came a roar of rage, and in the next moment a hand caught Kestwick's collar and flung him backward. Jessica looked up and saw Richard.

He swept his arm around her and pulled her off the ice. Kestwick let out a wordless scream of anger and frustration and charged forward, slamming into Richard and sending the two of them falling backward onto the frozen surface of the pond.

"Richard!" Jessica screamed.

There was another, louder crack when the two men smacked into the ice. Then it broke, and they fell into the water. Jessica screamed Richard's name again and started forward, but a man caught her arm and thrust her aside. It was Lord Westhampton, and he ran to the pond, where the two men were still struggling in the icy water.

Kestwick was trying to squirm away from Richard, to reach the ice and climb out on it, and Richard was grappling with him, attempting to drag the other man back to the shore with him.

The ice broke off everywhere they touched it.

Kestwick shoved Richard beneath the water, but he came up, grabbing Kestwick and throwing him backward against the ice. Jessica watched, frantic with worry, as Michael arrived at the pond and reached for Richard's shoulder. Richard was just out of range, and Michael glanced around quickly for something to use to grab his friend.

Jessica heard the sound of someone behind her and turned to see Mr. Cobb chugging through the snow, and farther behind him came Rachel and Gabriela. Cobb carried in his hand a foot-long cudgel, his weapon, Jessica assumed, but he used it now as a stick, handing it to the longer-armed Michael, who stretched out, holding the cudgel to Richard. Richard grasped the other end of the stick, and Michael pulled him toward the shore, leaning down with Cobb to grab the duke by the shoulders as soon as he was near enough to haul him out of the water. Richard flopped down in the snow, coughing, and Jessica ran to him, throwing herself onto her knees beside him.

"Are you all right? Oh, Richard!"

He nodded and sat up, pulling her into his arms and holding her tightly. "Jessica…Thank God. I have never been so scared in my life. I thought—I thought I was going to lose you."

"No. Never."

Richard tilted her chin up and kissed her, and suddenly Jessica felt far less cold.

Behind them Cobb and Michael turned to try to pull Kestwick to shore, as well. But Kestwick turned and swam away, ignoring Westhampton's shouts. His movements were labored, slowed by the cold that had penetrated him, and by the water that had soaked his clothes and filled his boots, dragging him down. He reached the edge of the sheet of ice that covered the pond and grasped it with his hands. He heaved his body out of the water, but at the sudden weight on it, the ice broke, and he slid back into the water. The large chunk of ice he had broken off slammed into his head, and he disappeared beneath the surface.

"Kestwick!" Westhampton shouted. He turned to Cobb, and Cobb shrugged. It was clear that there was little they could do. Kestwick was much too far away for them to pull him in.

"Richard! Jessica! Are you all right?" Rachel was upon them now. She pulled off her cloak and wrapped it around Jessica. "You poor thing. You must be frozen."

If she found anything odd in the sight of Richard holding his ward's governess as if he would never let her go, she did not say anything.

"Miss Jessie! Miss Jessie!" Gabriela was there, too. "Are you all right? I saw him carrying you out of the house, so I ran to tell the duke!"

"You were a very smart girl," Rachel told her, pulling the girl to her and hugging her. "If it had not been for you, there is no telling what might have happened."

"Why did he carry you out here?" she went on, turning to Jessica. "Is he the one who killed that other woman?"

Jessica nodded, shivering and clinging to Richard. They all turned to look at the pond where Kestwick was floundering. Lord Westhampton was running around the side of the pond, Cobb puffing along behind him, shouting discouragement.

"You cannot try it, my lord! You'll go under just like him!"

"I cannot stand here and let him drown," Westhampton expostulated. "Whatever he did."

Michael stepped carefully out onto the ice and began to make his way across it. Rachel, suddenly pale, ran toward Mr. Cobb. "No! Michael, no!"

Kestwick's head bobbed up to the surface, and he flailed, his hands hitting against the ice but sliding off slickly. There was a groan in the ice, and suddenly a crack began to form, splitting right in front of Kestwick and running toward Michael. Rachel shrieked, and Mr. Cobb had to grab her to keep her from running out on the ice after her husband.

Michael, who was now only ten feet from where Kestwick was spluttering and trying to stay afloat, lay facedown on the ice to distribute his weight more evenly and crawled forward. "Take my hand!" he shouted to Kestwick, creeping toward the edge of the ice and extending his hand toward the other man. Kestwick floundered toward Westhampton, grabbing the ice beside him with his hand and trying to slide along it to safety. There was another loud crack, and the ice in Kestwick's hand broke off. He sank again and never reappeared.

A crack appeared in front of Michael, and he scrambled quickly backward. Mr. Cobb crawled on hands and knees out onto the pond, grabbing Michael's foot and yanking him back just as another crack opened beneath Michael. The two men crawled rapidly toward the rear as the ice in front of them broke off and floated across the pond. They reached the shore and tumbled into the snow, panting.

Rachel, who had been standing as rigid as a statue,

dropped to her knees, covering her face with her hands. Gabriela ran to her, putting her arms around her and helping her up, and by the time Lord Westhampton and Mr. Cobb got shakily to their feet and turned to trudge back to them, Rachel had pulled her face back into a semblance of calm.

"I am freezing," she said shortly, and turned and walked back to where Jessica and Richard had gotten to their feet and were looking out across the pond. There was no sign of Kestwick. Everyone stared blankly, and a long moment passed. Still there was no sign of the man. All of them knew that there was no way Kestwick could survive now. He had been under the water too long; he could never fight back up under the dragging weight of his clothes and boots.

"The fool," Richard said shortly. "He's gone. Let's get back inside before we catch our deaths of cold. Then we'll try to sort this all out."

So it was that an hour later they were seated in the sitting room. Jessica, whom Gabriela, Rachel and one of the maids had hustled into warm, dry clothes and given a cup of hot tea liberally laced with brandy, now sat on the couch beside Richard, also dried off and warmed up. Everyone else was scattered around—Cobb, the Westhamptons, Miss Pargety, Mr. Goodrich, Darius Talbot, and even Radfield Addison, whom Richard had declared deserved to hear whatever they could find out about what had happened to his sister, despite his status as Cobb's prisoner. Gaby had fussed about being excluded from the discussion, but both Richard and Jessica agreed that the subject was not one fit for her young years.

Each of them held a steaming cup of hot chocolate and listened as Jessica described what had transpired in her bedroom earlier, and how Lord Kestwick had inadvertently revealed that he had killed Mrs. Woods, then admitted that he had also been responsible for the destruction of Jessica's jewelry box, as well as the break-ins at the General's house and here in the nursery.

"But why?" Radfield asked, his voice wavering pitiably. "Why would he want to hurt Bets?"

"I think she threatened to reveal something about him. Apparently she knew him from before…in London. But he would not tell me what it was…or why that box was so important. I don't understand it at all."

"And we may never know," Lord Westhampton said heavily.

"Don't blame yourself, Michael," Richard told him. "You did everything anyone could do to save him. He signed his own death warrant by swimming farther out into the pond."

He turned and fixed Darius Talbot with a cold gaze. "However, I think that we might be able to learn a little more about what Kestwick was doing. Mr. Talbot?"

Darius, who had been sitting in his chair the whole time like a man turned to stone, shifted nervously and grew even paler under Cleybourne's stare. "I don't know," he said, his voice coming out in a rasp. He cleared his throat and repeated. "I don't know. I swear."

"Did you help your friend Kestwick break into my home? And the General's house?"

"No!" Darius clasped his hands together in his

lap. "I tell you, I knew nothing about what he was doing. I—he—I met him in London at my club. It was shortly after his mother's death, and I offered him my condolences. He said that he was going up to Norfolk to tell an old friend of his mother's death—"

"Norfolk?" Jessica repeated. "Do you mean—he went to see General Streathern?"

Darius nodded. "Yes. I—I had no idea that you were there, of course."

"Then Kestwick's mother must have been the old friend whose death upset the General so," Rachel mused. "It was when he read of her death that he suffered an apoplexy. He was...very fond of her." She saw no reason to mention what the General had told her of his love for the woman.

Darius shrugged. "I don't know. Kestwick didn't say much about it. He just said he had to see the General and he asked if I would like to come with him. I was—" He looked slightly embarrassed. "I was rather pleased. He is an earl, and his father was an important man in the Government before he died. I knew Kestwick to chat with and so on, played cards together some, but we were not what one would call close friends. I was flattered that he had asked me to go with him."

He faltered to a stop, and Richard said, "Go on, Mr. Talbot. What happened then?"

"Well, we drove up to this town, Little Pilton."

"That's not far from the General's house," Jessica put in. "But when was this? Kestwick didn't call on the General."

Darius looked at her, surprised. "Yes, he did. He called on the General the night before the old fellow died. We heard about it the next day, and Kestwick was most astonished. He said the man had seemed in fair health the night before when he told him about Lady Kestwick's death. He was afraid the news had upset him more than he had let on.''

"The General already knew about her death," Jessica said flatly. "He'd known about it for over a week. Kestwick killed him. I don't know how or why, but I saw it in his eyes when he was talking. He killed the General. I accused him, and he did not deny it.''

"That's nonsense!" Darius exclaimed.

"Is it?" Jessica retorted. "Kestwick didn't come to call on the General. At least, not openly. No one in the house saw him. He must have entered secretly. And killed him." She paused, then added, "But why?''

"From what you have said, he wanted that box that the General left you," Rachel pointed out.

"Yes. But why? What about that box would have been worth killing someone for?''

"He was powerfully interested in some box," Darius agreed. "He—I think that was why he wanted to come this way on our journey back to London. We stayed in an inn near here for a day or two before it snowed.''

"That gave him the chance to break into the castle to look for it.''

"I guess," Darius said miserably. "I wasn't aware that he had gone out at night. I couldn't understand why we were here. It was damned dull. But, well, Kestwick wasn't the sort one questioned." He paused and sighed, then added, "I think he arranged to have the accident with the mail coach. I—it seemed to me at the time almost as if he headed toward the thing. I decided that he must not be a skillful driver, and, of course, one wouldn't want to criticize a friend's driving skill.''

''Mmm. Especially one so important,'' Richard added.

Darius colored. ''Perhaps I was foolish. But I had no idea. How could I?''

''He wanted a way to get into this house so he could search at his leisure,'' Richard surmised. ''Was it he who suggested that you make a pest of yourself with Miss Maitland?''

Darius's color went from pink to a bright red. ''He, well…'' He buried his head in his hands and said in a muffled tone, ''Yes. He—he asked me to try to find out about what sort of box Jessica had received from the General. He told me that he had read Streathern's will. I didn't know that he meant he had broken into the house to do so. He said that the old man had left Jessica money and this box in his will, and that Jessica and Streathern had—the two of them had been—'' He broke off and cast a glance at Richard.

Cleybourne returned his gaze stonily. ''I suggest that you do not finish that calumny, Mr. Talbot, or you are very likely to find yourself out in the snow, bag and baggage…and nursing a number of bruises. I trust I have made myself clear.''

''Um, yes. Yes, certainly. I understand, I assure you,'' Darius told him quickly. ''I would never repeat such a lie, I swear. I realize now how wrong he was. But at the time, well, I did not know. I believed him, trusted him. I agreed to talk to Jessica, to see if I could persuade her to tell me about the box.''

"But why?" Rachel asked, puzzled. "What is in that box that is so important?"

"That's just it!" Jessica exclaimed. "There was nothing in it but a few old keepsakes of the General's—a few of his medals, some old-fashioned jewelry, not anything terribly expensive."

"But it was obviously important to him. When Talbot failed to woo you, Kestwick stole your jewelry box from her dresser, doubtless thinking that it was the box in question."

"But why did he tear it up?" Rachel asked.

Darius shook his head quickly. "I know nothing about that. I did not even know that he had taken it until Miss Maitland said so this evening."

"I imagine he was expressing his frustration and anger," Richard answered. "Whatever it was he wanted, he had the wrong box, so he obviously did not find it. So he smashed the box in a fit of rage. Whatever he wanted, the man was a lunatic."

The group broke up soon after that, drifting away to their rooms to dress for supper. Jessica, tired and rather frustrated by not knowing why Lord Kestwick had done what he did, rose from the chair and started toward the door, but Richard came forward to stop her.

"Wait, if you would, Miss Maitland," he said formally. "I would like to speak to you for a moment if you don't mind."

"No. Of course not." Jessica turned back to him. His face was very serious, and her heart sank a little. She wondered if he was going to tell her that he regretted what had happened between them, after all, that he had reconsidered it and saw that it would be too likely to create a scandal—or that he could not do it, given his memories of Caroline.

She walked back to the sofa and sat down, composing herself. When the last visitor had left, Richard closed the door and walked over to Jessica. He sat down on the couch, turned so that he was close to facing her. For a long moment there was silence. Jessica looked up at him, steeling herself for whatever he was about to say.

"Miss Maitland, you must be aware of the regard in which I hold you," he began.

Jessica looked at him blankly. "What? Why are you talking like that?"

"I—well, it is a…a formal occasion."

"What is?" Jessica sighed. "Please, Richard, just tell me. If you do not wish me to be here anymore, simply say so. I understand. But I cannot take all this introduction."

"Not be here?" he repeated blankly. "What do you mean?"

Jessica frowned. "I mean, if you do not wish me to remain as Gabriela's governess. If you want me to leave the house."

He looked at her, a faint smile playing on his lips. "Miss Maitland, you are difficult to the end, I see. Yes, it is true that I do not wish you to remain as Gabriela's governess."

Jessica looked down quickly, unable to meet his eyes anymore. The pain in her chest was so searing it took a moment for his next words to register in her mind.

"However," he went on, "I do not want you to leave the house. Now or at any other time. Jessica…I am asking you to marry me."

Her head snapped up. "What!"

"I am asking you to marry me. To be the Duchess of Cleybourne."

Jessica was glad she was sitting down already, for she thought her knees would have given out. "But...but...you can't!"

"I can't?" he repeated. "And why can I not, I'd like to know?"

"Well, it—it's absurd. I am not your equal in station."

"What nonsense. You come from a perfectly good family. And, anyway, I don't know why it should make a difference to you if it doesn't to me."

"I am a governess."

"It is not your fault you fell upon hard times," he pointed out. "It is scarcely as if you had spent the past few years as a bird-of-paradise."

"But a duke does not marry a governess."

"Ah, but a duke does if he wants to. That is the best thing about being a duke, you see. I can marry exactly whom I choose. Who is going to reprimand me for it?"

"But, Richard, my father. The scandal. It would cast a cloud on your name."

"My dear girl," Richard said, standing up and reaching down to pull Jessica to her feet. "I am honored—and, I must admit, somewhat surprised—to find you so concerned about the Cleybourne name. However, I have to tell you that I do not think one scandal ten years ago—caused by your father, not you—would cast an enormous shadow on my family or title. And if it did, I don't care. I don't love my name. It doesn't make me quiver with longing as you do, nor does my heart speed up whenever I see my coat of arms, as it does when I see you. I love you, Jessica. I want to marry you.''

"Richard..." Jessica looked at him, torn, unable to say anything. Everything within her cried out to accept, yet she knew that it was not right.

"Well, I have discovered how to render you speechless, I see. I suppose that is something.''

"But, Richard—you—I cannot replace Caroline. You still love her.''

"I'm not asking you to replace Caroline. Frankly, except in your beauty, you are nothing like her. You are not her. I am not looking for her. It is you I want. You are the one who keeps me awake at night, wanting you. You are the one who aggravates me so I want to shout. And you are the one who has brought me back to life. I was a shell when you came here. I was wallowing in my own misery, unable to pull myself out of the swamp I was in. Then you came in, and you—you brought light back into the house. Into my life. Oh, I sound like a moonling, I know, a lovesick calf of a boy, but that is how you make me feel.

"Yes, I loved Caroline. I still love her, in a way. But that does not mean that I don't love you. I love you in an entirely different way. Caroline was a beautiful woman and I was a young man. I fell head-over-heels in love with her. I thought she was perfection. But the sad truth is that I didn't even know her. I loved the woman I thought she was, but I don't think that was really her at all. I thought we shared a love, but she never really loved me. At the end she was desperate to leave me. I couldn't let go of the ideal I had of her. That was what I was trying to keep, not Caroline. My dream of her and my daughter. It wasn't real."

He took Jessica by the shoulders and pulled her to him, kissing her for a long, long time. When at last he pulled away, she was breathless.

"That is real. You are real. I know you. I don't have to wonder if you are as I think or not. You will tell me exactly what you are and what you think, as well as precisely what you find wrong with me."

Jessica could not keep from chuckling. "I thought that was why you disliked me."

"It is. It is also why I love you to distraction. Jessica, end my torture. Tell me that you will marry me." He paused and looked at her, then added a trifle uncertainly, "Do you...not love me?"

"Oh, no!" Jessica cried out, flinging her arms around his neck. "I do love you. I love you so much I was willing to stay here as your mistress!"

"I think I would prefer it if you stayed here as my wife," he told her.

"Yes!" she cried. "Yes, I will marry you. I only hope you will not regret it."

"I know I will never do that," he responded, and closed her lips with another kiss."

19

Jessica gave herself a final look in the mirror, experiencing a moment's doubt that she looked the part of a duchess. Perhaps Rachel would take pity on her and guide her through it.

She smiled a little to herself. She was still fizzing with excitement inside. She imagined she probably would be for a long time.

Jessica walked over to her dresser and looked down at the box the General had left her. What had interested Lord Kestwick so about this box?

At that moment there was a tap on the door, and Jessica called, "Come in."

The door opened to reveal Richard standing there, dressed for supper. "I thought I would escort you down to the dining room. What are you doing?"

"Just looking at this box, wondering why it held such meaning for Lord Kestwick."

"And have you arrived at any answers?"

"No. Not really." Jessica opened the box, and Richard came over to look down at it. "Except, perhaps, this locket." She reached in and picked up a locket which, when opened, revealed a lock of blond hair. "I think this might have belonged to Lord Kestwick's mother. The general was in love with her all his life, you see. He told me so just before his death—except at the time I did not know that she was Lord Kestwick's mother."

"Surely that would not be enough to cause Kestwick to murder people—or even to try so hard to get the box," Richard said reasonably. "No one would know to whom the hair belonged."

Jessica pulled out all the contents of the box one by one and piled them on the dresser, saying, "Perhaps there is something else here, something that we cannot see."

"A false bottom perhaps?" Richard asked, trying to slide a fingernail between the felt-covered bottom and the side. "You know, it does look rather larger on the outside than what it seems inside." He closed the lid and turned it over, looking for some sort of join on the bottom.

"Perhaps that is why Kestwick smashed my jewelry box. Perhaps he took it apart looking for a secret compartment. It wouldn't have to be large, you know. It could hold a—maybe a letter. Maybe Lady Kestwick wrote the General a love missive, which Kestwick was afraid would cause a scandal."

She subsided. "That seems a trifle strange, too, doesn't it? How horrible a scandal could it be? Anyway, why would it get out? Even if I had found it, I would never have revealed anything that would have hurt the General's good name."

"Kestwick would not know that. I imagine he

judged the world by his own standards, and obviously he was wicked enough to ruin a name or anything else.''

''That's true.''

Cleybourne rapped his knuckles sharply against the bottom of the box, working his way across. ''It sounds rather hollow.''

''Are you looking for the secret compartment?'' came a voice from the door.

Richard and Jessica swung toward it in astonishment. Gabriela was standing in the door, watching them.

''There's a secret compartment?'' Richard asked.

''Oh, yes, the General showed it to me once. It's terribly clever.''

''Obviously we should have let Gabriela attend the discussion this afternoon,'' Richard said ruefully.

''Yes, you should have,'' Gabriela agreed, coming across the room to join them. ''Why?''

''There is something important about this box. It is why Lord Kestwick tried to kill me...well, one of the reasons.''

''He thought the General hid something in this box?'' Gabriela asked, wide-eyed. ''What?''

''We don't know. That is why we were looking in it.''

''See, this piece of wood moves.'' Gabriela pushed her finger against one piece of the inlaid wood, and it slid out, revealing a tiny lever. ''Then...''

Gabriela tugged at the lever, and a hidden drawer in the bottom of the box glided slowly out. Inside the drawer lay two folded packets of papers. One was addressed to Jessica in the General's shaky, aging hand. The other was addressed to the General, also in a hand Jessica recognized.

"My father..." she breathed. "That is my father's handwriting."

She reached into the drawer and pulled out the packet of papers. Both were sealed, the one from her father with his seal, which had been broken, as well as another, unbroken, wax imprint of the General's seal.

With fingers that trembled slightly, Jessica broke the seal on her father's papers and opened it. First was an official-looking document, stamped with the insignia of the navy and dated ten years earlier. Jessica looked at the date.

"Why, that is just a few days before my father died. What is this?"

Richard, looking over her shoulder, said, "I'm not sure. It looks like something to do with the war—movements of the fleet, men and material, rather secret sort of stuff, I should think. Wait!" He reached over her shoulder and snatched the paper out of her hand. "Look." He pointed at the name written in flowing letters across the bottom. "Lord Kestwick!"

"His father?" Jessica asked. "The present Kestwick's father?"

"Yes. He was quite high up in the government. My guess would be that this was a government document, probably meant to be kept secret. How did it get into your father's hands?"

Jessica still held a sheet of paper in her hand. It

was a letter in her father's handwriting. "Here," she said. "This explains it. It is a letter from my father to the General. Apparently he sent it with the document." She read from the letter "'As you can see, the secrets are slipping out through Kestwick's office. I believe that he knows nothing of it, but he takes many of his documents home to look through and stores them in a locked safe there, believing them well kept. It is his son who is the traitor. He has been stealing them from his father and passing them to the enemy for money. I have managed to infiltrate the group, and that is how I got this. He meets the French agents at the house of a courtesan named Marie Mac-Donald.'"

"That is why he killed Mrs. Woods!" Richard exclaimed. "She knew what he used to do and when she saw him, she decided she would make a bit of extra money by blackmailing him. So he killed her."

Jessica nodded, reading on. "'Many of the young officers and other young gentlemen frequent it. My operation is now complete, and I can assure you that I wait eagerly for this terrible stain to be lifted from my name.'"

Jessica lifted her face, tears standing in her eyes. "This is what Kestwick wanted. Proof that he was a traitor during the war."

Richard nodded. "No wonder he was so eager to have it. This would have ruined him."

"It ruined my father," Jessica said.

"Oh, my dear." Richard wrapped his arms around her, pulling her against his chest. "I am so sorry. This was why your father was cashiered from the army, wasn't it? It was a ruse so that he could infiltrate a gang of traitors.''

''Yes. Of course. I should have known. That was why Father could not tell me the truth of it. It was highly secret.''

Gabriela observed her guardian's arms around her governess with interest, but it was the age-old scandal about which she spoke. ''But what happened? Why didn't anyone know about this?''

''The General must have,'' Jessica said, her voice tinged with bitterness. ''My father must have been found out and killed by Kestwick—or else he simply had the bad fortune to have been caught in a tavern brawl while he was acting out his charade of having fallen from grace. But obviously General Streathern received this letter, for it is in his possession.''

''So Gramps knew and never said anything?'' Gabriela asked in a troubled voice.''

''Yes, I am afraid he did,'' Richard told her. ''I cannot imagine why.''

''I know why,'' Jessica said in a leaden voice. ''Because he loved Kestwick's mother. Remember?''

She tore open the other letter, the one to her from General Streathern, and began to read:

''‘Dear Jessica,
By now you no doubt hate me. You have every right to. Not only have I kept this secret all these years, but it was I who sent your father to his death. Please believe me when I say I did not intend to. If I had had any idea who the traitor was, I would never have set the investigation in

motion. Thomas was the best and brightest man serving under me, the one I trusted most completely. When we needed to find out who was leaking secrets to Bonaparte, I knew that he could do it better than anyone. For that reason, we pretended that he was cashiered from the army under a cloud of guilt, so that he could work his way into the gang of traitors. As you can tell from this document, he was successful. He discovered the traitor. I received this letter shortly after his death.

"I told you of a love I had for a woman all my life. It was Lady Kestwick, the mother of the traitor Thomas discovered. When I received your father's letter, knowing he had died in the tavern fight, and saw who he had caught, I was devastated. I wrestled with the problem for some time. I could not, as it turned out, bring myself to condemn the woman I loved so much to the life she would have had if her only son had been revealed as a traitor. I took Lord Kestwick aside and showed him the document. Together we went to his son and made him disband his operation under threat of being exposed. His father, of course, resigned from his position immediately.

"I know you must blame me now for what happened to your father and for the cloud under which you have had to live for the past ten years. You have every right to. The things I have done for you, which you counted kindnesses, have been my poor attempt to compensate for the wrong which I did to you and to your father. I hold you in true affection, and it has been a bitter grief to me to see you having to make your way in the world. I should have told you time and again over the years; every thanks I received from you was like salt to my wound. But I could not bear to tell you and earn your enmity. So I have taken the coward's way out, which you may feel is fitting, and I have left you these documents, which will prove that your father was wronged and that the present Lord Kestwick is a traitor. It will ruin my name, as well, but that is no more than I deserve.

"I beg your forgiveness and pray that you will remember someday the love that I felt for you. You have been like a granddaughter to me.'"

"But how could Gramps do that?" Gabriela asked plaintively. "It is so cruel!" She looked at Jessica with some trepidation. "You must hate me now."

"No! Of course I do not hate you. Don't ever think that. I love you dearly. Whatever your great-uncle did or did not do could not affect the way I feel about you." Jessica enfolded the girl in a hug. "And though it does grieve me sorely that the General did not remove the stain from my father's name, I cannot find it in me to hate him, either. I know quite well the things one is willing to do because of love, even things that are wrong."

She cast a glance at Richard as she said this, remembering the way she had longed so much for his touch, wished so much to be with him, that she had been willing to throw away her reputation and live in sin with him.

Jessica saw Gabriela's interested gaze follow her own glance to Richard, and she said, "Now, would you like to know something that no one else does?"

"Yes, of course." Gabriela brightened.

It was Richard who answered. "Miss Maitland is no longer going to be your governess."

"What?" Gabriela looked horrified. "But that is not good news at all!"

"The good news is that she will be your guardian's wife."

Gabriela's jaw dropped, and she swung toward Jessica. "Truly? Oh, Miss Jessie, I am so happy for you!" She threw her arms around Jessica and hugged her enthusiastically. Suddenly she stepped back and looked at Richard. "Does that mean you are not giving me away to Lady Westhampton?"

"That is right. Rachel will be most unhappy about it, but I shall tell her that she must content herself with being your aunt."

"Oh, thank you!" Gabriela said, her eyes beaming. "I promise you, you won't regret it."

"I am sure I will not."

"May I tell Lady Westhampton?" she asked, fairly quivering in her excitement.

"That I am going to be your guardian? Yes. As to the other, no, it is still a secret. You are the first to know."

"And you want to tell her yourself. I understand. I won't breathe a word, I promise."

With another impulsive hug for Jessica and then, as though she could not resist, for Richard, as well, she ran out of the room.

"I wonder how long that secret will last," Richard mused, smiling.

"I think she will not tell Rachel. Gabriela will consider it a point of honor. However, I would not be surprised if Rachel guesses from her manner that something more than your being her guardian is afoot."

"We shall tell her and Michael the news as soon as we can get them alone. And we can tell them what we discovered. We will need to clear your father's name, and I imagine Michael will have an idea how best to go about it. He's a brainy sort."

"Richard...I am not so sure about clearing my father's name."

"What?"

"What about Gabriela? The General's name will be even more tarnished by this than my father's ever was. I mean, yes, I would love to have his name restored, but it has been ten years, and many people have forgotten. But Gabriela's name will be hurt by it, and she will be making her coming-out in a few years. It will hurt her chances terribly...whereas I have dealt with it long ago. Of course, it would be better for your family," she added, realizing that it would mean his marriage to her would be less of a shock to the polite world.

"The devil with my family," said Richard. "I have very little family, except for a few cousins who will doubtless be most disappointed to see that I am remarrying at all. I have told you, I am free to do as I please, and I please to marry you, scandal or not. I want to restore your father's good name for you. You do not deserve to live, and he did not deserve to die, under the cloud of suspicion. He was an honorable man, and he did a very good thing. He probably died in the service of his country. For while the General may have preferred to believe that he died in a common tavern fight, I find it difficult to believe, given the circumstances. We know that Kestwick is a killer. I see no reason to think that he was not one back then, too. You may forgive the General for what he did for Lady Kestwick, but I do not. He allowed you to live in poverty, to suffer the rejection of society, to have to work to live. And if Gabriela is harmed by this, that, too, will lie at his door.''

He looked at her and smiled. ''I know. You are too tenderhearted to think of her being hurt. Well, do not worry. In four years' time, when she comes out, with a duke for a guardian and you and Rachel guiding her through her season—as well as the very substantial fortune she was left by Streathern and her father—I will probably have to beat the suitors off with a stick. She will be fine.''

Jessica smiled and reached up to place a light kiss on his lips. ''I love you.''

''And I love you. Now, I suggest we find Rachel and Michael and tell them our news.'' He kissed her brow, then nuzzled into her hair. ''Although, now that I think of it…there is a little bit of time before supper, and Gabriela will doubtless keep Rachel occupied for the next few minutes.''

"That is true," Jessica agreed, bending her neck to the side to allow him access. "Can you think of a way we could spend that time, Your Grace?"

His chuckle was muffled against her neck. "Indeed, I can, Miss Maitland."

Turning, he strode to the door and closed it, turning the key firmly in the lock. Then he walked back to her, a slow smile spreading across his face. Sweeping her up in his arms, he carried her across the floor to the bed. This time their lovemaking was slow and gentle, an easy exploration with hands and tongues and lips that built gradually, until at last they exploded into a white-hot burst of passion. And as she eased back into reality, her heart still hammering, her body slick with sweat, Jessica knew, with a happiness that had no measure, that she had at last found love.

The roads were passable in two days' time, and, to everyone's great relief, their visitors were able to leave, Lord and Lady Vesey taking Darius with them in the carriage to London, and the coach passengers continuing, much diminished, to York. Mr. Cobb escorted Radfield Addison to gaol and set off with the jewels for Mr. Gilpin.

The house was then in a stir for Christmas, only two days away. Christmas Day dawned bright and clear, with enough snow remaining to provide a picture-pretty scene.

The Yule log was dragged in in the middle of the afternoon and placed in the cavernous fireplace in the Great Hall. Richard lit it with a splinter saved for that purpose from the last year's log, something which his servants never failed to do, always wishing good fortune on him and his house even when he was not in attendance.

Afterward they sat down to a groaning table covered with a Christmas feast far larger than they could eat. There was roast beef and venison, as well as stuffed goose and pheasant, and a variety of vegetables. There was mince pie, a Christmas staple, one of which would be eaten every night for the Twelve Days of Christmas, thus insuring twelve months of good luck for the inhabitants of the house. The meal was finished off, of course, with a huge round plum pudding, made on the first Sunday of Advent, with everyone taking a turn at stirring it for luck. There was gingerbread, as well, and sugar plums and ginger nuts, so that by the end of the meal, no one could eat a bite more.

Everyone retired to the Great Hall, where the servants were given their gifts, and the gentlemen toasted the coming season from the wassail bowl, the ladies with wine.

"I think this is the best Christmas ever," Rachel said, smiling at Richard and Jessica.

"Splendid," her husband agreed, and his eyes rested on his wife's face for a moment. Then he smiled and added, "A wonderful feast, and good friends and family."

Richard slipped his hand through Jessica's and tugged her away from the group by the fire. She followed him, looking questioning. He reached into his pocket, smiling down at her, as he said, "I have a gift for you."

"Richard! But how—" She and Gabriela had knitted some simple gifts for the others during the past few days, but no one had been able to venture forth to the village.

He smiled, holding out his hand and opening it up to reveal a ring lying nestled in his palm. Jessica's eyes widened. "Richard!"

"A betrothal ring," he told her. "I thought of the one from the Cleybourne emeralds, but I did not think you would care for that. This sapphire, though, is beautiful and not quite as, shall we say, noticeable. It came to me from my mother, and from her mother before her."

"It's lovely. Perfect." Jessica picked up the ring. It was set with a pure blue sapphire, surrounded by tiny diamonds, far smaller and less showy than the Cleybourne emerald that she had seen on Caroline's hand in the portrait. He was right; she would not have wanted that ring, with all its memories of past tragedies. But this ring was beautiful and suited her far better. "Thank you."

She held the ring out to him, and he took it and slid it onto her finger, then raised her hand to his lips. "I love you, Jessica. Until you came, I think I was only half-alive—if even that much."

"And I love you." The glowing face she turned up to him showed the truth of her statement.

They linked hands and looked back to where the others sat before the fire, Gabriela showing Rachel a book that Jessica had given her, and Michael quietly watching them. Jessica sighed. "I only wish that Rachel and Michael could be as happy as I am."

"Well," Richard pointed out, "you have changed my life. Perhaps now you can start on Rachel's."

Jessica smiled faintly. "No. I am afraid that happiness is something each person has to find for himself...or herself."

"Well..." Richard leaned down and pulled her into his arms for a kiss. "I can only say I am glad that you found me."

"That we found each other," she corrected, and twined her arms around his neck for another kiss.